TRANSITUS

BRIAUNA MARIAH

TRANSITUS

BRIAUNA MARIAH

Heart Ally Books, LLC
Camano Island, Washington

Cover design: Josef Bartoň
Lab rendering: Najla Kay

Published by:
Heart Ally Books, LLC
26910 92nd Ave NW C5-406, Stanwood, WA 98292
Published on Camano Island, WA, USA
www.heartallybooks.com

ISBN-13: (epub) 978-1-63107-066-2
ISBN-13: (paperback) 978-1-63107-065-5

1 2 3 4 5 6 7 8 9 10

For you,
and the interconnectedness we may or may not share
on this tiny planet.

Gods of Tomorrow

Diane Marion, 2031

I AM NOT WHO I thought I was.

I thought I was a mathematician, politician, physician, technician. Maybe a geologist or psychologist. After three years of "Major: Undecided," I became a journalist.

I had finally found my calling. Found myself.

"Boucher! Dr. Boucher!" One of the dozen other reporters bellowed to a man who was being hustled up the steps by police.

The man, Dr. Geoffrey Boucher, stumbled. He had that next-day-o'clock shadow, disheveled hair, and now a scuffed left shoe.

I was sorry for the shoe. And the priceless tailored suit he'd almost dirtied.

Givenchy.

That would've been a crime.

I held my breath, fixed my dress, braced myself in the sea of chaos, and thought, this is it.

A reporter shoved a mic at the doctor. "Who did you think your work would benefit? Did you consider the moral implications?"

"Dr. Boucher, is it true you involved your newborn son, Louis, in your genetic experiments?" The reporter's smile could slice bone.

Dr. Boucher ignored the bombardment. I kept my mouth shut until he was close. Close enough that I could smell the heavy cologne wafting off him.

I knew his type.

The wandering-eye type. The girlfriend-wife-and-mistress type. I had one foot planted firmly on a stone step and the other planted at a crossroads between Morals Avenue and Promotion Street.

I knew what I was doing this morning when I donned my Stella, the dress I wore with nothing but boob tape. The dress with the neckline that plunged like the Titanic. The dress with just one purpose—make my tits look fucking fantastic.

Dr. Boucher blinked a double take at me, looking like some French actor with haunted hazel eyes. When he did, a vision flashed in my mind that was gone as quickly as it had appeared: a girl submerged in water. I didn't know if she was alive or dead, but one second she was there and the next, I stood blinking at Dr. Boucher, wondering why I had paused.

I wasn't nervous. I stared back at the doctor and twisted my lips, the moment was gone from my brain—no lingering memory of it. As if it hadn't happened at all.

I had the Doctor's attention.

Here was my chance.

"Geoffrey." I used his first name to throw him off guard. My voice hung as low as my neckline, making him work to hear it. My eyes were locked on his. "Some sources say you were justified in your actions, using genetic manipulation on those embryos. They say it's been done before. But no one has ever altered DNA as severely as you have. Some say it was a gross crime against humanity. Do you believe what you did was right?"

"There's no right or wrong in evolution, babe." His voice oozed like grease. Heads turned. A shutter snapped. The crowd held its breath. Even the police paused.

"What about equity? Did you think about the millions of impoverished people without access to this progress? Who will protect them from the billionaires of the world?" I stretched my mic toward him as far as my arm would go.

His attention locked on my face and lips, suspended and spellbound.

It was a big question. But I didn't really care about the poor. Or genetics, for that matter.

His eyes flicked down to my boobs, then back up.

I feigned disgust.

"The gods of tomorrow need no equity."

What does he mean by that? I didn't expect him to make me think. I faltered on my next question. "Did you intend to…?"

I stopped, realizing what he had just said.

"Are you implying the billionaires of the world are gods?"

With a sleazy smile, Geoffrey shrugged.

FIVE

Felice Karuli, Sunday, March 24, 2250, 5:52 a.m.

FORTY METERS UNDERWATER INSIDE an old repurposed SCUBA habitat, Felice Karuli sat shackled to her mother's ever-present disappointment. Disappointment that lingered long after her mother left the domed metal lab. Disappointment that days, weeks, and years were eking by, and still there was no cure for Pneumaphage.

"Carmak, how's your station doing? I'm out of new Cas9." Anxiety cracked Felice's voice. It was a tired, dusty-sounding voice. Felice searched her own station, the sink of Dome Four, to find what she needed, but Gina Carmak's station, opposite of her own, always had extra supplies.

Carmak didn't respond.

"Hellooo?" Felice juggled needles, test kits, bottles, vials, and Cas9 mixes. "Carmak, do you have extra mix to give?"

Felice stopped digging through the sink. She massaged her temples.

The silence was annoying—enough to make Felice bitter. Not enough to get her to stand and turn. Motivation didn't just magically appear.

Didn't she hear me? Elbows by the sink, Felice looked out the dome's only window, waiting for her lab partner's response.

A rockfish stared in. She stared back.

Maybe the smells of disinfectant and desperation dulled Carmak's ability to perceive sound. Maybe they bleached her brain. Or maybe she had her brain-wave ear com on some loud New World Alliance station.

The New World Alliance, the global government formed after total climate-induced devastation, only talked about Mainland issues. Politics, mostly. And heated debates about who would be the new face of the NWA unity campaigns. Or if the current face had one too few wrinkles to really exude the right message of wisdom and authority. None of that was relevant here. Not in warm, iceless Antarctica.

NWA decisions rarely affected what went on here. Except for one.

Felice tried to stop the flush of guilt burning in her cheeks. The NWA refused to cure, or even try to cure, the *transitus* population of Pneumaphage. Because *transitus* were granted speciation as *Homo transitus* in 2144, officializing their non-human status, the NWA claimed it a moral responsibility not to interfere.

Down here in this other world, Felice and her mother, Lamia Karuli, who headed their efforts against the disease, bent every rule to interfere. It was sick, really. Experimenting on kids' monthly blood draws to see which kid might be a candidate for invasive, highly illegal injections. Kids like Elpida Enosh, and her brother, Krimsey. If the NWA ever found out what they were really doing, the Humanoid Preservationist Organization would be shut down faster than hellfire. But that's not why she squirmed and rocked in her seat now. The threat of being shut down was a concern, of course. Where would *transitus* go to seek refuge? But that's not what kept her up at night. What kept her up at night was the little girl. Rumi.

No. Don't go there. Not now. She focused on relaxing the fiery knots in her belly.

Felice thought she heard the tiny, irritating voice of news anchor Jordan O'Keefe coming from Carmak's com. For good reason, Mainland com channels were banned here, inaccessible to the general public. At Lamia's request, Carmak tuned in to them to monitor the relevant headlines. She would be horrified to find out that the daughter of the woman she sucked up to knew she enjoyed it. Felice wasn't judging. She had her own guilty pleasures.

In a lot of ways, Carmak reminded Felice of her mother. A gentler, more timid version. But Carmak was similar enough; she sucked up all life from this place like a leech.

Slowly. Spread out over years.

Carmak even wore the same style braid as her mother, pulled so tight that the skin on her forehead was sucked back. As if ties could wrangle her hair into submission. The curls wanted to be free.

Felice took another vial from the sink. Examined it. Wrong mix. She held it to the side. "Carmak?"

She glanced behind her.

Carmak was hunched over her stainless-steel station on the other side of the table between them. Compared to Felice's messy, inoperable sink, full of whatever she decided to throw in it, Carmak's station was organized chaos.

"Y-you're not gonna believe…" Carmak's voice swung high, then low. "Holy Mother of Earth…"

"What happened?" Felice's grip slipped. The vial clattered in the sink and broke.

"The DNA shifted," she sang with surprise. As if shifting DNA wasn't what they dealt with. Every. Single. Day.

No shit the DNA shifted.

Felice picked glass out of the sink. "DNA tends to do that when you pair it with new instructions—*ow! Ahh…*" A glass sliver stuck Felice in the hand. She used her black manicured nails to pull it out. "Can you be a little more specific, please?"

"Is this from Five?"

Dehumanizing their most promising child subjects with numbers instead of names made Felice's skin boil. She put the rest of the broken glass into a jar and kept her tongue imprisoned behind clenched teeth.

She got it. Using numbers helped to cope with what they were doing.

But they fucking had names.

Felice put the jar down and turned. Tension in her face dropped.

Carmak's face had the most expression Felice had ever seen on it. Puzzlement. Pride. And the stark paleness of someone who held an Earth-shattering secret.

"Well, that's a face." Felice pretended not to be perturbed.

"It's Five's, isn't it?" She held up a vial of blood, turning the label toward Felice.

"Stop calling her Five. She has a name. It's *Elpida*."

"But it's hers, right?"

It was hard to stay mad at Carmak and that incredulous look. "You answered your own question… Have we made progress on her?"

"I had to be sure it was hers. I-I can hardly believe…" Carmak's voice jumped so high it practically scraped the ceiling. "She's becoming more human."

Felice's heart leapt to her throat faster than her ass left the chair. The two back legs scraped the tile. It tipped backwards and she caught it before it fell.

"Is it a breakthrough?" She placed the chair firmly on all four legs.

Elpida Enosh. That "more human" vial of blood was hers, what they'd been waiting for, the pot of gold at the end of Felice's out-of-reach rainbow.

"Not yet." Carmak placed the blood sample in her mini fridge, turned, and faced Felice. "But I think we're close."

Felice let out a breath. She met Carmak's still-stunned stare, skepticism slowing her pulse. "We also said Rumi was close. And look where *she* is. Her genes are spiraling."

"Elpida is closer than Rumi. She's nearly human and that's only from the preliminary test."

"What do you mean, nearly human?" She moved around the six-person table toward the workspace. She had gotten her hopes up before. She knew this game. She leaned over the countertop. Cold metal seeped heat from her palm. Liquid strings of genetic material in clear vials were labeled with numbers.

"You won't see anything that way. Just look at the data."

A message from Carmak pinged Felice's ear com. It was a soundless notification, like a blink of light in the back of her mind. She opened the message, unlocking it with a flicker of thought.

The com showed her images. Through her brain-waves, it displayed data to her visual cortex. Blindly staring through Carmak, she viewed the analysis.

Elpida's DNA had, of course, shifted. But it wasn't just a shift. The DNA was much more human now than it was *transitus*. Practically overnight, the DNA of the girl had completely transformed.

Her heart hitched. But before her heart could catch, before it could snag on the barbs of hope, she stamped the hope out like a flame. Before her mother could.

"She's a long way off." Her words tried to be sure and strong, but her mind reeled at the data. Only a few scattered letters of non-human code remained.

Like the miracle they had hoped Elpida to be, the girl was now human.

Almost. Almost human.

There was much work to be done.

Felice messaged her mother Lamia through her com. *"Progress on Five."*

Her mother's voice through the waves—a ghost of the real thing, liquid and leaking—was immediate. *"Get her."*

"Lamia's gonna ask you to bring her here."

Felice refocused her eyes and her tight lips stretched into a bladed smile. "I know that, Carmak." Her words were clipped.

The unsaid taboo hung in the air between them. *Abduction.*

Carmak must have sensed the shift in Felice and not wanted to deal with it because she turned away and started on more tests.

Felice turned back to the data, both amazed and appalled that they were finally getting somewhere. She knew this day would come. She knew this day would slam her morals against the wall. Shattering them like her clay-pot bones.

This was the result they had long been hoping for. She should be elated. But after all this was over, she would be left picking through the pieces.

This was her burden.

Because no one else was going to cure Pneumaphage.

When someone with the *transitus* gene developed Pneumaphage, it was always deadly.

The *transitus* gene was an accidental, man-made genetic mutation. *Homo transitus.* Not human. A completely new humanoid species that emerged most prominently in the twenty-second century.

Some *transitus* people were "viable."

Viable kids grew into aquatic lungs from their air-breathing lungs the same way baby teeth were replaced by adult teeth. The kids transitioned from air to water and went to live in the ocean as late as age twenty.

Viable *transitus* never got Pneumaphage.

But the *transitus* gene had a fatal flaw. Some *transitus*, like Elpida, were *non*-viable. Non-viable *transitus*—NVTs—would never develop aquatic lungs. NVTs were as stuck on land as humans. And their strings of messy part-human, part-*transitus* DNA were susceptible to error.

Scrambled DNA would fuck up.

If scrambled DNA fucked up enough, if the DNA got it wrong, the NVT got Pneumaphage. The disease gave them faulty genetic instructions. Instructions that told healthy, air-breathing lungs to transition. Since NVTs were non-viable—physically unable to transition—their confused lungs consumed themselves.

No one who got the disease lived.

It didn't discriminate.

If a five-year-old got it, they died. If a sixty-five-year-old got it, they died. Didn't matter if they had it for days or for years. Didn't even matter if they got a lung transplant.

They always died.

This secret project to cure Pneumaphage, combined with the will of her mother, tested Felice's limits. Tested how corrupt she would become to help save lives...

Save lives one day.

Right now, all she did was mess with them. Because Elpida Enosh did not have Pneumaphage. She wasn't dying. She was just unlucky enough to have a perfect gene mash-up.

Years ago, Felice's mother had figured out that they needed to reverse the gene of a young, non-viable *transitus* in order to stop the disease. So as years dragged by, they conducted their experiments and tweaked the genes of the kids, tested on Rumi Yen, and waited for results. To find a way to turn non-viable *transitus* human. Making them human would stop Pneumaphage.

But how does someone that is *transitus* become human?

That's what they had to figure out.

Several months ago, to speed up their progress, her mother mandated that they administer more aggressive genetic testers—instead of just mild genetic probing—to all the NVT kids living on the island as well as ramping up other trials on the viable kids. These new testers were now given during monthly nutritional checkups and blood draws.

Hence Elpida and Carmak's discovery.

They would have never found out how promising Elpida was without the aggressive testers.

Now Felice would have to actively pursue abducting a twelve-year-old resident. Unlike Rumi. With Rumi, she merely happened upon a perfect opportunity. When Rumi disappeared, it was easily waved away.

Just a kid who fell in the pinnacles... a rare but tragic ending.

Damp memory crawled into Felice's ear like a bug. Her shoulder twitched. She shook the feeling and rubbed her hands over her arms as if her creeping memories could be brushed away.

This was her mother's endeavor, but Felice had been tits-deep in this shady shit for fifteen years. And if she ever resisted, ever defied her mother, ever wavered or contested any part of the last fifty percent of her life, her mother unleashed an invisible assault of guilt. It raided her spirit. Pressed and squeezed and snuffed out any and all rebellion.

The taste of iron spread over her tongue. She had gnawed her cheek raw.

She closed the open file of data and squeezed between Carmak and the bolted table, toward the sealed chamber door.

"Where are you going? We're not done," Carmak said.

"No, *you're* not done. Keep running tests on that sample. I'm going to get the girl."

"How?"

"For me to know, Carmak."

"You worried about the mother?"

Felice stopped by the chamber door. "No."

"The brother?" Carmak's question mark sounded like it had a stroke.

"Yes. I'm worried about the brother." Thinking, she popped a knuckle. "He's very protective…"

Her mother pinged her again, as if on the exact same thread of thought: *"Can you expedite Krimsey Enosh, please?"*

The request made her sick, but she knew it would be necessary.

While their illegal operation couldn't reverse the *transitus* gene yet, there were a lot of other things they had figured out. Example: how to speed up a viable *transitus* to transition sooner. Make them no longer able to breathe air.

"Yes." Felice pinged back.

"Thank you, Daughter."

Maybe it was the cold, disembodied voice of her mother, maybe it was guilt, maybe it was both, but Felice had to pause at the door to restart her heart. Force-feed air into her lungs. Maybe it was the fact that she would now have to push herself to commit multiple, very deliberate, very intentional crimes. Crimes against a family she genuinely loved.

Here on the East Antarctic Island, the Humanoid Preservationist Organization—the HPO—took *transitus* in from Mainland. Families came here for refuge from harsh realities of life on Mainland, and to get out from under the thumb of the NWA.

Upon arrival, each family was assigned a guide. Guides helped ease families into their new lives. Helped them get used to the strange, day-to-day living of life on the side of a cliff—a dark crack between mountains. Most of all, guides helped new families ready their *transitus* children for the lives they had ahead.

Felice had been a guide to the Enosh family for five years and had been their glue when their dad died.

Pneumaphage.

Their connection made the sting of Felice's betrayal so much worse. Because Krimsey and Elpida and their mother, Sanjana, had practically been *her* family for a time. Felice was rubbing salt in a wound they weren't even aware they had.

Or maybe it was the other way around.

Maybe her contemptible decisions over the years had given *her* the wound. Tiny lacerations everywhere there was skin. And it was *her* wounds she rubbed salt into.

"Transition Ceremony is this week." Carmak snapped her back to the present.

"What?"

"You know, Krimsey Enosh? Maybe he'll just happen to transition in time for this week's ceremony? It would help, right?"

"You and my mother both have a strange way of reading my mind."

Carmak shrugged. Nonchalant, almost modest. Her face was irritating. It was inert and irritating and didn't look sad enough.

Carmak had no clue. No clue how awful it had been for Felice to rescue Rumi, who had merely gotten herself into a bad situation. To then see her relief wriggle into worry into fear into dread. Because, instead of taking her to her parents, Felice had brought her here.

She opened her mouth to speak, then a high-pitched alarm set off. Bounced and blared off metal walls. The dome amplified the sound like a speaker. Her com echoed the alarm.

At first, its meaning was lost in the spine-crumbling screech. Screeching so loud it ripped all thought from her mind. So loud that, for two terrible seconds, she forgot. So loud that her feet trembled, melted, stuck to the floor when she realized.

It was the alarm hooked to Rumi's vitals.

"Rumi." She could barely speak. The name snapped her spine in two, but she couldn't just stand there.

Rumi was dying.

Then she stared, blinked, turned, lunged. Adrenaline nearly kicked her legs out from under her. She slammed her hand into the keypad on the wall by the door.

Don't die. Rumi. Please don't die.

Seconds passed.

The keypad flashed red.

She swiped sweaty palms on her dress. She tried again, pressing a sickly hand to the pad, shaking. Her breath was ice. The green light finally flashed. The seal clicked. The door slid open. It banged against the stopper.

Inside the connecting chamber, she had to scan her hand a second time. She held her breath. Excruciating.

Green light. Go.

She swung the door open and sprinted into the central habitat. Her sandals struck the metal grating placed over the moon pool. Unwitting marine life darted from her shadow.

She pressed her hand against the keypad to the middle door, left wall, which required two-person authentication. She frantically searched over her shoulder.

"Carmak!" She screamed, raising her voice above the alarm. Carmak was fumbling with Dome Four's doors, trying to seal the chamber. "Fuck protocol! Close them later."

Carmak had managed to pull the second door half-closed before abandoning her attempt. She was now running toward Dome Two in slow motion. Felice's ears were ringing, the weight of each passing second compressing her joints.

Carmak reached the door and pressed her hand up against the other keypad. Together, they opened the outer chamber door to Dome Two, the inner door still shut. Felice pressed her hand into the right scanner, Carmak on the left. The door clicked open. Felice shoved it aside.

Inside was the image she feared.

Rumi Yen's small, blue-hued body sprawled on the floor, spasming by the bed. Carmak rushed to her. One foot over the threshold, Felice froze. She stood in the doorway, leaden with indecision.

Carmak knelt down and touched Rumi's forehead. She looked up at Felice. "She's rejecting the treatment."

Felice swallowed the terror rising in her throat and fought tears threatening her vision. *What do I do?*

Rumi's eyes roamed beneath her shining lids. Locks of red hair clung criss-cross over her forehead and cheeks.

"Aren't you going to do something?" Felice shouted.

"Only Lowery knows how to—"

"Do what Lowery did."

"Felice, if I take the wrong steps… it could be fatal."

"She's dying anyway!"

Carmak shook her head. "Her body might beat this without—"

"*Do something!*" Felice screamed. Rumi's struggle against death beat in her ears. She felt sick. Felice turned to the chamber supply wall behind her. She tore into the storage.

She searched every container, drawer, and compartment, filling the tiny chamber floor ankle deep with equipment. She searched for anything to jog her memory. She had seen Lowery save the girl before, injecting her with life-saving genetic material, keeping the body from rejecting the earlier tests.

Felice could hardly breathe past the nauseating lump building in her throat. She spotted a blue and green vial in a lower cabinet. She held it up to the light. The word scrawled along its side was too complex to decipher, but it was Lowery's writing. And it looked right.

She spotted a second vial. Also familiar.

"I have to mix it just right," Felice said. She stood, entered the dome, and approached Rumi, wielding the needle in one hand and vials in the other. Felice uncapped the vials with her teeth. Her hands shook as she made an attempt at measuring by luck.

"We should—"

"What, Carmak?" Felice spit a plastic cap onto the floor.

"Should we see how her body adapts first?"

"You mean just watch her die."

The cap rolled under the bed.

"No, I mean—well, how do we really know if it's working? What if—"

"Carmak. She *will* die if we leave her. Let me just remind you, this is *your* watch. *You'll* be the one telling my mother about this if she dies. Think about that."

Shaking, she tunnel-visioned onto the vials, drawing careful measurements through the needle.

Rumi's chest heaved.

"Keep her still," Felice said.

Carmak watched her in silence and braced Rumi, holding her flailing limbs and tiny webbed hands in place.

Felice held her breath. She jammed the needle into a twitching arm and released the mixture into Rumi's frail, sea-blue body. The spasms stopped immediately.

Rumi sighed, her breath slowed.

"Put her on the bed," Felice ordered. "*Quickly*. Be *gentle!*"

They took Rumi to the middle of the bed. Carmak placed Rumi's limp body on top of an ocean of white silk sheets.

Sitting on the edge, Felice loosely tucked a sheet around Rumi's middle.

Felice hovered, unblinking, feeling each puff of breath with the palm of her hand over Rumi's lips. Rumi inhaled. The intake of breath flowed cool between her fingers. A slow puff of air escaped Rumi's lips in an everlasting moment.

Time stopped.

Carmak said something. Felice had no concept of how long she waited for the next breath of air to draw into Rumi's body. Her hand shook, waiting. She was acutely aware of the dried sweat dusting the girl's unmoving eyelids.

There was a hand on her shoulder. Carmak. "What?" Felice asked.

"She's gone."

"That's impossible. No, it worked, see? She's—"

Not breathing.

Carmak gently tugged Felice away from the lifeless body.

Viable

Zeph Carmak, Sunday, March 24, 2250, 8:02 a.m.

ZEPH LOVED WORKING WITH crop seed variants in The Bowl—the lush, green terraforming valley past the pinnacles at the foot of Karuli Crag. They loved being elbow-deep in the only dirt on this sweltering, sun-ravaged East Antarctic island rich enough to grow anything.

But the long, strenuous hike along the sheer cliff of Karuli Crag to get there was always miserable.

Many *transitus* teens on the island fought each other relentlessly, as though life were an ugly game for survival. In a world sharply divided between human and *transitus*, between viable and non-viable, everything had to be black or white. Either you *were* or you were not. Anyone who was different in any way would be targeted and bullied. Divergence—of any kind—was wrong.

Zeph was a divergence.

When it came to gender, Zeph didn't fit labels. And while their fluidity would have been widely accepted in Mainland communities—here there was strong backlash.

"You would think that the hatred Mainlanders have for us would bring us together," Zeph growled, loud enough for the nearby kids to hear, while navigating a steep switchback down Karuli Crag. "You are bullies. All of you."

They knew the other teens were listening because being *transitus* came with the ability to sense the emotions of every *transitus* in a three-meter radius. Everyone around them, hidden within precarious plastic homes along the cliffside, was currently seething. Ill will seeped into Zeph's skin like smog.

"It is polite to keep your emotions contained," they grumbled, but most didn't, not when it came to Zeph.

Seething glares from glassless window holes followed their descent.

Not only was Zeph gender non-conforming, but they were also from Up Top, the top of Karuli Crag—not on the cliffside. It was a brutal combination. Up Top was where human families lived. Not *transitus* families. The fact that Zeph lived there was enough for less fortunate kids to justify their hate.

This morning's commute was particularly jarring in the emotional-assault arena. Which was why Zeph had no patience for Jules, the young terraforming intern, after arriving to work. They were together in the temp-controlled greenhouse and Jules was breathing. Right now, that alone was enough to be irritating. Zeph had planting to do. Had to care for several new seedling pots. Had a long list of things to do and none of the patience to delegate. There was no time for things like questions or sneezes or audible breath.

Jules flitted inside the greenhouse like a bee from flower pot to flower pot, minus the productivity. "Why do you work in terraforming? Don't you have human parents and live Up Top or something?"

Can she not see I am busy?

Her question grated. Tingling, tickling sweat dripped down Zeph's neck. Mashing a seed into the soil, their hand shook. "You know that's a stupid question, right?" Their words snapped like twigs.

Ignorant. Baseless. Frankly, discriminatory. As if living Up Top on the flat vista of Karuli Crag mountain or having human parents precluded them from the inevitability of NVT career assignments. As if human parents couldn't have *transitus* kids. Zeph loved the job, but that did not mean it was a chosen path. Testing into terraforming was the only reason Zeph worked here. Same way any other air-and-land-bound NVT tested into a lifelong career. Same way Jules tested into terraforming a year ago.

Internship Day was an inevitable fate, regardless of parentage. Never mattered how human a parent was. Sooner or later, every non-viable *transitus* kid had to face Internship Day. The day the HPO decided the rest of an NVT's life. If they weren't going to transition into the ocean, they were going to go to work.

It kept the HPO's East Antarctic community growing and thriving.

"What question?" Jules's voice was small and squeaky.

Normally, Zeph was much more forgiving. They liked Jules. A lot. She was a sweet, smart kid. Quick on her feet. But today was not the day.

Heated emotion oozing from their pores, Zeph moved the pots aside and scraped moist soil from their rubbery, blue-black palms. The wet earth was stuck to the loose webbing between their fingers.

Zeph turned to Jules. "What do you mean 'what question?'"

"I didn't say anything," she said. Barely fourteen, Jules was well put together. Her red bob was tucked and pinned tightly behind pale, blue-tinted ears and she wore an impressively clean white shirt. Embarrassment reddened her face.

You have never been this moody before. I wonder what's wrong, Jules's squeaky voice said—but with an echoey sound, reverberating in the forward part of Zeph's mind. Her mouth did not move. Zeph felt the sound rather than heard it. A sound that was not a sound. The words emanated from the same area of the brain where they sensed and received floating bits of *transitus* emotion.

"Excuse me?" Zeph asked. The noise of gulls and early morning chatter outside was drowned out by a rushing in their ears.

Zeph almost thought… well, no. Hearing Jules's thoughts? All *transitus* had the natural ability to sense other *transitus* emotion. Never tangible thought. That would be impossible.

"I am sorry, Jules." Zeph didn't mean to smirk, but their cheek twitched. Lips stretched. The growing smile split their mouth uncomfortably wide. "For a second, I thought I could tell what you were thinking." A snort escaped. Turning back to the shelves at the rear of the greenhouse, Zeph picked up a tray of tiny empty containers. "It has been a rough morning. Alright. I think you are ready to—"

The other transitus are still attacking you. Doesn't it get old assaulting the same person every day? The HPO really should do something about emotional bullies....

Zeph swung the tray around. Several of the black containers toppled over. Their eyes landed on Jules's thin but eager smile.

"You *did* say something."

Jules's smile—more a delicate, straight line than a smile—turned into an upside-down curve of curiosity. "Is everything okay? I haven't said anything."

Zeph did a quick mental check. Besides being irritable and flushed, their body felt fine. No queasiness. No shortness of breath. Didn't Pneumaphage cause hallucinations?

Oh, Earth, do I have Pneumaphage? What were the first symptoms again? Chest pain and pressure near the heart?

There was definitely a pressure. But it was probably being caused by the breath they were holding out of frustration, or it really was Pneuma—Zeph released the breath slowly.

I do not have Pneumaphage.

"You look..." Jules looked up at the greenhouse ceiling as if the words she was looking for would be there. "You look sick." She had a motherly stare. One that had no business being on the face of someone her age.

"Shut up, Jules." Zeph shoved the tray in front of her. "Take this and plant some of those new seedlings. No, not those ones, the other. The ones in the big bag. No, labeled—" Zeph took back the tray. More little containers toppled on it. "I will do it. You get the fertilizer."

"Maybe you should—"

"Maybe you should do as you are told. Fertilizer. There is a new mixture next door."

Jules clamped her mouth and left through the plastic greenhouse flap. She was gone all of five seconds before a blurry silhouette appeared again through the opaque entrance.

"Zeph Carmak."

This was not Jules. The voice belonged to Walmor, lead terra-former of The Bowl. He burst through the flap in a sweaty gush. The sudden flurry of movement made Zeph drop the tray completely.

"You scared me." Zeph picked up scattered containers.

Walmor was a pompous, boastful jerk. He was also human and, according to him, at the bottom of the HPO totem pole. He had an unhealthy relationship with power.

"Don't you check your damn com?" His voice was like a sack of rocks.

"You know I do not check when I am working," Zeph shouted back at him. Big mistake.

Rosacea red flushed his round cheeks, ready to explode. Instead of rupturing a fuse, Walmor's lips lifted into an ugly, not-quite-a-smile expression. "You're fired."

"What? You can't do that."

"I can. I did. Know why?"

"Careers are for life, you cannot just—"

"You're viable, Zeph Carmak. You'd know that if you checked your com." His nasty grin split wider.

"That is impossible."

"Thought so, too. Just check your com. Pack your stuff and get out of here." Walmor wrestled the greenhouse flap out of his way. "Whole damn HPO looking for you, *puh*. Won't turn on coms, for Earth's sake...." *Good luck, Earthforsaken crackcase*, he added. The insult was a sound. But not a sound. His lips did not move. Zeph was perceiving Walmor's thought. It was not just from Jules. Walmor's back disappeared from view.

Zeph was too stunned and confused to move for a full minute. When Jules came back with the fertilizer, Zeph was still staring at the door. Blinking at Jules, Zeph finally reached for their thin cardigan on the top shelf and picked a com from its pocket. Jules was staring, asking concerned questions. The questions went unanswered. Zeph sent a flick of thought into their com's settings.

With vis mode turned off, there was no visual stimulus. Just direct information feeding into their brain. Notifications in Zeph's com tumbled forth haphazardly. Little soundless message counts poured in, each message with its own sender and time stamp.

Fifteen messages awaited. Zeph's throat constricted, their pulse drummed, and the pressure in their chest burned as if on fire. They opened the oldest message first. It was their mother, Gina.

"Z, dear? I know you probably already left and maybe you have your com off, but don't go to work today. Please meet me in Medical. Everything is okay but something is going on."

Five more messages from their mother with the same tone and ambiguous concern revealed very little tangible information.

Zeph's heart tripped over the sixth message. The sender was *Lamia Karuli*. Unbelieving, they double-, triple-, then quadruple-checked the sender. Even then, it *had* to be a glitch. Lamia often sent big statements or announcements to everyone's coms at once, but this was not a bulk message. The credentials on this message indicated it was sent direct to Zeph straight from the president of the HPO.

Flicking a thought command at the message, Zeph made it open.

"Zeph Carmak. House H of Footpath Main, Up Top. Report to Medical Wing B for immediate re-classification."

Re-classification? That was impossible… no one had ever been re-classified. Walmor said they were viable… was that true? More messages awaited from the stores of the com. A lump formed in their throat. Zeph fought back tears.

What is happening to me?

Survival Daily

Krimsey Enosh, Sunday, March 24, 2250, 3:58 p.m.

KRIMSEY'S TOES DANGLED OVER the precipice. Preparing to drop like the rock in the pit of his stomach, he remembered why he hated Survival Daily. It wasn't the artificial light in the bottom of Glacier Lake, which stung his eyes. It wasn't the occasional *dwop* of bat guano striking the surface. It wasn't even the hunger that would soon gnaw at his stomach.

It was the awful reminder.

The reminder that he was different. That he did not belong above water—a part of him he was desperate to ignore. Without warning, his viable *transitus* mutation was going to force him to leave his sweltering-but-safe East Antarctic Island home and his cherished non-viable sister, Elpida. His lungs were going to transition, and he would become a permanent, involuntary resident of the ocean.

Unlike most *transitus*, Krimsey didn't want to leave land.

He took half a step back. Rocks were loose and sharp and awkward under his feet. He swallowed, trying to push down the terror. He hated that he let the reminder of his looming transition have so much power.

"We don't have all day!" A pressure on his back shoved him over the ledge.

The back of his throat burned with bile. He was heavy and weightless all at once. On Krimsey's way down, Cris Langly's nefarious glee skittered across the cave walls. Krimsey's body pitched out of control. His gangly limbs fought to right his angle of belly-first descent. Continuing to topple, he braced himself for the painful slap of impact.

Splash.

Contact with the surface bruised his ribs. Water smashed into his ears just before his world became muted. The mocking echoes of side-splitting laughter disappeared. A dose of water burned up his nose. His face contorted.

For a moment, he was furious. Anger blurred his vision. *What? What are* you *going to do to* Cris Langly, *Krimsey?* Even his own internal dialogue mocked him. He surfaced.

On the pebble beach, the stern Professor Rellington's seated shape looked unamused. One leg crossed over the other. Thin white lips. Clearing his throat, he brought his tired, intent eyes up to Cris.

Cris's laughter stopped, but its echoes continued on into the silence.

"Sorry, Professor Rellington." Cris was barely audible.

Rellington was the only *transitus* professor on the entire island. All the other professors were human. And he was the only one who monitored Survival Dailies. Krimsey was sure it was some form of discrimination that the only *transitus* teacher was sent down here for the dirty work, but Rellington seemed to enjoy it. Torturing all the viable kids, twenty-four hours at a time.

Once a month, Krimsey and other young, viable *transitus* kids had to practice survival for oceanic living. For Krimsey, that meant twenty-four hours of misery. No one ever seemed to mind Survival Daily as much as he did. Currently, there were forty-five other viable kids who lived under the guidance of the HPO. Rellington staggered small groups of them throughout the month to keep the schedules manageable. Rellington was down here ten times a month, living in a less-than-glamorous shack. Ten times too many for any sane, healthy person, according to Krimsey.

Rellington returned his uninterested stare to Krimsey.

Krimsey wiped water from his face, knowing he had left his confidence somewhere up on the precipice in his pile of sweaty clothes. He wished he could go back up and put it back on. At least then he'd be wearing more than just his underwear. He pushed his bangs aside and swam out of the way, under the shadow of a rock.

One by one, his classmates jumped in after him. First Bobby, the most opinionated *transitus* he had ever met, dove headfirst, surfaced, and whipped his blond hair in an exaggerated arc. Lucie followed next. She was too young for him to have spent enough time with her to know her, but he knew enough to stay away. Cris jumped last, whooping on the way down, hugging his pale, knobby knees to his chest.

The blue surface foamed white where Cris entered. His red hair popped up, undulating in the water like tendrils of blood. His brows and lashes were dewy and sharp; his nose protruded from his face, mouselike. Joining the others, he smiled an extra-wide, toothy grin. Krimsey couldn't help but imagine it was meant for him. A warning.

On the beach, Rellington stood. Hands behind his back, he waited. Pressed his lips together. Relaxed his shoulders. Gave each viable kid a good, long stare. Above, on the precipice landing, a panting huff and the sound of footsteps trickled down to the water. Rellington stopped the interrogation with his eyes and looked back up at the precipice. "Zeph, lateness can only happen once. Join them, please." The Professor projected his long, enunciated words toward the overhang where one of the many underground Karuli Crag tunnels came to an end.

Movement from above caught Krimsey's eye. A fifth *transitus* shuffled to the ledge. Krimsey felt vague, unfiltered impressions of excitement coming from this unfamiliar classmate. Confusion from Bobby, Cris, and Lucie mixed into the soup of *transitus* emotion. They all exchanged stares, then smirked.

Krimsey, keeping his own confusion close so others didn't sense him, drifted from his rock for a better look.

The new classmate's dark face and form glittered in sharp relief against the LEDs shining up from the lake. The smooth bald head and solid stance, from a distance, made this classmate look like a boy. But they had a delicate, feminine elegance, too. Krimsey was confused; he knew there was a gender-nonconforming *transitus* on the island, but they were not viable, so what were they doing here?

Regardless of identity, Krimsey was worried. The other kids were going to eat them alive. The best they could hope for was for the bullies to quickly lose interest. The new classmate leapt from the ledge headfirst. Strong, wide shoulders and thick calves rippled in the light and entered the water so smoothly, there was hardly any wake.

"Everyone, meet your new peer, Zeph Carmak. Zeph Carmak, meet everyone." Rellington's voice was pancake-flat.

Bobby and Cris motioned to Zeph with smiles.

Here we go.

Zeph swam toward them with a tentative flash of teeth, white foam bubbles trailing behind. The classmates pounced on the newbie with questions.

Bitter and still nursing his ego, Krimsey treaded back a meter, keeping to the fringe of the social circle, deciding he needed to stay far away from Zeph. For self-preservation reasons. Krimsey kept his mind shuttered from detection.

Zeph's dark yellow eyes caught him staring.

He looked away, noting that Zeph didn't partake in the chatter and didn't answer any questions. Surely, this nonchalant behavior would soon elicit harsh insults. Insults didn't come. The others looked at Zeph with genuine interest. Maybe Krimsey's initial impressions were wrong. Maybe Zeph and the bullies were a natural fit. Maybe Zeph would be popular. Krimsey's next nemesis.

"Be quiet. All of you." Rellington cut through the boisterous talk.

Cris shut up and the rest of the group fell silent.

"Not that you'll be doing any speaking tonight, but please note Zeph uses they/them pronouns." Rellington stated in a bored drawl. "You kids love to size each other up and count your differences so you can use them as projectiles against one another. I do not care for bullies, but I know you'll do as you do, I suppose. And I know there won't be anyone to look after you but yourselves after you transition, so there's that, and I don't know why I'm even saying all this, but for Earth's sake, respect the pronouns." He paused with a sigh, looking between all of them. "Now, you have questions. You may be wondering, 'Have I met them before?' 'Why have I never seen them?' 'Aren't they too old to be new to Survival Daily?' Let's clear all of that up now so we are sure to have no distraction."

Zeph drifted several centimeters away from Cris and the others and half-submerged their head beneath the surface. From this angle, their face looked like it had fallen several shades in hue, becoming dull.

"You would be correct," Rellington continued. "Zeph Carmak is much too old to have never done Survival Daily before. How can this be, you ask? Well, somehow, someone, somewhere misclassified this viable *transitus* as non-viable. Zeph grew up non-viable, took non-viable classes, trained into an NVT career, and now they're here. Viable." Rellington said the word with such disdain, he all but hocked up a ball of phlegm. "So yes, Zeph is new. No, they're not a fifteen-year-old newbie. And no, you probably have not met them before. Tonight, you can help them. Don't help them. Up to you. This is Survival, after all."

Rellington paused, landing his gaze on Zeph. His chest moved as if taking a long, steadying breath. Then, he folded his hands in front of him and, skimming over Krimsey, shared a stare with every other classmate, whose faces were in various states of shock.

How could a viable *transitus* ever be misclassified? Krimsey knew they were all wondering the same thing.

Then, of course, once the next question presented itself in Krimsey's mind, he couldn't be rid of it: could a non-viable *transitus* ever be mistaken as viable? The mere thought of this possibility made his pulse quicken and his hands go cold. Though he knew it was irrational, impossible, and unlikely that *he* was non-viable, that *he* could possibly escape his inevitable fate of transitioning, he clung to the idea for dear life.

"You all know the rules. But since it is *their* first time,"—Rellington unfolded his hands and listed the following points on three fingers—"absolutely no spoken word whatsoever... do not leave the confines of the lake... and you have twenty-four hours.

"This is *Survival* Daily. Use this time however you want but just know, there will be absolutely no outside interference during this time. If you are hungry, find something to eat. If you are tired, go to sleep. And if you are thirsty... canteens await you on the shore. When you are fully transitioned, this is not something you will have to worry about; as you know, your lungs will absorb the hydration you need.

"If you did not hydrate before coming here today... take this as a lesson to come better prepared next time." At this, the Professor's attention drifted toward Zeph.

Cris, clearly now interested in earning Zeph's attention, leaned over to them as Rellington droned on. He whispered something, then snickered. Krimsey watched the back of Zeph's bald head for a reaction but there was none.

Rellington was counting down. "Three... two... one.... And, begin."

The lights dimmed. Cris, his face deepening in the low light, continued to glance at Zeph. To Krimsey's delight, Zeph did not seem to return interest in Cris. Krimsey couldn't help but take some small satisfaction from that. About time someone gave Cris a healthy dose of indifference. Not that it changed Krimsey's interest in the new classmate. He was still strictly *uninterested*. In fact, Krimsey was slightly bitter toward Zeph and even less interested in them now. That is, had he had a drop of interest to begin with.

This wasn't fair. This kid was dodging every ripe opportunity to be bullied, things that Krimsey would have been absolutely demolished for. Because, what? Zeph was just interesting enough? So extremely different from the norm that they were now exotic? Zeph didn't seem to be a match for the bullies or the bullied. So they got to float in some place in between. And that was just not fair.

Krimsey breathed in. Closed his eyes. Light faded to dark.

He felt the presence of all but one slip away into the water.

He opened his eyes.

After a minute, two dark spheres appeared in his vision. Watching him. Only Zeph remained after the other classmates swam off. Gliding toward him in the tippy-toe depths, Zeph had a presence that demanded attention. High cheekbones, unwavering eyes, an emotional aura like a black hole... Krimsey couldn't help but be drawn in. In their presence, all of Krimsey's fuming ruminations suddenly lost steam.

"**Hello.**" Zeph greeted him, kicking more quickly than they needed in order to keep their hands free for signing.

Krimsey faltered, blinking back at the beach. Then he looked at Zeph and spelled out his name by letter in Universal Sign Language. "**I'm K-R-I-M-S-E-Y.**"

"**I go by Z.**" Zeph struggled to sign and swim at the same time, so their hand movements were jerky.

"**Z. I guess we haven't met before.**" Krimsey was curious. Even though he would never admit it.

"**We have now.**" Brilliant teeth shining, blue-black skin stretched ear to ear, Zeph's smile spread in the dark. Genuine. Attractive.

Yet somehow irritating.

Because the smile seemed to want small talk. Small talk was unproductive and it kept Krimsey from getting on with the misery of the next twenty-four hours already. The blinking red com light on the beach didn't help. Pulling at his attention and reminding him that Rellington could see, with the data from his com, exactly what he and Zeph were doing and signing.

He just wanted to slink out of Rellington's com's sight. Swim away to the cave half a kilometer away—one that Rellington didn't know about. The quicker Krimsey could get away, the quicker he could sit in his discomfort, and the quicker Survival Daily would end.

But the curiosity he was currently denying begged him for the answers to several questions. Questions he didn't plan to ask. These questions kept him in place. *What is it like to not be what you thought you were? What if the HPO misclassified their misclassification? Could I be non-viable?*

"**I blame myself,**" Zeph signed.

"**What?**"

"**Sorry. My USL… is not very good.**"

"**You blame yourself for what?**"

"**Blame,**" Zeph's head tilted with their ear to the water, "**might not be the right word. But I blame myself for not knowing sooner. Being viable.**"

The red light on the beach blinked, blinked, blinked in his periphery. "**How could you not know?**" Those weren't the right words. **"Sorry, that was—"** Krimsey sunk to his nose under water and blew nervous air.

"Rude?"

"Sorry."

"Not rude. I understand your question."

Did they? He wasn't even sure he understood his question. A plastic crackle came from the beach. A sniff.

"Yes." Zeph intently stared at him.

Krimsey's attention again wandered to the beach.

"You want to know if *you* could be non-viable. That is it. Right?" Zeph signed with a wave of their hand in front of Krimsey, which brought back his attention.

"I thought you said your USL was bad," Krimsey signed with a huff and a dip of his shoulders.

Zeph shrugged. **"Bad. Rusty. Have not practiced since I was a kid. So?"**

Avoiding their eyes, Krimsey looked at the beach again, trying to discern what Rellington's silhouette was doing based on the movement of his com light. Krimsey's heart did a little flip like it was trying to slip away when he saw the com light move to the right and out of sight. Rellington had turned his head and was probably looking their way now. Krimsey didn't like the attention. **"He can see what we are signing."**

Krimsey rolled onto his back but caught Zeph signing the words, **"Can I come with you?"** as he moved to leave.

He rolled forward and rubbed his chin, pretending to consider the question. Zeph's eyes were incessant. And so were their questions. Krimsey didn't want anyone bombarding his space for the next several hours. So he averted his gaze, wondered how many times he had looked away, looked back at them, and signed, **"I prefer to be alone."**

Zeph's eyes flickered, just for a moment. A dash of defeat.

Krimsey dropped his shoulders below water level. **"Sorry."**

"Why?"

The judgment in their eyes made him uncomfortable. As did the way Zeph didn't move when they looked at him. How still they kept their head. Krimsey glanced over his shoulder. **"Fine. Follow me."**

Krimsey swam off. Wide, webbed feet propelled him along the cavern outskirts. Zeph followed. The glacial lake stretched farther than either of them could see. After some time, Krimsey turned into a shallow cavity along the cavern wall, climbing on top of an ankle-deep platform.

Turning back to Zeph, who was hovering neck-deep just outside the shallow cave, Krimsey sat on the platform. **"This is where I come during Survival."**

The water was so shallow here, and Rellington's com's view of him so obscured, he'd often lie here on his back and only get out when the light flashed to mark the twenty-fourth hour's end. At nineteen, he didn't care that he was unprepared for his transition. He never thought he was one of the ones that would live long in the ocean. After transition, it was assumed that twelve percent of *transitus* kids died. Natural causes. Transition gone awry. Food chain trouble. Krimsey doubted he'd even make it to the nearest *transitus* city, which was somewhere off the West Antarctic coast.

Far enough from the HPO to maintain an air of mystery and to weed out the weak.

Zeph looked the cavity opening up and down, patted the shallow opening, as if testing it, then they huffed a little, signing something Krimsey didn't understand. With Krimsey's blank look and questioning hand gesture as a reply, Zeph slapped a palm on the water. Zeph looked around again, almost signed something else, gave up, then crawled into the space beside Krimsey on their hands and knees.

Dipping a set of webbed fingers on the shallow platform, water level just reaching their knuckles, Zeph managed to sign **"This is cheating,"** with a mocking smile.

"We're still in the lake."

"Yes, but…." Zeph put their fingers knuckle-deep in the water again and shrugged.

"What Rellington doesn't see, doesn't hurt him." Krimsey crossed his arms and looked over the lake. He glanced sideways twice at Zeph, who continued to give him a judgmental smile. **"Hey. It's in the lake…. That's the rule. It's still 'surviving.' Still twenty-four hours and starving."**

"Whatever you say."

"**Rellington never checks up here.**"

"**Alright. I believe you.**"

"**Besides,**" Krimsey continued, his face getting hot. He knew this would happen. Everyone was always so uptight. He shouldn't have invited anyone into his space. "**It's up to me if I live or die. Not Rellington. Not the guides. Not the HPO. Just me.**"

Zeph looked as if they had only caught part of that; their expression didn't change.

"**You're judging me,**" Krimsey signed. He wished he could wipe that look off their face. He flicked a splash of water in their direction, as if to make light of building tension. Laugh it off.

"**I did not sign anything,**" Zeph signed.

"**I see that look. You're judging.**"

"**Alright, but only because… you do not practice your skills?**" They asked. "**It is called *Survival* Daily. That is what it is for. Just practice. Not a big deal.**"

Krimsey blinked. *I knew I shouldn't have invited them.*

Zeph held their palms out and shrugged dismissively.

They sat side by side and looked out the cavity's opening. "**Why aren't you practicing with the others, then? I'm not going to help you.**"

"**Others were too clingy.**" Zeph's smile softened, a sort of twinkling, intelligent smirk. They emphasized their point by waving their hand, signing "**C-R-I-S,**" and imitating a perfect impression of Cris smothering Zeph with questions. Zeph crossed their eyes and lolled their tongue with their hands around their neck.

Krimsey stifled a laugh. "**They were all over you.**"

Krimsey had dreaded having this strange new person as a visitor, but he suddenly didn't mind it. Small talk, one thing he normally hated, could actually help make this time go by faster.

"**So why do you want to be non-viable so bad?**" Zeph signed.

Nope. No. This wasn't happening. The moment was gone. Small talk was fine, but this? Zeph was being nosy. Krimsey doubted they even cared about his answer. They just wanted to feel special about themselves, he was sure that was it. Maybe they weren't scared about transitioning and wanted to rub it in like the others.

The water rippled from some far-off break in the surface. He was thinking how best to tell Zeph to kindly bug off and mind their own business.

"I do not mean to be overbearing," Zeph signed, as if reading his mind. **"There was a time I wanted to be viable. Now I am and I am not sure it is for the better."**

Krimsey shrugged, aiming to be casual, watching mini waves in the middle of the black lake get so small they were almost imperceptible. If Zeph was going to stay here, the two of them were going to need to change the topic. **"Okay."**

He wanted to sign, *Okay, I don't really care*, but he was trying hard to not be rude.

"How long do you have?" they asked.

According to the last five DNA analyses from monthly blood draws, Krimsey had eight months, give or take a day, before his lungs would no longer breathe air. He wrapped his arms around his knees.

"I have a month and a half. According to Medical," Zeph continued.

Krimsey spared Zeph's distant eyes a glance. They met his with an unreadable stare. Blank, but alert with attentiveness. A month and a half was no time at all. No time to plan or practice or prepare. How were they going to manage? He found his heart aching for them.

"That's really bad," he signed with one free arm, keeping the other around his knees.

"My mom is not taking it so well. But me? I am fine. I have never done Survival Daily, but I did the equivalent when I was a kid. Pretended to do Survival in Gianvante Lake."

Krimsey found their eyes again, read their body language. Zeph was cross-legged in the shallow cave water. Shoulders stiff, barely angled toward him. No hint of angst in their face. But there was nothing pleasant there, either.

"I know, pretending is not the same. But I was a great swimmer. I am still, but just rusty. At everything. Like my USL."

"Your USL is better than mine."

Zeph's thin smile dropped. **"No, it is not."**

"It is. Your signs are precise. And I understand you, which, you know, I've heard is useful."

The edges of their lips twitched. Zeph's eyes followed his hands.

"I, however, am antisocial and hardly keep up. Too many subtle social cues that I miss."

"So. Why do you not practice?"

Krimsey hunched noncommittally. "I don't *not* practice...."

He could have told Zeph about his family. Not wanting to leave his sister for the ocean. Why he was her only reliable guardian. He could have told Zeph about his skepticism. That he didn't think thriving communities could actually grow and evolve in the ocean. He could have told Zeph that he just didn't care.

Ultimately, he landed on shrugging and signing, "I'm sure I'll just be eaten by a shark." He tried to smile jokingly, but the smile fell and belly-flopped.

"You know that is not true." Zeph looked him straight in the soul.

"How would you know?"

With a straight face, Zeph replied, "Too skinny. I would be eaten. But you?" Zeph's dark eyes and smooth face held their ground. "Can I help you hate Survival less? Come on, we can go for a swim."

"No."

"Come on, I can help. I am good at this."

He shook his head.

"I am *really* good at this."

Krimsey was getting irritated.

"If *transitus* could be guides, I am HPO-would-never-let-me-go good at this."

"N-O." He punched each letter in the air.

"What are you scared of, really?"

Krimsey suddenly stood. "I'M NOT SCARED." He mouthed the words, signing with jerky motions, puffing his chest.

His eyes flicked to the black lake surface and back to Zeph. He sat back down, facing the wall, pressing his face against his webbed fingers. He swallowed a terrible knot of solidified stress.

The fact was, Krimsey *was* scared. And he was a coward, which he hated. He simmered on this thought. A fire in his belly ignited.

Anxiety, fear, pain, dread—all its fuel. A minute passed. Longer. But then something shifted. The fire dimmed. The searing burn cooled. Sensations of warmth spread like a blanket, moved to his muscles, worked at the resistance like knots, and loosened his resolve.

It was as if an external presence guided him into a state of self-acceptance and suddenly urged him to take a dive. He closed his eyes, sighed, and turned to face Zeph.

Krimsey stood. Zeph looked up. **"Fine, let's do this."**

"You are sure?" The surprise was a fleeting flicker across their face.

"Yes. Before I change my mind," Krimsey signed, then reached his hand out. The blanketing presence continued to stifle his thoughts and fears.

"Take me somewhere you fear the most."

Just as his mind was about to refuse, Zeph took his hand. His heart pounded, spiked with adrenaline, but his body remained still. **"Okay. I will."**

Together, they walked to the mouth of the cave and walked off, plunging into the deep water outside. They sank downward into the salty, metallic water, equalizing their ears as they descended. Zeph's muscled body sank gracefully, as if having done this a thousand times before. Together, their knees settled into the sand. They bobbed just over the bottom of the lake. They faced each other.

Though their lungs were not yet transitioned into breathable aquatic lungs, *transitus* could hold air sometimes as long as fifteen minutes.

"Lead on," Zeph signed. **"Somewhere you really hate."**

Sand settled onto Krimsey's lap. He knew exactly where he had to go. Past Zeph's shoulder, he saw one of the lake's many trenches—a terrible black rip in the sandy floor. Grains of sand cascaded over the edge.

His lungs shook with panic. He looked up, swallowed hard three, four, five times. There was a push and pull of emotions. But the presence, his mental guide, was there, encouraging. And it won the internal battle.

I can do this.

They swam to the trench and together they plunged down.

BURIAL

Felice Karuli, Sunday, March 24, 2250, 7:08 a.m.

RUMI YEN'S BLANKET BRUSHED Felice's thigh. The too-young face was motionless. Carmak tugged at Felice's arm, trying to pull her away from the body. Felice couldn't wrap her mind around the fact that a kid was dead. It was too much.

This is not okay. I am not okay.

She seized up as if possessed.

Felice ripped herself from Carmak's groping hands and turned to the chamber connecting the dome to the main habitat. She needed supplies. She needed to resuscitate. Rumi couldn't be dead. She wasn't supposed to be dead.

She stumbled into the small chamber and collapsed to her knees. She tore open shelves and drawers, ignoring Carmak's protest. Priceless, medical-grade equipment tossed in a fit of panic.

Felice latched on to a defibrillator.

"That won't work." Carmak came up behind her and barred her way back into the dome, prying the defibrillator from Felice's grip. "She's gone. Stop."

"I have… to try." She hyperventilated. Snot ran past her lips. Behind Carmak, Rumi lay on the bed as if asleep. "I have to… Fuck. She can't be dead. No. She can't be."

"She's gone." Carmak jerked Felice by the shoulders, snapping her attention momentarily to meet her eyes. "She's gone, Felice."

She placed the defibrillator down in the pile at their feet. "Let me clean this up. Go."

She knew Carmak was right. But she gave one more bleary-eyed attempt at getting into the dome. She ducked. Tried to fit under the arms that blocked her. Carmak caught her, muttered, and guided her into the main habitat. With force.

The moon pool sloshed in the middle of the room. She turned to argue and the door to Dome Two was promptly sealed in Felice's face.

She was pathetic and she knew it. She didn't wipe her snot. She didn't wipe her tears. She didn't leave the chamber door. She didn't even breathe. Dizzy, she just sat on the cold, groaning metal floor.

This is the first and last time I let this happen. There was no cure worth the sacrifice of a young, healthy child. She would talk to her mother and put an end to this.

But she knew her mother wasn't going to give up on Elpida. Now that more progress had been made. Now that they had crept ever closer to reversing non-viable *transitus* genes into human genes. She banged her forehead against the chamber door. It was two-way authentication to get in, but only one was needed to get out. Safety measures. There were a lot of those in this souped-up lab. They needed the precautions.

Eventually, the door opened. The body was nestled in Carmak's arms. Though Felice's old tears had crusted, new ones threatened to burst free. The lump in her throat fought to choke her. And it put up a good fight. She nearly forgot how to breathe again. She nearly let it win.

Carmak and the body were a blur, swimming in her drunken vision. Felice blinked away the liquid clouding her eyes but the edges of her periphery remained hazy.

"Someone needs to close down Dome Four so we can go bury her." Carmak's voice sounded far away; Felice had the sensation of floating away from herself. Carmak looked down at Rumi, then at Felice.

"I'll take her." Felice sniffed.

"Are you... sure?"

"Yeah. Lamia will have a fit if we don't close down Dome Four properly before leaving. You need to do it. I'll miss something." She sniffed again and wiped her nose on her arm. "Hand her to me. I'll wait for you in the exit chamber. We'll leave the lab together." Despite Carmak's hesitations, she handed Rumi to Felice's reaching arms. Felice watched the transaction through her numbness. The metal sound of Carmak's footsteps cut across the moon pool. The final punctuation to Rumi's death.

Hugging the still-warm child, clenching her teeth, and trying not to think too hard about it, Felice swayed along the edges of the grated rectangular moon pool. She didn't like walking directly over it if she didn't have to.

At the far end of the habitat, directly parallel to Dome Four, was the safety chamber that led into the exit chamber. The safety protocols for exiting were strict. For good reason. If both safety chamber doors were open at the same time as someone arriving and opening the transport exit door on the other side of the safety chamber, water from the moon pool would shoot up and flood the place.

Felice knew all this. But her tired, weary brain ignored the little alarms in her subconscious as she opened the first safety door and left it open. With one arm wrapped around a dead child, with thoughts too distant for protocol, she went straight ahead to the second door.

She adjusted the body, then placed her hand on the keypad. The second door opened to reveal the exit chamber. Her ears crackled at a slight pressure change. The final door, at the end of the claustrophobic exit chamber, currently sealed shut, was the one that opened into an elevator-like transport. The one that, if opened at the same time as the other two doors—currently open—would spell disaster. Disaster and a rather sick end.

Felice sat on the cold metal bench next to the transport door and looked back at the moon pool, hardly registering her omission. Though it did register—she acknowledged that the thought did float somewhere in the back of her mind. She just didn't care.

She looked down at Rumi. Her mind was too numb from the morning's events to worry about such protocols and breaches and the possibility of flooding the place by mistake.

She cupped Rumi's body in both her arms.

Felice could hardly care if she herself died.

Besides, no one was coming to the lab today. No one but Carmak and herself, and they were already here. No one was going to open that third door.

Rumi's skin had already turned waxy and grey. The eyelids were closed. It was off-putting not seeing the eyes beneath them flutter.

Despite feeling repulsed by the empty lifelessness and its simultaneous fullness, she forced herself to take note of the state of Rumi's body before burial. The hair was the only thing that looked natural. It had not gone limp. It had not lost color. It had not changed in death. She smelled the lavender wash that still permeated the beautiful locks.

But her hair was missing something.

Her bow is gone.

"Carmak?" Felice stood, repositioned Rumi, and looked back through the safety chamber into the habitat. *She's still cleaning up Dome Four.* Felice stepped back through the two open chamber doors and into the habitat. Rumi loved that bow. Felice needed Carmak to open Dome Two back up.

"Carmak...." Felice hefted the body up her shoulder like a burping baby. "She needs the bow," Felice shouted, knowing Carmak wouldn't hear her through the closed chamber. She felt her mind slowly slipping. She watched it go, with nothing to do but strap in for the ride.

Felice stood at the edge of the moon pool, waiting, heart rate ramping up into her throat. The moon pool was blue and green and clear. The sandy bottom of Ross Bay shimmered with critters nuzzling themselves into a state of camouflage. Grey and white swirled shells scraped little trails across the sand in slow motion. Occasionally a fish swam by. Some even lingered to open their mouths and taste the habitat air.

The room overwhelmingly smelled of old metal and seaweed. The grate that covered the old SCUBA moon pool entrance dipped slightly downward. The bolts that used to fasten each edge had long since turned to dust. No one was supposed to lift the grating up and take a dive, but Felice thought about doing exactly that at least twice a day.

Carmak emerged from Dome Four and closed the door into the main habitat after her. Felice switched Rumi to her other side. "She needs her bow." Felice pressed her free hand against the pad to Dome Two. Her other arm shook. It felt as if the whole room trembled.

Her mind and body drifted apart again. She was watching from afar, in slow motion. Carmak sighed. She seemed to hold her tongue as she strode over the grating toward Felice. As she did so, the water in the moon pool sloshed and vibrated. Not normal. Felice didn't care. Ripples expanded in all directions. Carmak froze over the grate and looked down at the water.

"She's slipping. Help me," Felice said through lips made of rubber.

The water sloshed up the sides of the moon pool and splashed Carmak's sandals as if it were boiling. Definitely not normal. Still, what normally would instill Felice with a sense of foreboding and urgency in this moment was broken.

"Why is the water moving?" Carmak asked.

"I need Rumi's bow. Help me open this damn door." She'd worry about the water later. Her mind was too slow to pick up on Carmak's fear.

"Shit. The doors."

Right. The doors. Beneath Carmak, the water sloshed, gaining ferocity, scaring away the abundance of life in it. The water rose and fell repeatedly as did the pressure in Felice's skull.

The doors were left open. She had completely disregarded the protocol. The reason for that protocol—the reason for needing to keep all doors firmly shut after using them—tickled the back of Felice's mind.

She heard a soft popping sound coming from the exit room.

"Is someone coming down?"

"Yes, your mother, you idiot." Carmak hissed and lunged at Felice, yanking her free elbow. "Run."

The water continued to slosh in a fervent crescendo.

They sprinted across the habitat toward the exit chamber, Carmak dragging Felice, carrying Rumi's limp body over her shoulder. They scrambled through the chamber. Carmak fumbled with the door, which screeched on rusted hinges.

The transport tube out of the underwater lab was like a giant straw to the surface. Unstopper the straw, open up the doors, and the water would lose equilibrium. Open the transport door, open the safety chamber doors, and—*slooop.* The moon pool would flood upward into the lab instantaneously.

Death for everyone inside.

Felice felt the incoming transport slide over a pocket of air. Someone flew toward the lab in it, who would arrive any second. The transport system was only used and known by a select few people. It led here—to the lab—to the beach at Ross Bay, and to the underground tunnel network of the HPO.

Her ears popped. Her skull swelled. Metal pulsed. Carmak closed the rusted chamber door in slow motion. Behind the door, water jumped as if an ancient, angry kraken spewed from its depths. Sweat poured down Felice's sides. Her hands were clammy and slick.

Rumi's body was too heavy. She was petite, but she was one-arming it and—

Thud.

Felice felt three things simultaneously. The body slipped. Hit the ground, landing on Felice's feet. Limp. Dead. The door Carmak was struggling with finally crunched closed and sealed, just as water slapped the door, moments from flooding the lab. The transport locked into place at the end of the exit chamber and its door opened.

Felice's mother stepped out with a grim line etched across her face.

Considering her mother Lamia was the president of the HPO, considering her mother monitored and saw nearly everything that happened both in the lab and in the East Antarctic community that lived about fifteen kilometers from the lab, and considering the look on her mother's face, explanation was unnecessary.

Felice only met her mother's eyes to avoid looking at the body crushing her feet. It was a short-lived exchange. Standing on the lower step that led to the transport, Lamia's eyes snapped onto Carmak, who opened her mouth to speak.

"Close that door," Lamia said before Carmak could lay herself to rest with pitiful words. Carmak stepped out of the safety chamber into the crowded exit room and closed the second of the two safety chamber doors behind her. Lamia closed the transport door. She turned back around and motioned to Felice. "Pick it up." She referred to the body.

Felice's heart wrenched in two when she looked down. The limbs were frozen in dance, the angles all wrong. Felice wanted to squeeze tears from her blurry eyes, but they were too dry. Instead, she leaned down and hefted the body into her sore arms and held tight.

Lamia pushed herself between Felice and Carmak and checked the sealed safety chamber door. Her chin tucked toward her neck, Lamia stole a heavy breath and said, "Come on. We have to bury it." She turned back to the transport door, unlocked it, and they crammed themselves in wordlessly.

The transport took them up and outside to the black sand beach of Ross Bay. It was a quiet, still morning. The surface tension of high tide was broken only by a fish nibbling a bug. Trees lining the beach hardly whispered in the wind.

When they buried Rumi Yen between the trees, deep in the forest by the bay, Felice's hands shook. She cried and she fell to her knees.

Tether

KRIMSEY DOVE DEEPER, DEEPER, deeper. Into the darkness of the water he went, relying only on a single, precious breath of air, and Zeph, holding his hand. This was way past his comfort zone.

I can't do this. I can't face this fear.

Why had he agreed to this? It wasn't safe. It wasn't natural. *I'm too young to die.*

Yet, here he was. The infinite unknown pressed all around Krimsey as the two of them dove hand-in-hand into the glacial seawater trench.

The trench swallowed them both whole. Up-and-down and side-to-side were all wrong. All around them was just black and more black. Black so dense, all his other senses were crippled.

I can't go any further. I won't.

His orientation was lost except for Zeph's fingers wrapped around his palm, steadfast and reliable. But steadfast and reliable were not enough. Krimsey's wrist tensed, his hand unclamped, his eyelid twitched. His pulse *thwumped* in his ears; he felt Zeph's beating under his thumb. Together, their hands made a tether and Zeph was pulling Krimsey into the unknown.

Directionless, he tried to dart away from Zeph.

Zeph responded to his resistance with a hard squeeze, which sent Krimsey's heart into overdrive. Dots swelled and shrank in his vision. He knew he could go at least five more minutes underwater, but his lungs screamed at him to go back.

Zeph gave Krimsey's hand a swift yank that almost snapped them apart. The thought of losing his connection to Zeph sent the dots in his vision bouncing and sparking. Mini atomic explosions.

He swung back to Zeph.

Now, he gripped Zeph's fingers more fiercely. He stopped resisting, shoulders no longer creaking at the seams with tension.

You can *do this.* It was a smooth, confident thought.

Within himself, he suddenly felt a hollow, safe space. Space that was still, silent, and secure. A part of his mind went there, curled up, softened, then settled down.

Heart rate calming, Krimsey swam on with new, more confident energy. The pressures at this depth compressed his lungs and pressed into the sides of his skull. He equalized his ears with his free hand.

Krimsey felt something squishy, soft, and loose against his outstretched hand. They stopped. *Have we reached the bottom?* Sand as fine as silk invited them like a soft bed after a long journey.

Was that so hard? mused the part of him that had curled up comfortably in its safe space.

Using his free hand, without breaking their connection, Krimsey turned himself upright at the same time as Zeph so that his knees were planted in the sand. They had reached the trench floor. He couldn't believe it. Even more surprising, he wanted to stay. He was relaxed, his mind lingering on their connected hands. This connection. He imagined they were old friends. He could almost, *almost*, picture a life under the surface. Did he just need someone to picture it with?

As they sank into the sand, a tiny speck of light appeared. Another speck seemed to land where their hands were. He blinked. Had he dreamed the light? He blinked again and saw movement. A tiny galaxy of green pinpricks shaped into an arm waving in the dark, then dissipated like the tail of a shooting star. Tiny lights were clinging to and drifting around Zeph's body, forming a fluid, vaguely humanoid shape.

Then he heard it. As his heart thudded to an unexpectedly slow pulse, the beating in his ears softened.

Signs of life whispered. Whispered secrets meant only for him. There was a *swish*, then a *gurgle*. *Clack-clacking* of what could only be tiny crustaceans. Squelching, squishing, swooshing. Bubbles popped, sand scraped, and the low drones of Earth vibrated below them.

Krimsey raised his other arm through the bioluminescence. He formed a sign to indicate being awestruck. It was a failed attempt. He couldn't help but smile as the bioluminescent blob he formed faded.

This is incredible. Freeing his emotion so Zeph could feel it, he felt their awe as well. Tiny tendrils of thought fed them both with wonder. *How have I never been down here?*

Zeph's glittering outline shifted, ready to ascend.

Just then, a blur of movement caught Krimsey's eye. The bioluminescence streaked above them, stirred by something swimming through it. Giant fish? Seal? Shark? Croc? He had definitely heard of saltwater crocs. It started small, dashing in the distance, but then it grew. Some creature, some monster of the deep outlined in bioluminescence, was coming straight for them.

His pulse sped like an electric shock. He tried to remind himself that no sharks or other dangerous animals lived here. The HPO would never do that. They were just kids. Still, the elongated shape of the disturbance stirring the bioluminescence seemed predatory.

The HPO wouldn't do that to us... right?

Krimsey tried to keep calm. The approaching blur of movement was quick and taunting. Dashing in every direction, disappearing past the bioluminescence, then moving towards them. He knew the moment Zeph spotted the streak of movement because their confusion seeped and mixed into his own. *Don't panic. Don't panic.* He tried to steady himself. He closed his eyes. Just for a moment. Then he opened them just in time to see the moving swirl above them turn upwards. A trail of light followed as it streaked up and out of the bioluminescent layer, looking like a shooting star.

The sudden *whoosh* from its current battered them and pushed Krimsey over. He nearly lost his tether to Zeph. He grasped their hand tight, pulling Zeph with him.

The force that disturbed the water, whatever it was, seemed to be gone.

Lightheaded, heart now racing, Krimsey kicked his legs to right himself. In the shuffle, the two of them had floated off the sand. There was no telling which way was up. His body blasted through his remaining oxygen. The adrenaline was a flight response, but his veins grew hot, his jaw clenched, his hands turned to fists. He wanted to fight.

This was not the reaction he was expecting. Pure, primal anger zapped his insides.

Was this what Zeph felt? It certainly wasn't coming from him... right?

They were in such close proximity to each other, he could hardly tell which feelings were his own. While their emotions intermixed, one thing was certain: there was an uncontrollable anger growing and growing and it frightened him. Floating white spots crowded his vision and—despite being clearly underwater, not breathing—the smell of stale earth washed over him. He tried to dampen the anger by squeezing Zeph's hand.

In response to this, the anger shifted its attention onto him like a snarling animal.

Krimsey sent urgency toward Zeph to ascend, which Zeph acknowledged with a mental nod. Together, they found the bottom of the lake with their feet and kicked off the floor. They swam a meter before the glittering mass of bioluminescent terror appeared again. It glowed and drifted in their direction without shape, traveling toward them at a lazy prowl.

Then it sped to the left, ramming past Krimsey's shoulder. The mass circled them. It closed in.

Zeph stiffened, then kicked up to get away. Krimsey's frozen grip held tight. Zeph's upward momentum pulled their arms taught. Krimsey clung harder and swam after them, unable to keep up. Zeph's frantic sprint toward the surface pulled their hands apart. Krimsey felt their fingertips touching, sliding away. He was grasping. Kicking. Trying not to lose them. But a weary, heavy weight held Krimsey down. Zeph's fingertips slipped free.

No.

The mass continued to circle. Like a whirlpool, it dragged him downward.

A kick from Zeph's foot to his ribcage forced air from his lungs. Bubbles escaped and tickled his face. He couldn't breathe, couldn't see, couldn't move. Oxygen was precious. Was there enough left to get him to the surface?

He had seconds. Not minutes. Zeph's kicking foot brushed by his face. The will to live was a desperate, clawed beast. It sunk its razor talons into his belly. Blew a cold breath down his spine. Krimsey tried to reach out, to find Zeph and grab hold. He knew he might take them down with him. But in the moment, he didn't care. Survival was animal. Filled with pure panic, Krimsey had lost control. He reached and felt the fleshy heel of Zeph's foot, clamped his hand around it. But the circling currents continued to hold him down and Zeph slipped away. Krimsey flailed his limbs in all directions. He strained. Kicked. Jabbed. Spread his fingers and pulled at the water like a rope he might climb.

Z!

Just when the force was about to win, it vanished. Like a faded dream, all that was left behind was the bitter taste of memories, confusion, and salt.

Krimsey choked on the brackish water pouring into his mouth. His lungs strained and heaved. He kicked up so hard his legs tingled. His arms tingled. His fingers, splitting the water over his head, tingled, too. He wasn't even sure he was going the right direction until the promising, grey-black light of the surface came into view.

Krimsey's eyes blurred.

Just.

A little further.

He saw a commotion above, and thrashing water, just before he lost consciousness.

The sound of a splash startled Krimsey and he jerked awake, coughing and spitting up water, gagging on his own thick tongue. Sharp, unyielding rock dug into his belly. His toes skimmed the cold, glassy water. He was slumped over a house-sized boulder back at the surface. For a second, he forgot where he was and wondered how water could be so black and foreboding. He spit up a lungful of water, looked for where the sound came from, and remembered. The sight of Zeph's blue-black skin sparkling at the surface of the water jolted his muscles to move again. He pushed himself upright. Zeph was surrounded by active, thrashing water. The lake's surface tilted in Krimsey's vision. Swaying, determined to help his new friend, Krimsey scrambled back into the water. He swam toward the action. He smelled stale Earth and iron. Zeph's searing anger, so vicious he dug gouges in his palms with his nails, sizzled over Krimsey's skin.

Zeph lunged and slammed a body-sized something into a sharp outcropping. They snarled, breathing heavily on top of the struggling form. All Krimsey could see was their back. Zeph grunted. The victim of their attack slapped the surface. "I will rip you to shreds," Zeph screamed aloud. They thrashed in the water, a predator dancing with prey.

Through the furious splashing, Krimsey caught glimpses of the something Zeph had attacked. Only it wasn't a some*thing*. It was a some*one*. An arm. A shoulder. A dash of blood-red hair.

Cris?

Cris slipped down from the rock Zeph pinned him to, but Zeph slammed him back.

A blinding light—the one used rarely, only to add extra time to Survival—lit the cave for five terrible seconds. In those five seconds, he clearly saw Zeph latch onto the pale, scrawny Cris Langley and tear through his skin with their teeth and nails. Cris struggled against Zeph's coily might, trying to swim away, but Zeph was all muscle.

In the light, the water shone bright red. Clouds of blood streamed in all directions. Cris kicked Zeph in the gut. Then the light flashed off. Krimsey was temporarily blind. His eyes needed to readjust to the sudden darkness. The surface went quiet. The only sound he heard was the thudding in his ears and the tinkling of ripples in the water.

What. Just. Happened?

He tried to make sense of it. Zeph was like an animal that just ripped right through Cris. And Cris? When did Cris come into the picture? How long had he been unconscious? What in the actual Earthforsaken hell was going on?

The silence was eerie. He heard the papery whisper of a leather wing above. *Tinking* at the surface far away. His breath, wet and ragged and short.

They both went under...

A hollow, gutted squirming in his insides made him dizzy. He had to take several quick breaths to psych himself up enough to put his face back into the water. At first, he only saw outlines. The black trench dripping sand directly below him. Island-like boulders jutting from the floor. The calm, unmoving water. Hiding things. Lying to him. Deep, unsettling stillness. A chill racked through him.

He had dreamed nightmares about Cris before. This could be a dream. Krimsey could still be underwater, suffering wounds from the attacking creature of the depths too great to rise back up from. He could be dying.

Or maybe he was awake. Maybe he had managed to escape the lurking danger by throwing himself on that rock and he had just endangered himself by re-entering the water. Maybe the creature was on its way back, responding to the vibrations and ripples his body made, ready to kill. Cris and Zeph were the dream, their fight too vivid and irrational to be real.

Krimsey blinked again, catching movement in the corner of his eye.

There they were, flashing back into view. Cris swimming for his life and Zeph in pursuit. Zeph's terrifying aura of anger returned, clouding Krimsey's thoughts.

What?

Watching Zeph snag Cris's leg and actually bite him—with their teeth—then watching Zeph's rippling muscle and crushing thighs, and hearing their breathless underwater growl, Krimsey knew. Cris's life was at stake. Cris was a bully, but Krimsey had to help.

Zeph dragged him back down, out of Krimsey's range of vision. He didn't even hesitate.

He dipped under the water and jetted to where he had last seen Cris, ears popping and crackling as he descended. If anyone would have told him this morning that he'd be bailing Cris Langly out of a brutal fight with a mysterious, alluring new classmate, he'd have choked on his powdered eggs.

Finding them was easy.

He followed Zeph's scalding, angry essence like a scent trail. Cris was attempting to kick free. Krimsey swam toward the fight as fast as he could and snuck beneath them, hoping to catch Zeph off guard.

The manifestation of boiling anger worming its way into Krimsey slammed Zeph through the surface of the water like a breaching whale.

In midair, Zeph looked stunned. Their dark yellow eyes were blank, unrealistic, un-*transitus*. Splashing back into the lake on their back, Zeph shook, rubbed their face, and glared at Krimsey.

The shared anger boiled and tipped. It spilled everywhere, spewing spittle in the form of words at Zeph's face. Krimsey screamed. "What the fuck is wrong with you, Z?"

Cris swam to the big round rock Krimsey had found himself on not moments ago. Zeph paced the surface like a trapped animal, paused, opened their mouth—

"You almost killed him!" Krimsey's lips cracked and his head pounded.

Krimsey felt Zeph's sudden shock, but he didn't care. The collective, confused anger cooled to a low simmer before blinking out completely. It turned to wild embarrassment. Zeph's open mouth curled into a sneer and they dashed away.

Cris pulled himself limply onto the jutting rock island. He flopped onto it. Water and blood dripped from his back down his sides. On all fours, Cris coughed up water. Seeing Krimsey, he narrowed his eyes and whispered, "The fuck is wrong with your girlfriend?"

"Z's not my—" Krimsey hesitated, out of breath with spots in his vision. "Cris, are you okay?" He swam toward him.

Cris pushed himself upright, wincing. He twisted to look at his side and sucked in his breath. Smeared across Cris's pale skin was a jagged, deep cut from armpit to waist. The base of Krimsey's spine prickled with empathy.

Flashing light from the other side of the lake stung his eyes like knives.

One, two, three…

Four. It flashed four times.

Krimsey switched to signing. **"He added twelve hours. We should be quiet."**

Cris signed several expletives. The movement was jerky and aggressive. Cris gasped in pain and clutched his side.

"Do you have any idea why Zeph would have attacked you?" He looked around, as if Zeph might appear again and do them both in. **"Were you the one that helped me out of the water?"**

Cris didn't answer. He didn't meet Krimsey's eyes. He just stared at the lake past Krimsey's shoulders. The thoughts fogging up the space between them oozed with guilt.

Realization hit like a punch in the face. There was no monster. Just an awfully unimaginative bully.

"It was you!" Of course it was. The worst of Krimsey's nightmares had come true. But he couldn't even be that angry. Cris was in such sorry shape after his battle with Zeph that he swayed on the rock as if slowly turning to gel.

Cris deserved it, though. The pang in Krimsey's gut solidified. Maybe he shouldn't have yelled at Zeph… He shuddered, involuntarily recalling the image of Zeph biting Cris. Savage. Both of them. **"Why the hell did you mess with us like that? There's something seriously wrong with you."**

Krimsey was about to chew him out more, but Cris tipped forward and would have splashed face-first in the water had Krimsey not stopped to catch him. Once he was stabilized and stopped swaying, Krimsey quickly let him go.

"You need help," Krimsey signed. **"We need a needle. Urchin. And thread. Eelgrass."**

Cris's laugh stuttered. **"No eelgrass here."**

Krimsey looked at the wound helplessly.

"You really are a wimp," Cris signed. **"There are urchins at the rear of the lake, about two meters down. You can get a grassy twine there, too."**

In all his years of doing this, Krimsey had never been to the far end of Glacier Lake.

Seeing the look on his face, Cris signed weakly, **"Yeah, it's a trek. If you don't want to, I'll do it myself."** Cris grunted, moving to dislodge himself from the island and tipping forward dangerously.

Krimsey was ready to let Cris handle this himself. He was ready to swim aside, swim away, and put Cris out of his mind. He was ready to never look at or talk to Cris or Zeph again.

But his dumb brain did something else.

"No. You can't do that," he signed, defeated by moral obligation and something else he couldn't quite place. Like some mix of sympathy and… admiration? No, that couldn't be right.

He chewed on the inside of his cheek. His eyes wandered over the black abyss. His shoulders leveled. It was a different kind of conviction. One that was motivated, wholeheartedly, from within himself. No adrenaline or external goading. No one there hounding him to face his fears.

He wanted to do this. He wanted to help Cris. He wanted to prove he wasn't a wimp.

"I'll do it."

Body Language

Krimsey Enosh, Sunday, March 24, 2250, 6:46 p.m.

Upon Krimsey's return—maybe an hour, maybe less—Cris hadn't moved.

The far reaches of the lake hadn't been so bad, not after what he had just been through. He prodded Cris, who looked dead but then groaned and sat up with effort and eyed the rudimentary tools Krimsey had acquired. When Krimsey approached, Cris leaned away, his knees pointed in the opposite direction Krimsey was coming from.

"What if it gets infected? It stopped bleeding. Isn't that bad?" Cris signed over his shoulder.

Was Cris... this steel-hearted antagonizer... *scared?*

In their studies, Krimsey was sure they had both seen images of injuries worse than this. Krimsey swam around the other side of the rock and climbed up, so Cris could see him. **"Cris, our bodies are designed to bleed less in the water. Calm down."**

Krimsey reached toward Cris, who instinctively jerked back, eyes wide and bloodshot and watery. **"Do you think Rellington would...?"**

"You know we're on our own," Krimsey signed with the urchin spine between his teeth, his shoulders rounding, softening. **"Turn your back to me."**

Cris's gaze moved away. Krimsey secured the makeshift thread to the makeshift needle. He clenched his teeth so hard his jaw became sore. Cris was too vulnerable, too real, too fragile—breathing, existing, centimeters away. Being here, helping him, felt wrong. It made his insides squirm.

Krimsey rubbed his thumb up and down the spine of the needle, seeing that it would hold up to pressure. Not break inside the skin. Leaning forward, he inspected the wound. Cris shifted. Body heat radiated between Cris's side and Krimsey's fingers. He placed his fingers beside the wound. A twitching shudder ran through the skin he touched.

"Brace yourself," Krimsey whispered, hoping the sound did not reach Rellington's com.

Then he pierced the edge of the flay.

"Sorry." Krimsey's face puckered, expecting Cris to flinch or yelp.

Cris sat motionless, holding the rock under him for balance, chin resting atop his bent knees. Feeling more uneasy than his subject, Krimsey sewed Cris up.

"This looks better," Krimsey signed to Cris when he turned around. **"It's not perfect. My hand... well, I'm hungry and unsteady but you will be okay."**

Cris bared his teeth, looking down. **"You're right. It's not perfect,"** he signed. There were bumps and knots all the way down Cris's side. Medical Daily—their daily hands-on medical class—and book-smarts only went so far.

"You're alive," Krimsey signed to him.

"I'm alive," he nodded. **"How long has it been?"**

Krimsey changed to a more comfortable position on the rock. **"Three?"** He guessed. **"Time goes by so slow down here."**

Cris looked away, his face hardened.

"Why were you attacking us?"

"Get off it already." His signs were frustrated, irritable, but with that same hint of vulnerability. Cris picked at his knees. **"I never planned for it to.... For Earth's sake, you *did* see what Zeph did, didn't you? It was like..."** He shuddered and shook his head.

Krimsey was silent, thinking Cris kind of deserved what he got. Though, Zeph *had* gone berserk.

"I'm…"

"**What?**" Krimsey looked at Cris, who seemed to be wrestling with his thoughts. Cris's hands hung low in front of him.

"**I'm sorry,**" Cris signed, rubbing his hand through his hair. He glanced at Krimsey, then glanced away. "**For always treating you so badly.**"

Krimsey half smiled, waiting for the punchline. It didn't come. He opened his mouth and closed it and scrutinized the way each muscle in Chris's face behaved. Though his education on body language had focused mainly on possible cues one could send to another underwater rather than above it, Krimsey's memory quickly flitted to a particular lesson of attraction.

Language Daily. The class consisted largely of learning about the complexity of sign language. It also included lessons in body language, the study of the vocal cords with brief, purely anecdotal guesses as to how *transitus* might adapt to underwater living, and a large dose of paternalism. Krimsey's least favorite class, assuming Survival Daily was more of a personal damnation than a class.

Signs of attraction. Stealing glances whenever Krimsey looked away. Check. Cris rubbed his arm. Nervous or excited fidgety behavior. Check. Leaning forward and leaning in to be closer. Cris was hunched, one of his knees up and propped under his chin, more so than leaned in, but still seemed to gravitate by the millimeter toward Krimsey. Check? The fact that Cris was opening up to Krimsey at all—vulnerability, openness, a crack in his defenses—also check?

No way. Krimsey was imagining it. Cris would crack. He'd pull away and jab Krimsey in the shoulder with a solid fist. Then he'd laugh-screech at Krimsey and jump in the water and swim away.

Am I seeing what I want to see? Am I attracted to this?

The question surprised him. The fact that Krimsey was even asking it of himself was appalling, but his stomach was doing a little flip, his heart doing a little *ba-bump*, his ears growing a little hot. The question had to be asked.

Something about Cris's vulnerability struck a nerve. His eyes were dewy and soft. Not mean and malicious, as they normally were. His thin lips hung slack, creating a little 'o' that could almost be heard. His cheeks were rosy, wetness still clinging to the peach fuzz of his face.

Krimsey was leaning over the rough piece of rock between them a little too far. Staring. Equally slack-jawed and as perplexed as Cris looked. The topic would need to be revisited. Krimsey fought the urge to give Cris a punch in the arm himself.

Krimsey cleared his throat, about to speak. Coughed out half an audible letter, even. Before he remembered where they were. He scratched the irritating hem of his underwear, rubbed his belly, then finally thought to sign, **"Why?"**

Cris frowned and readjusted his position on the rock, crossing his legs in front of him. **"Why am I sorry?"**

"Sorry, no." Krimsey scratched his head and hunched lower. He raised his arms. **"I meant why were you mean to me, then?"**

"I guess I just can't wait to get away from here. From humans. From the HPO. To finally get to one of those underwater cities they all talk about," Cris signed. **"I don't know, maybe taking it out on you helped. Again, I'm sorry."** Krimsey scrutinized Cris's new body position for signs but came up blank. He was just a teen *transitus*. Sitting on a rock. Being nice to the other teen he'd spent hundreds of hours torturing. Not a big deal.

Small talk. Make small talk. Nod. Krimsey nodded, distracted by a line in Cris's cheek he'd never noticed. **"That makes one of us,"** Krimsey signed. **"I doubt I'd make it alive even to the closest underwater city."**

"Of course, you're just a wimp. No one expects you to—" Cris's face dropped. **"Sorry."**

"You don't have to be nice to me just because I helped you." Krimsey exhaled out a long breath, realizing for the first time he had been holding every intake several seconds too long. Cris's insult put Krimsey's questions at ease. He liked it more when Cris was his own personal, one-dimensional bully. Less confusing.

"Yeah, I do." Cris's face softened and looked at Krimsey. **"You're alright. I'm just an angry, cooped-up asshole. Don't tell anyone I told you that."**

A few minutes passed. Krimsey was too tired and confused to move, and Cris showed no preference to be alone. **"I should stay to make sure you don't die."**

What little color there was in Cris's pale face drained.

"I'm joking. You're not going to die." Krimsey leaned in. **"Can I look?"**

Cris nodded and turned his face to the water, his jaw working side to side.

Krimsey touched the wound with light fingers, tracing the handiwork up to his armpit. The wound was not bleeding much but was dark red with inflammation. The scar would be nasty. Cris's gaze moved, looking down at the wound, and then he stole a halted glance at Krimsey.

Krimsey snatched back his hand, too aware of how he lingered next to Cris, too aware of how Cris's eyes did the same. **"You'll be okay."** The signs were hasty. **"So I guess we...."** A moment of hesitation. Could he and Cris be friends after this? Despite his confusion, Krimsey felt oddly bonded with him in a way he had never felt with anyone before. He didn't want to leave. He didn't want to stay, either.

"I guess we go back to hating each other, then?" Cris grimaced.

Krimsey's heart skipped a beat. He really wanted to say no. Instead, he remained frozen.

"Now *I'm* joking," Cris signed. His lips twitched. His shoulders stiffened. **"If you weren't so afraid of transitioning and leaving land, where would you go? If you could go anywhere after you transition?"**

Of all his nineteen years of life, the years he should have spent musing and preparing, practicing and planning, Krimsey had never thought about this question. He had never thought about where he'd *want* to go. Because that would assume he *wanted* to go at all.

Instead, he had wasted his time. Languishing and moping and thinking things only cowards thought. He always figured he'd give up and be one of the kids who died. Why consider the possibilities if that was to be his fate? Why consider? Why try? Why prepare?

"I know where I'll go," Cris signed. **"I hear there's an underwater city by the Mariana trench and it's thriving. That is where I'll go."**

What a foreign thing. To want to live by a gaping, bottomless gash in the sea. **"Why?"**

"I'm really fascinated by evolution." Cris became animated. **"Imagine a thousand years from now what that city might look like. Naturally, some people would explore deeper and deeper, right? Like the Bajau. Genetically, it would make sense for them to start to adapt. What would that life look like?"**

Krimsey had to admire the enthusiasm. And the Bajau? Had Cris actually spent a fraction of his time studying?

"Our bodies can't handle those pressures." Krimsey's heart rate quickened. The images his mind fed his body were all too convincing. He imagined sudden deep-sea pressures that would crush bone. He imagined putting his body—literally—through hell. Or as close as one could get to it. He imagined—or tried to imagine—a city by the Mariana trench. **"Those are just rumors. Why would anyone start a city by a trench?"**

"That's what *they* want us to think."

"It's impossible."

"We could totally adapt." Cris's eyes glazed over as he signed and his eyes darted up as if accessing an impossibly grand future. One Krimsey could not see. **"Have you ever wondered why the HPO only skims over what we're capable of? They always deflect our questions. They tell us we can hold our breath longer than humans and we bleed less because of our rubbery skin. Ten percent of new babies are being born with aquatic lungs. Our genes were built to evolve fast—what else can we do? Our lungs turn *aquatic*. That is *amazing*. What other things can our bodies do? What secrets do our DNA hold? What if we are more capable and more amazing than we ever thought possible?"**

Krimsey could hardly keep up. He tried to interject. **"The HPO says our bodies don't—"**

"The HPO doesn't tell us *SHIT*," Cris huffed, signing the word *shit* by the letter. **"And the only way to find these things out for ourselves is by transitioning and testing our limits. On our terms. Not theirs. Survival Daily?"** He raised both arms toward the cavern walls. **"This is pathetic. Not a true test of our power. I think they're afraid of us."**

But they do. They tell us everything we need to know. Krimsey didn't feel like arguing. He felt both invigorated and disturbed by

Cris's passion. **"I still think you will have to rethink the trench idea. It is not physically possible."**

"That we know of."

"No human has ever—"

"No *human*. Do you forget we are not human?"

Maybe I do forget.

Cris had a million and one ideas. For a few more minutes, they bantered. A back-and-forth ping-pong. Cris signed about one bizarre, completely removed-from-reality idea. Krimsey playfully countered it, then crossed his arms, then imagined, with a flickering image, the fanciful idea Cris had just shared. Letting the image morph and transform in his mind's eye.

What would that look like? How might that taste? Where could that happen? Krimsey soon became immersed in Cris's fantastical reality. *Transitus* becoming cartilaginous beings who communicated solely by light and touch. *Transitus* swimming hand-in-flipper with dolphins, learning how to communicate with them, and then banding together to build immense coral cities. *Transitus* becoming nomadic, forming close family tribes, and communicating through touch so seamlessly it was like reading minds. Some *transitus* would prefer going solo, adapting to counter the ocean's might with strength and fortitude.

Krimsey stopped countering the ideas. He just let them wash over him. One of them lay down first, Krimsey wasn't sure who. Together, they looked into the dark, cavernous ceiling and instead saw the color of the ocean at sunset, as if they'd jumped into the interface of a com and were watching a movie. Arms held up above him, Cris shared his ideas until, to Krimsey's surprise, the ideas ran dry.

Then they just stared upward. Then to the sides. Avoiding the clunky awkwardness of each other's gaze. Krimsey was smiling, a sort of sloppy, half smile. He dropped the tension from his cheeks, frowned at the water, and he tried to figure out if the creatures moving in his belly were butterflies or snakes.

Memories

Felice Karuli, Monday, March 25, 2250, 4:41 p.m.

DIRT FROM THE UNPLANNED forest burial of Rumi Yen was still stuck beneath Felice's nails. She picked at her thumbnail and wiped it on her hem. The silence of the dining room enveloped her thoughts in a vacuum, impossible to escape. The silence buzzed as if she had just suffered a blunt force trauma to the head. The silence was deafening. When she was done distracting herself with the state of her unkempt nails, a polished knot in the table kept her focus. She rubbed a thumb over it until her thumb lost all sensation.

A shadow fell over the table.

Felice looked up. Lamia was rejoining the table with two glasses of cold water, placing one of the glasses in front of Felice, looking at her expectantly.

"Did you say something, Mother?" Felice's voice was tinny and far away.

Lamia sat and started on her dinner. She chewed her roasted grouse and broccoli, then swallowed. A sheen of fat coated her lips. She stared at Felice. "I asked if Lowery had anything to say? You know, our head researcher?" Lamia stabbed another bite.

Felice pushed bits of meat around on her plate. She consumed the smallest bite of meat. It tasted like nothing.

"Felice?" Felice knew that tone, quiet and demanding.

"Oh? Lowery...."

"Where is your head, Daughter?"

"At the beach. Thinking."

"Is that why you were late? You went back to Ross Bay?"

"Yes. I was cleaning up Rumi's things and then walked home through the woods. I needed some time to myself."

Lamia shot her a glare of annoyed disbelief. "Rumi's things hardly needed attention. Where were you really?"

The cold, heartless tone with which her mother was able to say those words, as if Rumi was nothing, was unbearable. Felice stared at her plate. If she looked at Lamia, she would vomit. Or throw the plate at her. It was all she could do to keep breathing.

Lamia was right, though. She hadn't really been through the woods. The walk from Ross Bay back to the HPO Underground— the network of tunnels inside Karuli Crag—was four hour's worth of overgrown brambles. Instead, Felice had visited Rumi's grave long enough for the sun to peak and to have begun its descent. When she left the grave, Felice took the transport back and, instead of going home, spent some time with her lover, Ive. To get away from Lamia. Instead of sorting out her feelings or planning the tasks ahead or figuring out how to tell Lamia to do this shit herself.

Lamia had promised the girl would not die. She *promised*. Felice looked at the dirt between her nails and all she saw was blood. She'd believed she was doing something right, when she took Rumi. Saved the girl. She had *helped*. Unlike anyone else in the world, she and Lamia cared about the *transitus* enough to attempt a cure for Pneumaphage. Mainland wasn't even *trying*.

Rumi was not supposed to die.

But now, she was here, Lamia was asking questions, hounding on her appearance, and she had come no closer to coming to terms with the fact that the last fifteen years of hard work had just led to a little girl's death.

A long exhalation startled Felice, as if she had been asleep and Lamia's angry tic blew stale life back into her. A bite of food had lodged itself halfway down to her stomach. It took everything she had to keep it from rising up.

"So you did not talk to Lowery then? We need to know why the girl died."

"I don't need Lowery to know why she died." Rumi's death was not blameless.

Felice's gritty, between-her-teeth tone was not lost on Lamia. Lamia set down her utensils.

Bracing herself for what would surely be a stern lecture, Felice squared herself in her seat. Lamia's braid was more taut than ever, pulled back so severely her whole face lifted. Felice wouldn't dare mention the single thread of hair that escaped.

"You're right, of course," Lamia said.

The breath Felice was saving for rebuttal escaped in a small puff. Felice licked her lips. "Does that mean you agree?"

"About?"

"Elpida...."

"What about her?"

"We can't take her in."

"Oh. No, that's not what I meant. We still need her. But don't worry about that anymore."

Felice's spine stiffened. Her fork paused over the bland broccoli. Don't worry? Someone died. How was her mother so calm about all this?

"When you were trekking through the woods...." Lamia's eyes passed over Felice's ruffled hair. "Well, your com was off, so I had Carmak put some things in motion for me."

"What did you do?" Felice stabbed a broccoli, with no intention of eating it. Her stomach bubbled. Right now, her mother had never been more fearsome. The thumping in her chest ramped up.

This can't go on. It can't. How can I go on pretending?

"Five applied for early admission for Internship Day, which takes place tomorrow," Lamia explained with joyous enthusiasm. "You won't have to worry about her anymore. It's been arranged. As for Krimsey, he's already in motion as well. He's currently in Survival, otherwise we would have already scheduled him for a checkup. Though it's a wonder his transition was going to be in eight months... *really*. For his age? Late bloomer, I suppose." Lamia paused and seemed to get sucked into her thoughts. Shadows deepened the creases around her tired eyelids. She blinked and smiled, a small shake moving through her. "At any rate, his timing will be better now. For us."

Felice wanted badly to feel relieved. Relieved that *she* wouldn't have to concoct the ploy to kidnap Elpida.

Instead, Felice's heart rate made her forehead sweat and her hand wobble. Her fork felt slick in her hand. She let it clatter onto her plate along with the broccoli.

Lamia's eyes snapped and narrowed on Felice so quickly, Felice would have thought she had just scraped her nails on a chalkboard. Then Lamia relaxed.

"I'm so proud of you, Daughter." Lamia's tight smile curled in the corners, leaving her grey eyes untouched. She brought her cool glass of water to her lips, watching Felice through the cup. "Five is much further along than we could have ever imagined."

Felice hated this feeling in her gut. She wanted to escape. She wanted to vomit. Her heart and mind were still reeling from the death of an innocent child and her mother was talking logistics.

"We can't take Elpida." The tough conviction Felice was going for in her voice fell short and shook. She folded her hands in her lap to clench the fists that formed. "You told me, when we started on Rumi, she wouldn't die. What if the same thing happens to Elpida? That would be...."

"Immoral?"

"Contemptible. Tragic. Unforgivable."

"Is it immoral to systematically quarantine hundreds of people? Is it immoral to attempt genocide? On those same people? Tell me, where is the morality in that? Is that not a tragedy?"

Felice knew where this was going. The argument that the NWA had done much worse. "That was almost two hundred years ago."

"Is it immoral to systematically kill, oppress, experiment on, strip rights from, and—when all else fails—send away to a far-off island as somebody else's problem, those same people for almost two hundred years?"

"Just because the NWA has treated *transitus* poorly does not mean that we have a golden ticket of purity." Felice dug her fingers into her palms so hard, they had to be bleeding by now. If they weren't, it was only because she had gnawed most of her nails to the quick.

"We're saving lives."

"We just *killed* someone."

"Think of Annabel."

Annabel. Lamia's firstborn. Just an infant when she died of Pneumaphage. Felice was having déjà vu. She'd had this fight before. But never had her mother defended the death of a *transitus* child.

A line had to be drawn.

Felice couldn't look her mother in the eyes. "Annabel is already dead. Elpida is alive. How can you justify—?"

"*We're saving lives.*" Lamia hissed, just over a whisper. That was the closest Felice had ever come to seeing her mother lose composure.

It was the closest Felice had ever come to screaming her next words. She swallowed hard, hesitating before asking her mother how she'd keep Elpida's kidnapping from detection. Being president of the HPO did not come without scrutiny.

"I have someone," her reply was hard and final. Her mother's ghostly eyes seemed to move right through her.

"What are we telling Elpida's mother?"

"That she died of sudden-onset Pneumaphage. It's really perfect, actually. Transition Ceremony and Internship Day. All in one. Who would have thought Five would request early admission?"

Felice would have thought it, having practically raised Elpida and Krimsey. The girl was brilliant. She didn't deserve this. Rumi hadn't deserved it, either.

Her mother continued, "The brother will be out, we'll have the girl, and there will be no room for questions."

"Just one."

"Hmm?"

"Sanjana Enosh will ask to see the body."

"Oh that's easy enough to dismiss. It'll all happen while she's at work. We can simply explain we—"

"Burial pod."

"Exactly."

"You do realize she works in relations?" Was she really letting herself get pulled back into this bullshit? *But the HPO can't be compromised....* "If she suspects anything, she may have the power to destroy everything we've—"

"That won't happen."

Lamia was right. Sanjana was as interesting as cardboard and as bright as a rock. She'd lost all personality, all spark and joy of life, when her husband died.

Felice took another bite of grouse, now completely cold, and immediately regretted it. She swallowed it, half-chewed, forcing it to her stomach with her entire glass of water. It did not sit well.

Lamia cleared her throat. "There is something I'll need from you. We have a ship of new arrivals docking tomorrow. I'll need you to handle logistics for the non-viables aboard."

"You mean the viables? I'm starting them off with their guides, right?"

"We are going to try something new." Lamia shrugged coolly.

At last, her mother's intention tumbled before her.

"We're doing testers on the new NVT kids? To check their genes as well?"

"Not exactly."

"What, then?"

Lamia's eyes leveled with hers.

"Daughter, you're not going to leave me stuck up to my nose in logistics on my own are you? I see it in your eyes. You've checked out."

"What is the plan for the kids, Mother?" She chewed the raised flesh of her inner cheek.

"I *know* yesterday was difficult." Lamia danced around the answer. Her mother must have sensed—or anticipated—Felice's trepidation. "You just have to keep reminding yourself why we do it. Wouldn't you do everything in your power to prevent more deaths like Annabel's from happening? The Enoshes' father? Just yesterday, a ten-year-old child succumbed to Pneumaphage. Right here. On this island." She sniffed.

Lamia reached out with her pearly, trimmed fingernails and touched Felice on the arm. Felice's skin tingled as if Lamia's touch held an electric supercharge. Resisting the urge to pull back, cheeks burning, Felice asked again, "What is the plan for the kids?"

Felice could guess the answer. Her ears rang.

"Progress has been slow, as you know. Rumi was a one-off. She was us taking a chance. Elpida is much more promising because of the testers. We know she's close. She could be the key."

Beneath the table, her hands had lost feeling but continued to quiver in her lap. She shoved them between her legs to get them to stop.

"I was exchanging ideas with Carmak the other day and—"

Her ears were roaring. Her mother's voice was launching an offensive against Felice's senses. An all-out assault. "Just say it!" Felice burst like a grenade.

"We will be taking the four new NVT arrivals in to the labs."

"Impossible." She stood and the rushing blood made her woozy.

"The longer we take, the more *transitus* will die of this disease. Four NVTs is a small price. We need them in the lab in order to try several of our theories, in case Elpida does not work. If the NWA refuses to attempt anything noteworthy against the disease aside from lung transplants, which don't work, if no one else will take it upon themselves to—"

"The NWA will be on us like flies on shit. This will raise suspicion. And, and, but... the fact that you would even suggest—"

"*There is no more time!*" The table shuddered under Lamia's fist. Cutlery *tinked* against the plates. Felice winced. The lack of grace took her by surprise. Lamia dabbed splattered sauce off the back of her hand with a cloth. "Just do it. They're our easiest target. The families will arrive at the port town. You will concoct a story. The kids wander off in the middle of the night. I don't care, just make it convincing. Are we clear?"

Felice was clear on one thing.

What her mother asked of her was impossible. She would not do it. She sat back down. "Clear."

Not only was it wrong, but it put their entire community at risk. This community was here to help *transitus*. The New World Alliance touted ideals of utopia, but the reality was that the outside world, the Mainland, under the NWA's governance, was riddled with problems.

Mostly problems for *transitus* people.

If the NWA had reason to shut the HPO down.... If the NWA found out about the lab and the experiments and the kidnapping and death of Rumi Yen, the HPO *would* be shut down. The *transi tus* families seeking refuge and guidance would have nowhere to go.

Life on Mainland for a *transitus* was shit.

As Felice tried to finish her meal, the memories of Rumi and Elpida and the Enosh family fed a downward spiral. Each memory was like a rock in her palm. Not stones smoothed by the liquid flow of time, but rocks that were sharp and battered by wind and sand and ground into something fatal.

The two of them finished their meals. Standing and straightening her dress, Lamia beckoned to Felice. She obliged, going obediently to her mother, whose embrace nearly shattered her, and whose chilly "I'm proud of you, Daughter," was pointed and painful.

Felice returned a practiced smile, wished her mother a good night, and sat back at the table to contend with her thoughts alone. The kitchen was dim. For a long time, she just stared at her reflection on the table.

Inside her was a deafening battle. If she defied her mother, Lamia would find another, less tactful way to get what she wanted. If she obeyed, she'd hate herself and she'd risk exposing them to the NWA. She certainly couldn't shut the lab down—not on her own. She wouldn't win. Whatever decision she made, there was no winning.

Only losing.

The quiet, deadly chaos inside her needed to be quashed. But how? It took everything she had not to end her pain right there with a kitchen blade.

Well that's pointless, Felice; you're no use if you're dead. Who will do the right thing then?

Finally getting up from the table, Felice drew herself a lukewarm bath, undressed, and submerged herself as if water might draw from her body the toxins of sin.

But she couldn't escape the thought of the blade in the kitchen. She couldn't escape the memory rocks ripping open her skin, burrowing into her. Dripping, she stood out of the tub. A puddle collected at her feet. She gathered her cowardice into a single driving thought and padded naked and wet into the kitchen to retrieve the blade.

She couldn't escape the way it clung to her skin. That putrid smell of death.

THE CLAY

Élodie Le Goff, 2049

I THOUGHT I WAS a mistake.

Mother and Father had said so, so wouldn't it be true? Wouldn't the two humans that brought Élodie Le Goff into this world know whether or not they had made a mistake?

I was crying when I met him on the outskirts of Montpellier along La Mosson river. Father was angry. Mother was sad. And I was a dumb, emotional, crying seventeen-year-old. Nothing new here. Except—

Him.

I lifted my head. "Hello?"

The man was scruffy and scrawny and suited in something dirty, two sizes too big. My hand reached for the empty water jug in the sand beside me. He walked between the bushes toward the river like a regular.

But this was my spot. And he was not regular.

"Who are you?" I sniffed. He didn't look alarming to me. He didn't look like he could snatch me and stuff me in a bag, let alone pick me up. He looked weak. He didn't look like he'd ensnare me.

But Mother always said to keep my guard.

"Geoff." His reply was gravelly.

He crouched by the river and his jug *glugged* to the brim, filling with cool, crisp water. Then he tipped it up to take a swig.

"You're supposed to clean the—" Water dribbled into his salty grey beard. "Never mind." I felt him come closer and sit. I scooted away, trying to pretend I wasn't concerned.

I wished I had brought that knife Father always told me to keep in my pocket.

"I love the water." The man's eyes followed the swollen, streaming river. His voice had changed, become something new, something fluid, something melodic. "What's your name?"

I didn't answer. Mother said not to talk to strangers. Not with how fragmented and fraught the world was. I was sure I should have been running, screaming, kicking adrenaline into my fingertips by now.

"How old are you?"

I should be careful. My hips inched away. I scratched the sand and clutched my empty jug.

"Do you ever imagine what might be next for us?" He asked in that softened, low voice. He looked over at me and I didn't shy from his stare, though I wanted to. "Fantasize what could be? World without all this hurt. Without all the heat and death and raw humanity? Too raw." The man shook his head like a bear.

I didn't know what he was talking about. I was frozen but intrigued. Drawn like a moth too scared to fly.

Then he said, "I can make you whole," in a way that sounded both insane and reasonable. Like he'd just asked me if I'd like some salt for my soup.

So he was a crazy person.

I need to go.

But I stayed.

And he continued.

I thought I saw something too, as he talked. Thin, smiling lips. Gold-flecked eyes. The sky-blue dress of a girl I didn't know. Water. So much water, blurring the vision. But as soon as I squinted my eyes, the memory faded like an unremembered dream.

Geoff was telling me stories.

I listened, listened, listened, never once saying a word. I listened to his ideas and did not hear Mother's dinner bell *dong dong dong*. I listened to his stories and rode on the soaring rhythm of them. I listened to his science as the sky—still and swaying with leaves, graying with night—became dark.

I listened without realizing that the old man had lured me. Without realizing I was ensnared. Without realizing I'd be the first to feel that science, live that story, be the clay to his idea.

Her Mother

Zeph Carmak, Tuesday, March 26, 2250, 4:40 a.m.

EXHAUSTED, ZEPH STOPPED OUTSIDE the Carmak residence, just getting home from Survival Daily. The floodlights Up Top had recently turned off, with the sun hovering just beneath the horizon, ready to breach. Being in Antarctica meant it would stay there, providing faint blue-grey light, for several more hours.

Tense voices came from the house, through the wide, open window hole. Zeph paused by the sill.

"I know you're mad. I know. I shouldn't have gone behind your—"

"Carmak, I'm not *mad*, I'm just trying to decide whether or not to trust you now."

The voice speaking to their mother sounded like the HPO president, Lamia Karuli. Which would not have been unusual, since Zeph's mother, Gina Carmak, worked for Lamia, but both voices from inside were off. Zeph's mother sounded submissive and scared. She sounded frayed. Lamia's voice was stiff and strained. This was so far from business as usual, Zeph had to stagger back a step, moving out of view.

"Of course you can trust me," their mother said. "I've been by your side for eighteen years. This was just—"

"Just what?" Lamia seemed more interested in interrupting than hearing what Zeph's mother had to say. "You conducted unauthorized bloodwork on Zeph. You compromised our entire operation. How do you think this will look to the NWA?"

A hard, tight dread in Zeph's stomach took hold. Bloodwork? What was that supposed to mean?

"A non-viable has never become viable before. Maybe if there were records of it happening, we could pass it off as a fluke. But this was intentional and clearly so. You're on a very short rope, Carmak."

"I'll make it right."

"You had better. Time is short." Lamia sniffed.

"I understand." Zeph's mother sighed. "What's going on with the Enoshes? Is Felice still able to finish what you need?"

"Felice is recovering. I could use your help with logistics on the Enoshes while she is out of commission, but that doesn't get you out of the water on this Zeph issue."

"I know. I know. I'm going to fix that issue. The NWA will never find out. I promise."

What was so wrong with them the NWA couldn't find out? What had Gina done? The dread in their belly oozed upward, climbing toward their throat. This was clearly a conversation not meant to be overheard. Wanting to leave but unable to peel away, Zeph kept listening. Something monumental was going on here. And it involved them.

"Her mother can't know, either." Lamia's voice got pointed and low. "You know that woman will use this as leverage with the NWA. What? Why do you look so surprised?"

Zeph retreated into their own thoughts, completely lost. *Are they talking about me? Whose mother can't know what?* When Zeph returned their attention to eavesdropping, the voices had gone quiet. There was a long pause in conversation. A moment of silence. Tense. Palpable.

There was a sound of fabric rustling. It sounded like someone was coming to the door. Zeph's limbs went weak. Their feet melded to the mountain beneath them.

"I would never tell Zeph's mother about any of this." Gina's voice came to them as if from a great distance. Zeph heard the lie resting between the syllables of her words. Whatever "this" was, Gina would absolutely be telling "Zeph's mother" about it.

"Oh, don't act like you haven't been in touch with that damned woman. I don't have rocks in my skull. We've seen the signatures." The conversation continued, but Lamia's tone faded in and out. The rest of the conversation blurred. A small white flower growing out of the foundation of the house bounced from a light breeze. Its petals swirled.

Zeph staggered back a few steps and caught themselves against the house. This confusion, combined with their already empty belly and tired body, was like a lethal drug. Both women had referred to Zeph's mother as if one of the speaking participants *was not* their mother.

Gina and Lamia stopped talking. Or if the conversation continued, Zeph did not hear it. Terrified of being caught, Zeph moved around to the other side of the house. The back side of the house paralleled another. It was dark and the energy units that cooled the water and ran the electricity from solar panels hummed.

Zeph leaned against it, the box vibrating their skin and teeth and bones as if attempting a sort of dismantlement from the inside out. Swallowing, shaking, crying, and trying not to make a sound, Zeph slumped to the ground between the house and the box.

A lump in their rear pocket dug into their hip. It was their com. Zeph took it from their pocket and glared at it, as if ready to toss it down a very long drop. They sighed. They could not blame the com for their life coming unraveled. Zeph placed it in their right ear to track the time, leaned their head back, closed their eyes, and fell asleep.

A seagull pecked at Zeph's feet. They jolted awake as if stopping a fall and the gull took flight. Confused as to why they had been asleep in a back alley, Zeph staggered to their feet and watched the gull circle over the Up Top houses against a wildflower-blue sky. Then they remembered coming home, and the overheard conversation between their mother and Lamia. Words trickled into their thoughts like a leaky faucet.

Her... mother... can't... know... either.

Being misgendered by the president, who never disrespected Zeph's pronouns, was not even the most upsetting thing about that statement. *Mother...* The word sat dry and stale on the back of their tongue. Their breath went sour.

I want to wake up from this nightmare.

Zeph instructed their com to pull up the Day In Review, a community-run feed of happenings in Karuli Crag and the only reliable, HPO-verified news source. Just before they were leaving home for Survival Daily, it had been flooded with talk of Zeph Carmak, *transitus*, 17, child of Gina Carmak, human, 52, a high-level medical field worker, and Terrance Carmak, human, 56, a high-level operations manager. The headlines had all claimed various takes on Zeph's viable versus non-viable status. Some interpreted Zeph's change in status as an incorrect diagnosis, left uncaught for years. Others boldly stated Zeph was *transitus* evolution at its finest. Speculations had run rampant.

Today, already 9:30 in the morning, the feed buzzed with the latest. There was a countdown guesstimate of when the new ship of supplies would arrive—between three and seven hours. Talk of the supersale from the last shipment three months ago—a last-ditch attempt at making slightly chipped glass bowls sound appealing. Reminders of the upcoming Transition Ceremony. Mention of the full moon. Nothing useful. Nothing interesting. And zero word of Zeph Carmak. Not even in the archives from the other day. Zeph looked for traces of scrubbing. Looked for any leftover tidbits of the news. Any mention of their name at all. Nothing. Bizarre. Like it never even happened.

What did that mean? They shook the feeling of dread slipping down their spine and crept out from between the houses to their open door. Zeph was too sore, their brain too scattered for none of this to have happened. What was going on? Who was moderating the news, and to what end?

Her... mother...

They entertained the thoughts that the words *her mother* conjured. Zeph was darker than both their parents. They had never questioned it because Zeph was *transitus* and their parents were human. The differences between them had to do with the genetic mutation. That was all. Maybe Zeph had a godmother. They had never heard of having one, but maybe there was a long-lost relative from Mainland. Maybe somebody was coming in on the new arrivals ship. And the bloodwork Lamia referred to... it seemed related to their change in classification. For some reason, Lamia was upset with their mother for this whole thing. For Zeph changing. Which could explain why someone could have scrubbed the news. Lamia did not want word reaching Mainland, she even said so.

But why?

Gina sat at the lacquered table in the dining area that had just enough room for three people. Standing in the doorway, Zeph noticed right away that their mother carried a huge mental weight. Gina's frizzed braid curved with the hunch of her back and the hand against her forehead shook, carrying more than just the weight of her head. She heaved a breath as if unable to get enough oxygen under all that heaviness.

Zeph stepped inside. Their breath shortened, pulled out by invisible fingers. Inside the house, everything got three shades darker and Zeph felt a shift in their core. This was what it felt like to have a huge burden sucking up all the air in a room. This was what uncertainty felt like. This was what unwelcome, unfathomable change felt like. Zeph suddenly feared all those things and the reasons behind them.

"Mom?"

Gina looked startled when she looked up. She had a com in her ear. She looked around the house as if expecting someone, then back to Zeph.

"Who are you looking for?" Zeph wondered about the theoretical godmother and walked, weak-kneed, to the kitchen.

"No one." A warm, pleading smile stretched out the wrinkles on Gina's forehead. She stood from her seat and paced around the table, stealing glances at Zeph.

From the kitchen, Zeph poured a large, cold glass of water. Glugging the glass down in one breath, Zeph stared at the textured plastic ceiling.

Her... mother... can't... know... either. The way Lamia had said it... Zeph blinked. "So we are not expecting anyone?" Zeph poured more water into their glass and took a long sip, watching how their mother avoided eye contact.

She narrowed her eyes at the doorway. Gina had eyes and ears like a cat, at least from what Zeph had seen from Mainland documentaries. All brown and black and sharp angles, with an uncanny focus. Her shoulders twitched at every turn of the wind and clink of a neighbor's dishes two houses over. Her com flashed a blue ping and she tugged her braid over her shoulder.

"I see. You are busy." Zeph poured a new glass and offered it. "I am going to get some rest."

"Wait. Honey, will you have a seat please?" Gina took the offered water as she paced. She showed her teeth with an unfriendly smile. "We need to talk."

"Are you going to sit, too?" Zeph asked. "You are stressing me out." Gina continued to pace in tight circles next to the table. Her com flashed blue again. "Is that Lamia?"

Gina's shoulders lifted, her neck stiffened, and she looked up from her pacing. She met Zeph's eyes with a cold, metallic stab.

Zeph shivered, no longer wishing to linger. Some things were best kept unknown. "I should let you work."

"Sit." Her voice was dark and abrupt with an unfamiliar grain. "Please."

Zeph regarded their mother for half a second before cautious curiosity won over. They walked to the table and collapsed into a chair. Even with the nap behind the house, the last two days had left Zeph weak. Water from their cup sloshed onto their shirt.

"Oh." Gina stopped pacing and examined Zeph. "Honey."

"What?"

"You must be exhausted from your first Survival. I'm sorry. I didn't even ask how it was." She was stalling.

"I am fine," Zeph said, not fine at all. They tried to stay stoic. Their lower lip twitched.

"Zeph." Gina looked down and held her glass in two hands, as if it provided her a calming effect. The condensation dripped onto her manicured nails. "I know that face. You are not fine. Do you want to talk about it?"

"No." *Yes.* They did. They needed someone to confide in. Survival had been a nightmare come true. But right now, Gina was scaring them.

Their chin broke into wobbles, giving them away. Then, wet salt ran into the corners of their lips. "It was awful, Mom."

"Oh, hon." Gina looked at the doorway again, then set her glass on the table. She knelt by them. "Shoot. Okay, come here." She leaned over and took Zeph in her arms. On a normal day, the embrace would have been comforting. Today, it was not. They cried harder, feeling trapped. Their mother's arms wrapping around them was a vise of lies.

Lamia said Gina did bloodwork on me.

Six months ago, she had been fighting the medical office administrators to be put in charge of Zeph's monthly checkups instead of their regular nurse. Zeph had never had emotional outbursts like the ones they had been experiencing in the past two days, but they remembered their emotions and anxieties started feeling off six months ago.

That can not be a coincidence. Gina changed me. Not for the better. Why did she do this? Who is Gina Carmak, really? Am I even safe? Heat brewed like a sunburn across their cheeks.

Gina rocked back and forth, arms firm across Zeph's back, saying nothing. Zeph waited for her to pull away before releasing the tension in their shoulders. When she pulled away, there were tears in her eyes waiting to spill. The two of them searched each other's faces for several seconds, scouring the features for information, before Zeph spoke. "Do I have a godmother?"

Gina wiped at her eyes and stood back up. She looked away. "Why would you ask a question like that? You have your dad and I."

"I know, but no one from Mainland or anything?"

"Where is this coming from?"

Do I say it? Do I want to say it? She is being defensive. More reason not to trust her right now. Their heart raced. The precariousness of this conversation was imminent. Zeph was about to jump off a ledge.

"You know you can talk to me about anything, right?" Gina said.

"Can I?" Their voice was sharp.

"Of course you—"

"Do you know what time Survival ended?" Zeph asked.

"What time did it end?" Gina asked as her com flashed blue for the third time since Zeph came inside. Her eyes shifted out of focus slightly.

"It ended hours ago." *Is she even listening?* "I heard you talking to Lamia." Their heart rocketed into their throat. What if they did not want to know what was going on? What if—?

"I see." Gina nodded, looking just past Zeph's face with an unrecognizable grimace. Her eyes flickered and her com went green, which meant vis mode had just been switched on. Just when Zeph was going to open their mouth and demand answers, Gina bellowed, "Don't you dare, woman! Don't you even—*bitch*. Zeph, give me that—" She reached down to where Zeph sat and batted their com from their ear as if it were a cockroach.

Zeph flinched and leaned back, knuckles gripping the seat of their chair. Before the com bounced against the floor with a hollow plastic-on-plastic sound, a verbal message pierced through their notifications without even being selected. *"It was Gina's idea, not mine. Remember that, child, when she turns you against me. She's going to—"*

The voice was deep and salty like the sea. It conjured images of ocean foam that coated rock. It conjured the unstable feeling of an earthquake. It had an earthy flavor sprinkled with nostalgia.

Shocked, Zeph held still. The shock wore off slowly, like paralysis lifting from one body part at a time. First, the toes. Zeph blinked. Then, the fingers. They looked between the com and their mother. Then limbs, tingly and numb, awoke. "You just hit me." Soon, their whole body buzzed with hot and cold tingles. They leaned down to pick up the com, flinching and pausing when their mother reached toward them as if to stop them. Gina dropped her arms to her side.

"I'm sorry. I didn't mean to. I was trying to protect you." Gina's face showed as much shock in her expression as Zeph felt. "Please don't pick up that com. She shouldn't have contacted you. I told her—"

"Who is she?" Zeph picked the com off the floor and rolled it between their fingers.

"It's not my place to say." Zeph could see the fear in her eyes.

"Are you...." Zeph sighed and closed their eyes, as if it would steel them for any answer they did not like. "Are you not my mother?"

Gina sucked in a breath. She looked out the window for the millionth time.

That was all it took. In that half-second non-answer, Zeph's world crashed like the ocean. Blood roared in their ears. All they could hear was the rushing white noise. It was deafening. They clenched the com. Its plastic shell creaked under the pressure.

"What did she tell you, Zeph?"

"Why haven't you answered my question? It should be a simple answer."

Gina sniffed and crossed her arms. "Whatever that woman told you just now, you can't trust—no, don't do that—"

Zeph put the com back in their ear and stood. "Are you or are you not my mother?"

"For Earth's sake. Hon… This isn't how…" Gina's shoulders slumped. "Okay, but you were never safe here, Zeph. And we aren't safe anymore. That's why we need to talk."

"I need you to say it." The words itched the back of their throat.

Gina squared up and took Zeph by the shoulders. "I love you, Z. You need to trust me. Go pack a bag. There's an arriving ship today. We have to get on it and leave."

The roaring in their ears drowned out several of her words. "Trust you? You hit me. You kept secrets. You—" Their voice cracked and heaved. "You want me to *leave* with you? What is going on? Are you taking me to my real mother?"

"No. Definitely not." Her jaw set hard lines into her face.

"Then it is true. You're not my real mother."

Gina was stone.

Their vision swayed. This couldn't be happening. Could they believe this was happening? What *was* happening?

"What was your idea?" Zeph's voice steamed. They latched onto the first next question they needed answered. "That voice on the com. She said it was 'your idea.'" Gina said nothing. She pursed her lips and looked to the side. "You have to tell me what is going on."

"Zeph, you there?" It was the voice again. The voice like ocean rocks. It should not have been possible to send an audible message like that, having it bypass all the internal messaging storage. Zeph tried to mentally grab the message and examine it, but the message did not leave anything to grab. *"Zeph? There are two sides to every story, Zeph. You must hear mine out. She's going to make up lies about me."*

The voice rang in their head after it was gone.

"Why are you contacting me?" Zeph asked out loud, simultaneously directing a thread of mental energy to the com, grasping at the tail end of the voice message. "Who is this? What was her idea?"

There was a long pause. Gina opened her mouth to speak but nothing came out. Shaking, her face melted, soft and scared. Then, the voice whispered as if the answer were painful, *"To make you viable, Zeph."*

So they were right. Their fears confirmed. *Gina did this.*

"Zeph, please." She must have seen the change in them as Zeph's body coiled and tensed. "We have to go."

"You made me like this?" The question was a whisper, but it hissed like rain over hot coals. "The extra checkups, the secrecy, this whole time you were, what? Experimenting on me?" Their voice rose like hungry flames.

"*Shhh.*" Gina stepped toward Zeph. "If Lamia—"

"So you got in trouble with your boss. And now you want to take me away because you messed up?"

"The Karulis have been—"

"*You.* You have been. You have been changing me." Zeph's shouts made the sounds from the neighboring house stop. Their fingers twitched, remembering the satisfaction of unleashing a similar flurry of anger onto flesh. Cris's flesh. They could still taste the iron of Cris's blood on their tongue.

Zeph stood, facing Gina, and wanted to rip, tear, bite.

"But you weren't safe. It was only a matter of time before Lamia—"

"I do not care about Lamia!" Zeph screamed, stepping toward her. Towering over her. Tears that had been clouding their vision until now tumbled down their cheeks, spilling onto their shirt. Zeph rammed past Gina and walked to the doorway.

"Stop." Gina touched Zeph's shoulder.

Zeph turned around, ready to explode. They blinked and shook and imagined the euphoria of letting loose their anger—but also the regret that would follow after. Whose body was this, to react with such severe anger to a soft touch? It was not their own anymore. It belonged to someone they did not recognize.

What am I doing?

"Let go." An animal lurked behind their words. "I will hurt you." *I do not want to hurt you. I do not want to hurt anyone.* Gina snapped her hand back and shrank. Zeph ran. They did not know if they should have trusted Gina and fled with her. They did not know what would happen next. They did not know who or what they ran from. But they ran because they had no choice.

They could only think of one place that was safe.

Internship Day

Krimsey Enosh, Tuesday, March 26, 2250, 9:10 a.m.

After the worst Survival Daily in history, Krimsey slept on his flimsy mattress on the floor. Although *slept* isn't the word he would use. Flopped. Rolled. Languished. He ached from pushing himself too hard in Survival. Sore muscles kept him turning over in bed every five minutes. By the time he was startled awake by a pouncing, overexcited little sister, he was completely twisted and tangled in the sheet he barely slept in.

With the full weight of his growing twelve-year-old sister on his chest, Krimsey was reminded that Elpida wasn't a little girl anymore. She felt like two thousand kilograms crushing his ribs. Her teeth gleamed like lighthouses. Blue hues reflected up from the lake at the bottom of the chasm outside through a bay window–sized hole. The brilliant blue tinted everything in the house, including Elpida's tan skin. It made her look very *transitus* and very viable, despite being the *least* viable *transitus* he knew.

Her dark brown curls tickled his nose.

"*Gurroff,*" Krimsey grunted as he pushed her off him.

Elpida stood aside. Her smile misted over, lips pulled taught. "You know what day it is, right?"

"Oh no," Krimsey groaned.

While twelve was a little early to be testing into the Non-Viable *Transitus* Internship Program, Elpida Enosh was not waiting around an extra year. Today, Elpida was taking her early application.

"It's Internship Day."

"What time is it?" He had lost so much time to Survival, it was easy to forget two days had passed. He should have known better. He should have kept track of the time. He should have set an alarm.

"It's 9:12."

Nausea settled in the pit of his empty stomach. They barely had enough time to haul up the cliffside. He needed to check her in *by* 10:00 a.m. Lateness factored into her test results. Though it would be Krimsey's fault and not Elpida's, the HPO didn't take kindly to excuses. Unacceptable. He plucked his com from yesterday's crumpled clothes that lay on a shelf in the living room beside the mattress.

He pushed the tiny button on the side. It powered on with a flash of white light. A ping from about an hour ago opened in the visual display. Dailies and various orders from the HPO came through an official channel throughout each day and did not reveal the rest of the com's interface until they were read. His brain registered the latest message.

"Reminder: All transitus are to report to Karuli Dome for the Transition Ceremony today, 4:00 p.m."

Another thing he had forgotten. Ceremony Day. A monthly ritual the HPO hosted. When the names of viable transitus whose blood showed they were close to transition were called out. Those kids got sent to port to ready themselves. Based on his past checkups, Krimsey knew he had eight more months, minus about thirty-six hours. He wasn't counting.

He mentally swiped the message away, revealing the visual interface of his com. He blinked once, the interface disappeared, and he focused on his sister. "Where's Sanjana?" Krimsey hadn't called Sanjana *Mother* since the day she had disappeared into her job. Since she stopped *mother*ing Elpida. Since Father died.

"Mother's *working…*" Elpida crossed her arms and tapped her foot in the middle of the room. "I'm going to be late."

"I'm so sorry, Ellie. I feel terrible." He rushed to throw his old shorts and t-shirt on and shove stale, wheat-and-protein-based trail mix into his mouth and pockets. "If we hurry we'll only be a little late."

"It's *Pida*."

"What?"

"You keep calling me Ellie like I'm a child. It's *Pida* now."

Krimsey refused. *She's growing up too quick.* "Sure, yeah, whatever." He wasn't going to call her that. "Let's get you checked in." He tripped over a dining room chair on his way out the door.

If the air was stuffy inside their cramped cliffside home, outside it was ruthless. The humidity in the rift between the parallel cliffsides was likely ninety-eight percent. At least, that's what it felt like to Krimsey. Like he was perpetually drowning. Their steps crunched along the ledge to Footpath Main and they followed the switchbacks of Main up the cliffside.

At the top of the cliff, the morning mist had evaporated. The prowling ocean views lay in wait over the east and west edges of Karuli Crag. A twinge of blue begged for Krimsey's attention. He resisted. With the ocean in his peripheral vision, he could pretend that it was just sky. That its depths didn't beckon him ominously.

He owed his future to the ocean. That didn't mean he owed *this moment* to it. This moment was a happy one. This moment belonged to Elpida. Belonged to *her* future.

And they were still running late.

"Elpida." Krimsey turned to his sister, avoiding calling her either Pida—which he hated—or Ellie—which *she* hated. They had pushed through the morning market that skirted the cliff and paused outside Karuli Dome. "Are you ready?"

She looked ready. His sister was always bright-eyed, but today her skin glowed with anticipation. Her oval face had filled out, sharpened with more definition. It was as if she'd sprouted into an adult overnight. The last remnants of her childhood were the innocent sparks of joy that lurked behind every expression. One of the qualities he cherished most about her.

"Of course I am." She brushed her curly bangs from her face.

He looked away when he started to recognize traces of Father in her brown curls and eyes. In her high *transitus* forehead. Father died when Elpida was a baby. But even after all this time, Krimsey spent much of his energy tip-toeing his thoughts around how much he missed him.

At the top of Karuli Crag, Up Top, was the morning market, Karuli Dome, and low-lying recycled plastic homes that dotted the trails forking off Footpath Main. The iridescent glass of Karuli Dome glittered in the low-lying spring sun, towering over the middle of the narrow mountain plateau, overlooking the small human community. Footpath Main bent and wound all the way around the dome. The dome's west side was flanked by a stone courtyard and Ross Bay Overlook.

Elpida stared at the dome and hesitated, chewing her lip. "What if I don't test into the internship I want?" Her voice had an upward tilt to it.

"Ellie, I am sure you will do *great*. But you don't have to test this year if you don't want to. You could spend more time preparing. You are allowed to change your mind. Do you want to change your mind?"

"No." She shook her head confidently. "What I mean is they only accept a small number of NVTs in the terraforming-based tech-developer program," Elpida mused. "What if they don't even have a position this year? Sometimes they don't. I know Sonya retired last year so this might mean there is an opening but I don't know."

"Who is Sonya?"

"She was a terraforming-based tech developer."

"How many people do they normally assign to terraforming-based... uh... that job?"

"Last year? No one. It's a very limited job. Only three people have gotten it in the past four years. If accepted, I would get to be the one making and running simulations for what to grow and where. Every decision I'd make would impact the terraforming operations."

"That's fantastic. Is anyone else so awesome that they're taking an early application?"

"No..."

"Is anyone else so awesome that they practiced four hours a night after studies and assignments for three years?"

"No," she said.

"Well, it sounds like you've done your research. You've done so much preparation. I am sure your gut is leading you right. You'll get it. Come on. Less delaying, more moving." They walked briskly to the glass revolving doors and pushed into the airy, white-tiled interior of the dome. The main hub, the grand foyer, the pride and joy of the HPO. Inside was refreshing circulated air. Humans and *transitus* bustled across the tiled floor. He looked down at her as they hurried across the foyer. "Are you *sure* you're ready? You don't get second chances with this. If you fail this one, they'll give you the generic test and then put you wherever they want you. That's it. You'll be in your tested profession for life."

"I want to make a difference... You think I'll make a difference?"

"Elpida Ray Enosh. You are beyond intelligent, you are thoughtful, and you already make a difference. The terraforming program will be lucky to have you."

"Terraforming-based tech development. That's the test I'm requesting. It's very specific."

"Right. That," Krimsey said. Elpida was frowning, withdrawing into that overactive mind of hers. "Hey. Listen, if they slap you with the generic test after you're done and you don't test into your dream career, I promise I will take you on a weekend hike to port." Krimsey raised his right hand for emphasis. She'd been dying to go to port and hike through the valleys for some time now. Mother hadn't let them go. Elpida was "too young," she said.

Someone bumped his shoulder. "Watch it."

Krimsey muttered an apology.

Elpida eyed him.

"What?"

"You're not going to say something?"

"No, Elpida, that's not how things work around here."

Elpida *humphed* and clicked her tongue. She said something under her breath and Krimsey knew it contained her signature snark.

"See? You're already making a difference. You're calling your brother out on being a wimp."

Elpida laughed. "You promise about the hike? Because I'm not sure I'll get it. I'll hold you to it."

"You have my word. I'll even carry you on my back if you get tired. And you're absolutely sure *today* is the day?"

"Yes." She gave him a sideways glance. "*Yes*," she emphasized. "I *am* ready. Stop asking already." Elpida sighed as they clambered down the main stairwell in the middle of the dome.

The stairwell was full of people spilling, hurrying, ambling down it with just as many others emerging. Straight into the tunnels and into the mountain. Krimsey and Elpida barged down the staircase. He held his sister's arm to keep her from being jostled. At the bottom of the staircase was a broad, dim gallery. Hallways, tunnels, and doors lined the walls.

It was easy to feel trapped in the HPO Underground and even easier to get lost. They turned down the tunnel opening that led to the sector of rooms and tunnels dedicated to the separate education of non-viable *transitus*. Very different from the preparations viable *transitus* underwent. Elpida never had Survival to worry about. Non-viables would never transition. Never live and breathe in the ocean.

They found room 244, checked in, and received a stern reprimand for lateness. Elpida waved back at him nervously, disappearing through a door past registration and into another hallway.

Krimsey's anxious heart thudded in his chest. He sat, reclined his head against the hard wall, and rested his eyes.

The rest was short-lived. "You're viable," the man sitting next to him said, clearly surprised.

"I am." He offered his hand deliberately in the space left between them. "I'm Krimsey."

The man took Krimsey's hand but didn't seem in a hurry to let it go. "A little old, aren't you?"

"Um...." The awkward encounter made his blood simmer with anxiety. He tried to say something polite. Nothing came out.

"I've never seen a viable around here as old as you are. Shouldn't you have transitioned by now?" Before Krimsey could process what was happening, a new com notification pinged him.

"Krimsey Enosh. House D of Footpath 91. Report to Medical Wing C."

Retracting his palm, Krimsey said, "Excuse me."

Thankful for any excuse to leave, Krimsey stood up, walking quickly, wondering why he was being called to Medical, why *Wing*

C when he'd already done his bloodwork checkup last week, and why *nobody* had any *Earthforsaken manners.*

And walked straight into the wall. Before embarrassment could leak into the room, Krimsey clamped up his emotional defense. Hot-faced, aching, and more tired than he had any right to be, he slinked out of the room.

This is going to be a long day.

Krimsey scrunched his nose. The medical wing always smelled of sweat, mold, and disinfectant. Air vents rattled along the dim stone tunnels. Unused to seeing wing C so empty, he almost passed right by the door.

"Good morning," he cleared his throat. "I was called to wing C but I think there's been a mistake or glitch or…"

"Krimsey Enosh?"

He nodded.

The woman at the desk was wrinkled and pale with bags under her eyes. Tattered green scrubs were pulled taught over her squat form. Poor posture gave her the shape of a mushy melon. The receptionist looked right through him, accessing her com.

She blinked. "Go right ahead."

"But—"

"Go on. They're waiting in the third room down on the left."

The woman clearly had no interest in any eye contact, let alone answering his questions. Krimsey passed through the door behind her and found two people waiting for him in the room down the hall.

Both humans wore those same green scrubs, but the brown-skinned woman with black eyes and a severe braid donned a crisp new set. Hers hadn't faded. She excused the woman next to her, who scurried out.

"Hi… I think there was a mistake. I already had my checkup last week." Krimsey glanced at the kit of vials on the counter. "Did they forget something?"

"Have a seat, Krimsey. My name is Gina Carmak." Her voice was hoarse. The bags beneath her eyes were caked with a slightly off-shade makeup.

Krimsey sat. He fidgeted in the seat when Gina brought out a needle.

"Have you ever had a follow-up before?"

"No."

"It's pretty simple. We have follow-ups on any *transitus* whose tests come back deficient in important vitamins or minerals. We noticed your levels of zinc and vitamin C are essentially non-existent. We'll be administering a vitamin cocktail to help balance you out."

"Oh." He relaxed a little, though the woman herself still seemed tense. Zinc and vitamin C seemed important.

"Alright. Are you ready? You look a little green in the face." Gina chuckled. "Well, you know what I mean. You don't like needles, do you?"

Krimsey *felt* green in the face. Needles were his worst enemy. "I'm deficient even after the regular dose last week? Is that common?" He stalled. The needle and syringe in her hand seemed to glint with menace. Rancid juices in his empty stomach stewed.

"Very common." She cleared her throat. "You're old enough now that, as your body changes and adapts and readies your lungs for transition, it's common to see these deficiencies. Your body is likely about to go into overdrive and it's using up your stores. We have to be sure you have the proper nutrients for a smooth transition."

"Does that mean I'm transitioning? Don't I have eight more months?" He breathed deep and even, to distract him from the settling panic.

"On average, a viable *transitus* like yourself transitions into their aquatic lungs around sixteen. Your estimations predict that you have eight months, yes. But timing has been known to change if the *transitus* is under a lot of stress. Are you under a lot of stress?"

Who lives on the literal side of a cliff and isn't under a lot of stress? "Of course I am. So how long do I have, then?"

"We're still sifting through the recent bloodwork for the Transition Ceremony tonight," she continued. "If your expected time of transition has changed, we will be sure to let you know." She stepped forward. Krimsey turned his head to look at the bland grey wall and offered his arm. "This'll pinch a bit."

Krimsey squeezed his eyes, bit his tongue, and held his breath. His face tensed. His chest tensed. Even his belly tensed. She touched his arm and it went limp with fear.

A tiny squeeze pinched his skin. His mouth tasted metallic.

"There. That was it."

He looked down, coughed, and said, "Oh." He swallowed hard at the bile that had risen. "That hurt less than usual."

Gina looked down her long nose at him. Her smile melted across her face. "Yes, well, you're all set."

Unravel

FELICE'S BREATH TREMBLED. HER belly churned. Her nails bit into her palm. She was being taunted in her dreams by Rumi Yen's small blue gaze looking up at her. She woke to her own pleading whimpers and wild, throbbing pulse. She opened her eyes. The dream gave way to a piercing white in her eyes and the smell of sun-warmed sheets. Felice blinked away the persistent fringes of sleep, swallowed, and held in her tears.

"Ive?" she whispered to her not-quite-boyfriend. Ive was re-clined with her in bed. He seemed asleep, breaths slow and deep. Shafts of window light streamed in and strands of his hair splayed brilliantly across her chest in every hue of red. One of Felice's arms was pinned beneath Ive and her other arm shot stabbing pain from wrist to elbow every time she moved.

Ive was fully clothed—he wore plain green work clothes—and his left arm was strewn over her collar bone. She saw that his sleeve was completely sheared off, and she knew why.

She looked at her stinging arm. Ive knew how to dress a wound, but he probably didn't know where the gauze was stored in her house. Her arm was wrapped nicely. But wrapped in that *green....* Conspicuous, repugnant, regretful *green....*

Resolving to change the green cloth wrapped around her crusted, self-inflicted gash the first chance she'd get, Felice's eyes glazed. She wondered how she'd get out of this nonstop nightmare if she couldn't even kill herself right.

"I wish I could tell you the things I've done," Felice whispered, stroking Ive's angular *transitus* face. Her thumb traced down the bridge of his long nose, around his lips, up sharp cheekbones. "I know we all have our secrets. You have yours. Lamia has hers. We all have them. It makes us more human. But mine? My secrets kill me. Every day they kill me." Her body was anchored and heavy, but not from the weight of him.

Ive stirred, lifted his head. "You're up," he said softly.

"I forgot you were still coming," she said under strained breath.

Ive was older than she was, by fifteen years or so. She never asked his age. Ive's jawline rested in the nook of her neck. His face was like silk. He was masterfully chiseled. He was cool and pale, with blue tints of transitus pigmentation. She loved all these features but loved the look of age on him most. The lines by his mouth. The sprinkle of grey hairs at the back of his head. The years of both good times and bad set in the gaze of his eyes. She pulled him in with her arm that was wrapped beneath his back; his body was a refuge.

"I'm too numb to even feel embarrassed," she said.

"No, you have no reason to feel embarrassed. Please don't feel that way." His voice soothed her bleeding thoughts. "Tell me how I can help."

"You should have let me die. If you knew what I've done...." Her voice cracked, her throat and lips were dry as sand. "I don't want to feel the pain anymore."

"Stop," he whispered, tucking the cool touch of his legs and feet neatly around hers, his chest hugging her closely. "Does this help?"

"Better if you were naked," she chuckled weakly, savoring all the spots where the cool skin of his leg touched hers.

"I can make that happen." He kissed her neck.

Felice stiffened.

"What's wrong?"

"Ive? Where's my com? I had it with me when—"

She sat up, looked about in a panic, patting the tangle of sheets.

"Felice..."

Felice stood, swaying out of bed. "No no no no no. Where is it?"

"Felice!"

Felice stopped. Her head pounded.

Ive's eyes lit up a brilliant blue in the slanted gold light pouring in from outside. She followed his gaze to the dresser against the black, high-gloss accent wall. Her shoulders loosened. Felice plucked the little black com off the dresser.

Ive got up and prepared to put her in his arms. "It's… busted, Felice. The bathwater… last night… you never took it off. It fell into the water." He tiptoed around the topic of last night as if she would break.

"I need my com. Damn it. This is too much," she croaked under her breath.

"Breathe. We can get you—"

"NO. I need it now!" Felice shouted and forced herself from his enclosing embrace. "I need it… today… I have to greet them…" She reached for a slinky black dress and muttered incoherent nonsense. Something about arrivals and port and Sanjana and—

"Felice you know I work in coms, let's get you a new one together." His inflection strained.

It must have been hard, seeing her unravel. *Ive doesn't know hard.* She angry-sighed at the ceiling.

"Do you love me, Ive?" Her mind felt thick and heavy, as if the pressure inside it were building to a crescendo.

"Of course I do."

"Say it."

"I love you."

"If you love me, you'll stop meddling."

"I wasn't—"

"Just stop! Stop it! Stop saving me. Stop helping me. Stop it. Stop loving me, Ive, just stop."

Felice crumpled to her knees against the wall, half dressed. Her chest heaved and her heart fluttered. Fluttered and somersaulted upside down, falling into the pit of her stomach and rebounding into her throat.

Her body shuddered. She felt sick.

Weak.

Ive crouched and kissed her wobbling chin and kissed the tears.

"Go," she said, unable to contain the love that leaked.

Ive stood and padded barefoot out of the room. Seconds later, he was back with a cup of brown liquid and a fluffy white roll. Sitting next to her, he first handed over the cup, cool and wet with condensation. She took a tentative sip. Orange blossom black tea. Dash of honey. A luxury to have. Even for a Karuli. It was her favorite.

"Thanks," she said, now accepting the roll and biting into it and drowning it with a gulp of cold brewed tea. She finished both and handed him the empty cup. Felice stood, feeling as if her body were floating and untethered.

"I have to go," she said. She dressed. "You should leave before my mother sees you." She walked to the doorway of her bedroom and paused. "I'm… sorry. I shouldn't have said those things to you." She turned around and gave him a tight look. "You're more than I deserve."

Then she left.

In Danger

THE SHOT KRIMSEY RECEIVED twenty minutes ago in wing C did not hurt at the time it was administered. As he made his way through the HPO tunnels, however, the spot the needle stuck grew hot and uncomfortable. He returned to waiting room 244 to wait for Elpida. He expected to have to put up with a full room of parents including the man with poor manners, but the room was empty.

He double-checked the numbers outside to verify it was the same room. It was. Everyone was gone. Even the receptionist.

Krimsey peered across the reception desk. No one. Confused, he took a seat. *Maybe the receptionist stepped away.* The other kids must have already finished their tests and Elpida, working diligently on her advanced test, was taking her time. He checked the time.

"Don't go to Medical." An abrupt voice blared in his com. A voice with robust complexities, like coffee. Deep, ambiguous, and utterly unfamiliar. He flinched at the message and blinked. He looked around, as if the receptionist would pop out and begin laughing. At first, he wondered if it came from the official HPO channel. But the sender was untethered. No notification. No name. Krimsey flicked a thought at his com to examine the sudden verbal message, but as far as the com could tell, it hadn't even existed.

His right eye twitched and he held in a dry cough. He would ignore the message. Besides, he had already been to Medical. The com system had obviously sent a fluke, a glitch.

The vent system for the room shuddered loudly to a stop. The absence of sound was eerie. Hairs on his forearms and the back of his neck rose. The tunnels always echoed with sound. The *tap tap tap* of shoes. Hushed murmurs or boisterous chats. When all else fell quiet, *clang-clanging* vents were almost always the music of the HPO Underground.

It was too quiet.

Krimsey shifted in his seat, and the worn grey cloth on his body rustled.

Rapping his fingers on his shorts, Krimsey's nervousness for Elpida made him feel a bit sick. He leaned over the left arm of his chair for a clear view into the reception window again. Still empty. Krimsey was about to stand—sleepy, impatient—and search for assistance, when the com voice appeared again.

"Elpida Enosh is in danger, Krimsey."

It disappeared before he could snag the message and reply to the sender. Krimsey bolted up and whipped around in the still room.

"Who's there?" The silence following his outburst was deafening. He rubbed his eyes, as if clearer vision were the solution. This time, it did not strike him as a glitch. The message was too specific. What did it mean, Elpida was in danger? Elpida was taking her test. In danger of failing? The air vents clanged back on, sputtering with effort, then after a moment, a smooth stream tousled his hair.

"Dear?" The receptionist appeared in the window. "Can I help you, dear?"

Then, on the com, *"I am sorry. Stay out of trouble and disregard."*

Krimsey straightened. "Yes," he answered the receptionist, concern straining his voice. He had to put his hands in his pockets to keep from shaking. "I'm waiting for Elpida Enosh. Do you think she'll be much longer?"

The receptionist looked surprised. "Honey, Enosh finished early. She's already left."

"Oh." Krimsey turned to leave, stopped, turned back. He wondered now if someone was pranking him. If Elpida was pranking him. He looked again at the displeased-with-her-job receptionist and found his voice. "But she wouldn't have left without me. Are you sure she's done?"

A green com light flickered on from her ear. She had switched her com to vis mode. Her eyes scanned invisible rows of information only she could see.

"Nope, dear, she finished," said the woman.

"Alright. Thank you. Did she tell anyone where she went? Was she looking for me?"

"Don't think so."

"Can you tell me what she tested into?" He wondered if Elpida's tech-terraforming request had been rejected. Maybe she tested into something undesirable, like maintenance or admin. Maybe she left to pout.

"Can't do that. Sorry, dear."

Krimsey blinked, his vision tunneled. Muscles tensed just perceptibly, squaring his shoulders. Mostly, he was annoyed at Elpida, but the woman was hardly any help herself.

Why didn't she wait for me? This is wrong.

"Why not? She's going to tell me anyways," Krimsey pressed, risking reprimand.

"Confidential."

Queasiness in his belly bunched into several knots. "She's my *sister.*"

The woman pursed her lips and her brows glowered down at him, casting sharp shadows over her face.

"Sorry. It's just… I'm worried about her. She must be upset. Can you just tell me if she passed her tech-terraforming test or not?" The tension set in his face loosened. He didn't want to earn the reputation of an ill-behaved *transitus* teen. The message in his head nagged him. Elpida in danger? Whether she was in danger, which he found hard to believe, or not, he was beginning to wonder if he should tell the receptionist about the com messages he had just received. Explain why he was becoming so concerned. Why she should be, too.

The woman shook her head.

She probably wasn't the one to tell. For one, she didn't seem to care much. About anything.

At the woman's stern non-reply, Krimsey added, "Did she say if she was going home or...?"

Impatience seemed to creep into her body—rigid, twitching, sighing, and breathing audibly.

"Okay, well, thanks for your help," he muttered. As he left, Krimsey forced the exit door open with a kick. It hit the outer wall.

Bang.

A little too reckless. He cringed but didn't look back because he was afraid that if he did, there would be discipline. *Why did I do that?*

"Sorry," he muttered quickly and hurried back toward the underground gallery.

Krimsey rose from the gallery stairwell into the dome. Through the wide, triangular glass panels of the dome walls, he saw several young people loitering and laughing in the courtyard outside. They looked around Elpida's age.

The courtyard was made pretty by several standing stone sculptures and a well-maintained gravel path with benches. Some of the kids dangled their legs over empty air off the cliffside ledge.

Krimsey pushed through the revolving door, greeted by sweltering Antarctic temperatures, and approached the group.

"Have any of you seen Elpida Enosh?"

Everyone shook their heads, looking at him like he had lost his mind, then leaning in to each other with whispers and flashing teeth.

He left, clutching his sweaty, twitching thumb in his palm. She wouldn't have Dailies today. She'd have the day off. She most likely would have gone home.

Krimsey sighed and shook his head. Maybe he had lost his mind. The stress of Survival Daily had taken everything out of him and he still had not recovered.

Krimsey crossed from the courtyard to Footpath Main and followed it down the cliffside to go home. His knees creaked in protest as he descended the footpaths. Every time someone passed him, he stopped. He looked over his shoulder. Glared at the back of their head. His neck prickled. He still could not rule out that the messages earlier had been a prank.

Who knows how to hack coms?

Of course, the only person he knew who was possibly skilled enough to do something as elaborate as sending a prioritized, untethered voice message was Cris Langley.

Why *him?* Sharing an awkward, intimate moment with a bully during Survival was certainly the fastest way to become the biggest target on the continent. Krimsey tried to recall if he'd seen a flash of vibrant red locks today. He hadn't, but this theory felt more and more reasonable by the second. Would Cris go so far as taking Elpida away just for a scare? For a few laughs at Krimsey's expense? At Elpida's expense? To save face?

Yes. He probably would.

The thought of Cris messing with his sister made Krimsey's ears burn. His breath heaved. The air felt too thin.

The Enosh residence was the second to last home on Footpath 91. He turned down 91, stealing stares through the open doors of his neighbors. While theirs were lively with chatter, his home was hollow. No actual doors existed—every home had just a plastic rectangular frame. He stepped inside. Bumps rose on his skin. Elevated hairs tickled his forearms.

"Elpida?"

Inside, the home was L-shaped, without any walls dividing the rooms. So he knew right away Elpida was either not here, or she was hiding. There was a small table by the entrance and two small mattresses in the crook of the *L*. At the bottom leg of the *L* was a cupboard filled with utensils. Beneath it, the hard plastic counter jutted from the wall, home to a one-burner electric cooktop and a small, crooked refrigerator. Sanjana, his mother, had a bed and rug and dresser crammed at the top of the *L*.

"Ellie, this isn't funny," he said.

Rippling blue light from the empty window opening overlooking the cliffside flitted across the table top. The light danced inside the open kitchen cupboard. Jigged in the shadows between the cups and bowls. Hit the ceiling. Slithered across his shirt like a snake. The light only moved wild and fast like that when kids played in the lake below.

He hurried to the window hole and looked down. Below, Gianvante Lake laughed. Water swayed and settled. A parent dried off two ant-sized kids on the pebble beach by the grass.

They were tiny. Too tiny. They weren't Elpida.

His heart *tha-thumped*, skipped every third beat. Lungs rattled audibly.

Elpida wasn't here.

"Where are you? Where are you?" Krimsey tore the house apart. "Where are you?" He searched and seized every nook of the house, looking for her, for clues, for anything to calm him down. "Where are you?"

Sheets, pillows, mattresses and cupboard doors flew. Bowls clattered to the floor. He kicked one. It slammed against the wall and cracked. He imagined the loud *snap* was Cris's bones. If this prank was Cris's doing, if Cris so much as touched her... He shuddered. Well, Cris was going to die.

"Where are you, Elpida?" His voice crackled like caked mud.

He didn't even know where Cris lived. For all he knew, Cris lived Up Top, had human parents and thirteen sisters. Cush life with cush things in a cush house with plenty of time to learn frivolous things.

Like hacking.

Partly because he had no idea where Cris lived and partly because a tiny, fractional, infinitesimal part of him wanted to give Cris the benefit of the doubt—very, very deep down, in a chasm—*wait*.

Chasm.

The pinnacles.

He had to rule out one more possibility before full panic mode set in. What he would do then, he wasn't sure. Elpida was his responsibility. She knew better than to do this to him, but if she had been upset, she could have gone to the pinnacles. The pinnacles, where there was a crumbling, perilous trail leading to the terraforming bowl that supplied them all with fresh, plant-based food. Where that trail wound around a mess of tall, spiked rock formations and gaping chasms. If Elpida didn't test into the tech-terraforming job, maybe she would have gone down there. To pester the workers. An unauthorized field trip. As far-fetched as it was, it wasn't out of the realm of possibility. Kids got lost down there. Fell down deadly voids. Dropped straight to nowhere-land.

He decided if—as much as he hated the idea—if he did not find Elpida there, he would alert the HPO. Before he became personally responsible for the murder of one blood-red-haired *transitus* boy.

You can be rational, Krim. Be rational. His stomach was still sick. It was all the stress. *Damn it, Elpida.*

Cold sweat collected on his scalp and dripped into his brows. Krimsey wiped his face. He bounded down Footpath Main. He would scold Elpida for being so reckless. She was the smartest kid he knew, but sometimes she was just careless. Too free-spirited. His downhill momentum carried him as he took a giant leap over the last switchback. He landed on grass that covered the bottom of Karuli Crag.

He told himself Elpida was fine. But the little-girl-sized cracks along the pinnacle path were vivid pictures in his mind. He cursed and ran harder.

He kept the glittering Gianvante Lake to his right and headed south toward the pinnacle path. The path wandered like a mischievous snake, sneaking cracks and deep, hidden holes between sharp inclines and dramatic drops. A snake's den. Waiting to gulp down the next kid.

The pinnacle path was the same place Rumi Yen, an unsupervised NVT like his sister, had reportedly perished, over two years ago. Her body was never found. All that had been found was a torn green scrap of the shirt she had been wearing.

It was dark down here. Little blue lights lined the thinning trail. Sun never touched between Karuli Crag and its towering neighbor, but the sun and its nutrients were artificially brought there with old-world technology. Krimsey heaved at the top of a steep incline and stopped where the path leveled off. Sky-scraping spires surrounded him and the terraforming bowl stood in the distance.

"Elpida?" It was a lonely whisper.

He listened for an answer. A drafty whistle replied. The gust of wind whined and whirled, whipping his hair back.

"Elpidaaaaa!" Krimsey shouted. The pinnacles bounced his voice back at him. He clambered up a steep side trail. He scrambled and searched up and down the sprawling web of trails, earth cracking and crumbling beneath him, until the network finally spat him out next to the entrance of The Bowl.

Stomach churning in ways he hadn't felt since his father died, Krimsey checked the great bowl of green grass, where terraformers planted and toiled and studied. Each person shook their head at him. No, they had not seen a small twelve-year-old NVT. No, they had not heard anyone call for help. And, *no, you are not allowed in here.*

Krimsey left The Bowl and wandered the path toward home. Again, he thought about Cris and his murder. *Be realistic, Krimsey.* He pushed himself to think beyond personal emotions. The voice on the com provided him a warning. A warning from someone who sounded nothing like Cris. A warning that told him Elpida was in danger. Now Elpida was missing. What did that even mean, then? The voice had said not to go to Medical. Could Medical have been a distraction? If Medical was a distraction, that would mean… That the HPO was corrupt.

Not possible. What if she just fell? Krimsey couldn't get the horrifying story of Rumi Yen out of his mind now. *Just fell.* As if that was the best possible scenario. He landed once again on the more hopeful idea that he was being pranked. He refused to believe in anything else. He leaned against the base of the crag beside him and mentally opened up his com interface. He began composing a message to his mother.

"Don't be alarmed, but have you seen Elpida? I haven't seen her since…" He stopped. Given the urgency of the situation, he changed the recipient to the HPO's crisis link and started the message over. *"My sister, Elpida Enosh, has been missing since this morning and may be in danger. Please advise!"* **Send.**

One anxiety-inducing minute later, a remorseful message appeared in reply. *"We regret to inform you of the sudden, tragic passing of Elpida Enosh of House D, Footpath 91. Deepest condolences."*

His blood fell from his head down to his toes in a hot, rushing cascade. He shivered. *"No, you have it wrong. She was just with me. I think I may be getting pranked,"* Krimsey sent immediately back, his breath short and fast.

Another message arrived in reply. *"Deepest condolences, dear. There will be a memorial service and support for family who are grieving."* With it, an attachment. He opened the attachment.

It had Elpida's obituary. *"Elpida Enosh was born October 3rd, 2238 and regretfully died—"* He closed the attachment, squeezing out tears.

"That's wrong," he began his reply, trying to come at this with a rational mind. He had just seen her this morning, alive and well and healthy. She was not dead. *"Can you just send help? This person knows how to hack coms really well. He's faking her death to get on my nerves. It's not true."*

The operator did not respond. By now, his breathing was speeding as if he'd just run the entire length of Footpath Main. He looked back down the path toward home. If she had seen the obituary, Sanjana would be—what would she be? Krimsey was sick thinking about what Sanjana might be or do. At best, she'd be hysterical for weeks. At worst, she'd stop eating and drinking and turn into a husk. Sanjana would be home soon. Krimsey had to reassure her that the HPO's information was false. That he'd bring Elpida home. That he'd show the HPO this oversight.

Cris would be punished.

He took three steps. Then, a sweaty gush of air buffeted him, followed by the firm pressure of a hand on his shoulder blade. Krimsey jumped at least a meter out of his skin.

Arrivals

Felice Karuli, Tuesday, March 26, 2250, 12:45 p.m.

Felice traded her airy office at the west edge of Karuli Dome—with its breathtaking views of Ross Bay, hundreds of jagged clifftops, and loosely swaying foliage, thick at the foot of the Ross side of the crag—for the smells of pungent seaweed and sunbaked shore. This was Felice's farthest idea from fun. A long tumble down Karuli Crag would have been more pleasant.

Felice pasted a smile across her face to mask her inner musings.

She stood at the shore, watching passengers from the sleek, white, eighty-meter-long supply ship take a final, tumultuous ride across the shallow waves in a small launch boat and dock.

Felice pinged her mother with the refurbished com she'd obtained from her office. *"Arrivals docked."*

Then she promptly turned off her com, in case any stray thoughts about her mother and her mother's plan mistakenly bled through the com waves. Stray thoughts had been known to send messages. It was outdated tech, in need of an upgrade, but the HPO didn't have the budget to spearhead tech that actually worked.

Sea-battered, sun-weathered faces crowded the boat's gangway and peered out at Felice and the eight guides who flanked her. The eager faces then turned from Felice and the guides to look at the small ocean town.

Port was a rickety old town. It was quaint. Quiet. It served its purpose, which was to mediate people and provisions between Mainland and the HPO. But it was much worse for wear than the battered families who had just arrived after a month of bouncing blue waves. Majestic mountains gently hugged the rolling outskirts of the port town. Away from the town center, small homes nestled between valley folds.

The families disembarking looked green and ready to finally find their feet again. Choppy waves sprayed them. Felice shifted her feet on the rocky shore, clasped her hands behind her, and made her smile warm and pleasant.

Eight families in total.

They clung to their young and grabbed the gangway as it lurched. Smiling, unfaltering, Felice's focus flitted from one family to the next.

She counted. *Four of these transitus kids are non-viable.*

She counted two infants. Felice guessed the babies were too young to assess whether or not they carried the full *transitus* mutation. She counted the rest, assuming that the babies could be overlooked. Eight children were under the age of ten; the remaining *transitus* were at least thirteen and up; and one family had a human child. At a glance, the parents appeared predominantly human. Humans were always more difficult to handle than *transitus*.

The families clamored in relief, stepping roughly over matted wet seaweed, planting their feet between wobbling black rocks.

"Hello, families." Felice forced welcoming warmth into her voice. She donned her pearly whites like jewels. "We are *thrilled* you've chosen to join our family here at the Humanoid Preservationist Organization. Your guides here will formally greet you."

Felice stepped forward and shook hands with a parent she was most interested in. A mustached man with black eyes and a distracted scowl. She met his gaze firmly. The father introduced himself and his partner with a drawl. He blinked though drips of sweat, made a funny little comment about the heat, and shifted his toddler in his arms.

The toddler blinked blazing blue eyes at her, but it was the hair that had drawn Felice.

"What a gorgeous head of red curls," she said, to which the girl responded by burying her fiery hair in her father's chest. Behind them, the guides were finding and greeting their families with enthusiasm.

"Is she viable?" Felice wondered out loud.

The man scratched a balding spot on his head. "Ah, no—I—we don't know yet."

She sighed through her teeth, relieved the girl would not be on her mother's radar. At least, *not yet*. She still had not decided how best to refuse her mother. Felice passed her reaction of relief off as a hearty smile. She cleared her throat. "That's alright, you'll have answers soon. We're here to help you navigate this tumultuous time. Your last name is…?"

"Turnhill." He was annoyed and gruff, wiping profuse sweat from his face.

"Thank you. Now, let's see." She looked at the guides behind her.

Felice quickly flicked her com back on, faltered when she noticed, and then promptly ignored, a new message from her mother, then searched for the name Turnhill. When she found the name of their assigned guide, she ushered the impatient family toward them. Only then did she tentatively open the new message.

"Something came up. Everything is in motion, but I'll need you to tell Sanjana about Five yourself, as soon as she is off work. 2:00 p.m. please."

Felice lost her firm smile.

She thought up a reply and sent, *"Is everything alright? I'm greeting the arrivals."*

"Fine. The brother is taken care of. Everything is as planned. Just correcting a few hiccups. I'll need you to manage Sanjana before the Ceremony. I'm proud of you."

Feeling as if she had been knocked over the side of the head one too many times, Felice drew in a deep breath, exhaled, and fixed her smile back on straight. She turned to the group of beaming but tired faces.

She drew their attention with a wave and a booming voice. "I am Felice Karuli." She had the whole bit memorized—the smile, the speech, the tone. "It seems many of you have already found your assigned guides and I am loving the smiles I see. I am sorry my mother, Lamia Karuli, could not greet you today. I promise, you will meet her soon. I can only hope I am a sufficient replacement for her today.

"Today, you get to rest. Explore the port town. Adjust to solid land beneath you. I know it's a long trip from Mainland to Antarctica. We have lodging awaiting you, and together we'll depart for Karuli Crag first thing in the morning. There, you will settle into your new lives. Your guides will be a part of your family for the next four years. Ask them questions. They will assist you in adjusting to your new lives as quickly and smoothly as possible. It is a steep learning curve, but I promise you, things can and will only go up from here."

Groups following their guides toward town began to cross the rocky, low-tide beach. Felice lingered behind to help the remaining families. The three remaining guides, being new and confused, lagged on introductions.

A breeze whipped her hair. Felice approached a blended family and asked for a name. The mother, who might have been *transitus* herself, held an infant. The father, definitely human, carried a *transitus* toddler. A third child clung to his pant leg.

They were the Ogier family.

Felice called over their struggling guide, who came tripping toward them across the slimy beach.

The guide began introductions. The mother rattled off questions. Felice knelt and smiled at the little one clinging to her father. "What's your name?" She asked the girl.

The girl's face had a typical *transitus* slope to it, resembling her mother. Her skin was white and freckled. She appeared very human. Human, except for her webbed hands. Honey eyes widened at the sight of Felice. She tucked herself behind the man's leg. His first name, she had just overheard, was Thomas.

"Sorry," he said. "This is Prae. She's jus' shy."

"Oh, that's alright." Felice cracked open her smile and stood.

The man sensed an opening for his own question—his wife was much too chatty—and he asked, "Will Prae still get the same treatment?"

Felice's heart bottomed. Her stomach churned. *The girl is non-viable*, Felice thought, confirming her worry. "Is she… viable?"

"This guy is," he said, unaware of the visceral drop in Felice's face. He hoisted the small child in his arm. "We're not sure about the baby yet. How soon do we know? We jus' heard the HPO can, uh, classify much sooner than Mainlanders. And how does the education for unviables vary?"

"*Non*-viables. More often though, we use the term NVT." Felice cleared her throat, which now felt slick with bile. She kept her plastic smile while she inwardly cursed her mother. *She's too young. I don't care what Lamia says, I'm not doing this. I'm out. They're just kids.*

"NVT," the man corrected. "Sorry about that, ma'am."

"No need for apologies. How old are they? When did they each get classified?" Her heels dug into the ground.

"Our baby is eleven months. This guy is four. We didn't know he was viable until jus' a week ago. Ship medic told us. And Prae is six. We knew she was, uh, NVT when she was three."

Her smile faltering, Felice ignored Prae's big, staring eyes. It was like she was looking right into Felice's soul. "It's... possible we can classify your baby in as little as two or three months. You are correct in that the HPO capabilities and equipment are vastly superior to Mainland. As far as curriculum content, your guide will help you through those specifics. While your children *are* all *transitus*, they are preparing for two very different lives. On one hand, your little viable ones may transition and leave as early as twelve or even eleven." The man sucked in his breath. "On the other hand, NVTs have long, productive lives on the island, assisting our cause, which is *their* cause. But I assure you, while education varies, *all transitus* are treated equally. You are in good hands.

"If you don't mind, I have to step away, but I look forward to seeing you in the morning. It will be a long hike to the HPO; it's at the top of that mountain..." She pointed at the Karuli Crag mountain. "So rest up." She excused herself, noted the remaining families were now paired, and headed toward the cluster of buildings nestled just off shore.

The group of arrivals were clustered between two buildings, separated from the beach by a small stone staircase. The guides were happily engaging with their assigned families, slowly meandering their way to the overnight lodging in one main group. Felice climbed the steps, shimmied between bodies, excusing herself as she went, and crossed the main footpath. The main port path was parallel with the beach and it extended from one end of town to the other. The north end connected with the zig-zagging trail to Karuli Crag.

The trail was the main route back, and the most publicly known one, but it was not the route Felice intended to take to get to Sanjana's home in time. There was another, shorter one that only a select few workers knew about. The transport system.

A hand touched her shoulder. "Excuse me."

Felice turned to face a man who was backlit by the low afternoon sun. He wore dark, stuffy clothes and his eyes sagged. "Can… I help you?" She offered.

Where did he come from?

She checked the time. *1:07 p.m.*

"I was hoping you could direct me to the port office?" He said *office* in a snake-like, trailing way.

"Are you a parent? Where's your guide?"

"I am. Port office?" He raised his chin so that he was looking slightly down at her. Felice didn't have time for superiority complexes. The office admin could deal with him. She waved a hand down the path. The man thanked her and headed toward the green building two down.

The town was awakening with the long-awaited arrival of goods, and Felice was careful not to be seen as she made her way to a side alley. Muscled laborers, mostly NVTs, hauled empty carts toward the dock, clattering noisily across the beach as several small boats ferried in supplies. Children of all shades and shapes and ages, innocent and free, giggled in the streets.

Felice took a turn down an empty supply route and walked to the dead end. The uniform building before her was as green and sun-bleached as the rest. Nondescript. She pulled a key from her pocket and entered the empty building, locking it behind her. There were no windows. The only light inside was the faint outline of a cart-sized side door. Later in the day, brimming carts could be hauled in to Karuli Crag this way. She tapped her com light on. It glowed softly, illuminating a bland interior.

In the middle of the room was a wide hatch. She opened it and descended. A ramp led her into the dim stone hallways. Her footfalls whispered angrily at her. Her mind hissed, *why are you doing this? Why are you doing this? Why are you doing this?*

Felice panted up a steep tunnel, feeling like her brain was being incrementally boiled alive in contradictions, self-loathing, and indecision.

Are You Her?

Zeph Carmak, Tuesday, March 26, 2250, 11:08 p.m.

ZEPH KNEW ALL HPO-ISSUED coms were tracked with hidden location responders. As long as one had their com with them, the HPO could find them. It was a well-kept secret. This was how the HPO found missing children who wandered into the dark, too far from home. They found adults this way, too. Ones who had, emotionally, had enough. Ones who had run off to cope. Shirk responsibilities. Or those who had attempted to—or succeeded in—doing much darker things. It made sense, in such a rural, maze-like community, and no one ever questioned why the HPO was so good at locating people. Most residents had their suspicions. Most didn't care.

Zeph had known about the tracking since they were a child.

"Your com, Mommy," Zeph had said, finding a banged-up com on the kitchen counter one day, running to their mother, only to discover that their mother already had a com in her ear and that this second com was supposed to be a secret. It took their seven-year-old brain two months, two of their own broken coms, and nearly two hundred questions, to finally figure out why Gina had two coms. Mommy had a throwaway com to hide her location. It acted as a decoy, keeping her location from the people who monitored the responders. Little Zeph always assumed Mommy was just deeply concerned with personal privacy. Today, they knew there were darker reasons behind Gina's secrecy.

It seemed Gina—the woman who was *not* their biological mother—had been keeping things from the HPO. Now she was in trouble, and her actions had put Zeph in the crossfire. Zeph didn't know if the HPO was going to be looking for them or if Gina had access to the location grid, but they kept their com firmly lodged in their ear regardless. It was the only thing that tied them to the woman who had sent those untethered voice messages. Zeph needed answers and hoped she would reach out again. So far though, the com was silent.

Zeph climbed down from the top of Karuli Crag to their safe place near the pinnacles. The crevices they lodged their fingers into were sharp and narrow and tore fresh texture into their calloused skin. As they sank their fingers into the next handhold below them, they knew that anyone who would track their whereabouts would not pursue them here. For now, they were safe. They would have time to think.

It was dark down here in the crag. They lowered themselves down and found their next hand and foot placements by the light of The Bowl and the firm guidance of muscle memory.

Zeph's safe space was a small nook in the cliffside. They settled into the nook and rested their body while their mind ran circles. Up here, they had their birds-eye view of The Bowl, the pinnacles, the valleys, and dangers beyond. They were high above the towering spikes of rock, the pinnacle trail, and the yawning monster-maw pits between them all.

For the next hour, Zeph waited. At first, just hoping for inspiration to come—some realization that would inform their next move. Nothing came. They were clueless and exhausted and hungry and angry and terrified. But after some time, which included seriously considering throwing their com into the pinnacles, they realized the only thing they wanted was for the voice to come back. They waited and waited. Hoping that, if the voice belonged to who they thought, she'd come back to them. Zeph lay back. Sat up. Shifted to their side. Dangled their feet. Threw a rock. Scraped the newly sharp bits of skin, dry and dead, from their palm and fingertips. For another hour, Zeph simmered; their belly growled and begged for them to go home. They wanted to go home. They wanted their mother to be their mother again and they wanted their body to be their body again.

Impossible.

The voice didn't come. Zeph lingered on their growing frustration. If this woman was who they suspected, this entire situation was awfully inconsiderate of her.

So, what? She was just going to leave Zeph hanging? Drop a bomb of truth and dash before she got burned by the radiation? Maybe Zeph was wrong. Maybe they should have trusted Gina. They were banging balled fists into the wall of their nook to let off steam when the voice returned.

"Are you safe?"

"Are you her?" Zeph shouted into the com. They imagined the shape of the woman behind the voice. Well rounded. Big-boned, but rough at the edges. All sharp cheekbones, elbows, and knees. *"Are you my biological mother?"* It was not what Zeph thought they would say right from the top, but it *was* what they had been thinking from the moment of first contact.

The reply did not come immediately. Zeph closed their eyes and imagined her, dark and tall and firm and stiff, deliberating on her answer before delivering the news. *"Yes."*

Zeph let out a long breath. They cupped their hands over their overheating ears. Their eyes were hot and blurred. Zeph had spent enough time up here alone to have regained control of their wild mess of emotions. Now, the anger came screaming back. Speeding through their blood, thin and hot, pricking their eyes with tears.

"Where are you? I am going to come see you." The question escaped and was sent as a message before they had time to think.

"I will tell you how to find me. But first you need the truth. Are you ready for truth?" The voice rumbled with gravel.

"How am I supposed to answer that?" Zeph asked out loud.

"I know. I'm sorry; that is not a fair question. How about we start small? How do you feel? Are your physical symptoms manageable?"

Zeph couldn't even tell if they had physical symptoms. They assumed everything they felt within their own body was just a product of their mental state. Sweaty palms. Increased heart rate. Churning stomach.

"My own mother experimented on me. None of this is manageable." They composed this message mentally. Could the woman on the other side hear their voice when they spoke like they heard hers? They didn't want to be that vulnerable. Not yet. *"You helped her, right? That is why she is lying to Lamia and why you know about all this and why you told me it was her idea. You wanted to save your own butt."*

Zeph pinched their bottom lip nervously, waiting to see if a mental message still worked.

"I am not innocent of your suffering, Zeph." The woman's message was a whisper. *"Yes, I helped your mother change you."*

Zeph's blood pressure spiked. Their heart rate bumped two times too fast. Their ears burned. They had hoped to be wrong. They breathed and counted to five, considering how to react. Angry? Yes. Uncontrollable? No. Who was this woman who made choices based on her concept of them, a false version that existed only in her mind? Could you betray someone you've never met? To their surprise, Zeph realized they were not mad. The fact that they had breathed all the way to five, still in control over themselves, was proof of that.

"But you were not the one that stuck me with the needle each day." They were calm.

"I suppose not. But Zeph—I had a heavy hand in the research. I do not take any decision back because I acted in your best interest, but what I helped Gina do to you is inexcusable."

"Did I say I was excusing it?" That was a bold assumption. *"No. I am not excusing. But you were not the one that lied to my face. She was my mother. I may never forgive either of you for what has happened to me. Will you tell me how to find you now?"*

"Are you ready for more truth, Zeph?"

They didn't want to answer that question.

"I will only tell you if you consent to the information," she said. *"I am not without demons. And neither is this island."* The voice was steady, practiced, as if she had said this a thousand times before.

"Alright. Tell me," Zeph said. They looked at the rock ceiling and let out a tense sigh.

"Are you sure? There is no backing out of knowing." She paused. *"Evil things happen on this island. I am being selfish. I should be telling you to flee this island with your mother. I can't help but admit I'd like to see you."*

Everything the woman said continued to reinforce that she was driven by the desire to show Zeph truth. Not pulling the dark, comfortable blanket of lies over their eyes. Hard, cold, bare truth. Truth that was raw. Painful.

"Earlier you asked me if I was safe," **Zeph said.** *"Well, my answer is no. I do not feel safe. And the fact that this was the first thing you asked—"* their throat got a lump and their eyes swam. *"My home is not safe. Gina is not safe. There is no one I feel I can go back to. I do not care about your demons. Do you want me safe?"*

"That is all I want."

"Then we want the same thing. Tell me what you need to say." This woman on the other side of the com messages was just a disembodied voice, but she was the only promise of something stable.

She did not respond right away. Zeph looked out at The Bowl. Reflected on how much had changed in such a short period of time. Change was supposed to be gradual. Small victories and failures navigating the battlefield of life. Personal growth moving at such incremental speed, it went unnoticed. Stripped of gradualness of change, Zeph was… well, Zeph was scared. Terrified.

When the woman's next message came, it was a long, unbroken string of unbelievable words. Had Zeph heard all this two days ago, they would have rejected it as absurd lies. Their heart rate crescendoed as they listened.

"The HPO experiments on children. They have experimented on you, your peers, your closest friends. Two years ago, they kidnapped an NVT named Rumi Yen. She was taken in. Caged like an animal all this time. Two days ago, she died. I don't think she ever saw the sun. Gina and I did what we did to you because the HPO is interested in the blood of NVTs. We believed it would have only been a matter of time until you could have become a target.

"I wish I could tell you you're special. That there is a reason for all this change in your life that makes sense of it. Something, anything, that makes it all worth your pain. Unfortunately, bad things just happen. We made you viable to save you from them."

They wanted to say something, anything, to what they just heard. But when they opened their mouth, nothing came out but a dry hiss. Their pulse throbbed at the base of their thumb, their knuckles stretching tight as they gripped the rock beside them for stability.

"Zeph, I want to tell you more. About why I had to leave you, but things here are getting very urgent now and I'd like your help."

"What do you need?" They sucked in air.

"They've already targeted several new victims. They are bringing these children to a secret place, possibly to their deaths. I'll tell you how to get to me but you must bring me Prae, a six-year-old NVT who just arrived on the ship with her family. I'll help guide you. Will you do that for me?"

"You mean… you want me to kidnap her on your behalf, before they do?" They sent this message mentally, unable to unclench their jaw to speak. *Forsaken Earth, a six-year-old?*

"Yes. It's part of a plan to put all this to an end."

Zeph's blood pumped so fast now that their breathing was hot and heavy. So fast that when they brought their shaking palms in front of them, they saw not two, but four. So fast that they swayed and swallowed and focused on the top of a pinnacle outside to keep the bile down. This shouldn't have been happening, but it was. No one should have to go through what the woman described. It was worse than death. It was worse than a stab in the back by a mother.

They didn't like the idea. Kidnapping a kid. It felt wrong. But would they do it to save her? Fuck. Of course. Maybe they weren't so different from Gina. Maybe everyone was just morally superior until the best of two bads stared them in the face.

"You won't do anything to her if I do this? You promise to keep her from Rumi Yen's same fate?"

"Yes. Yes, she will be completely safe. And when all is done, she will be returned to her family," she breathed. Her voice was bell-like, as if touched by hope.

"I will help."

"Thank you, dear child."

"Not for you. For her."

Thoughts

Zeph Carmak, Tuesday, March 26, 2250, 1:22 p.m.

"Can you climb down *from where you are?*" Zeph's mother asked.

Their biological mother. Their real, biological mother was talking to them right now and the two of them were going to meet and Zeph was going to break several laws for her. Zeph was sure the strangeness of the situation had yet to hit. What had hit, though, was a hot, impending rage. It simmered just beneath the surface of their skin. Crackling rocks and a ghost-like whisper from the pinnacles below caught their attention. Zeph stopped, their next message to the woman whose name they still did not know left unsent.

"*Elpidaaaaa.*" A long-winded shout. Zeph looked down the side of the cliff. A figure below wandered the pinnacles, moving through dangerous side-trails toward The Bowl. Someone must be lost. They checked the Day In Review feed on their com and scanned for missing children. No one seemed to be missing, but the same name that had been shouted appeared in an obituary. Elpida Enosh. Sept 1, 2238 to March 26, 2250.

"*Zeph, are you there?*" Her voice was light, undemanding.

"*Yes. I am still here. I can climb down.*" Zeph wiped their palms, swung their legs over the ledge of their nook, and began to descend.

Considering the woman had the ability to reach Zeph through com messages in such an unusual manner, it was not a surprise she also knew Zeph's whereabouts. She was not only tracking Zeph now, but may have been doing so for years. The thought was disturbing.

"Let me know when you reach the bottom."

Zeph heaved down to an awkward foothold and held their position to look over their shoulder. The figure below climbed the steps into The Bowl. *"I will. What is your name?"* Zeph asked. It seemed like something they should know. Something they should have interest in. They didn't know why it only now occurred to them that they didn't know it. Maybe the newness of everything was still catching them off guard. Maybe they didn't want the woman to be any more real than just a voice on a com. Not yet.

"You can call me Mother, can't you?"

Zeph didn't reply.

"Take a joke, child. My name is Cyn. Cyn Jones."

"Cyn Jones." Zeph repeated, focusing on their climb.

Halfway down to the semi-solid terrain, Zeph stopped. They felt a familiar *transitus* presence. They looked down. The figure that had entered The Bowl earlier was now walking out and heading down the trail, directly toward the spot where Zeph planned to land. Amorphous thoughts from the figure reached them like the smell of baking dough.

"Why did you stop?" Cyn asked.

"Is it possible for transitus *to mind-read?"* they asked.

"Not exactly… well, not specific to transitus.*"* Her answer wavered.

"What about the changes in me? Could that have triggered something for me to gain…" Zeph felt ridiculous saying it out loud. *"Abilities?"*

"You have inherited the ability from me. I believe what you are experiencing is a genetic anomaly."

"I thought I was going crazy."

"You are not crazy, Zeph."

The figure below was now so close that Zeph could almost hear them as if directly speaking to their ear. *Where is she? Where is my sister?* The tone was familiar. The presence of the figure was warm, but also worried and frazzled, and it gave them a slight sense of dread. Zeph knew this person. It was…

Krimsey. Oh, no. They groaned internally, contemplating waiting him out so they didn't have to face an awkward encounter.

Below, Krimsey was in distress. He heaved and sighed and muttered. Bouncing emotion wafted off him and it was nauseating. The thoughts plaguing him were like a ticking bomb. *If Cris is behind this…* Krimsey's thoughts seeped loudly into Zeph's own. *I'll murder that two-faced fool,* he continued. *Hacking my com just to get back at me. For what? For being nice? Saving his life? Think about this logically. Think. Think.*

Krimsey was uncomfortably close in proximity to Zeph's landing spot now. If Zeph came down, they'd both have to face an awkward encounter. There was no way around it other than to stay up here. After making a total fool of themselves at Survival, Zeph preferred avoidance. They could wait. Zeph tried to tune out Krimsey's thoughts, but they kept coming like a barrage.

The voice on the com provided a warning. It sounded nothing like Cris. It told me Elpida is in danger. Now Elpida is missing. What does that even mean, then? Is the HPO corrupt?

This piqued Zeph's interest. Because, well, the answer was a resounding yes. The HPO was corrupt. Was Elpida Krimsey's sister? She died… the obituary said as much. So why was he looking for her?

Poor guy.

That's just not possible, Krimsey continued. Zeph huffed and rolled their eyes. *They are under strict regulations. This is ridiculous. What if she just fell? I can't stop thinking about the story of Rumi Yen falling in the pinnacles.*

Zeph's breath froze. *Rumi Yen? As in the Rumi Yen who Cyn said was taken?*

It was common knowledge that these things happened. Children fell. "Fuck," Zeph whispered, as a memory resurfaced and dots began to connect. Two years ago. Coming out here to their overlook. Someone hoisting a kid out of the pinnacles.

Zeph saw the rescue. Happy for the child, they went about climbing to their outlook and didn't give it another thought. Who paid attention to the news at their age? If they had, they would have known what Krimsey was dwelling on now—there was a missing kid two years ago named Rumi Yen and that missing kid was never found. Not rescued.

But a kid *was* rescued. *I saw it,* Zeph thought.

They should have checked the news.

"Fuck," Zeph whispered again. "Cyn was right. They kidnapped her. The evidence was right in front of me all this time. Are they doing the same thing with Elpida?"

"Still there?" Cyn asked.

"I need to check something out. Just give me a minute." Zeph took out their com and put it on a ledge; they would come back for it later. They climbed further down the wall. They were being impulsive. But this correlation to Rumi couldn't be ignored. Besides, Krimsey seemed like he really needed a friend right now.

Krimsey jumped when Zeph landed beside him. There was a small scrape on his forehead mostly covered by a mop of dry, reddish-brown bangs. The bangs looked good on him. Zeph hadn't noticed them before, when his hair was soaked in lake water.

"Zeph!" His body was stiff. His eyes were red. Crusty tears dried to his face with the blowing breeze.

"Mm-hmm. Z, remember?" Zeph felt Krimsey mentally roll the sound of their voice in his head, like tasting a sweet.

Why does your voice sound familiar? The thought drifted from Krimsey as he took his eyes off them. "What are you doing here?" He looked up, mouth wide, at the side of the cliff. "You climbed down that?"

Following his gaze, Zeph said, "Of course. It is my shortcut. See those three ledges? There, there, and there. I used to come down here all the time." Zeph pointed at the rock wall where Krimsey had, until recently, been standing. "Before I found out I was viable. I was a terraformer."

"What are you doing here?" Krimsey stepped backward over a crack in the trail. His anguish came clearly through to Zeph: *I need to get to Sanjana and tell her about Ellie.* Zeph was also acutely aware that, behind Krimsey, there was a *transitus*-sized chasm. It was deep. Swallow-him-whole deep. Fall-to-his-death deep.

"Well…." *Where to begin?*

You ripped another kid to a bloody pulp, they heard Krimsey think as a shudder moved through him. The movement was only perceptible because Zeph experienced Krimsey's inner turmoil much more deeply than they should. It was a dangerous, distracting situation to be in, considering both Zeph and Krimsey were just a couple shuffles away from that pit. Maybe showing up was a mistake. Too late now.

"Careful, Krimsey," they said. Krimsey took tiny steps backward, not looking back at the path behind him. "I just heard you looking for your sister. I wanted to help. Maybe make amends?"

Mid-step, Krimsey stubbed his heel on the jagged trail and stumbled. Suddenly, his thoughts roared, making all sorts of far-fetched connections and assumptions, screaming into Zeph's head. Krimsey's fingers curled into fists. "It was *you*," he said.

The only audible sound was the wind whistling through the tall black spires. But Zeph heard tsunamis of thought roaring, crashing against their own walls of defense. Krimsey's thoughts hit Zeph like punches. *It was you. You were the voice on my com,* he accused. *It wasn't Cris. You took her.* Krimsey's lips did not move. Still, the thoughts echoed. His eyes were the only thing that moved, his hands clenched at his sides.

Zeph breathed deeply, standing still but feeling bruised. They could not think clearly. Could not concentrate. Why had they even come down here? "Enough!" The echo ping-ponged off their chest into the spires and Krimsey's thoughts shut down like a crashing computer. "I did not take your sister. But I think I know what happened to her," Zeph said, veins pounding with electricity. "I can help you." Massaging one shoulder, closing their eyes, convinced that every personal thought was on display, Zeph's nerves cooled. "But not if you are going to be like *this*."

"You just gave yourself up," Krimsey said.

"What?"

"There's no point in denying it! I didn't even say you took my sister, but you're already saying you didn't do it. How would you even know I was looking for her if it wasn't you? You must have been up there, spying on me, getting in your sick kicks. You're worse than Cris."

Zeph clenched their fists. "You were screaming her name for nearly an hour. The entire HPO knows you're looking for her."

"I am going to report you."

Krimsey managed to cinch up his emotional walls like a dam, so Zeph could only guess that the look on his face was pure rage. This was going nowhere. Krimsey shifted, sending a rock rattling down a fissure. His eyes, hesitant to leave Zeph's, followed the rock down the descent. Thunking into oblivion.

"Will you please stop? Calm down and listen to me." Zeph opened a crack in their emotional barrier. A tiny opening. Just enough to let Krimsey feel the hurt that colored their words. Punctuated by a firm but gentle message to just be still.

"I don't trust your feelings." Despite the firmness of his words, Krimsey's body relaxed. He shifted in place, staring down at the threadbare seams of his old, floppy sandals. "Why did you attack Cris like that, Z? It was awful...." He finally looked up at Zeph. "Why were you spying on me? Is this some sort of game? Where is my sister? I thought we'd be...."

He stopped but Zeph heard the word in his head and it stung.

Friends. So they were not friends, then. Understandable. But... *ouch.* "I am sorry for what happened," Zeph said, looking at their hands, then clasping them behind their back. "I barely have any memory of what happened. I was scared at first, then angry when I realized it was Cris attacking us. Then, nothing. Just a hard, cold blackout and then I woke up to find Cris all bloody, and you yelling at me. I am sorry. You have no idea how sorry. I was not spying on you, Krimsey. I was hiding from someone. From the HPO, actually. I think they are the ones who took your sister."

"You were clearly hanging out meters above my head, watching and listening to my every move."

"Krimsey, no—" Words caught in the depths of their belly like barbed wire. Zeph felt anger bubbling. Beginning to steam, tip, spill. They took a deep breath, but breathing only made their cheeks grow hot. "Do you know the story of Rumi Yen?" Of course they knew he did, but Zeph wasn't about to admit they could read his mind.

Krimsey said nothing. His walls kept his thoughts in check.

"She disappeared here in the pinnacles two years ago. That spot up there is where I go to think, nothing else. I saw a little girl get rescued from the pinnacles from that spot—two years ago. Have you ever seen reports of a little girl getting saved from the pinnacles?"

"No," he said.

"That's because she was kidnapped. By the HPO. She died days ago. She was imprisoned for two years."

"Why are you telling me this? How do you know this?"

"I was talking to the woman on the com. I am going to go find her."

"So it really was you, then," Krimsey said.

"What? No, I—"

"It was your voice on the com. How do I know you didn't take Rumi Yen, too? How do I believe anything you're saying? How else would you know about the woman on the com? It was you."

Zeph yelled at the sky. It echoed. "I know about her because I hear your thoughts. You think it's me because you think I sound like her."

Krimsey paused. Blinked. Then he laughed. Not just a short, fake, mocking chuckle. His eyes rolled back, head tipped toward the sky, face split wide, and laughter erupted deep from his belly, rolling by like a passing cloud. Tears poured down the sides of his face.

"Look at me." Zeph stepped forward and leaned close and the blue trail lights gleamed in Krimsey's eyes. "I can *hear* you. I hear your thoughts. Like emotions. What on Earth is so funny?"

This sent Krimsey deeper into the fit of laughter. He hardly breathed. He gulped down air and bent over, a hand on one knee. He looked sideways up at Zeph, face shaded with heat, lips twitching in the corners. "You… are a terrible liar," he said between spurts of dying laughter. "I'm sorry… sorry… it's not even funny… it's just…" he burst into laughing tears again and struggled with his breath. "You are so dead." The laughter sent his voice into another dimension, as high-pitched as air escaping from a teapot.

"Well, Elpida might be, but I will go where I'm wanted." Zeph creaked into motion, realizing they had been holding themselves so stiffly they ached. Zeph turned around and walked up the trail toward The Bowl just to get away from him.

"What did you just say?" His voice reentered this dimension with a snag and he coughed. He was no longer laughing.

Zeph kept walking.

"Where are you going?"

"Leaving so I do not hurt you."

"You won't hurt me." He said the words like a threat. "Where is my sister, Z?"

Zeph's teeth pressed together painfully. "For Earth's sake, you are stubborn."

"*Transitus* don't read minds, Z. Where is she?" His voice was dark, hoarse from the laughter. He coughed into his shoulder.

Zeph stopped and turned around. Earthly smells of boulder—black and dull like soft tea—mingled with their senses. "If you want answers, join the party. I do, too. Some shit is going down at the HPO and that is about all I know. Maybe your sister got caught up in it, taken like Rumi Yen. Maybe Cris is getting back at you. Maybe. Sure, maybe she is fine. *Maybe* she *is not* dead. I do not know nor do I now care. You know what I do know? That woman on the com has answers and *I* know where to find her. Not *you. Me.*"

"Dead?" Krimsey snorted. "That was a good one, I almost believed it for a second, too. How did you do it? How did you fake the obituary?"

Zeph's heart skipped a beat in anger. "I did not do such a thing." Their muscles twitched.

"Wait, do you think Cris did this?"

"No, *you* think Cris did this. Hearing your thoughts, remember?"

Conflict scoured Krimsey's face. Twisted his features. He looked like he did back in Survival, when Zeph had offered him help, but he was too scared to face his fears. The way he stood—tall, but held up only by twigs—the way his eyes flickered away from Zeph and back, it was exactly the same. Krimsey turned and walked back toward the HPO.

"Where are *you* going?"

"My sister isn't here. I have to go get ready for the Transition Ceremony."

"Wait, do you believe me now?" Krimsey kept walking. "I can take you to the woman from the com messages. We can work together to find—"

"I know a hacker. I'm going to trace the message."

"Who?"

"Cris."

"You are joking, right? You *just* accused him of taking your sister. I could take you right to the woman and you are going to ask *him* for help instead?"

Krimsey barked a laugh. It could have passed as a humorless, dry cough. "I wish I was joking. Cris Langley, however much we hate each other, knows a thing or two about coms. His dad is head of coms security. Sorry I'm having such a hard time trusting your delusions."

Zeph sprung forward and grabbed Krimsey's wrist so he would not disappear around the bend. "You cannot do that."

Zeph was angry now. Fuming. Furious. Flat-out boiling. They felt the monster beneath the heat trying to take hold, but Zeph fought for control.

"Let go of me!" The racing pulse in Krimsey's wrist spiraled, beating so fast Zeph wondered if he would faint.

"You cannot tell *him* about this. This is dangerous."

"Why? Because you're afraid he's going to lead me straight to you?"

"No but—" Zeph's blood pressure spiked and there was a low, consistent whistle in their ears.

Zeph did not want to hurt Krimsey. Or for him to look at them with those wide eyes. They did not want to be seen as the monster they felt inside, the one they felt lurking in the dark. But Krimsey was being stupid and reckless. Zeph *had* a resource. Someone who might have more answers than either of them even wanted. But he was just going to turn away? Ask his *bully* for help and not them?

Zeph's fist hardened.

On a normal day, feeling Krimsey's fear response, feeling his urge to yell, to move, to lunge, feeling his anticipation—he was sure they would toss him down a rift—would have kept Zeph from even approaching him. It was not a normal day. Those days were gone.

The tendon on the top of their middle knuckle clicked from skin being pulled taut. The moody monster inside them took hold of their fist. Wrapped scaly fingers around each muscle like a marionette and lunged it into Krimsey's belly.

The blow put Krimsey in his place. Flat in the hard dirt.

He doubled over in a fit of coughs. Spit dribbled and sprayed from his mouth. Krimsey clenched his abdomen, wrapped himself tightly, and tensed for more.

"Stand up." Zeph yelled, or tried to yell. The words petered out in their throat, letting out a noise like a dying bird. Krimsey's coughs sprayed the ground with blood. Red flecks stained their left sandal.

Krimsey, struggling to breathe, looked up.

Zeph stiffened and focused on the wet blood on the ground.

"You are transitioning," Zeph said quietly, avoiding his eyes. Their mouth hung open.

Krimsey snapped his mouth open and shut several times to say something. Instead of words, a severe fit of wheezes bubbled forth.

When he caught his breath, he squeezed words past his gravelly throat. "Forsaken Earth, Z. You—you just punched me—"

Zeph closed their mouth, eyes still wide and staring. "We need to get you help."

A new fit of coughing crescendoed into gasps for breath.

"You need the ocean. We need to get you to port. I need to get someone. *Shit.*"

"Don't…" Krimsey coughed and spit out more specks of red. Zeph could tell he was keeping his distance as he pushed from the ground, and this time Zeph gave it to him, stepping back. Krimsey coughed and wobbled, propping himself against the edge of the cliff wall. He cleared his throat. "Don't touch me. I don't need your help."

Krimsey assessed his route—fingers gripping the wall behind him. He hoisted himself up.

"Krimsey, I…." Digging their clipped nails into their palms, Zeph clenched their fists at their sides.

Krimsey whipped around, his hair like a flicking fire. His eyes flashed. "Something to say?"

"I did not mean to hurt you."

"Doesn't matter." Krimsey's jaw clenched. He sucked in a breath. "I'm going now." He turned away.

Smiled-Out

Felice Karuli, Tuesday, March 26, 2250, 2:27 p.m.

FELICE DONNED THE FAKE smile she had been using all afternoon, sure it had been stretched too thin. Positivity. That was the HPO way. Even in—no, *especially* in—the face of adversity.

Overthinking herself to numbness, hating herself for following orders, certain that Mrs. Sanjana Enosh would see right through the lie of her daughter's death, Felice approached the Enoshes' cliffside home. Determination turned her bones to cold steel.

Don't feel.

Don't cry.

Don't be weak.

Keeping her eyes on the home, she walked the footpath as close to the cliff wall as she could, one hand up against it for balance. She was already terrified of heights, and the scale of things from the side of the cliff was dizzying. A dark, winged animal soaring below could have been a meter-wide monster of an eagle or it could have been a bat. Her perception of depth was shot. She tried to ignore the straight drop down mere centimeters from her feet. Her stomach sloshed emptily. She did not envy those who lived on the narrow, winding ledges of Karuli Crag. But she accepted the necessity of this way of living.

When the reigning organization on Antarctica passed leadership on to the Karuli family in 2155, there had been a dire need.

Transitus people *needed* escape. Despite the Antarctic colony having as mottled a past with *transitus* people as the NWA, this island and its tall cliffs and deep chasms had been the only safe place to hide from prying government oversight. Now, hiding from the NWA was no longer needed, but the structures here still stood. Rebuilding was not just expensive. It was impossible. Neither the funds nor the compassion would ever be provided. Not for the sake of *transitus*. Cliffside living it was, then.

Through the open doorway of the Enosh residence, Felice could see the house was a mess. Kitchen cupboard doors were wide open. Cups scattered on the floor. Bedsheets tossed to the side of the mattresses they belonged on. The place had been much cleaner when Felice spent every day here as a guide, but it was still like looking through the doorway of a time capsule.

Sanjana, at the dining table with her back to the entrance, had become more grey. Her exposed arms, the nape of her neck, and the flesh hiding within the depths of her oversized cottons more bony and frail.

Felice knocked on the frame of the doorway. Sanjana Enosh and her frizz of grey-blonde hair turned, her face making a surprised half smile. Sanjana stood. "Felice." She glanced at the mess around her.

"Hi. I'm… sorry for the impromptu visit." Felice screwed on a neutral expression to keep out her sad terror. "I… have some news. May I come in?" Felice's broken eye contact twitched sideways a second too long.

"Of course. Come in." Sanjana frowned. "It's been ages, Felice. It is so lovely to see you. Is everything alright?"

Felice sat at the table and watched her scuttle into the kitchen. Something wooden skittered across the floor. "I'm sorry for the mess. I…" she sighed and smiled. "Well, the kids, you know." Sanjana brought over a pitcher of water in one hand and two cups were pinched together in the other. She set them on the table and poured them each a cup of water.

"Thank you."

"Miss Karuli, you look perturbed."

Felice faltered when Sanjana called her that. Called her Miss *Karuli*. The formality of it made her cringe. She blinked and recomposed herself, placed her hands in her lap under the table.

"I only just got home. Do you mind if I...?" Sanjana pointed to the fridge.

"Actually, Mrs. Enosh," Felice said, returning the formality, "it's quite a sensitive matter. Will you take a seat?" Felice stared at the water in her glass, finding a suitable position for the downturned muscles over her eyes.

Sanjana leaned stiffly against the wall. Felice stared. She stared until the woman's expression, as perfectly as a mirror, matched her own fixed, neutral sadness. *Forsaken earth.* Was she really as good at this as her mother was? Felice took a tentative sip of water as if it were poison.

Sanjana pulled up a second chair and sat. "What is it? Did my daughter cheat on her test? Oh no, she cheated, didn't she? Is that why she's not home?"

"No—no... Sanjana... that's... not it," she said, halting.

Felice convinced herself the emotions choking up her words were not real. They weren't supposed to be real. Because Sanjana's daughter was, in fact, alive. But hot tears were hiding just behind Felice's lids. Two messages pinged Felice's com at once. She set the com to 'off' and placed it in her breast pocket.

"Your husband, as you know, had a rare condition within his *transitus* gene. This morning, we discovered that same gene in Elpida." Felice wrung her hands under the table.

Sanjana's gaze was fixed on a spot just above Felice.

Felice continued, her throat tightening. "Unfortunately, we discovered... that... your daughter had Pneumaphage..." Felice took a deep, shuddering breath, realizing her use of the past tense put Sanjana on alert. "Elpida did not take her test because she came down with a very sudden, very rapid case of Pneumaphage and... and... I'm so sorry. She didn't make it."

A horrible expression twisted over Sanjana's face. As if the air was now putrid and volatile. She sucked in a breath.

There is no way out of this now.

"She—?" Sanjana's voice broke.

A line of tears dropped into Felice's lap. She trembled, holding her shoulders and her neck stiff. She was thinking of Elpida. She was thinking of Rumi. She was thinking of the kids that would die. Her lies did this. An icy block of self-disgust threatened to climb up her throat. Elpida wasn't dead. But she might as well have been.

"I am so sorry, Sanjana. So, so sorry. She's already been prepared for a burial pod. They didn't...." She sniffed the runniness draining from her nose and stood, looking away. Sanjana looked like she saw a ghost. "If you need anything, you know where to find me."

"I didn't get to say goodbye." Sanjana's lips cracked, tears spilled, her whole body collapsed onto the table. She shook with silent, violent tears.

Felice dared to reach over and place a hesitant hand on Sanjana's arm. "I know this is hard." She reached deep, determined to find within herself words with delicate, profound meaning. Words that would soothe a suffering soul. Words that would mend this mess.

Instead, the knotted muscles around her smiled-out mouth collapsed.

Felice said nothing.

Quarantine

Gianvante Dasulorn, 2078

I THOUGHT I WAS somebody else.

Same dream did it to me every time. In it, I was a child. Sick, hungry, and motherless. Hidden away in the Ardèche mountains of France. Then I'd wake up. In a different body. Different home. In solitude. Confused at first, disoriented.

I opened my eyes. Nothing looked familiar.

But then wind howled. Battered my 3D-printed recycled plastic home. I remembered my name. I remembered that my home neighbored the thawed pole of Antarctica. The winds were strong at the coastal port town which had previously hosted researchers but was now inhabited by seventeen squatters and refugees. As the wind screamed by, I remembered I was the first to migrate from town to the protected cliff a few kilometers inland.

The first of many.

It was lonely up here.

I sat up from my blow-up sleeping pad in the narrow, one-roomed abode. Salted sweat dripped into the corners of my mouth as the grip of my night terror receded like the global coastline.

Slowly. Painfully.

I stretched and shuddered involuntarily. The images my brain concocted, fresh from my nightmare, were ghastly. Too much news did that to a person, I guessed. Gave a person radical visions.

Those poor damn kids.

I reached over and clicked on the satellite radio for the news anyways—the channel I listened to was obscure and very underground. Mainstream channels didn't speak of the mutant kids, or even know they existed. The world spun on without knowledge of them. Oblivious of the unfolding horror. Unlike the rest of the world, I knew what was going on and I knew that listening to that news would only make me feel worse, but that never stopped me. I fed off the anxiety the stories gave me. I had a purpose. It was an obsessive, unhealthy habit. I had to stop. Maybe then the dreams would stop. But I couldn't just stop thinking of them. I couldn't abandon them, replacing them in my mind with bright things. Not when the existences they lived were so dark.

"… another escaped mutant," a female voice said through the white noise of the speakers as I stood, waiting for my tingling leg to wake up, "… got as far as Les Vans, frightening a human couple, who found the mutant eating apples from their farm… this mutant, a sixteen-year-old who goes by the name of Turray Nelson, was returned to quarantine by NWA authorities. In other news…."

"Jeezus."

My mind wandered and saw the pinprick of a memory. A rusty metal door opening. Vaguely familiar. A little girl in a dress looking back. I shuddered. She was gone, the little girl. The memory faded like ink on a sun-bleached paper. As if it was never even there.

The radio continued its reports regarding the NWA's horrific quarantine.

"Quarantine." How bad do conditions have to be for a sixteen-year-old kid to run forty-five kilometers through the wilderness? And how desperate is the damn NWA to keep these poor kids contained? They should be getting reintroduced back to society, not hidden like Earth-forsaken mutts.

Grabbing a mug of water off my small table, I perused the collage of notes that littered my wall. I added little notes to it almost daily. Grey pieces of homemade paper covering every bit of surface area.

The NWA kept these kids in quarantine because they didn't want the human genome to get tainted with their experimental DNA. But that was goddamn inhumane. If that was what it meant to be human, maybe it was better to just embrace the tidal wave coming for us.

I heard the crunch of gravel outside.

A knock rapped on the makeshift piece of wood that leaned against the door hole. I switched off the radio and grabbed my pack. I slid aside the wood that covered the entrance.

Captain James Earl stood on the trail between my house and the cliff wall. "You still listen to that NWA garbage?" His beard trembled in the wind.

I grunted at him, stepping outside with my gigantic, tattered hiking pack. The path outside was so narrow, James had to step away to make room. I pulled the wood back over the hole and turned to him. "You ready?"

"Yeah, ship's nice'n ready, too. That's the important part. Good sailin' for a short while."

"Good. Let's break some mutants out of quarantine," I said. "Before the NWA turns this shit into goddamn genocide."

Transition Ceremony

Krimsey Enosh, Tuesday, March 26, 2250, 2:35 p.m.

BREATHLESS, KRIMSEY RAN, LEAPT, and tripped through the pinnacles with renewed energy. There were three things he knew for sure. One. Zeph, not Cris, was aware of the disappearance of Elpida, and they were his primary suspect. Two. The HPO reports indicated Elpida was dead. Three. Elpida was in danger. Not dead. Before the encounter with Zeph, he had been just about ready to spiral. Elpida was just *gone*. Plucked from his life so abruptly, his head was left reeling. Spinning round and round, still searching for her big little eyes, because she had just been right beside him. He had hardly blinked twice to process. Now, though, he had a clue. Now he knew that the voice on his com might lead him to his sister, if only he could trace his com history and find the person behind it. Not only that, but tracing the voice would provide him evidence he could use when the HPO—in their piles of paperwork and legions of uncaring receptionists—denied his claims. Now, he was not without direction.

"Mother, I'm almost home." He sent the com message to Sanjana. He wanted to add a more comforting note, but he didn't want to alert her in case she hadn't looked at the feeds yet. Calling her "mother" was alarming enough. *"Don't do anything stupid 'til I get there,"* he added, thinking this note was more in character.

A sliver of grey-blue sky hung over the depths of Karuli Crag and he heard the happy echoes of kids playing like otters in Gianvante Lake. The lake was a beacon of liquid light in the distance. It was central to the lives of anyone who lived on the lower half of the crag, the hub of the lower HPO. Not only did the blue lights embedded in the lake illuminate day-to-day living for the cliff-dwellers and provide artificial sun for the greenery, but the lake itself was where people came to unwind. Krimsey passed the tunnel openings at the foot of Karuli Crag that led into the HPO Underground and walked along the lake path back to the bottom of Footpath Main. Families socialized by the grassy beach and their children played and laughed and danced. A knot formed in his belly. He looked away with a hard jaw. Normalcy was an odd sight when his world had just been turned upside down.

He looked up at Footpath Main. It was crowded. Today was Ceremony Day. So people were getting off early, pouring out of the tunnels onto the grass, ambling up Footpath Main, to get ready and dress up in their formals. His mother Sanjana worked Up Top, mediating communication with the New World Alliance on Mainland, so they lived on the upper half of the cliff face for convenience. It was a long, slow trek home.

He was annoyed that Ceremony Day was today. The people on the path slowed him down. *Everyone already knows which kids are ready to transition. Why do they always make a big deal of it?* Krimsey hated that the HPO glorified transitioning with this monthly ritual. Even more so now.

He took a deep breath, realizing that dwelling on the topic was making his pulse explode. Zeph thought he was transitioning because they punched him, but he still had eight months before he had to worry. Eight months before his name would be called. None of it mattered, though, until Elpida was found. The rope of anxiety growing in his belly was so tight, he could use it to bungee.

Turning onto the trail his home was on, Krimsey finally freed himself from behind a line of slow, tired *transitus* adults.

He was so engulfed by his own thoughts, he didn't realize someone passed him on his right, walking away from the houses at the end of Path 91, until he was hit with a wall of earthy, floral perfume. He turned his head to catch a glimpse of long, bone-straight blonde hair. Sallow, red-rimmed eyes glanced back at Krimsey before the woman disappeared around a jutting precipice. The woman's face impressed itself in his mind. The look of the woman was pale and sad and helpless. She looked like she'd been through hell. An administrator, maybe? Come to tell Sanjana the terrible news?

Krimsey hurried forward.

It wasn't until after Krimsey was approaching his home that the image of the woman registered as someone he knew. He looked back, his heart picking up, his gut lurching. She was gone, of course, but Krimsey glared at the path as if she might reappear.

Felice Karuli. Daughter of the president. His old family guide. What did it mean that Felice had come by? It made sense for her to be wrecked by news of Elpida. To be the one, who was so close to each of them, to deliver it. She had been his friend and care-taker for years; his childhood images of her were plastered and unmoving in his memory. That sorry state of a woman was far from the animated, young Felice he knew. What had happened to her? Wouldn't she know it wasn't true? He almost turned back to find her when a sob emanated from the house.

What if it is?

His gut twisted like a snake.

He looked inside. Sanjana cried, face down at the rickety wood table.

Krimsey went in, accidentally kicking a kitchen utensil. Sanjana gasped and staggered to her feet, wiping bloodshot eyes with her palms. She stood like an old, crooked tree. One of the ones that had grown, young and hopeful and green, on the side of a cliff, but had aged, all grooved branches and knotted, shallow roots, and died in place a long time ago. Krimsey couldn't find the words to dampen the sadness in the room. There were none. He turned and retrieved a dry, clean cloth from the kitchen floor.

He held it like a talisman of hope in his hands. "I'm sorry for the mess." His voice croaked, sympathetic to the squeaks of held-in sobs coming from his mother.

He stepped toward Sanjana and held out the cloth. She looked at the cloth in his hand but didn't take it. Her lips pursed, form-ing a shelf that captured the watery snot running from her nose.

Krimsey considered tossing the offering aside, but today he would choose patience over frustration for his mother.

"May I?" He raised the cloth between his fingers. Sanjana said nothing as he wiped the snot from her upper lip, but the tears increased, flooding her face as if turned on by a faucet.

"Felice came. She was—your sister… she's dead. She's gone," she said, with such brittleness he thought she would crack and pull him down with her as the pieces fell. She swayed.

Even though these were the words he expected, Krimsey's heart lodged in his throat. He swallowed hard, but the lump doubled in size, threatening to choke him. He coughed. The agitation made him feel as if the lump grew spikes for arms and legs.

"She isn't dead. I came to tell you." He spoke around the spikes piercing his soft flesh. "What did Felice say?" His voice came out weak and wet. Barely audible over Sanjana blowing her nose into the cloth his hand held. When she was done, he threw it to land in the pile of old laundry by his mattress. Krimsey's voice of doubt came creeping in. His ideas were so far-fetched. So far out of the realm of possibility. The HPO confirmed the death with an obituary. Felice Karuli confirmed it by coming here.

"She said it was Pneumaphage," Sanjana whispered.

His heart bottomed out in the pit of his stomach. He nodded and swallowed. The beating lump of spikes in his throat blocked his breath. "What else did she say?" The words pushed past the blockage and were sucked back in like a gasp. If he was going to prove the HPO wrong, he needed to know everything.

"Her funeral," Sanjana said, stepping toward the kitchen and leaning all her weight onto the counter, "is scheduled for four days from now." Her palm slipped and she bumped a loose cup off the counter. Shaking, she leaned over to pick it up. She opened the cupboard Krimsey had flung it out of earlier today and put it away.

Krimsey tried to speak through his rising panic, but only a muffled sound came out. His tongue was swollen, battered by the sharp lump in him that refused to dislodge, and slick with spit that tasted like bitter metal. He picked up the water pitcher from the counter and drank a swig from the spout.

"What… what else did she—?"

"What else?" Sanjana shouted, slamming the cupboard door. Everything inside toppled in a domino of hollow crashing. "'What else, what else?' What else do you think? Your sister is dead. She came in, told me Elpida had your father's same fate, that it was sudden and quick and she is dead, that her body is already in a pod, and when she herself was too bereaved to leave, she told me that Elpida didn't even get to finish her coms technology test she'd requested. Felice couldn't even tell me if she would have passed Internship Day or not. Got sick. Right there in the middle of that damn test."

Krimsey choked on another swig of water. His mother flinched. He stared at her, setting the pitcher back down. "Terraforming tech."

"What?"

"Terraforming," he said, a pinprick of hope warming his belly.

"What are you on about?" She asked, hand poised like a question mark.

"Terraforming. I said terraforming," he yelled, casting his gaze about and seeing their home in a whole new light. Same old blue light, only the illusions were shattered. Shapes in the shadows. They had always been there. Now he could see them with clarity. Who on this island had enough power to generate lies this big? Certainly not Cris. Not Zeph. "Terraforming-based tech development. That was the test Elpida requested."

"No, I'm very certain it was coms tech. It's what Felice told me," Sanjana said.

"Are you sure Felice said that?" He had to be absolutely certain.

"Yes. I know the difference between coms tech and terraforming tech. Earth's sake."

Felice lies. The walls were coming down. "And Felice said she didn't finish?"

"No," she said, "she didn't finish her test."

Krimsey didn't know if his sister had finished her test, or hadn't. But he knew someone was lying. He knew for a fact that the woman at the reception told him she had finished and he now knew that Felice told Sanjana she had not.

Who had the power to fake a death? Sure, the voice on the com had power. She couldn't have contacted him in the manner she had if she didn't. But fake a death? One so convincing that the HPO had a body that matched up to Elpida Enosh?

No.

There was only one possible answer. He had just caught the HPO in a massive lie. They didn't have a body. And his sister *wasn't* dead—she really wasn't. They took her. It was just as Zeph had said. Damn. He should have gone with Zeph.

Where Krimsey should have been filled with empty despair, where he should have been hopeless and hollow, he was filled with energy. His bones buzzed. This was proof. Proof that couldn't be used, true. But enough proof to keep hesitation at bay.

He looked at Sanjana. Her dry, quivering lips formed a hard line, so pale and colorless that the flesh blended in with the rest of her skin. Her hazel brown eyes grew deep with worry and several more lines appeared on her face. "She's gone." She crumpled against the counter and dripped her despair all over the surface.

"She isn't dead," Krimsey said. A quiet tinkle of an alarm sounded in his head. His 3:10 p.m. alarm. He brushed past Sanjana. Her lips moved, her eyes reddened, and she tried to grab his hand. He shot away from her reaching arms and went to his pile of laundry, watching her as he peeled off sweaty clothes. He was afraid she might implode.

"K—Krim—s-sit down." Sanjana burst into tears. "Where are you going?"

"Transition Ceremony," he said, pausing with his flowing, slightly stained dress shirt half on. "You should stay here." He finished dressing in his all-white formals and cut up half an apple for Sanjana. He kissed her on the forehead, picked up her com from the counter, and placed it in her palm. "Keep an ear out for me. I need you, Mother. Don't forget that." She was still red and puffy and withered as he left.

When he reached the top of the crag, Krimsey was seething, blood warmer and faster than ever. He didn't know what the HPO was doing, but it certainly didn't seem like they were doing *transitus* any favors. This ceremony, for example, was a sadistic ritual performance, for who? No one enjoyed the Transition Ceremony. Not even the parents. It was a solemn thing, sending off their kids into the ocean, into Earth only knew what dangers lurked. *Mandatory attendance.*

Why?

And segregating humans to live in nice homes atop the cliff, with all the essential amenities, while *transitus* families lived like trolls, always centimeters from falling to their death? They said it was because humans had permanent residence, while *transitus* were coming and going. Never meant to stay and live on the cliff forever. What about the families that stayed? What about the non-viables? What about Elpida?

Elpida, with the dreams and the passion and the drive? Stuck with some land-locked career she didn't choose, never allowed to change or decide for herself. Never allowed to live. This island was where *transitus* were sucked up and spit out to die.

To what end?

What was the HPO doing, if not helping *transitus*? Was helping *transitus* a front for something else? Something illegal? Something sinister?

He didn't have answers. But he knew who might.

He entered the iridescent glass dome. Inside was a sea of people wearing dark green or blue or red, sprinkled with those who could afford silky whites. Voices hummed in the vast, airy dome, the ceremony being used as a once-a-month social hour. Rows of old brown metal chairs faced a small podium in the middle of the white-tiled foyer. Behind the podium were the stairs leading down to the HPO Underground.

"Hey, Cris," Krimsey called.

Cris Langley stood out like a beacon with pale, sallow skin, long green sleeves, and bright head of fire. A sickly sheen and purple bags hung beneath his eyes. He looked worse now that he was out of the lake than when he had been in it. Under the spotlight of fluorescent lights, the toll Survival had taken on him showed. Cris was talking to a man who resembled him. He looked directly at Krimsey, said something to the man, and crossed his arms as the man left the dome.

Krimsey's temperature rose. He fought the urge to look away from Cris's piercing stare. Instead, he made his way toward him. When he was close, Krimsey said, "Cris. I need a favor."

Cris looked away, pretending not to hear. His line of sight landed on a group of *transitus* teens Krimsey recognized as the "cool" gang. But Cris's electric attention stayed behind, keeping his awareness on Krimsey with interest. Cris let his *transitus* emotion leak like noxious gas.

Krimsey reached Cris and touched his shoulder with the tips of his fingers.

"What do *you* want?" Cris flinched as if Krimsey had sent a tiny bolt of lightning through him. Cris's eyes returned to Krimsey.

"I wouldn't be coming to you if it wasn't important."

Krimsey expected the look on Cris's face to turn sour. Expected a forced laugh, dodgy eyes, and a punch to the gut. Cris did look away. But not in apprehension. Krimsey couldn't read the look. Cris's eyes turned back to Krimsey. "You're serious? You're not just trying to get at me or something?"

Krimsey shook his head and swallowed, fighting the urge to dash. "Uh-uh. I'm serious. Trust me, I don't want this any more than you do." The twitterpated stress flooding his bloodstream and the speed of his breath rising at the proximity of Cris's body told him otherwise. He *did* want to talk to Cris. He wanted *his* help. He wanted Cris to *want* to help him. The din of gathering families rose and fell.

Cris sniffed and looked behind him, body language stiff. He snapped back around and hissed, "Alright. Spit it out."

"Over there." Krimsey jutted a chin toward the office cubicles that flanked the west side of the dome. They needed privacy from prying ears.

"No. No way." Cris crossed his arms.

"We need privacy. This is life and death."

"Do you know how that'll *look?*" Cris's cheeks were flushed and he pulled down the hem of his shirt.

"I don't care—" Krimsey stopped. The cool crowd was staring. Whispering to each other. Cris cared how it looked. *Interesting*.

They were interrupted by a hurried *tap tap tap tap tap* of high heels. The families quieted to a low murmur and there was a commotion of metal scuffles as people found their seats. Lamia Karuli, the president of the HPO, strode from the back of the crowd at the dome entrance to the front podium. She wore a slinky, over-the-top, exposed-back dress of the most luxurious white silk. Krimsey scrutinized her for clues. Lamia had always been mysterious, but now the veil was lifting. The president of the HPO held a slithering stride and piercing gaze. She didn't want to be here. Her eyes slid over her audience analytically, as if seeing only zeros and ones. Krimsey saw through the wide, tooth-sparkling smile.

"Okay," Krimsey whispered to Cris. "I can't explain now, but I need you to hack my com."

"I'm confused." Cris frowned. "You're already in your com."

"I need to track a sender."

"Did you forget how to use your pings? You are trying to get back at me. I'm a jerk," Cris lowered his voice to match Krimsey's and tugged again at his shirt. "Don't stoop to my level."

The sound of Lamia clearing her throat echoed across the tile.

"This is serious," Krimsey said. "This sender is like a ghost. You're the only one who can hack it. Just... meet me after Ceremony. Please?"

"Please be seated," Lamia said, clearing her throat again. More metal scuffles.

"Fine. If this is a joke, you're dead."

Krimsey left to find a seat in the back. The only free spot in the back row was five seats in. He shuffled past a few pairs of knees and sat. The chair creaked, piercing the now-hushed quiet.

His chest felt full of air as thick as brick. Transition Ceremony felt wrong. It felt wrong to sit nice and tidy and well-behaved when his world had gone so wrong. His knuckles were white as he clenched the edge of his chair and listened to Lamia's droning introduction. Not deciphering individual words, but just hearing the syllables tap the inside of his skull like those high, high heels she wore. *Tap tap tap tap tap.* He examined her more closely than he ever had, as if expecting snakes to come out of her eyes. Her dark, sparkling eyelids were a cloak over her grey eyes, which pored over each family in the audience one by one. How had he not seen it before? He looked around at the families. They were oblivious. How did no one notice that dullness in her face? She was ghoulish and always had been, but he only now saw the truth.

"Anthony Dafforn. Would you please step up?" Lamia called after a while, squinting past the rafter light that illuminated the podium. Her reluctant lips pulled into a deceiving smile.

Anthony Dafforn, barely thirteen, was clapped all the way to the podium. More names were called. Krimsey was so lost in the dark depths of Lamia's demeanor that he lost track of who else was made to do the walk of shame.

Then, the stuff of Krimsey's nightmares emerged. People were suddenly whispering, pointing, and staring directly at him.

"Enosh? Krimsey Enosh. Would you please join us?" Lamia's amplified voice rang in his skull.

Did she just call my name?

"The kid has waited so long, he's stunned." Lamia called out. There was a chuckle. "Let's give this nineteen-year-old a welcoming ovation." There was clapping. A lurching in his belly. He found Cris's familiar gaze and Krimsey locked onto it, full of fear. Cris's eyes met his with what Krimsey could only interpret as a sigh of relief. Slack mouth, slack eyes, slack brows. Was that a smile, or a trick of the light? "Don't be shy, Krimsey. It's been a long time coming… You're a bit early, but sometimes our calculations can be off."

Zeph was right. I can't believe Zeph was right.

Bile in his belly hardened and churned, forming the most potent soup. Nausea made him melt into his seat. He didn't want to believe it. He couldn't. He still had eight months… didn't he? He needed time. Was this another lie? He didn't feel different. One by one, more and more faces found him and gave him tight nods.

"Come on dear," Lamia said, her voice losing its high-pitched charm. Krimsey stood, shaking, unwilling to peel his eyes off Cris just to have a familiar face. He tripped on the leg of his chair and scooted past the happy, hostile faces surrounding him.

The intensity of the room and its stares sabotaged any chance Krimsey might have had at keeping his cool. His scalp burned. He waded stiffly through the dense *transitus* emotion emanating from the room, eyes darting, shoulders locking up, thanking his body for at least keeping its contents on the inside.

He got to the end of the row and walked slowly to the podium, finally looking away from Cris. He nearly blacked out when he joined Anthony and the other *transitus* kids at the podium.

The other kids at the podium hardly looked prepared for this. Or strong enough for it. Or solid enough to withstand several atmospheres of water, let alone the predators that roamed it.

Krimsey fidgeted back and forth, trying to piece together an impossible puzzle. Three more *transitus*, all much younger than Krimsey, were also put on display.

"Thank you all for being here tonight." Lamia's voice was decadent, smooth, the kind of voice that rolled like a river.

Krimsey examined his blueish webbed toes sticking out from his sandals while his ears rang.

"We are gathered here to celebrate the transformation these *transitus* will soon embark upon. It is bittersweet. Inevitable. Most of all, it is a moment that never ceases to give me chills.

"Before me stand six strong souls who, during their time preparing, following guides, attending Dailies, have been equipped with the tools and knowledge of survival.

"Before me stand future sons and daughters of the sea. Their eyes will witness worlds we don't dare to imagine. For, strapped to the confines of our own established reality, our own past, present, and future, pre-written into the blueprint of humankind, our imaginations fall flat. Our genes deny us that freedom of imagining. Of re-writing. That is, until now. Now that humanity is no longer just humanity.

"*Transitus*-kind, our fledgling seeds of humanity, will write their own story. For us to dream up the world in which our children will exist would be putting words to an unspeakable feeling. An impossible feeling. It would be telling a story we can't possibly tell. It has to be told for us.

"Before me stand perfect little glimpses of tomorrow."

Lamia looked each of them up and down. Her frame was stiff and still and soft. Her dress swayed as she shifted her stance. "Now, you have worked hard to prepare yourselves. I know it is a little scary. And it's okay to feel frightened. Anthony looks uncertain. Milos looks a little shaky. Yessie is beaming but I know you've done only one Survival since turning fifteen.

"Your bodies have entered the phase where things will start to feel different. I know you have studied, but knowledge doesn't prepare you for this. It's not supposed to. Reading static words like *congested*, or *tingling*, or *tightness*, is just that. They're just words. Words other *transitus* have experienced in their own ways. Just as we cannot imagine how your future might play out, you cannot imagine or anticipate or even describe how you'll begin to feel. All of it, however, is normal.

"Now, just because your bloodwork indicates you have entered your transition phase, it does not mean it will happen tomorrow. Or the next day. Or the next week. Many transitions occur slowly, over several weeks. For some of you, like Krimsey, given his age, it can take days. Even hours. Every body is different and develops their aquatic lungs at different paces. For this reason, you must be ready and near the ocean.

"Dafforn, Enosh, Finn, Henderson, Kendal, and Sutter families, please join us by the podium to receive your gifts and say your goodbyes. Your children will be going to port now."

The volume in the dome rose and everyone stood at once. Lamia stepped from the podium. A parent caught her attention and started speaking before she could turn away. Her arms were crossed patiently behind her back.

More parents wanting their turn at dialogue with the president pretended to converse amongst each other, while casting attentive side-eyes at Lamia.

His eyes milled the crowd. Krimsey's mouth went dry when he saw a flash of Cris, moving toward the exit. Krimsey struggled to breathe evenly. A growing feeling of urgency pummeled his belly.

"You look worried." A hand landed on Krimsey's shoulder. He looked up from the crowd to find Lamia standing beside him with a semi-pleasant smile. "Anything I can do to ease your mind?"

"Actually, I... I was looking for my friend. I wanted to say goodbye." When he moved forward, Lamia's hand slid off him like a limp eel.

"Careful who you let into your life." Lamia said.

Krimsey looked back at her, his heart already thumping too fast to keep up with the stress of the day. His mouth formed a hard line. Did Lamia know he knew? Was he compromised? Why did she look so happy?

"When you transition," she added. "Everything will be different."

Krimsey let out the breath he had been holding. "Yeah, of course. I plan to be a loner, anyways." Krimsey coughed out a meek *ha ha* and turned to look for Cris, hoping Lamia's interest in him would redirect onto someone else. It did.

Cris, where did you go?

At the thought of his looming transition, warmth plumed from his chest and his nervous heart sputtered. He tried to calm his nerves. Wrung his hands. Wanted to swallow but his mouth was a desert, then he coughed at the effort and stood on his toes.

In front of him were empty chairs and chattering families and a small stream of people exiting the glass dome. Lamia, who had walked off to his right, had forgotten him. The end of her braid flicked back and forth as she talked.

The warmth that spread from Krimsey's chest to his belly to the tips of his fingers grew hot. He smelled the reeking sweat that poured down his sides.

He took a step back, tripped on the edge of the podium, and caught himself before anyone noticed. He could already feel his body giving up on him. Changing. Becoming other. He had to find Elpida.

He took another step back, trying to get a better vantage of the crowd. He saw a flash of pale skin and red hair. Cris locked eyes with him. So he hadn't left. Krimsey rolled his head in the direction of the stairs behind the podium to indicate that Cris should follow him. Then he slipped down the dark, empty staircase.

He hoped Cris got the message.

Downstairs, there was a soft blue glow and the wide gallery full of pillars was empty. Noise from the winding-down ceremony trickled down. Every sound that stood out pricked the back of his neck. There were twenty-five tunnels and doors that branched from this gallery. Plenty of places to dash to if things went wrong, but also plenty of places to get lost. Krimsey hid behind a pillar and listened for Cris's approach.

A soft sound scraped the back of his skull. On the bottom step of the gallery a silhouette appeared. A white high heel, back lit by the Ceremony lights. His blood flash-froze, his heart halted, and his eyes darted to the Medical entrance, the tunnel that was closest to him.

Before the white-adorned president could take her final step and look into the gallery, Krimsey had to jump-start his heart to move his feet and run from his cover. He ran to the entry and slammed through a pungent wall of disinfectant.

The serpentine labyrinth of Medical was also empty of people. Krimsey turned down a hallway once, twice, three times, four—then realized he was lost. Dashing in and out of dead-end hallways and rooms, Krimsey wondered if Lamia had seen him come down the stairs, or if someone had told her of his escape. His heart refused to incriminate Cris until further notice.

As Krimsey ran, his heart burned and worked overtime and his belly felt singed. As he ran, a new fear tugged at him. That his body would soon betray him. Lightheaded, sluggish, and dizzy, Krimsey wasn't sure how much longer he could continue. The burning sensation in his heart grew. Krimsey pushed and pushed and pushed against the feeling, but his vision began to flicker and fade.

He had to find somewhere safe. Where no one would find him. Where he could stay until danger passed. Except, in his delirium, Krimsey forgot some very important details. That he was in the HPO Underground. That he *was lost*. And that Lamia Karuli had every advantage.

Prae

In the shadows of two large port buildings, Zeph huddled among the sounds of bubbling laughter, crashing waves, and the nerves that pounded in their veins, roaring like a hurricane. They ducked beneath a dripping windowsill. The plastic wall against their back was rough and cold. The rain had stopped for the moment, but Zeph was already sopping wet. Mud had splashed up their ankles and rainwater had trickled down their back, soaking through their clothes, just in the short distance from the tunnels to port.

They were coming to terms with a lot of things today, including that apparently there were transport shafts that cut hours from the distance between HPO and port. Piece by piece, Cyn was exposing them to the deceitful nature of the HPO.

Multiple com messages had come from Gina. *"Where are you? I'm worried about you, Z." "Come home please. We need to talk."* Each plea she had sent drove an icy dagger deeper into Zeph's heart. She was the first person Zeph had always turned to when in need of love, affection, or advice. She was the rock Zeph had built their life around, the foundation of their understanding of the world. The only mother Zeph had ever known—until now.

Zeph ignored her. It was the only option.

Nothing felt right anymore. Nothing felt real. For Earth's sake, they were getting ready to kidnap a little *transitus* girl. Prae Ogier.

It was absurd. Yet this was the safest they had felt in hours. While Zeph trekked along the way to port, Cyn had assured them that she had masked their com's location responder; no one but Cyn knew where they were. It gave them the feeling of being invisible, covered in the cloak of a total stranger.

Commotion inside the building shook them out of their contemplation. Holding on to the sill beside them, Zeph peeked into the building. Dribbles of runoff splashed the sill and the table just inside. A book—*So, You've Got the Transitus Gene: Parenting Edition*—lay forgotten, soggy on the table. Cushy furniture lined the room. Splatters of rain soaked the arm of a sun-faded chair.

On the far side of the room, two men stood at the bottom of the stairwell beside the front door, engrossed in discussion. One man looked to be human. He wore a white button-up, partially unbuttoned, and held a *transitus* toddler in his arms. Another kid was at his feet, tugging at his pants. The other man, also human, no kids at his side, picked up a dropped book off the floor and nodded his head at something the other had said. Zeph tried to listen for clues, but they could hardly hear the conversation over the white noise of wind.

Zeph wiped their nose with a wet sleeve and grimaced at the seed of doubt trying to worm its way through their thoughts. It wasn't that they regretted deciding to do this. They did not regret a thing. But they did have to pause and ask themselves: What in the forsaken earth happened to their life? Was this the only option? They told themselves they were just wet, cold, and bitter. Oh, and Cyn was cryptic as a witch. Zeph was not having fun.

I do not have regrets. I do not have regrets. I do not have regrets.

"Have you identified where she is?" Cyn. *Finally.* She'd gone quiet while they muddled. And they had a few things to say. But Zeph was at Cyn's mercy; they could not contact the woman without an active connection back to her. They had no choice but to wait until she was ready to talk to them. It was infuriating.

"There you are!" Zeph crouched back under the window sill, shivered, and spat sand from their teeth. *"This is impossible. There are at least fourteen kids spread between three buildings. How am I going to identify one kid?"* Sweat and rainwater trickled down their back.

"Sixteen."

"What?"

"Sixteen kids."

Zeph sighed, suppressing the urge to scream. Maybe if they had help, this would not be so impossible. *"Why are you not helping, again?"*

"I am helping. I'm keeping an eye on security. You'll find her. I'll ping in another ten minutes."

"Wait!" Ugh. It was too late; the finicky com link to Cyn disappeared.

They closed their eyes. *I do not have regrets.*

The muffled voices inside continued. Zeph peered inside again. The father with the kids hanging on him was about to snap. The cheeks in his iconic flustered-parent face flushed with red. He tried to maintain composure within his conversation but finally broke. "Prae! Stop it," he shouted. "Go upstairs with your mom. I'll be right there."

Zeph's heart leapt. They immediately stood, taking careful peeks from the side of the window frame. The girl—*transitus* forehead, red hair, some variation of yellow in her eyes—wailed and stomped up the stairs.

Determined, Zeph took a deep breath and stepped out from the alley. A circle of flood-lamp light illuminated the soggy main path through the port town. The clouds closed up at that moment, as if it were an omen, and the rain torrented, slashing sideways in the gusts of wind pushing Zeph forward. Daring them.

"How about now?" Cyn again.

"This cannot possibly work," Zeph complained to her over the com, tripping on their own foot when another blast of Mother Nature pushed against Zeph's resistance. *"I am soaked. They are not going to believe me."*

"You found her? Great. You can do this."

If their so-called friend Krimsey had just listened to them, Zeph would not be doing this alone. *No. I do not need anybody.* An overwhelming flood of emotion took hold. *Screw Krimsey. Screw Gina. And screw Cyn Jones, too. I'm doing this for Prae. And I can do this on my own.*

Zeph closed their eyes, walked up to the unadorned plastic front door, and knocked.

The man who had been conversing with Prae's father opened the door and looked at Zeph.

Zeph cleared their throat, suppressed a shiver, and said, "Evening."

"You're soaked!" The man opened the door wider and stepped aside. Warm, humid air smelling of unwashed bodies wafted out.

Zeph forced a hesitant chuckle to cover the crinkle of their nose, remaining in place. "Umm," they said, trying to remember the lines Cyn had told them to use. Off-script. They were going to have to go off-script. Zeph cleared their throat, the same way adults did to sound important. "I am assisting this evening. Guides are working on some intake before departure tomorrow. The—"

"Please, please, come in."

Zeph stood there, dripping. Snot or rain or whatever quivered on their nose.

Zeph kept firmly in place. "We just need to see Prae Ogier."

The man who stood back a few meters raised his chin and poked his head into the conversation. "Prae?" he asked. "Is everything alright?"

"Mister Ogier, sir, yes, everything is fine," they said, their mouth beginning to twitch. "The guides just requested her for an... intake." They searched for a more convincing word than 'intake' but came up short.

"Intake? *Prae.*" The man turned and shouted up the stairs.

With red eyes and a teary, freckled face, the little girl from earlier stomped back down the stairs, sniveling. Zeph's heart jumped.

What am I doing?

"What's it for?" Mr. Ogier picked up a light rain jacket from a hook by the door.

"Oh, just routine. Something we noticed." Zeph shifted and smiled, channeling the energy Gina gave whenever working in Medical. Their joints creaked. "No need to accompany."

"She's a finicky child," the man said, stepping forward as the other stepped aside. "Come on honey, put your coat on." Mr. Ogier put one tiny webbed hand into a sleeve, then slipped the other in, and secured the hood.

"We just need Prae. You can stay." Zeph tried not to sound too forceful.

Mr. Ogier frowned at Zeph.

The other man, who had stepped back, nosed back in and asked, "So what's the routine for again?"

"Don't like leaving my kiddo on her own, you know? Better if I come."

Zeph gulped, then forced another smile. *I definitely regret this.* "Sure, no problem." There was no way out of this now, not without arousing suspicion.

Together, they stepped from the awning, Zeph thinking quick. The rain blared. Zeph blinked past the torrent.

"Aren't the guides this way?" Mr. Ogier asked, pointing the opposite direction Zeph had started off in.

"Equipment is over here," Zeph said, walking quickly away from the building, to the left, the direction Cyn had instructed. Father and daughter followed. Prae plopped into every puddle until her father pulled her up into his arms.

As they walked, an idea formed. Zeph turned down a path they knew would be a dead-end. The three of them plodded down to the building at the end, the same building Zeph had emerged from earlier. It led into the port transport tunnels which connected the port and the HPO. A shortcut to Karuli Crag. Cyn had helped Zeph navigate the tunnels, and when they emerged, they made sure to leave the building as they had found it. With the door locked. Zeph walked up to the door and jimmied the handle.

Mr. Ogier set Prae down, watching with great concern.

Pretending exasperation, Zeph sighed, knocked impatiently, paused just for show, then turned to Mr. Ogier. "Shoot. They are supposed to be here. Your guide has the key. Will you go let 'em know we are waiting?" Zeph pulled Prae close, under the small awning of the doorway. Smiling, "We will wait here. Keep her out of the rain."

The man's eyes narrowed. "Uhh." He looked at the building. Looked at Zeph. Looked at Prae. Looked behind him. "Where are the guides? They weren't in the building this evening but I know they were going to stay in the ground floor room."

"Port office. I'd imagine. Since the guide is not here." Zeph guessed. It didn't matter as long as he believed the lie.

Mr. Ogier relinquished his suspicion. "Damn place is a kook house." He turned around and obliged.

Zeph's shoulders released and they let out an audible sigh. Zeph realized they were shaking, and not from the rain. It was pure adrenaline. Zeph smiled. They kind of liked it.

As soon as Prae's father disappeared around the corner up the alley, Zeph leaned down to the nervous *transitus* girl and said, "Do you like piggyback rides?"

Both Zeph and the girl were gone before Mr. Ogier could arrive back with alarmed reinforcements.

Wrung-Out

Felice Karuli, Tuesday, March 26, 2250, 5:03 p.m.

FELICE SAT ALONE BLINKING in the dark with her com off. Her shallow breath snagged on the invisible fingers of despair curled around her heart. She needed to be alone and the supply tunnels linking Karuli Crag with the port town was the only safe place. She came here because she didn't know what to do and because she was afraid of what she'd do if she were anywhere else. The ends of her shoulder blades pressed into the smooth tunnel wall and the tears on her face were dry and crusted.

"There you are." A concerned male voice sounding a whole lot like Ive burst around the corner of the nearest intersection.

"Ive? Fuck." Her skin crawled at the sudden sound, ears prickling. She looked up. Ive's gruff face appeared, glowing from the com light in his ear. Next-day stubble peppered his jaw line. She put a hand over her pounding heart. "You scared me."

"I could say the same." His face was hard and soft all at once. Chiseled angles all warped by curved shadows.

"You think I'm going to off myself." Her voice was flat.

"Am I wrong?"

She had considered it, more than once today, but she didn't have to answer for him to know this. "How did you find me?"

"Coms." His voice strained. His Adam's apple moved down and up as he swallowed.

"My com is off." Her com should not have been trackable. A small pit of unease formed in her stomach. She sat straighter and pursed her lips. What was Ive doing here?

"I have my ways." Ive's shadowy, toothy smile was more ominous than inviting.

"They don't even work in the tunnels." That was only partially true. Sometimes, they did work in the tunnels, but only her special secondary com. She frowned, pressing her hands against the floor to prop herself up. She stood.

Ive shrugged. His lips were white and hard. "Why are you down here, Felice?"

They stared at each other for a moment, unwavering eyes seeming to each hold secrets. "You tell me first," she said.

"I'm helping. I know a thing or two about what's going on," he said, voice low. He sat down at the base of the wall and patted the floor beside him. "Are you going to tell me why you're hiding?"

Felice laughed. The kind of laugh that hurt. Not from the bottom of the belly, but from the top of the chest. Harsh and cold like a cough.

If Ive knew a thing or two, it was a thing or two too few. If only she could share her secrets. Tell him what was really going on. That the HPO was led by a corrupt woman and that woman's daughter. That, together, they were killers. Maybe he could help her... if he didn't immediately kill her himself, when he heard of the things she'd done. She bowed her head in her palms and sat beside him.

"Hey, now." Ive's cold hand brushed hers. He took her hand away from her forehead. He looked intently at her. When her attention focused back on him, his face, his eyes, his lips, he took her other hand. He pulled her in to him.

She folded herself tightly against his chest and let him stroke her hair but pulled back when she felt how fast his heart beat. "What's wrong? What aren't you telling me?"

"It kills me to see you like this," he said, ignoring the question.

"Stop looking at me like I'm going to break."

"Aren't you?" He looked like he was grappling with what to say next. His body shifted, pulling away and straightening against the wall. "Felice, what do you think head of coms security does?"

"You monitor the coms." *What does this have to do with anything?*

"*All* of the coms," he added.

"What are you getting at?"

"Your coms. Your mother's coms. Carmak's coms. Your decoy coms *and* your primaries." His mouth twitched with concern. "I know what happened with Rumi."

Felice's blood pressure plummeted; her fingertips tingled and stung. She was suffocating. All the things she'd said. All the horrible things they'd done. Ive knew. He told her as such moments ago and she brushed it off like he didn't know what he was talking about. "Fuck."

"Breathe, it's alright." His eyes darted in a game with hers.

Felice was reeling. Trying to mentally track exactly what he knew. The primary com she used was supposed to be off-grid. Only her mother, Carmak, Lowery, and a few others were supposed to know. The decoy com she kept on her was meant to be her on-grid presence. Trackable. Like everyone else.

Felice stood. Her knees creaked. She turned her back to him. His uniform rustled as he stood. Ive touched her shoulder.

"I've always known," he said. "I know about Rumi and the testers and the research and the lab. I was vetted for this job. I knew exactly what it would involve." Ive tried to chuckle but it died in his throat and Felice sobbed. "It's okay."

How could she be so blind? Of course he knew everything. Lamia needed someone to track potential threats. She needed someone who knew everything. Someone who could mislead the NWA when those Mainlanders nosed into the system to check up on them. Someone who could manage the entire mess she and her mother created.

She never imagined that this someone would be *her* someone.

"Fuck, Ive. I'm such a terrible person." She couldn't look at him.

"You're not a terrible person. Felice," he said her name sternly. "Felice." She turned, tears spilling. She yanked her hands back when he tried to hold them. "You're not a terrible person. Do you believe me?"

He swam in her vision.

"Why are you telling me this? Why are you here?"

"Because there's been a security breach. Your mother sent me to find you."

"My mother... fuck... she knows about us... doesn't she? Forsaken Earth. Don't answer that." Felice knew the answer. Had her mother planted her lover into her life, too? She didn't want him to say it. She wiped her face. "How can you even look at me?" Her heart thumped in her chest like a rock.

She turned to see a range of emotion flicker across his face.

"How can *you* look at me?" His voice was a musky whisper, an over-plucked bass. She could see that starting this conversation had taken a lot out of Ive. Now the dark under circles—the tired eyes—made sense. He looked at her like he had just broken all the bones in her body.

Felice was so worried about figuring out what Ive did and did not know about *her* that she hadn't stopped to think about how *he* fit into all this. Why was he helping Lamia?

"Do you know what she asked me to do?"

He nodded. "That wasn't fair of her to ask you to do that."

"*Fair?*" Her voice was shrill and rasped the back of her throat. "Fair isn't quite the word I'd use in this situation. So you know she wants me to *abduct* four kids."

"I do."

"Fair." She laughed, this time with a burning hiccough in her chest. She peeled away from him, to get a better look at his eyes. Did she even know him anymore? "Did you know I spent the morning mapping out the logistics of kidnapping those children, Ive? Did you know that? Curing Pneumaphage is not worth their lives. The fact that I even mapped out logistics is—And you know what? It's impossible anyways. Logistically, it's a nightmare. Logistically, my mother has lost her mind. I'm so stuck, Ive. What am I even doing? Can you believe I have followed that woman's orders for this long?"

"I can believe it. The work is so close."

"You sound just like her. What the fuck? Why are you helping her?"

Ive's face spun in a million directions. The sharpness of it warped into some weapon designed to pierce her heart.

"There are some things I came ready to tell you. And other things I can't tell you," he said. Hurt snapped his voice in half.

What was he leaving out?

Felice bit her lip and blinked away tears. "You can," she said. Firm, despite the tears. "What are you keeping from me that could possibly compel you to help Lamia do this?"

"It's not for me to tell." His pointed face faded in and out of her vision.

"My mother harbors other secrets from me, then?" She asked. He didn't say anything. "Alright. I see where you stand. You know… I know my mother better than anyone…. She's gone way too far. She's lost her mind. And you have, too."

"Maybe. Maybe not." A mud-red wave of hair clung to his sweaty brow.

"You're not who I thought you were." Whatever he was keeping from her, she needed to find out. But how? Should she raid the labs? But she had access to everything in the labs. There were no other secrets.

The muscles on the sides of his head seemed to work themselves out of an argument, shadows filling and unfilling his temple in the low light. "I am not who I thought I was, either," he said after a time. Then, "Your mother has a new request."

"And she sent you thinking I'd listen to you." The words left a bitter note on her tongue.

Ive cast a sideways glance, his temples still working overtime. "And she's a little preoccupied herself." His voice sounded as if he had ground his teeth to sand and swallowed.

"With what? If she can't even ask me herself—"

"We're dealing with an emergency, Felice, I'd appreciate some cooperation."

Ive sounded just like Lamia. Felice crossed her arms. Realizing it made her cleavage more prominent, she uncrossed them and fiddled her fingers at her sides. "What the hell is going on, then?" She breathed through her nostrils because she was losing her calm.

Ive's jaw clenched. It was a miracle there were still teeth in there at all when he spoke again. "There's a woman in the mountains trying to take us out. She's broken through all my security."

Felice snorted. "A woman in the mountains."

"Cyn Jones."

That name was familiar.

"I didn't know of Cyn until recently. Wish your mother had informed me sooner; so much would have made sense. There were clues… breadcrumbs. For years. Ghost trails left behind after hacks or messages. I didn't figure it out until today. This morning we pinpointed her signatures after she sent a few messages to Zeph Carmak. This is when I confronted your mother and she told me."

"Messages to Zeph Carmak? As in Gina Carmak, my co-worker's child?" This was news she could work with. The first clue to more of Lamia's secrets. Her shoulders loosened, but she still stepped back when Ive took a step toward her.

"Your mother has suspected sabotage for years now," he said, without blinking, without answering the question. "Seventeen years ago, Cyn Jones was the head of coms, the woman I replaced. Lamia was too distracted at the time to properly vet Mrs. Jones…"

Felice remembered Cyn now. Pregnant. Dark skin. Full of life. "I remember her…. She just disappeared. I thought she'd left the island or something."

"You were just a kid. Kids don't notice disappearances. They just get on with their lives," Ive said.

"So she did just…?"

"Disappear?"

"Yes."

"She did. Though it seems Cyn never left. Lamia suspected. She'd have heard of a stowaway leaving the island. She ignored Cyn, though, tried to forget her. Other things to worry about."

"Why contact Zeph Carmak?"

"Zeph Carmak is her kid."

"How is that…." The woman had been pregnant. "Gina took her baby?"

"I don't know the specifics. Lamia didn't tell me. I guess there was an exchange."

"Do you know what she told Zeph? What does Cyn know? If she was head of coms before you…" Cyn Jones must know a lot. She had hacked their coms systems and evaded detection for years.

"No. I can't view the messages. They disappear too quickly. But I'm close. It's possible Cyn has access to all our systems. There are signatures monitoring the power grid, the coms, our databases. The only place it seems she hasn't been able to touch are the labs.

I'm still unraveling the clues. Some of them are too old to reliably reference."

"So, what now? My mother wants me to go find Cyn?"

"Cyn Jones fucked us." Ive drew in a long, shaking breath. "She kidnapped a kid. The parents at port are going wild."

"What?!" She reached for her com, then stopped. Pressed her hand against her side. "Which kid was it, Ive?"

"Prae Ogier," he said. "One of the kids on your mother's list."

"She knows something about the labs, then, even if she hasn't broken in," Felice said. "She knows exactly what we're doing."

"That's speculation."

"Well, it's not fucking speculation. She has access to all our communications. Earth forsaken hell, Ive. She's going to—what the hell were the guides doing? When did this happen?" Felice had to commend the woman. She could only see Cyn's first move, but Felice already knew the woman was brilliant.

"It happened an hour ago," Ive said. "Your mother expects you to work damage control with the parents."

Felice paced down the tunnelway. Then back. "What's my mother doing that's more important than handling *this*? She expects me to handle it? We have security for a reason." Anxious steps down the tunnelway again.

Ive scratched his head. "Are you done?" Felice stopped pacing. Ive was irritated.

"What am *I* supposed to do?" Rising panic. Cyn Jones may have been brilliant, but she was fucking with the lives of everyone on this island. Chaos was not the answer to such a delicate ecosystem.

"Felice, Cyn Jones is unstable. She's a threat to every *transitus* living here."

"That much is clear," she said.

"Lamia would like you to figure it out. It's easier than bringing in the kids, right? She plans to handle that separately, now. That's the good news." He reached out and rubbed her shoulder.

Felice pulled away. "Such good news," she said with a vein of sarcasm. "You know what? Fine." She pulled out her com and turned it on. "But I don't want to see your face. I really don't. Just go. We're done here." The words stung on their way out.

Her vision flashed, showing her seven message pings. They glowed like an afterthought in the back of her mind.

Ive was still standing there.

"What are you waiting for?"

"There's one more thing," Ive said.

"Fuck's sake."

"Zeph ran off and ditched their com at port and is probably with her. With Cyn."

"Alright. Gina must be a mess but I honestly don't care."

"Just thought you should know. Oh, and I almost forgot. Here." Ive put his hand in his pants pocket. Felice's mind immediately jumped to all the times he had come by and smuggled her food at her office when she had been too busy to care for herself. On all her worst days, he was there. When she was too drained to even think of drinking water, he came. Now that Felice thought back on her day, she realized the last things she had consumed were the bread roll and tea he had brought her that morning. She was starving. Her heart skipped a beat, relishing the normalcy of Ive trying to take care of her. Even if just one last time.

Ive pulled out a rumpled ball of fabric and unfurled it in front of her. A thin black rain jacket.

"It's pouring out there," he said.

"Oh," she said. "Anything else?" Felice forgot to breathe. White noise swished in her ears as she took his offering.

Ive swallowed, leaned over and kissed her on the forehead. "Nothing else, except that I love you, Felice." She didn't believe him. He said, "You won't have to see me again. We're done." There was the truth.

Ive turned and left, leaving his musky scent behind. Felice stared into the dark. After a few minutes, Ive's smell faded and followed him down the hall.

In Ive's company, she had forgotten the cold, icy fingers clamped around her heart. She had forgotten the tightness in her chest. She had forgotten the dark despair. When he was gone, the fingers slowly squeezed, squeezed, squeezed, until all that was left was a hollow heart.

One by one, Felice began to open the messages waiting for her on her com. There was a mess for her to clean.

INNOCENT

Felice Karuli, Tuesday, March 26, 2250, 5:48 p.m.

WHEN SHE OPENED HER com messages, her ears burned. Frantic pleas from her guides stationed with new families at port described the evening as an unraveling wreck. Prae Ogier, the tiny NVT she had been so nervous about, had been kidnapped. She didn't know how she felt about the long-term implications of the news yet. Cyn's meddling was a sign. A switch inside Felice had been flipped. But she didn't have the time to work out its meaning.

Her fists clenched so tight, her nails dug into skin. Only a quarter of the way through the messages, she cried out in frustration.

She pinged her mother. *"Lamia! Need you at port, now!"*

"I am aware. Busy. Take care of it please. Delay them. I don't care," her mother replied.

"Your fucking mess. Clean it up." Felice sent it and switched off her com.

Felice knew her mother wasn't going to do anything. Not when she had already asked Felice to take care of the still-unfolding event. Felice had some time to simmer with her cooling thoughts on the way to port and realized that Cyn Jones, while she very likely had a vendetta against the HPO, could perhaps have been exactly what Felice needed to shake things up around here. Maybe Cyn Jones could be Felice's pawn, her own hidden checkmate against her mother. Maybe Cyn Jones could be... an ally? She was already brainstorming ways of contacting the woman.

No. She was getting ahead of herself.

She needed more information. She needed to understand the woman's motives. And she wasn't going to get the knowledge she needed by seething and crying. She wiped under her eyes, hoping whatever mascara that may have smeared didn't look too deranged. Grey rain dashed into her face and pummeled the wet gravel pathway. She wrapped the stupid rain jacket around her face tighter.

She arrived at port, where her thoughts were interrupted by an invisible, angry mob. Shouts broke through window openings from the middle of three two-story rooming houses, shouts that must have contained a whole lot of swearing and spit. With her heart stuttering, she straightened the hem of her dress, clenched her teeth, and approached the rooming house.

A small posse of parents from the building on the left popped out one by one. They gathered and huddled under the awning, then dashed, splashing toward the middle building, shielding each other from the cascading fall of rain.

Felice's approach slowed. She watched a guide she recognized as Aimie pop out after the parents and nervously scuttle through the rain into the middle building. The middle building with its wide, open doorway, had swallowed each of them whole. Crossing the intersection, Felice's steps squelched around muddy potholes.

The moment her right foot hit the rooming house lobby tiles, she was punched with smells of wet, dirty bodies. Fifteen or so parents, many of whom were supposed to be housed in the neighboring two buildings, crowded the small reception room.

Her ears rang with rising shouts. The reception room was large enough for twelve people at most. Not fifteen parents, their kids, and several guides. Two kids ducked between the legs of adults. Someone's teenager plopped on a damp couch. Six of the eight guides cowered in a corner, flinching at the chaos, wedged behind a decorative side table. The guide who had just entered, Aimie, trembled in front of Felice, not yet noticing her arrival. Aimie shifted on her feet, then pushed through the crowd to join the other guides.

Felice stood just inside the entryway, in front of the stairs that led to the upper bedrooms. Everyone was being jostled. One pair of parents were in heated verbal combat. Someone else knocked over a table vase filled with wildflowers from the valley. Felice watched the uproar unfold in horror. She watched, gaping at them, frozen in fear. Her rain jacket dripped water onto the floor.

One woman leaned beside the man next to her, pointed at Felice, whisper-shouting in his ear. One by one, faces turned. At first, it grew quiet. The volume of the crowd rolled low like dwindling ocean swells.

Before anyone could start back up, Felice seized the silence. "Now, before anyone jumps into further shouting," she called out, "I need to make one thing very clear: we are working on bringing Prae Ogier back to her parents and resolving this incident swiftly."

Felice took a breath and strategically placed her hands on her hips.

"As we work to resolve this... *astronomical*... and *unusual* calamity, we ask that everyone but the Ogier family please return to their assigned lodgings in their assigned buildings...."

"Now wait a minute!"

"Not a chance!"

"We need answers!"

"Do you know where she is?"

"Why won't you tell us?"

"Just what sort of operation are you—"

"As I said..." Felice strained to be heard over the rising hysteria.

"I jus' need a name, lady," Thomas Ogier barked, his square jaw quavered. "The culprit was tall—broad shoulders, blue skin, almos' black. Bald and dark yellow eyes. Never seen anyone like that before so you must have a name."

Definitely a description of Zeph Carmak.

The din grew to an unbearable level.

"When's the ship leaving? I want my children back on that ship."

"We don't feel safe."

In the corner, the guides bobbled their heads at each other in relief, having the attention of the families diverted from them for the time being. Aimie joined them.

"Yeah," another parent agreed.

Felice closed her eyes and breathed. She had gotten through worse, hadn't she? Wracking her brain for a solution, Felice recalled a run-in with Rumi Yen's parent several years back, just days following the missing child report. Only, this parent hadn't seen the kidnapper. Hadn't seen anything. No proof enough for accusations. The only words to rely on were the lies of the HPO. Her lies. And now?

"The ship doesn't—" Felice was interrupted by another shout. "Your transport to this island was contingent on the understanding that—"

It was ironic, considering. It wasn't even Felice who had done the kidnapping this time. Her mother had ordered it. She had all but refused. Yet here she was. Cornered. Caught. And innocent. Relatively speaking.

"We want to go back! Whose kid is next?"

"If the *transitus* you raise up are *this* lawless...."

"I don't want a part of this! Take us back!"

"Take us back!"

Felice's voice rose. "THERE IS NO GOING BACK!" The room was shocked into momentary stillness. "Your transport to this island..." she lowered her voice, repeating herself, "was contingent on the understanding that there is no going back."

Then, the outcry sparked and licked like flames, rebounding twofold. Wild theories of kidnappings—basically true, considering Rumi—and accusations of being unsafe, unruly, unorganized—also true—were all flung in her face. True, true, true.

"LISTEN!" Her voice cracked over the stressed voices and she cleared her throat. "Any desire to return to Mainland must be brought up with the New World Alliance directly. Of your own accord. If that is what you wish, I encourage you to do so immediately. It can be done at the port office down the street." As two parents pounded past her out the door, she looked at Mr. Ogier. Thomas Ogier was a head taller than Felice, and she had to crane her neck to look at him.

"Jus' want our little Prae safe."

The woman hovering at his shoulder with a baby in her arms scowled at Felice. Felice touched his elbow with her cold, brittle fingers. "I know, Mr. Ogier. We will bring her back."

"So you do know where…? I mean, has this happened—?"

"No," Felice asserted. "Disappearances, I assure you, do not happen at the HPO and we will get to the bottom of this. You can wait out here, but you have to give me and your guides some space. Lamia is coming. If you have more questions, and you don't want to bring your grievances to the port office, wait for Lamia." She still had to shout, as the noise in the room approached unbearable levels again.

This did not appease the parents. But it did stop their questions.

Felice flicked her attention to Aimie, who now hid behind a shroud of fading window light beside the other guides. "Aimie," Felice snapped. The guide was twenty-something—inexperienced, but had proved to handle pressure well in the past. She was actively being vetted to join Lamia's ring of insiders. Eyes skittish, Aimie hurried to Felice.

"Yes?"

"Contact my mother. Tell her she needs to get here immediately," Felice whispered urgently.

"But…" Fear flickered across the poor girl's face.

"Did you hear me?" Felice hissed. Would the girl stand up to this level of pressure, or would she cave?

"Yes, but—"

"Just do it."

A hard determination took over Aimie's short stature. She nodded, if still a bit hesitant. She stood slightly taller as she tapped the com in her ear; her eyes zoned out. Felice turned and slipped into the room by the entryway. She snapped the door closed behind her. The noise from the main room was muffled now but continued to ring between her ears.

The downstairs room was meant to house newly assigned guides. Four beds lined one wall. Belongings were scattered across one of them. On her left was a bathroom.

Felice rushed to the toilet. She hadn't eaten much, but her stomach had a lot to give. She shook and heaved liquid bile. And when she thought she was done, she dry heaved into the bowl for several long minutes.

Felice stood, trembling, feeling as if she might collapse. She propped herself up against the sink, rinsed her mouth, and stared into the mirror. The person who stared back was unrecognizable.

Mascara streaked beneath her eyes, making her look ghoulish. The under-eye darkness highlighted their puffy pink hue. Her hair, uncomfortably hot and damp inside the hood of her rain jacket, clung around her ears and jawline, curling in the humidity. Throwing the jacket aside, she saw that her black roots were showing, too.

Her eyes welled.

Her purple lips puckered hideously.

I look like my mother. She imagined Lamia chastising her for imperfect appearance. *Why can't I do anything right?*

There was a knock at the door. Then a voice.

Felice wiped at the mascara under her eyes, managing to make her eyes more red and irritated. She tucked the curling blonde locks behind her ears, flattening and smoothing as she crossed over to the door. She blinked away the welling tears and the knocking at the door outside became furious.

Tell them… tell them… Felice paused to stare at the door and the cracks of light coming through the jambs. *Shit, Felice, how are you going to fix this?*

Felice flung open the guide suite door. Aimie looked at her meekly. She was accompanied by a vaguely familiar man. His sharp nose and cheekbones were very red, lips chapped, hair thinning and windblown.

The man wore stuffy, starched attire, all black, clearly not from the island.

"Who are you?" Felice asked, guarded.

"Franklin. Franklin Boyd. My limbs are quite exhausted. Do you mind?" He lifted his chin, peering down his nose at her. His voice was low and slow, as if each syllable went through a cooker before being expelled.

Boyd… why does that sound so familiar?

Looking perturbed, Mr. Boyd strode in, found a light switch, and flipped it. He stood in the middle of the room.

Boyd, Boyd, Boyd…

"By the look on your face, Miss Karuli, you have yet to place my name."

Aimie slowly shut herself, Felice, and Mr. Boyd inside the room. Outside, it had grown oddly quiet.

"I'm sorry, Mr. Boyd, but what is your business here? Are you a parent?"

The man barked a short little laugh, as if she were toying with him. "Oh. You're serious." Mr. Boyd extended his hand to her, though disdainfully. "It's just that, you asked that earlier. I am a parent. But not one of yours."

I asked that earlier?

"Franklin Boyd. President of NWA *Transitus* Relations." He took his time to draw out the word *transitus* while his amber brown eyes slowly crawled up to meet hers. "This is where you—Miss Karuli—offer your own introduction. Or do you people not follow standard formalities on this... island?"

At Felice's blank look, he straightened.

"Very well. I hear a child has been taken?"

"Y-Yes, we're looking into Prae Ogier's disappearance, as I mentioned to the families, this is an isolated event and—"

"Isolated? Miss Karuli, I don't know of any Prae Ogier. So there's a second disappearance, then?"

"Second...?"

Her eyes widened. He was the man from this morning asking for the port office. How long had he been snooping around? What did he find?

"*Really*, Miss Karuli, by the state of things, you'd think this place was being run by a pack of animals." Felice's jaw gaped at him. "*Elpida Enosh*. Ring any little alarms behind that pretty face?"

Piece of My Heart

Tessa Darling, 2101

I THOUGHT I WOULD *die.*

It was the shock more than anything. Lon suspected dehydration, so he fetched a glass for me, dear soul. My breaths were shallow, and a glass of water is never not smart.

I took it, gulped it down, and my voice after was surprisingly sturdy. During childbirth, I had had a vision. There had been a child there. And a brackish, cold feeling in my chest. The vision was quickly gone. Like it hadn't come to mind at all.

I was feeling chilled and determined and I couldn't remember why.

"Lon? I'd like to see her again. Will you get me a towel?"

"Are you sure? Can you—stand?" He was now looking at the midwife, who was holding the small, strange creature of our love.

Hand pruned from the water in the birthing tub, I reached toward Lon and the uncertain grip he had on my clean grey towel. "I am fine. Bring her to me. I don't need to stand long. I just need to get out of this tub to say hello to my... daughter."

I let out a long, dizzying exhale. The bathwater I sat in had turned red and lukewarm. I felt the effects of adrenaline and my birthing hormones begin to fade.

The midwife approached me with the newborn bundle hesitantly. "Are—are you sure?"

I swallowed my resolve like a pill.

"Yes."

She looked to my husband, who pulled my hand with a heave. Feeling like a beached whale, I collapsed in the chair with the towel wrapped around me like a hug.

Lon's face followed the midwife and the bundle as she handed me a scrunchy, pruny thing that had the shape of a newborn. Half shaped like Lon. Half shaped like me. And half... something else entirely. The babe had been cleaned with a towel, so I finally had a good look.

"Aspen. Aspen Darling." I looked at Lon. "What do you think?"

"Well, I..."

Words caught in Lon's throat as I peeled back the cloth bundling my tiny joy. Lon was so green, I thought he'd die from the shock. My motherly intuition, however, took over and I examined Aspen with a speculative curiosity.

My daughter seemed to have several mutations. Instead of the purple-pink hue of a newborn, Aspen was blue. Almost green. I looked up. The midwife had a look on her face, staring at the baby, that I didn't care to interpret.

"Are you sure she's not ill? You've never heard of...?" I was at a loss for the right words.

I didn't finish my question, but she got the idea and said, "As far as I can tell with my training, Mrs. Darling, the child is perfectly healthy. Just..."

"Abnormal," I said.

"Right. Abnormal. Really, the only thing that seems to be wrong with her is that she's... well, blue. And I noticed some extra growth between the bases of her fingers. Like... like..."

"Webbing," I said.

"Yes. That. And of course the eyes. And the forehead is rather sloped, taking after neither you nor your husband. She does *seem* healthy, but you will, of course, want to take her to the hospital just to be sure."

"Of course."

BUTTERFLIES

Krimsey Enosh, Tuesday, March 26, 2250, 5:56 p.m.

BLUE. IT WAS THE last thing Krimsey remembered. Blue, and… a loud *thud.*

He had fallen. Blacked out. He'd pushed himself too hard. His name was called during the Transition Ceremony. No, that wasn't right. Was it? His name wasn't supposed to be called. But it had been. And… Elpida was dead. No, not dead. Missing. *Missing,* not dead. Taken. His mouth tasted like vomit. He didn't remember throwing up. But he did remember something else. After the ceremony, he was going to meet Cris. But Lamia followed him. He ran. He shouldn't have run.

Running looked suspicious.

Running was what the guilty did.

Was he? Guilty?

He remembered slamming into the floor, one of the blue lights along the restricted tunnel shone in his face, and the next second, he was out cold and hard.

But where was he now? How much time had passed?

Slowly, he opened his sleepy, crusted eyes.

Or, he thought he opened them. He only saw black. His senses were numb.

Am I dead?

His heartbeat thudded like a beast in his ears, so he wasn't dead. The smell of disinfectant was sour and pungent and made his groggy eyes burn. And… what was that sound?

Krimsey jolted upright. The movement tripped a sensor light. He squinted at the sudden, sharp brightness stabbing him between the eyes. He was on a bed. Someone with flaming red hair lay in a chair at the foot of it.

"Cris." Racing with adrenaline, Krimsey jumped off the bed.

"For Earth's sake!" Cris squinted at Krimsey with bleary red eyes and smeared drool from the corner of his mouth. He sat up in the chair.

"What are you doing here?" Krimsey examined the small medical room. There was a hazard bin on the floor. Supplies lined the counter across from him. There was a sink. Empty jars. Stuffed jars. An empty IV drip. Long, sharp steel tools. Hose-like tubes attached to unfamiliar boxes. "What happened?"

"Do you always wake up shouting?" Cris was still wiping the visible remains of sleep from his face and cheeks. "You gave me a heart attack."

A helpless, creeping dread crawled up Krimsey's spine. "Why are you here? Did you tell Lamia…?"

"What? No. She saw you sneak out from the Ceremony."

"Then why are you here?"

"They tracked your com, Krimsey," Cris said, his arms guarded across his chest.

Krimsey stood from the bed and swayed. His head pounded. His mouth was dry and sour and raw. His hollow belly clenched like a fist. He had definitely thrown up. Because if he hadn't, something would have come up now. The back of his throat tickled. He went over to the sink and spit out a yellow, watery glob.

"You're lucky they did," Cris said.

"Lucky they tracked me?" This was the worst news. Lamia had more power than he thought possible. He had often wondered, more a musing than something he believed an actual possibility, if their HPO-assigned coms were tracked. Now he knew.

"If you hadn't been tracked, well, Krim, you nearly died. They found and revived you." Cris said quietly.

"How do I nearly die?" Krimsey asked, turning on the water and wiping his mouth. He was frustrated that Cris was avoiding a direct question and wary of Cris's motives for being here. Krimsey couldn't flaunt his trust like a gullible child anymore. He turned the faucet off. "You either die or you don't."

The sound of faint footsteps perked his ears and he padded quietly to the large metal door. His ear recoiled from the cold steel of the door when he pressed his face against it. Krimsey thought he heard the footsteps getting closer.

As he listened, he noticed a wide helplessness in Cris's neon eyes. Krimsey pulled away from the door. "What?"

"What do you mean, 'what'? Nothing, I'm just—you needed help. Didn't want you to think I bailed," Cris said.

Krimsey shuffled away from the door. He put some distance between him and Cris, who slouched deeper into his chair. "So I nearly died and they just left you to stay with me? Where—?" His heart spiked painfully. Krimsey gasped. His mind went blank. He put a hand over his chest and doubled over.

Cris jumped to his feet. "Are you okay?" He sounded far away.

After seven long seconds of unbearable stabbing sensations where Krimsey's heart was, the pain subsided. He took a deep breath. The wind in his lungs tasted metallic. He coughed into his palm to see if there was any blood. Green specks of fluid came out.

It was happening. This was real. His body was changing. Terrified and vulnerable, still coughing, he looked around the room. His eyes drifted to the gadgets on the counter, landing on a surgical knife. Despite the waves of pain, Krimsey straightened as much as he could, slightly bent at the waist, and snatched up the knife.

"What are you doing?" Cris hissed.

Krimsey didn't feel safe here. And he felt weak. And the knife… What was he going to do with a knife? "I don't know," he said, walking to and pulling on the door with his free hand, knife clenched in the other. The door cracked open.

The stone halls beyond were unfamiliar. Smooth, dimly lit corridors. Generic curved walls. Ventilation. Blue light lined the floors. More tapping footsteps stood his neck hairs on alert.

Someone was coming.

He shut the door.

He wielded the knife as if he'd use it, held up and poised. His arms and legs tensed. Ready for combat—in poor form, probably—he waited. Cris took a seat on the bed behind him. It rustled with a metallic creak.

The two of them were so still, and waited for so long, the overhead sensor clicked the light off. When the sound of footsteps faded, Krimsey let his muscles uncoil, feeling ridiculous with a knife in his hand. The light clicked back on.

It was then that he realized he had been changed out of his formals into loose red medical cottons. Looking down at himself, he picked at the hem of the unfamiliar shirt, then looked at Cris.

"It wasn't me," Cris said with a rush.

"Wasn't...?"

Cris gestured at the new wardrobe.

"Oh." Krimsey's cheeks rose in temperature. "I didn't think you would have —that's not what I—" He sucked in a breath then exhaled loudly. Cris's proximity was suddenly very warm and prickly and he wondered if Cris felt the same heat. "I was just going to ask where my formals went."

Cris made a face, blew a breath of air, and pointed at the cupboard doors beneath the medical counter.

Krimsey groaned. "I threw up in them, didn't I?"

Cris nodded. Krimsey thought about retrieving the clothes, but felt even more awkward now and just shifted his feet and rubbed his arm. "Um. It's whatever... tell me again why they let you into my medical room?"

"I told them I was a concerned friend," Cris mumbled.

"Oh." Krimsey looked around the room for his com, pretending to be less invested in the conversation than he was. "Are you?"

"Am I what?"

"A concerned friend?"

Krimsey blinked at Cris expectantly. Cris, who had left too many questions half-answered, looked down at his feet. Several breaths of tense silence passed. When Cris turned his face back up at him, Krimsey's stomach gave a little lurch that wasn't entirely *un*-pleasant.

Cris looked away again. "Maybe I am," he said.

"Oh." It was Krimsey's turn to look away. Feeling inappropriate with a knife in his hand, he shimmied it into the deep pocket in his scrubs. "How long was I out?"

"I don't know, long enough for a nap."

"You've just been waiting for me to wake up?" He chewed on his top lip.

Instead of answering, Cris extended his arm, Krimsey's black com innocently displayed in his palm.

"I gave it a try," Cris said. "I was able to pinpoint that there *was* a ghost message but didn't find a way to send anything *to* your ghost or identify them. That's what you wanted, right? To contact the sender? Whoever they are, they're really good."

Krimsey picked up the com and pressed and held the "on" button. It flashed white once and flickered to life. Krimsey's eyes narrowed at him. "Come on, there has to be a way." He was more convinced now than ever that this ghost of a woman had dire information. Information he needed to save his sister from this corrupt place.

"There isn't. If there's a way, I'm not the one for you. I tried everything I know. I just needed you to know I tried."

Cris got up and turned toward the door.

"Wait." Krimsey's pulse quickened, not wanting him to leave and not knowing why. He shoved away the wriggling feeling in his stomach.

"What?"

"They took my sister," Krimsey said anxiously.

"What?"

"My sister! They took my sister. The HPO. I think... I don't know."

With one hand on the door, Cris met Krimsey's gaze. Butterflies came tumbling back into Krimsey's stomach.

"I heard what happened to her," Cris said consolingly. "I'm sorry."

"No," Krimsey snapped. "You didn't. They're saying that she died, but they're lying. I think they took her." He thought about his exchange with Zeph. He thought about all the lies. The disembodied gaze of Lamia Karuli. Felice. Stricken and red-eyed, passing by on the cliff. "No, I'm sure they did. They took her."

Cris blinked at him.

"Just… be careful. Don't trust the HPO."

Cris's teeth flashed. "I already don't trust them." He swung the door inward, stepped into the hall, and said, "See you on the other side."

After several minutes, the light sensor flicked off again. Krimsey kept still in the dark, wishing he had said to Cris what he really wanted to say. But instead, having no words to express the weird, twisted-up feelings inside him, Krimsey had opted to watch Cris close the door and leave.

He had more important things to worry about. How much time did he have? His lungs stung. He was changing. It was all happening so fast. He toyed with the knife in his pocket. The light flicked back on.

How do I find the woman from the com messages when Cris proved it impossible? How do I find Elpida? Krimsey remembered the look on Felice's face when she was leaving their residence. *Could Felice be an ally? No, I can't trust her. I don't know who is a friend and who is an enemy. But I need help.* He wished Cris hadn't left. *I could spend years searching these tunnels for Elpida. Shouldn't I at least try?* He stared at the door so long that the light flicked off again.

Who can I trust…?

His pulse sped up. The NWA kept the HPO in check. Just how involved was their oversight? Did they have eyes on Elpida? Krimsey spent his life believing he could trust the HPO—what made him think the NWA was trustworthy? *The two are in direct opposition to each other.* Trust had nothing to do with it. The NWA would seize any opportunity to search the HPO. They'd uncover the lies just as he had. They'd help him free his sister.

An idea continued to form. He knew what he could do to get the NWA's attention. Would he be able to pull it off, though?

He opened the door. He listened, starting down the tunnels, stopping at the intersections in order to route away from signs of activity. All the while, looking for numbers or landmarks, doors or rooms, or anything to hint as to where he was. He needed to orient himself. Get to the coms rooms.

He concealed himself around bends and corners any time he heard someone approaching. Each time he faced a choice, go left or go right, he led with his instinct. Whatever that was worth. What else did he have?

He took another turn and—

Collided directly into Lamia Karuli. Air whooshed out of him. The impact of their collision knocked Lamia back several steps and Krimsey flat on his back, reigniting the pain in his chest. She was accompanied by a human in traditional green scrubs. Krimsey reached on the floor for his com. It skittered across the ground.

"Excuse me," Lamia said.

Krimsey peeled his eyes from his com to look up. He blinked stars from his vision and wheezed.

Lamia stared at him down her long, thin nose. Recognition registered and her face contorted. "Krimsey... you caused quite a scare for us after the ceremony, didn't you? What are you doing down here? Come, you're lost." Lamia's sky-grey eyes glittered in the fluorescent light that hung overhead. She walked to the loose com, picked it up, and looked at her assistant. "Take this to head of coms security, will you, please? For decommissioning. He won't be needing it. Will you? Not where you're going."

The com switched hands and the assistant scurried down the tunnel.

Krimsey opened his mouth to speak but only a groan escaped. The wind was knocked out of him. Breathing was a struggle. His heavy lungs resisted every draw of breath. Lamia offered him a hand. When the stars in his vision faded, Krimsey took Lamia's hand and watched the assistant turn left into the fourth tunnel down.

"There," Lamia hefted him up with immense strength. "I don't bite." Her smile widened, creasing the aged lines in her face. "How are you feeling?"

He started to speak but his voice was muffled, the air in his lungs still strained. "I'm..."

Lamia wrapped long fingers around his bony shoulder. She directed him back down the way he'd come. Krimsey focused on his feet.

"As I thought," she said briskly, tapping down the hall in her white heels. "Breathless, you poor thing. You know, episodes leading to transition are common. Sometimes, instead of a mild episode, you may have a severe and painful black-out. These are typically brought on by great stress to the body. You're very lucky that we found you in time to revive you, Mister Enosh. Otherwise you'd be dead."

"Where are you taking me?" Krimsey found his breath. He looked back, counted steps, and hoped this was an opportunity to glean insight. He had no idea where he was. So he mapped each turn they took from the place of their encounter. He'd plan to head where the assistant had gone. Straight to coms security.

Lamia stopped and looked at him like he was an experiment gone wrong.

"Back to Medical, where else on Earth would I take you?" She let one eyebrow crawl halfway up her forehead.

Krimsey held his tongue, feeling a deep burning inside him.

"Right. Let's check for possible concussion. You're still recovering from the last one." They continued down the tunnel. "Then you are to go immediately to port for your transition. Further delay will kill you. Understood?"

"Uh-huh." Fifty-two strides straight; ten left; one hundred fifteen left; twenty right. Low murmurs at the end of the hall grew louder. His heart thudded and he remembered the knife in his pocket. "How long do I have?"

"What?" Lamia laughed. "You have somewhere to be?"

Lamia stopped to examine him, her hard stare turning cold in the blue light. "Less than twenty-four hours, I'd say. *Don't* try sneaking around again. You won't be so lucky next time. But before you go anywhere…" Lamia opened a door beside them. "Goodbyes are in order."

The room revealed a small, frail woman sitting on a bed. Sanjana.

"Krimsey," his mother exclaimed. "Oh Krimsey, I was so worried." She burst into tears, rushing to him, taking him in her arms, and squeezing the breath out of him.

When Krimsey pulled away to look at her, her cheeks were bright and shiny with tears. He felt Lamia's presence breathing down on them.

"I thought you were…" Sanjana lost her last word, wrapped in a hiccup.

"I know," Krimsey said.

Sanjana put a hand in his hair, patting it, then pulling him close again. "I need to remember this. How it feels to hold my baby." Sanjana choked on another word. "You're so grown up."

"I'm sorry I disappeared on you," he whispered, feeling a terrible knot in his stomach forming at what he had to do next.

Lamia cleared her throat from the doorway, letting her impatience be known. "Say your goodbyes. Time is short."

Krimsey kissed his mother on the cheek. "I love you."

He shoved his hand into his pocket and felt the cold steel weapon he'd stolen. Keeping his hand on the metal in his pocket, he barreled through the doorway into the corridor, expecting to surprise Lamia and knock her over on his way out. Her body was tough and sinewy and she stood her ground. An arm slashed out at him. He ducked, but she wrapped fingers like talons around his shoulder.

She was stronger than should have been possible. Grasping both his shoulders, she dragged him the rest of the way into the corridor and slammed him into the wall. The upward force of her grip had his toes brushing the ground.

"That wasn't very nice." Despite his screams of agony, Lamia's face was unmoving when her lips spoke. The inflection of her tone was how one might address a friend.

Eyes locked on his, piercing and cold, Lamia tightened her left hand, pushing him harder against the wall. With her right hand, the left still firmly pinning him, she wiped sweat from her brow.

He kicked forward to break the grip. *Pop.* A deep, agonizing sound, heard through the marrow of his bones, ripped pain through his pinned shoulder. He writhed against the pain, panting, kicking only air.

"Let me tell you how this is going to go," Lamia started calmly. "I am going to release your shoulder which, by the sound of it, is now dislocated—for which I am *truly* sorry. You are going to apologize to your dear mother here, who is appalled by your actions, and you're going to be accompanied immediately to port to begin your transition."

Her temple flexed.

He heard footsteps marching toward them. The sound bounced off the walls from all directions.

"You have approximately thirty seconds before things are about to go very differently, Krimsey Enosh," Lamia said.

Krimsey sighed, wincing through the pain, his hand still wrapped around the knife in his pocket. "Alright."

She let go. Krimsey's feet dropped onto concrete. His arm, and the entire socket adjoining it to his body, was on fire. He looked up to see her face, the marching footsteps nearing. Then, with his good arm, he slashed outward with the knife. Lamia moved, but too slow. Unsuspecting. The blade dug deep into the side of her thigh. She buckled as the knife came free, her knees thudding onto the floor, her mouth open in a silent scream.

Dripping bloody knife and all, he ran. As hard as he could, he ran.

Guilty. Definitely guilty this time.

Transitus

Felice Karuli, Tuesday, March 26, 2250, 6:42 p.m.

"Elpida Enosh? Oh yes," Felice said, blinking several times at the severe-looking NWA rep standing before her and casting a look in Aimie's direction. The guide made herself as small as possible near a closet door. *Why, yes, Mr. Boyd,* Felice thought, behind what must have been a very confused-looking smile, *every damn alarm in my head is currently screaming. Thank you for your concern.*

"'*Oh yes,*' indeed." In his stubbornly superior tone, he drew out each of his syllables. His eyes wandered down to Felice's muddy sandals and back up.

Thwarting further commentary on her disarray, Felice said, "But Mr. Boyd, sir, did you travel all the way here just for Enosh? There must be some confusion. Enosh died. Sudden onset Pneumaphage. She's not *missing.*"

"*Just* for Enosh? No, no, no, it seems quite a mess is going on here right under our noses. The New World Alliance sent me to 'crack the proverbial whip.' So to speak. Logs missing. Reports are always late or incomplete. Straying subject matter. Improper transition documentation. How are we on the Mainland supposed to keep supporting your operations if your protocols are consistently questionable? And I came just in time. It seems you have a riot on your hands."

"Riot? No, this is…" *Careful with your words.* "I have this under control." Just then, the front door to the lobby outside slammed shut. "Anyway, you're here now. You must be tired. We weren't prepared for your arrival—"

"You weren't supposed to be." He cleared his throat. "I wouldn't have had such an… *interesting* reception. Yes, show me to my room. It's, what, five? Six?"

"Almost seven," she said, checking her com. Felice forgot Mainlanders didn't use coms.

"Right, well. I'll bring my things by and you can show me around."

"I'm sorry?"

"You don't expect I came all this way unannounced just to give you time to clean things up, do you? No, I'll start my assessments tonight. If there's anything I feel we missed or glazed over, we'll schedule those for the remainder of the week."

Felice looked at Aimie.

"I need a Karuli, not a secondhand guide," Mr. Boyd said.

"I'm sorry Mr. Boyd, but as you can see, my time is a bit constrained."

"Lamia, then."

"She's on her way, but we're both quite—"

"Not a problem. I can keep up," he said with a toothy, upturned smile. "I will observe you and how you manage your… *constrained* time."

"Aimie?" Felice turned to the guide again, talking softly. "Will you please assist Mr. Boyd in obtaining his belongings and bring them here? Which guides are slated to sleep in this suite?"

"I can find out."

"Do. And relocate them."

"We'll be short a few beds," Aimie commented. "In the other suites."

"I know. They'll need to make it work." Felice smiled wide at Mr. Boyd. "We want to make sure our new guest is comfortable here."

Felice collapsed on one of the suite beds when Mr. Franklin Boyd and the guide left the building. She closed her eyes for a minute, which stretched into thirty. The sensation of falling jolted her back awake.

"Lamia," she pinged, rubbing her eyes. *"I need you. How much longer do I delay?"*

"Outside."

Felice peeked out the window. Lamia strode down the empty port path, holding a light windbreaker over her braid. Somehow, her sandals were spotless. Felice was almost surprised her mother wasn't wearing pumps. Then Felice saw the slight twinge in Lamia's face and the limp in her leg and rushed out of the room. The remaining parents, who impatiently sat on chairs in the lobby, stood when Felice entered.

She held up her hand. "A moment."

"But—"

"*A moment,*" Felice said, frazzled. Her mother entered, clearly in pain, despite the impeccable appearance. Felice lowered her voice. "We need to talk."

They closed themselves in the guide suite. Lamia sat on the far bed in the corner and beckoned for Felice to join her.

"We have about… five minutes," Felice said. "A rep from the NWA just arrived, but I'm assuming you knew that."

"I'm aware." Lamia's gaze bore holes into Felice's forehead.

"What happened to your leg?" Felice asked. Lamia's eyes were misty. "Mother, we need to fix this before he—"

"Fix what, Felice? All I see are disgruntled parents, a missing child—nothing we haven't addressed before—"

"We haven't addressed *eight families* before." Felice hissed under her breath. "They all know Prae was kidnapped and it wasn't even *us*."

"As I said, disgruntled parents." Lamia's tone was hushed and controlled.

"The rep knows about Elpida. How does the rep know about Elpida?" Her breaths were frantic. When was she going to put all this to an end? How?

"Elpida is dead. I'll show him the logs."

"And the rest of the NVTs you want? The lab? What if he finds the lab?" Her voice was increasingly loud. A half-crazed laugh escaped.

"That's impossible. He won't find the lab, we have it wrapped too tightly under control for that to ever be an issue." Lamia's voice was increasingly calm. Controlled. Quiet.

"Cyn Jones?"

"Yes, well she's the real problem here, isn't she? What did Ive tell you?"

Felice ignored the question. "What does Cyn have to gain by kidnapping Prae?"

"Shut us down, as you may have already suspected. I believe Mr. Boyd is her doing." She waved a hand. Felice knew her mother enough to know that she was hiding other truths behind that masked expression. The corner of her eye twitched and her mouth was stiff. "Don't worry about the specifics. But I do have a favor to ask."

Felice was done with favors. She wanted answers. She wished she could pull the information out of her mother. Make her slip. But Lamia would recognize the attempt if Felice tried. "Mother, I—"

"Krimsey Enosh."

Her mouth went dry at the mention of another Enosh. "What about him?" *What horrible new thing will she ask of me?* "He's transitioning. Did something go wrong?"

Felice focused on Lamia's tight lips when she answered. "He knocked himself out earlier. Almost transitioned and suffocated himself in the tunnels. I gave him a small dose of suppressant. It revived him. Quite effectively." Lamia looked down at her leg.

"Suppressant?"

Lamia stiffened. "What did Ive tell you, Felice?"

"Was Ive supposed to have told me about a suppressant? Why the hell are you keeping secrets from me? What did you tell him to make him so Earthforsaken devoted to you?"

"We need to focus." Lamia's knees pressed together and she tapped her thumbs like drums. She was nervous. The power between them shifted. "These details aren't important. I need you to—"

"What is the suppressant?" Felice raised her voice and stood, enunciating each word with precision. Her veins thudded, electrified. A mental fog lifted, like white noise coming to a stop.

She had the power.

Lamia didn't stand to meet her. She tilted her chin up, her eyes lifted, her hands folded in her lap. This was her attempt to keep control. Control she had already lost.

"Well? I know you have secrets." Felice shouted loud enough to hurt herself. "Tell me. Tell me, or—" Shuffling parents in the lobby stopped to hover just outside the door. Felice turned around and stomped toward the closed suite door and turned the knob but held it closed.

"Is that a threat?" Lamia's lips hardly moved, stiff, like her voice.

"Maybe it is. I need a reason. I need to know why I am helping you cover this shit up, or I'm not doing it anymore." Whatever the reason, whatever the secret, Felice had already made up her mind. Felice pulled the door open a crack. She peeked out. An anxious energy, tapping fingers, bouncing feet, was settling over the parents who remained. Several stepped away from the door and sat. Shouting their sins out the door would not be the way she exposed her mother. It had to be thought out. Calculated. Just like her.

Felice closed the door. Walked back to the bed. Crossed her arms.

Worry settled into Lamia's body. In the whites of her eyes. In the skin pulled tight over her knuckles. In the way she licked her lips before she spoke. "I'll tell you everything, my love. Sit with me." Her shoulders dropped, her body deflated. Like letting loose a long, deep breath. "You're *transitus*, Felice. You're dying," Lamia said before Felice could sit. "The cure we seek is for you."

Felice half-hovered over the bed, about to sit. She swallowed and collapsed, nearly missing the bed entirely. Every nerve screamed. Her throat was like sand. Her hair stood on end. Her ears rang. She adjusted herself on the bed, easing herself into an upright sitting position next to her mother.

This was another grab for power. An attempt at the upper hand. Lamia was desperate.

She cleared her throat but the back of her tongue was stuck, dry, to her windpipe. Instead, she gagged and coughed.

"Are you alright? This news must be—"

"Don't. I'm—" Felice looked at the white tile between her knees. *Leave it to Lamia Karuli to tell her daughter she is dying, right in the middle of a shit storm. All to gain back control.* "What, so I have Pneumaphage?"

"Yes." Lamia's tone was even. Hard. Not the rounded, kind, gentle voice she reserved for lies. But also not the voice she reserved for softening a blow.

"When you say suppressant... You mean you have something that delays transitioning." It wasn't a question, but a clarification. It made sense now. Crashing in her ears drowned out rational thought. The reason why Ive was so cool with Lamia's plan was this. He loved Felice so much, he didn't care what else came burning down.

Another unrounded, "*Yes.*"

"You haven't told me of the suppressant before because you're using it on me. How?"

"Do you want that answer?"

"Ive," Felice said. "He's been giving it to me."

Lamia sniffed and looked out the window. "The suppressant isn't working anymore. It's a bandaid to a fatal wound. You're running out of time."

"And you kept Cyn from me because...?" The connection was just there, out of reach. *Why?*

"She's trying to stop our cure." Lamia said.

"Why? Why does Cyn want to stop our cure?"

"Because of the children?" Lamia said. "Same reason you wanted to quit."

"There wasn't always children. There wasn't always Rumi. Cyn has been here long before then. Ive said her signatures go back years."

Half of Lamia's face glowed from the light coming in through the window. Felice saw it, then, as Lamia sat on the bed beside her, hands folded neatly in her silken lap. Pain. Her face was tightly wrapped in all the wrong places. Her lips curled slightly down instead of up. Her eyes were lined with subtle tones of pink instead of black and they drooped in the corners, as if she lacked the energy to pep up her gaze with her regular *zing*. Her cheeks were hard and pursed.

"Your guess is as good as mine, Felice."

"Okay." Fellice swallowed. *She's lying. Again.*

"Now," Lamia continued, "are you going to help me reign this woman in so we can finish our work?"

Felice consciously relaxed her shoulders, her skin still ablaze with shock. Blinking, smiling, ribs shaking, rounding her words into a palatable package, she said, "Yes. Of course. I don't want to die."

"Good. Because I can't lose you." Lamia's hand quavered by Felice's brow. Tucking a strand of hair behind Felice's ear, Lamia let out a sigh and a tear at the same time.

Felice wasn't sure whose lie was better.

"So, what did you need me to do about Krimsey?" Felice asked.

Lights Out

Krimsey Enosh, Tuesday, March 26, 2250, 6:35 p.m.

KRIMSEY RAN THROUGH THE tunnels until his vision began to turn purple with pain and cold sweat trickled down his sides. He hadn't gone far. He'd gotten all the way back to the turn Lamia's assistant had taken to get to coms security. He caught his breath in long, shaky gulps, leaning against the tunnel wall, trying to stay quiet. The marching footsteps that had approached during his encounter with Lamia hadn't chased him in pursuit. It was so quiet he could hear his pulse thudding in his ears and the burbling sounds in his gut. While he thought the silence strange, he was grateful.

He pushed sticky hair off his forehead, taking a few steps down the tunnel. He repressed his breath. Only allowing it to come in shallow gasps. Doing so helped to ease the sharp stabs his dislocated shoulder gave him if his chest expanded too much. Or if he moved too quickly. Or if he turned his head.

He walked slowly, turning down a new tunnel and following the sound of a faint electronic hum. He kept his ears perked. Every shift in the soundscape made him turn his head. Was that *tick-tick-tick* in the distance just the air vents turning, or was it the sound of a person planning to sneak up on him?

He walked down the tunnels long enough to relax a little, writing the sounds off for what they were. *Clicks, clacks*, and *bings* of machinery and electronics doing their operational duties. But why had no one followed him? He had stabbed the president. *Stabbed* her. Right in the thigh. The fullness of that realization had barely hit him yet. He feared the answer to why no one followed. He had an idea. He was probably going to die soon. He tried not to think about it.

Besides, he didn't plan to stay in the tunnels long.

He stopped. The door in front of him separated this tunnel and the section beyond. A slight depression in the floor indicated a downward slope. Buzzing electricity came from behind that door. He pushed it open with a wince, remembering he was in pain. The plan was first to find a new com to communicate with the NWA, and second to take out the HPO power. Cause chaos. The people working at the port office were hardly NWA, but they were close enough and would step in if something was off. They would investigate, seize, and search. They could find Elpida.

The doors lining the tunnels in this section were marked by numbers. Blue lights lined the sides of the floors. Krimsey distracted himself from his pain with the smooth surface of the walls against his palm.

He opened the doors of several com rooms, only going inside when he reached one labeled *515*. This room was dark. From what he could see, though, it was the one he was looking for. Light from the tunnel hall flooded around him, pouring into the room. Small, blinking electronics lined the far wall. And there were shelves stacked tall in the middle of the room, full of boxes. He was sure to find a new com to use in one of those. He'd need the com so he could listen to the com links for news of Elpida being found. And, if the coms were tracked by location, most likely someone from the NWA would contact him after he did what he was planning to do. They would have questions. He would give them answers. He felt his way along the wall for the lights. They came on, bright and fluorescent. Then, thinking better of it, he turned off the lights and closed the door. His eyes adjusted to the dim room by the light of electronics.

Looking and feeling inside a box on a shelf, he found a pile of decommissioned coms. He grabbed one, put it on, and peeked into the next box.

Boxes upon boxes were filled with old coms, cables, metal scraps, and unidentifiable junk. Nothing here looked like it would activate his new com, but he continued to rummage. He stopped every few seconds to listen for outside sound. He tossed his fifth searched box back on its shelf and started toward the black air-conditioner-sized boxes that hummed against the rear wall of the room.

Three rows of the machines were stacked on top of each other, three high and three wide. These boxes powered electricity throughout the entire HPO. He twisted the blood-crusted knife in his hand, eyeing the short, thick, color-coded wires at the rear of each box. Some wires connected the boxes together and some ran up the wall, joining at a corner in the room where there was a hole in the ceiling. If he jammed his knife at random into the cords, certainly something of the chaotic nature would happen. He hoped all the power would shut down. That would be a bright flashing beacon to the overseeing NWA. But was he really going to go at this with random hope? He didn't really know what he was doing.

Either way, he needed to first activate his com so he could confirm his plan worked. He wasn't leaving this island until Elpida was safe, without any doubt.

Krimsey walked over to the shelves of dusty boxes and rummaged some more, looking for a long, skinny device made of plastic and metal that would re-commission his com. After sifting diligently, one-armed, through the contents of every box in the room more than once, Krimsey began to lose hope in his plan. While he stared at the same box for the third time, tilting it toward the electronic lights to see better, the air conditioning kicked on. He released the box.

"Agh!" He heaved a sigh at the ceiling, the effort of the breath costing him a wave of sharp pain. Then, he caught a glimpse of something on the top shelf. He climbed up on top of the lower shelves, pushing through the swelling of his shoulder, and peeked at the dusty mess above. There was a jumble of junk up here he hadn't noticed earlier. He shuffled carefully through the contents, pausing occasionally at a new shushing sweeping sound outside. He ignored it. Mostly. His ears kept telling his brain to get out of here. Small doses of adrenaline spiked his blood.

Aha.

From the junk shelf, Krimsey pulled out a long, silver device with buttons and switches on one side, and two com ports on the other. He had only ever seen a com activation done jointly. With one com tech plugged in to one port, and the newly assigned com plugged in to the other port. But he knew a com could also be set up independently.

Krimsey climbed down from the shelves, trying his best not to do anything too jarring, and fumbled with the device, shoving the battered, old com from his palm into the port. A green light appeared.

That looks promising....

The green blinked at Krimsey, then turned a steady white. He examined the buttons and flips on the side, contemplating.

Now what? I'm screwed....

He tried flipping up a switch. It flashed red. Not sure if that was as bad as it seemed or not, Krimsey tried more buttons and flips, gently reaching out with his mind at the same time, seeing if he felt anything.

Then, a sudden jolt of electronic awareness buzzed around him, as if in invitation. Krimsey followed the flow of energy with his mind, and found himself inside the com settings. He toggled the settings a while longer, finding some mild success, but security barriers within the com blocked him at every turn. Just when he was ready to give up—either that or throw the whole thing across the room—he felt the com release a security barrier. He was linked.

Krimsey's heart flipped backwards in his chest. He popped the com out of the device. It fumbled between his fingers and dropped to the floor. He picked it up and placed it firmly into his ear. A message was waiting for him. Probably an old ping, left over from the previous owner. He turned back around to the wall of stacked boxes of blinking, flashing electronics. He stared at the wall, tentatively toggled some outer buttons that always seemed to flick back to the previous position, and sighed.

In the com, a new message appeared. His heart twisted.

Before he could open the message, a sound snapped his attention to the front of the room. At first, he associated the sound with the com, but his attention landed on the door, which had just swung open.

Light shot across the room, bright and piercing.

Krimsey's skin jumped at the sight of a greasy blonde head in the spilling light. Only one person bleached her hair so aggressively that it was as bright as the moon. Felice Karuli. He crouched and grasped the knife in his hand harder, concealing himself behind a large box on a low shelf in the middle of the room as the light switched on.

Had the HPO sent her for him?

"Krimsey?"

Blood turned to ice, throat constricted, vision sparking in his peripherals, Krimsey jumped and knocked a box off a shelf. Its contents spilled and clattered across the aisle.

Footsteps came around the side of the room and Krimsey shifted around the corner of the shelf to stay hidden. More footsteps. Krimsey made himself as small as possible. He looked at the knife gripped in his palm and set it on the floor as if it had suddenly become poison.

"I see your com light, dear. Reflecting off the metal shelving." Felice's voice rasped.

Krimsey heard a rustle and a second light switched on, illuminating the room like the inside of a fluorescent sun. His heart spiked and he picked up the knife again, his knuckles hardening around it. Krimsey stood.

Felice's blonde hair was wet and patted flat against her head in knots. Her eyes were dark and red and swollen. She wore a tattered black dress, muddied at the hem. Her sandals were brown and soggy. Chipped black polish poked out through the mud on her toenails.

Hiding the knife behind him, Krimsey stared back at the unmoving Felice Karuli.

"What are you doing in here, Krimsey? Did you get my messages?" She stepped forward once, then twice, and stopped. She sighed when Krimsey didn't answer.

Messages? He quickly pulled up the pings on his new com. Timestamps were both for today. The first, which had appeared as soon as he'd gotten into the com, said, *"Access granted. You're wel-come."* The second, *"Come outside. Promise I won't bite."*

Krimsey took a step back, his eyes suspicious, narrow and watering from the brightness of the room. "Why weren't you at the ceremony today? Were you with my sister?"

Felice raised a brow. "No...."

"Why did you help me activate the com?"

"I'm your friend. I wanted to show you that." That was the most suspicious statement Krimsey had ever heard.

"How did you know where to find me?"

Felice pointed up into the corner of the room. "You're in the most secure section of the entire HPO. There are cameras everywhere."

"I know she's not dead," Krimsey blurted, projecting strength, yet feeling smaller and smaller with each step she took down the opposite aisle toward him.

She rubbed her temple. "You're right."

"Don't even—wait, what?"

"You're right," she said. "She's alive."

He was falling through space. Earth dropped out from under him and he was lurching down, down, down. Relief spilled down his cheeks. He *was* right. A small part of him, the part of him that didn't *want* to rebel, the part of his psyche whispering doubt, thought that this entire scenario could have been all in his head.

"Is she okay?" His voice cracked past the tears of mixed emo-tion. It wasn't the question he planned to ask, but it was the one he needed to ask.

"She's okay."

"How can I believe anything you say? They sent you to get me."

Felice looked through the shelves and boxes to meet Krimsey's eyes. He stepped back. "My... mother." Felice sniffed. "She sent me, yes. Because you trust me."

"No one said I trust you."

Felice took three more steps. She was halfway down the aisle now.

"She sent me because she assumed you'd trust me. She wants me to help you find Cyn Jones. She knows you were contacted by her."

"Cyn Jones?"

"The hacker."

"I don't know anything about Cyn Jones. Where is Elpida?" Krimsey rasped.

"In a lab."

"Where?"

"I'm not telling you that because you'll die trying to get to it on your own."

"Lot of help you are, then." The electronic boxes behind him taunted him, the low hum was like a laugh.

"My mother did a number on your shoulder. Let me help you," she said, hyper-focused on his arm without the knife. When he didn't move, she added. "I'm not going to hide the fact that I was sent to earn your trust so I could use you and stop... whatever it is you're doing in here. That's what the president wants me to do. But I'm not interested in doing any of that. I'm going to help you. And in return, you're going to help me. I think we can both get what we need."

"Prove it."

"Let me fix your shoulder first. She told me it's dislocated. Put the knife down."

The light at the back wall flickered. Air sunk like ice cubes from a ventilation shaft at the fork. Krimsey was silent as he leaned against the wall. He put down the knife but remained wary. When she took a step, he sidestepped.

Felice clicked her tongue. "Krimsey, everything I've ever done for you has been to help you and your family with your successful transition. That hasn't changed."

Krimsey wheezed with tears in his eyes. Either he was transitioning, or the swelling shoulder was getting worse. "Then tell me where my sister is or I'll die looking for her. I will. I'm not leaving land until I know she's safe."

"Krimsey," her voice became hard. "I see that look in your eyes. You're feeling defiant. I see you're ready to take down whatever stands in your path that might be a threat."

He met her tired eyes.

"Save that Earthforsaken look for the real enemy. This is bigger than you know." Her words could crack stone. "I'm not the threat."

Alarmed, he blinked at her and tensed his good arm.

"Whatever you are thinking you can *do*—in less than twenty-four hours before transitioning, at that—it's an impossible task. There is nothing you can do. Not on your own. If you don't squash that fire right now, Krimsey? I will. I will destroy you if I think you're a threat to the livelihoods of the people on this island. Do you want to know who the real enemy is?"

She paused, perhaps waiting for a guess.

"The real enemy is my mother," she said. "I'm the only one that can get you out of this mess. And I believe Cyn Jones—the hacker that contacted you this morning—is the only one that can get us out of this mess."

"I don't know anything about Cyn Jones. If I knew where she was, I'd be there now," Krimsey said.

"We can figure that out together," she said.

"Alright."

"Can you trust that I am on your side?"

Krimsey mulled her words in his head and knew he had no other choice but to trust her. But could she somehow prove her loyalty? "Disable it." He jerked his head to the back of the room.

"Disable what?"

"All of it. Then you can help me with my shoulder."

"All of… what? The power?"

"Yes. Is there a problem?"

"No… I mean, yes, but why?"

"I want the NWA's attention. That's the only way I will trust you. Disable the power, alert the government. Unless you have other intentions?"

"That's not—" She sighed. Felice strode toward him from the other side of the shelves. Krimsey took a step away. She stopped and crouched to look between two boxes at him. "It probably won't get the NWA's attention in the way you're thinking, but it might do something else."

"Okay," he said, crossing his arms. She would not be able to persuade him from his plan.

"There is an NWA rep on the island. It'll get his attention. I don't know what the consequences will be." She looked up and to the right, then looked at the boxes behind Krimsey. "Fuck it. It's kind of brilliant." She reached through the shelves. "Give it to me. The knife. Give it."

Twisting the handle between his fingers, Krimsey weighed the pros and cons of trusting Felice. Pros, she could help him and they could work together. Cons, she could be bluffing and be doing exactly what she said she was sent to do. She could cost him his life and Elpida's. He had to trust that the conviction and concern in her eyes were real. He placed the base of the knife into her palm. The tip faced him, pointing at his heart.

"When I do this, all of forsaken Earth will break loose. It'll most literally be chaos. Do you know what you'll do next?"

Krimsey shrugged.

Felice let out a dry laugh. "Specific." She moved to the back of the room with the knife.

"Wait," Krimsey said. "How do I know you've done it?"

"Trust me, you'll know."

"How?"

"Emergency coms communication will stay live, so long as individual com batteries are charged. No tracking, though, which is a feature the HPO uses to keep tabs on everyone. And everything that's powered by our solar grid in a five-kilometer radius"—she opened the plastic face of a box—"will go dead." Felice slammed the knife into the wiring. The room went dark.

Defense

Zeph Carmak, Tuesday, March 26, 2250, 7:20 p.m.

SURROUNDED BY CABLES AND buzzing monitors in a house in the middle of a valley, a gigantic grin split across Zeph's face.

"Did he really shut everything down? That is so cool."

"Wait a minute." Cyn frowned at the line of numbers and symbols on the screen before her. "Someone is with him." Cyn's face dropped. "Felice Karuli."

"Do you think he is in trouble?"

"Can't tell. Maybe it's a trap. Shit."

"What? Is he okay?"

"Shit. No."

"What is going on?"

"No, *he's* fine but *we're* not. Forsaken Earth, motherfu—" Cyn sucked in a breath and furiously tapped on her keyboard.

Zeph looked at the screen. Numbers and letters raced three or four times as fast as they had been going before.

Cyn muttered something.

"Damn it."

"Tell me!"

"Bug off for a bit, why don't you?" Cyn snapped, looking at the screen, then paused, sparing a quick side glance at Zeph. "Fuck. I didn't mean to—damn it, you're crying."

"I am... *fine...* I cannot control it. The emotions. I will go wait outside."

"No, damn it, just stay. Stop asking questions." Cyn squinted at the screen, hit a string of keys, squinted again, and looked back down at the keys in her lap. "Shutdown punctured some holes in my defense. I'm holding them off but if I stop, they'll be able to find us. They'll use us to cover their asses with the NWA."

"What are we going to do?"

"Looks like it also bought Lamia a lot of time. *Fuck*, she's too good. She's already got the rep off her back."

"Can you just contact the rep?"

"Doesn't use coms. Besides, some undocumented signal contacting him? He might not even trust it and Lamia would be all over that. I have a thought."

"What?"

"How well do you swim?"

Do You Trust Her?

Krimsey Enosh, Tuesday, March 26, 2250, 7:25 p.m.

"Who the hell do you think you are?"

Krimsey's ears perked at the familiar voice in his new com. He trailed at Felice's heels, going down a tunnel. He didn't know which tunnel, or where, just that Felice was all he had right now.

Krimsey grasped at the message and replied. *"Cyn Jones!"*

"You should have just been on your way kid. I told you to stay out of trouble."

"I need to see her. My sister. I will not leave this Earthforsaken island until I know she's safe. Can you help?"

Cyn didn't reply right away.

"Be at port in thirty minutes. Lose Felice."

"Thirty minutes? Port is hours from here. I'd have to hike down the—"

"There's an emergency transport. It has its own power reserves. It'll get you here in ten. I'll tell you how, just loose Felice."

"Transport?" He had never heard of such a thing traversing fifteen kilometers in ten minutes. He had also never heard of so much corruption packed into a governing body. He clenched his jaw.

"Felice Karuli stays with me. She helped me."

"Lose her. Or no deal."

Krimsey frowned and looked at Felice. "I know where Cyn is."

"Where?"

"She doesn't want you to come."

"I'm coming." Felice's tone was not to be negotiated with. Then she added, even more serious, "Tell her that I shut the power off."

"She doesn't seem to be happy about that."

"Tell her I know about the suppressant. Tell her that's why I'm helping."

Krimsey relayed the message. Cyn's reply was delayed.

"Alright. Destroy your coms and come. Both of you. But hurry."

His heart pounded when he heard the white noise of waves. Grey light glowed just around the next bend. Together, Felice and Krimsey emerged from the tunnels onto a short platform high above a crashing ocean. Waves and wind rioted, booming against the rocks below and spraying their faces with salt. Gulls stood out against grey-and-blue-streaked clouds. The jutting precipice showed them expansive views of the island-dotted *Transitus* Bay. To their left, stark, looming mountains bordered the grassy port town of the HPO's East Antarctic community.

Krimsey was amazed. As promised, the emergency transport had gotten them from the HPO underground to port in just minutes.

A gull standing on the edge flared its wings at the sudden sight of them, squawked, and took a nosedive off the precipice. Felice carefully clambered across a narrow ridge to the left of the tunnel opening along the battered cliffside.

Together, they clambered across a narrow ridge, the only way to port. The sea frothed beneath their feet. Felice's erratic breath was audible. Clinging to the side of the cliff, her knuckles were white from strain.

A brooding cloud of emotion attached to Krimsey and stuck like sap. Unsure of its origin, he tried to mentally swipe at the emotion like a fly. Dissipate the coming storm. Distracted, he stumbled over a jagged step. His balance faltered, wavering on the edge of the cliff. Felice was quick to react. Her hand lashed out behind her, catching his elbow.

"Thanks." He grimaced.

She released him when his balance was restored. After a few more moments of labored breathing, she asked, "So where exactly *is* Cyn, then?"

"Port."

"Yes, but precisely *where?*"

"I don't know. Just keep your eyes on the ground. She has a plan." *I hope.*

Felice clambered up and over another large, jagged rock and offered a hand to Krimsey. When he refused to take it, she turned and said, "You do realize everyone and their mothers—literally—*and* the NWA—are out here today?"

"That's what you said."

"We need to steer clear of the middle of port." Felice hoisted herself over a large outcropping, wedging her sandals into footholds. Her black dress collected smears of grey mud.

"Why?"

"Because my mother is there, Krimsey." She sounded angry. "Do I need to spell it out for you? We need to stay out of the way of whatever mess is pooling around her. Trust me, you don't want to get caught after what we just did. Port may be a shitshow we can just slip through without being noticed, but you'd be surprised at how in control Lamia gets when handling shit. I don't know what Cyn has planned, but it better be flawless."

Soon, they intersected with the main footpath, which eventually turned into Footpath Main of the HPO. It meandered up a valley where two impeding mountains converged. The flat-top mountain on the left, sharp and boxed, housed the HPO and Karuli Crag, not seen from this vantage. The one on the right paralleled the cliffsides of Karuli and joined the left at the opposite end of the pinnacles and The Bowl. This mountain cascaded toward the ocean. Rolling hills skirted its foothills, which gently cupped the rear of the port town. The path meandering between both was smoothed by time and thousands of feet, and dotted with wildflowers. Krimsey started down the rolling, grassy hills toward town. Felice grabbed him. "What are you doing? I said we need to avoid the middle of port. This takes you right through the heart of it."

The sprawling, battered town seemed to snooze in the dim hours of the evening. The only sounds he heard were the crashing waves and the crunch of his own footsteps. "The town looks dead to me, Felice. We need to get there so we can find Cyn."

Krimsey yanked himself free of Felice and continued toward the town. As they descended through the grassy knolls, Felice cleared her throat. "Can I make a suggestion?"

"No."

Felice made a sound in the back of her throat.

"Fine. What is it?"

"May we at least avoid the most visible path around? Otherwise, you're just making it too easy for us to be caught."

Krimsey turned on his heels. "What would you suggest, then? Cyn needs to be able to find us."

Felice looked over her shoulder. Krimsey followed her gaze to a rocky animal path between a stack of boulders. He couldn't see where it led, but the path was filled with brambles.

"These boulders lining the foothills go directly behind the town. We'll blend in if we go that way and cut behind the town. It's that or...." Felice's gaze flicked back down the path. Between two sun-battered buildings, a dark blue figure started up the hill toward them. Tattered robes trailed behind the figure, head hunched down.

Krimsey snatched Felice's shoulder, scrambled up the path, and pushed her down into the brambles behind a boulder. He crouched in front of her.

"Good choice," she said under her breath.

Krimsey glowered back at her and held his tongue. He put his finger over his lips.

"Though that was definitely not my mother. Could that have been Cyn?"

"Do you ever stop talking? For Earth's sake." Krimsey sighed. The boulder concealing them was half the size of a house, but they were too close to the main path. He peeked around the edge. The figure continued at a brisk pace up the hill.

"We can hide behind that cluster of boulders and wait," he said, pointing behind them. "We won't be seen from there when the person passes by."

"Then what?"

"I'm figuring it out, ok? You're the one that said it's not safe. Just go," he hissed. "Over there." Krimsey pointed at a large cluster of black rocks. Felice started forward and he grabbed her. "Crawl. Otherwise we'll be seen."

He glanced up at Felice when she didn't get down to crawl. She looked at him sideways with a tight-lipped grin.

"What?"

She smiled wider, teeth flashing as she turned around and crouched forward. "Nothing."

Krimsey followed suit, crouching into the thorny bushes and belly-crawling along the damp animal trail.

"Why were you smiling?"

"You're just… different than I remember. More confident."

Krimsey was silent. The mud streaked down his chest, dragging his shirt, making it heavy. "Yeah, well, I'm not a kid anymore," he grunted. Felice's head popped up briefly. "Stay low!"

"There's a rock," she hissed back at him. "Watch it."

"Just be quiet."

Belly to the dirt, they shifted their weight on their elbows and knees. Krimsey paused several times to hear over the rustling of his clothes. He heard the crunch of gravel not far off.

"Hurry," he whispered, looking over his shoulder. His view of the main path was obscured. Nothing moved but a small bird that landed on a branch. It twittered a crisp birdsong and twisted its head. Krimsey condemned the bird in his mind. Ahead of him, Felice reached the hiding spot and ducked behind the cluster of boulders. Krimsey continued along the muddy path and quickly joined Felice. He stood and peered around the first boulder through the thicket from which they had come.

Minutes passed in breathless anticipation. He let his breath out slowly, trying to time the rattling wheeze with the *shooshh* of the wind to mask the sound. Felice was quiet, peering and patient behind him. Focusing on the sound of steady waves in the distance and sea birds, Krimsey realized that the methodical sound of gravel crunching had stopped.

A deep, mulling presence drifted over him like a sudden thundercloud. The sensation was like receiving unhinged emotion from another *transitus*, only this experience was gripping. As if two hands cupped over his shoulders and a breath blew down his neck. He shrugged his shoulders and twitched, turning back at Felice. He stared at her with his mouth half-open, brows springing into a frown. Felice looked back at him with an unchanged expression of curiosity.

"*Was that you?*" he mouthed the words.

Felice mirrored his look and shook her head.

Are you safe? A familiar voice boomed as if speaking directly into his ear.

He staggered against the rock behind him and froze. His heart did a somersault. His ears burned. Back and palms flat against the boulder, he thought this had to be a trick. A fluke. A glitch in the universe messing with his mind. He squinted harder at Felice. Her face hadn't shifted to reflect any acknowledgement of the voice. She eyed him with concern and tilted her head.

The voice belonged to Zeph. Zeph hadn't been lying. Telepathy and mind-reading?

That is correct. Will you come out of hiding now? Each syllable echoed like a crystal bell.

Felice opened her mouth to speak, but Krimsey stepped out from hiding and she squeaked and swiped after him.

A familiar *transitus* stared back at him through the bushes, peering out from the dark cloak, standing in the middle of the path at the top of the intersecting animal trail. Dark skin, dark yellow eyes, and a bald head that shined in the dark. Zeph. A slightly twisted smirk showed under their hood.

"You really can read minds." Krimsey gaped. He took a step, then tripped on a root and stumbled forward. "How is this—"

Zeph put a quick finger against their lips. "Shh." They looked over their shoulder at the town, then back at him. *Do not talk.* Their eyes shifted to focus on something behind him. Zeph's aura turned hostile. He looked back at Felice, who had stepped out of hiding.

I refused to believe them, Krimsey thought, remembering Zeph's earlier offer to find the com woman together. *They must hate me.* He took a step back. "Did she send you to find us?"

Shut up, Zeph said to him in their slightly frightening, ringing, telepathic voice. Zeph's eyes never left Felice. In the dark, Krimsey couldn't see them glaring, but he could feel the irritable expression creeping in the tension of their face through their emotional link. When he opened up his ability to partake in *transitus* emotion, Zeph's thoughts and emotion seemed to take on an almost extra-terrestrial, corporeal form. *Think your thoughts, do not speak your words. We are safe here. But not if we are heard.*

"Krimsey," Felice said, a line of stress cracking her whisper. "What's the plan here? Whoever your friend is, they're—"

"Giving you a death-glare. I know. Wait and don't talk."

How does it work then? Can you hear my thoughts? Krimsey thought.

Yes. Zeph's presence was malleable and soft.

Forsaken Earth, that's scary. How is this happening? He pressed his mixed brew of emotions—awe and sympathy and guilt joined with a bowl full of nerves like ramen—toward Zeph, hoping for an apologetic effect.

Cyn taught me a few tricks, Zeph answered. *And I do not need or seek sympathy or apology.* Zeph tilted their forehead at Felice. *Do you trust her?*

I never thought we'd speak again.

I could honestly care less about our fight. It is in the past. I aim to keep it there and move on. But are you aware of what Felice Karuli is capable of? I have read the things she has done. Stuff she has said.

Krimsey glanced back at Felice again. Her gaze darted from Krimsey, to Zeph, back to Krimsey, then finally to a place in the sky she seemed very occupied by.

Felice isn't our enemy. Krimsey searched Zeph's face for cracks. *I thought Cyn understood that.*

She did. We are not happy about it. "Come on," Zeph said out loud, their presence pulling back and turning to stone. A fortified mental wall solidified around them. A new drizzle of rain fell.

"What just happened?" Felice asked, brow tightly furrowed. Her jaw was slack and she held an arm up, as if her body had questions, too.

"I don't know. Felice, this is my friend, Zeph. They go by Z."

Friend? The single-word thought shot out from Zeph's wall like an arrow. Zeph raised an eyebrow. "That is not what you would have said this afternoon. Our fight is in the past, but I am not dead. 'Friend' is a strong word," Zeph said, casting a final glare at Felice. "Let's go." Zeph walked down the path between green foothills the way they had come.

"I think," Krimsey said to Felice, "We're being taken to Cyn."

CYN JONES

Felice Karuli, Tuesday, March 26, 2250, 8:18 p.m.

KRIMSEY STARTED TO SCRAMBLE down the animal path to follow Zeph, who Felice thought was a bossy bitch in need of an attitude rewire, but Felice caught his arm.

He stopped and turned, his mouth asymmetrical. "Hey, I know that must have been weird for you," he said under his breath. "I'll explain everything, but right now we have to follow Z."

"What? I don't care about that. I mean, I do, that was weird as shit, but I trust you. I just," Felice whispered, watching Zeph's back recede.

"Felice—"

"I need you to promise me something."

"I'm not in a position to—"

"Listen, I trust you, okay. Do you trust me?"

"I think so.... I don't know." He bit the inside of his cheek, kept looking away down the hill.

"Because they—" Felice jabbed a thumb toward Zeph Carmak's back, "—don't trust me. Which I'm sure means Cyn Jones doesn't either. I need to know I have someone on my side. I need to know I'm not getting stabbed in the back at the first chance. I'm here to stay and here to help. So long as I know. I ask you again. Do you trust me?"

"I don't know. Z—"

"I don't give a fuck what Z thinks. Do you?"

Krimsey swallowed, looked after Zeph, then gave her a brazen look. "Yes," he said. She could almost feel the heat of his decision wafting off him. "I do."

She raised her hand to push loose hair back behind her ear. She felt her hand shake, though the tremor was visibly impercepti-ble. She brushed her hair out of her face, then put her hand solidly on Krimsey's uninjured shoulder. She could feel the tremor grow, stemming from deep within her core. An iceberg melting, cracking open. Resistance. Breaking free. She exhaled, tension flowing out with the breath. "Thanks, kid."

Carmak's kid had found a way to Cyn Jones and now, despite the odds, led Felice and Krimsey behind the misty, post-rain slog of a town, straight to the woman. Felice had to admit, she got a slight thrill every time she thought about meeting the mastermind who had managed to light so many fires.

They kept the fragrant fields that flanked the town to their left and they crept past old buildings. Gusts of wind bent the flowery fields. Scraggly strands of hair whipped around her face. *Why is it so quiet?* Felice wondered where her mother had gone as she hopelessly fixed the flying strands. *To find me? To stall the rep? To restore the power?* Which fire was her mother currently running to quench?

Felice wondered how it could possibly be so quiet, when just hours before, she had struggled to contain the worst unraveling of the HPO's foundation she'd ever witnessed.

She wondered if Mr. NWA-what's-his-face was asleep. Or if he was having a heart attack realizing how many holes the official reports had. Or a hernia listening to Lamia drone about how well the *transitus* were doing…

Hot and cold warred at her extremities, and a shiver racked her spine. She stepped over some muddy cables behind a building. "Are you telling me Cyn's been hiding in town all these years? Is that—"

Krimsey turned and *shushed* her.

"Alright, alright," she muttered.

She knew that no one was out looking for them. Lamia had sent her to find Krimsey and help him get to Cyn, and Lamia currently awaited a signal. Sending Felice to Krimsey was her way of eliminating one fire. Eliminating one more variable situation that could blow up in Lamia's face.

Only, sending Felice hadn't eliminated the variable, had it? Felice was the variable now, and her mother didn't even know. Felice imagined she was the spark and Cyn the fresh, dry kindling. Or was Felice the raging, wet storm? Well, that all depended on Cyn. How would the woman react to Felice's help?

As they crept past empty back-alley footpaths, all Felice wanted to do was lie in the field of wildflowers and drown in their smell. Soothe the deep trembling in her bones. Instead, she peeled her gaze away from the field and paid close attention to the kids. Krimsey and Zeph were excessively quiet. Not stealthy—their steps were too loud and careless. But not a single word had been exchanged since they'd entered the town. The way Zeph looked over at Krimsey with a telling expression was creepy. Telling *what*, Felice could only guess. The odd pair was so in sync, it seemed they could read each other's minds.

A dark, dense fog rolled in from the ocean. The fog encroached upon the two HPO passenger ships on the horizon. Every crawl past a back-alley intersection revealed less and less of the ships until their hulls, then their lights, were consumed.

Krimsey stopped in front of her and she walked right into him. They had reached the edge of town. The last building on the outskirts of the flower field was small, squat, and lackluster. An exposed, winding path led up through the foothills.

The black-and-emerald foothills rolled and dipped for as far as the eye could see. The ocean met and crashed into the black rock crusting its shores. Sun-bleached homes were scattered about.

Very exposed.

Zeph glanced back at Felice, then to Krimsey. He returned Zeph's stare with a strained face she hadn't seen before, then he looked ahead and nodded. Felice wanted to scream at him: *"What the hell is going on?"*

For the first time in her life, Felice was not in control. Not in control of the HPO or the lab or the kids. Not in control of where the next step would take her, let alone the next hour. Not even in control of the automatic over-beating inside her own chest.

She bit the inside of her cheek. She held her tongue and the questions that sat on the tip of it. They started up the path. Hungry, confused, and tired as all forsaken Earth, she followed.

Felice dragged her feet. Soon, they turned off the path and climbed higher and higher into the foothills, heading straight up into steep, mountainous territory. Her thighs and lungs burned. They passed the last smattering of valley homes. Deeper they went, foothills finally giving way to black, looming crags. Approaching the sheer face of the mountain, which shot straight up into the sky, Zeph ducked, took an invisible step down, and vanished.

What on Earth?

Krimsey stopped and looked back at Felice. A smile lifted his features. A bright shock of emotion against a tired canvas.

"She lives in a cave?" Felice asked, her knees popping at the final incline. She came to his side, bent over with her hands on her thighs, and looked down into the hole. She pushed her sweat-plastered bangs aside and wiped the moisture collected beneath her eyes.

"No. But this is the way," he said.

"You all coming or what?" Zeph's voice echoed out of the hole.

"Coming," Krimsey said. His voice echoed into empty space. The sound of Zeph's footfalls rattled further away. "Ladies first."

"Oh no, you get your butt in there. You're going first." Felice was still breathing heavily. "No wonder my mother never found the woman. She's an Earth-forsaken bat."

Krimsey bent and leapt into the hole with a thud. He looked up, his face barely visible, but his eyes must have caught the light of the sky because they had a faint, cat-like glow. "You're not going to…?" he trailed off, looking down when the sound of clattering rocks pulled his attention away.

Felice crouched lower and crossed her arms. "I'm coming. I just need a moment to catch my breath. What, you worried I'll ditch and turn you in?"

"No. Not that," he said. "But I am worried we've put so much faith into a woman we've never met. And…." he trailed off again and blinked.

"Spit it out."

"Cyn really hates you."

"Okay." She drew out the word in a breathy huff. "What makes you think that?"

Annoyingly, Krimsey opted out of answering. "I trust you, Felice. I do. I know what side you're on. But...."

"But what? Speak your words, Krim."

"What's the plan if she doesn't pan out?"

Felice leaned down further, her knees hovering over the hole, her arm propping her over the ledge against an outcropping.

"What do we do," he said, a dry air of desperation marking his voice, "if she turns us away because of you?"

"If you have to choose me over your sister? That's what you're concerned about?"

A spark caught in Krimsey's eye. "I will choose my sister over any of you."

"I know," she said. "And I will choose this island. Move over, I'm coming down." She stood with a creak and shuffled her feet to the ledge. She heard rough echoes of Krimsey's shoes scrapping rock and grains of crushed rock falling like hourglass sand. "I have a feeling," she huffed, letting herself down in a controlled descent. "All our goals align such that," she grunted, scraping her knee against the ledge as she let go and landed inside the dark cave, "we won't succeed in any one of them unless we work together. That's how these things work, right?" She let a fake, gleaming smile break across her face even though it was too dark to see a thing.

"Hmm," Krimsey said.

Well, the smile was more for her, anyway.

If Cyn hated Felice, it was for good reason. There probably wasn't much the woman didn't know about her. But she had to believe smarts would win over hatred.

She had to believe that the smarts that had gotten Cyn this far in life would see a good opportunity when it presented itself. And Felice, daughter of the president, right at her doorstep? Offering genuine, honest-to-all-forsaken-Earth help? Insider intel like shortcuts and codes, wants and weaknesses, and access to, and the very good graces of, Lamia Karuli herself? That was a damn good opportunity.

Besides, she couldn't afford too many questions now. She was in it. They all were. Together. Whether they liked it or not.

Felice shivered and blinked several times. She heard Krimsey moving ahead of her. What would Cyn do to her, though, if it was hate that won? *No point in speculating, now, Felice. You've given up your control, remember?* Even if turning back were an option for her, she didn't want to. She liked this feeling. She liked that the responsibility for the situation they were all in was now shared. Slowly, her eyes adjusted to a faint glow that cast downward light straight ahead. She saw the dark outline of Krimsey and, ahead of him, Zeph and, further ahead still, the jagged traces of rock outlined by white light. Zeph reached the place where the light touched the rock wall and began to climb. Krimsey started shortly after.

This… This had to be a joke.

Gaping, she walked forward as both Zeph and Krimsey disappeared from her vantage. The ground beneath her feet was worn. Stamped down from years of someone going in and out, in and out. When she reached the rock wall, the space opened up above her. The source of light was a narrow crack high above. She watched Zeph, with Krimsey on their heels, clamber up the rock toward the light and squeeze through the crack at the top, each one of them passing through, casting Felice momentarily into pitch dark.

"Fuck this," she said, looking up. "You should know I don't do heights." She touched the rough wall with a finger. In spots, the wall was jagged and sharp. Untouched. In other spots, a pattern of grips and footholds had been smoothed and shaped by use.

"You can do it, Felice," Krimsey called down, an outline appearing in the crack above.

"Is there a back door?"

The outline disappeared. She heard unintelligible mutters. Krimsey reappeared, the shape of his curls bouncing. "This is the only way in. You've got to do it." There was a strain of worry that colored his voice. A downward pitch of doubt. For a moment, Felice herself was sure she was about to turn back.

She took hold of a solid handhold that was shoulder height. She hoisted herself up, finding two easy footholds. Then she looked up and climbed, sweat pooling near her mouth and eyes.

As she climbed, she tried to squash the whispers of doubt. Each time one of the whispers found purchase, and she let thoughts of giving up take hold, she took a deep breath and pictured Elpida.

Short, brown curls. Hands the size of sand dollars. Deep, pensive eyes with flecks of gold. The gold in her eyes was the *transitus* gene expressing itself in between human traits. Gold, though, was a thing to be mined. Exploited. Whittled down into little nubs until there was nothing left but grey. Grey, the color of memories that clung like a stench. Grey, the color of Rumi's withering skin. Grey, the color of death. Her image of Elpida was dated. She hadn't seen the girl in years. But it was an effective one. The last time she had seen Elpida, she had been the age Rumi was when she died. In her imaginings, the two girls became one, easily mixed up.

She would not allow a repeat. Elpida would live.

Her soles echoed against the deep rock walls. Checking her footing, Felice grasped the shining, slick rock and hoisted herself up again and again. Squinting against the prick of white light glaring down at her. Grunting past her racing breath. Gasping when she looked down.

Don't look down. From her glances, she could tell she was past any point of return.

The rock was sharp and slippery at the same time. She tested her weight on a ledge with her right foot. She pressed her fingers hard into the next handhold. Then, she pushed up with a shaking leg. Careful to place her free foot someplace sturdy, she flexed her biceps and pushed upward again. Her sandal slipped off the rock and her back slammed against the wall beside her.

She swung one arm behind her to catch herself. Her supporting leg wobbled. She couldn't control the slow deterioration of strength. The wobbling grew violent and her body, tense and tight, also shook. Her arm, weak like a noodle, gave out, but she caught herself before slipping off the edge completely. She repositioned so that her legs wouldn't cramp up. She let out a slow breath.

Felice looked up. The silhouette of Krimsey's head still just hovered, motionless. She gritted her teeth. She wished he'd do something. Anything. "Come on," Krimsey said. Anything but gutless encouragement.

Finding another handhold and different footing, she took several breaths and pushed up as hard as she could. She landed with her belly flat on a ledge and wriggled herself into a sitting position. Her breath was heavy.

"You're almost there." Krimsey, again. "See that foothold behind your head? If you get your left foot there, you can push yourself to the next ledge."

There was another flat ledge about a meter and a half up.

Felice shoved her hand into a fissure, positioned her left foot, then pushed with all her strength. Her hand snagged in the fissure and wouldn't release as the rest of her body propelled upward. She heard a pop and sharp pain burst from her wrist. Felice cried out, wrestled her hand free, and collapsed on the next ledge.

Tears of pain squeezed between her lashes.

The opening was just above her head. She stood, gritted against the pain, tears blurring her vision, and wriggled her body up through the crevice. She thrust her good hand forward to catch some final hold to heave herself into a standing position and made contact with a firm hand, which hoisted her up.

She blinked away wetness from her eyes. Rough stalks of grass stabbed her ankles. "Thank you."

It was Zeph, though, not Krimsey, who had helped her. For half a second, Felice was relieved. Finally. A slight hint of acknowledgment. A modicum of respect. An ounce of hope, blooming in her chest. Maybe setting aside differences wouldn't be so difficult. Maybe coming here wasn't a personal condemnation. But Zeph's face was stiff, watching Felice with unmoving, catlike stillness.

"I said thank you," she said again, shuffling away from the hole she just came out of.

Zeph said nothing, eyes slowly evaluating her. When their gaze paused on her wrist, Felice moved her injured limb behind her, letting the pain of the movement wash over her without a single groan or a wince. Her eyes only watered more fiercely.

"Am I supposed to do a trick?" Felice asked, looking to Krimsey for help, but was instead pulled into the incredible backdrop that surrounded him. Tall white UV lamplights flooded a grassy valley. Nestled in the center of the valley was a wooden home. Bees hummed in a bed of flowers bordering a nearby greenhouse. She couldn't see what lay in the dark past the concentric circles of UV light, but she felt confined. She imagined the mountain enclosed all sides of the valley, concealing this place from unwanted detection.

"Whenever you are ready," Zeph said. "I will check you for devices."

"Well there's nothing to check," she said.

"Arms out." Zeph stepped a bit too close, nose barely a few centimeters from Felice's forehead.

"Is this really necessary? I'm not going anywhere. Krimsey saw me crush my com."

"Arms out," Zeph said again, gaze shifting for the briefest of moments toward Krimsey. *"Please."*

Felice lifted her arms and Zeph lightly pressed down the sides of her dress. "Honey, I prefer a little foreplay before you go in on me like that." Felice cracked open a smile like a can of beans. "You do realize I'm wearing a *slip?* They have no pockets. The only place I could possibly be hiding anything would be—"

"Shut up." Zeph's steely resolve seemed to split for a second, eye twitching.

"I'm not really your type though, am—?" Zeph reached for Felice's outstretched arms, grabbed both by the wrists, and pulled them down. A cold gasp scraped down Felice's throat. Pain radiated past her elbow. "You little fu—"

"Both of you," Krimsey shouted. "Stop."

Felice's eyes stung with tears. She blinked them away and they streamed down her face, clearing her warbled vision. The only visible evidence of how much pain Zeph had inflicted.

"Fine. Come on," Zeph said with a sigh and an obvious eye-roll, grabbing Krimsey by the shoulder.

Krimsey sucked in a breath. A wordless howl escaped him. "Fuck, Z. I *told you* about my shoulder."

"I forgot, I forgot! Sorry." Zeph stared at him in horror, hand retracting, then looking at Felice as if she had caused the pain.

"Oh, I see, you only feel bad about inflicting pain when it isn't me. Message received." Felice raised her good hand in defense. But the interaction got her wheels spinning. She knew for a fact that no words had been exchanged about Krimsey's shoulder since encountering Zeph. *Fact.*

So how did Zeph forget something he never said? She was beginning to think they really were mind-reading.

"I'm fine," Krimsey said, though he put more distance between himself and Zeph. He started toward the ramshackle house. "I'm ready." Felice made a half-hearted attempt at smoothing her hair down before following the two across the grass field. She spared a couple of side glances at Krimsey, who repeatedly bit his bottom lip and stared straight ahead.

As they approached, she heard a voice through the open door. She stepped after Zeph and Krimsey onto a slanted porch and stood just outside the doorway. And, among coils of black wires and screens and messes of junk piled atop junk piled atop a buckling table, was Cyn Jones.

SPECIATION

Rich Klaine, 2141

"TECHNICALLY SPEAKING, I DID die."

"Oh," I said, absently straightening my stack of papers and my *'Rich W. Klaine, President'* plaque.

The woman on the other side of my desk, Julianna Beck, beloved icon, socialite, NWA unity campaigner, the most recognized woman on the planet, crossed and uncrossed her legs. She sat straight, twirling the rotating chair from side to side, looking at me seriously.

"Technically," she said, sparing a glance at my door. "Heart attack. Or something... But a full recovery, so that's good."

"Then you are feeling well, yes?" Her death could have been a devastating blow. Though she'd have likely become a martyr. Ultimately strengthening the New World Alliance campaigns.

Of course, such a thought was an atrocity. I nipped it immediately.

Pleasantries aside, I had an important meeting in five minutes and needed to get to the bottom of this impromptu get-together with Julianna. *Inquiry*, she had called it. She knew I'd always make time for her. But only her agent and my assistant knew she was here. Her husband was campaigning without her. And I was beginning to worry about this behavior.

"Tell me, Mrs. Beck." I leaned forward. Steepled my fingers beneath my beard. "How can I help you?"

"Is this room clean?"

"I assure you, my office is, and always has been, clear of taps. This place is safe. What concern plagues you, my dear?"

"I have it." She lowered her voice significantly.

"What is it you have?" My ears perked.

"You *know*...." Her mouth tightened and pursed. Her brows pointed behind her bangs.

"You don't mean...?" Pressure seemed to drop in the room, dampening the sound my aging ears picked up. I lost my senses for a moment, a mental weight pulling me elsewhere. I saw rushing water and felt briefly panicked, before the moment disappeared. I was staring at Mrs. Beck with incredulity. Past the office door, my assistant spoke quickly to someone. Surely my ten o'clock. "Mags?" I called.

"Yes?" My assistant's muffled reply.

"Reschedule, please."

Mags peeped in, slivering the door open. "But—"

"Close the door and reschedule." I turned to Julianna and examined her.

Nothing unusual about her. She was the most beautiful damned woman I'd ever met. Red lips. Thick ones that could blow a kiss a mile away. Fluffy, curled bangs and tight-cropped brunette hair framing an oval face. Medium dark, sun-kissed skin. Strong forehead and strong, willful mind on the other side of it, too.

"Transitioner?" I whispered. "You don't look...."

"Turns out, doesn't matter how you look. *Anyone* can have it. Goddamn terrifying, Rich." Her lip quivered.

I was confused. I talked to her monthly, sometimes even weekly, for campaigns, but our relationship was strictly professional. She looked down at her lap, maybe a tear dripped down, I couldn't tell. I repositioned myself in my seat.

"Julianna, I—"

"You don't have to say anything," she said, reaching into a bag and pulling out an envelope.

I opened it. A resignation letter.

"Read it."

I did. Her writing was small and looped.

"You want me to veto the speciation bill, or you'll…? Are you… blackmailing me?"

"Is it blackmail if it's mutually beneficial? Speciation would require me to acknowledge I'm not human. I'm human, Rich. It's not right to separate us out like that. Segregation was a thing, Rich, and it wasn't good. Besides, it'll be a bad look on you. On me. On everyone. The government icon can't be '*transitus*.' I can't be '*transitus*.'" She spat the proposed species name like poison. *Homo transitus*.

"But the entire council voted in favor…."

"You'll lose me, Rich. If you don't reject the vote. Don't make those damned people something that they aren't. I'm human. They're human."

"Eighty-five percent of transitioners want this. And the evidence in the DNA is undeniable. We *need* this law passed."

"Think about it, Rich." She stood. "I'll have to resign."

"It'll be a *civil war*."

"So be it. At least you'll have my beloved *human* face to plaster all over your next unity campaign."

The next day, I vetoed the vote. Speciation declined.

INSIDER

Krimsey Enosh, Tuesday, March 26, 2250, 9:01 p.m.

KRIMSEY ENTERED THE HOME in the middle of the valley. The first thing he noticed was the presence distracting him from taking in the single-room cabin. It pressed down on him, felt him as a blind person might, cupping his cheek in a palm. It felt the pain in his chest and curled around the throbbing in his arm, tracing it up to his shoulder. It recoiled from the hard, swelling knot there.

Your stunt tonight caused quite a ruckus. Not all of it good. It was the same voice he had heard on his com, only clearer. The same way Zeph had been speaking to him for the past hour or so. Ringing, like the crisp chime of a bell. He shouldn't have been surprised by the mind-speak, but he was. As the presence pulled away, Krimsey's attention did, too.

After first noting a lopsided ceiling, uneven floors, and a disastrous table in the middle of the room, his attention gravitated. A single chair that matched the dining set faced the far back wall. Dangling from the back wall hung a behemoth monitor. The technology looked ancient. A black screen about the span of his arms seemed to be held up by only cables. Below the monitor, where all the loose cords ended, was a black box. And in the far back corner, among all the cords and boxes and clutter on the floor, Cyn Jones crouched beside a crumpled pile of bedding containing a small girl, whispering comforting words as the little girl closed her eyes.

Krimsey's gaze flicked up when Cyn turned from the girl to look at him. She had deep skin dark as night, eyes as bright and yellow as day, and a crown of salt-and-pepper coils that brushed her shoulders. She held a webbed finger to her lips.

I just got her to sleep, Cyn's voice said in his head.

Cyn's eyes glowed like suns in the low light of the room. They shifted to focus on something behind him in the same calculated way Zeph had done to Felice in the brambles. The woman took a defensive step back and crossed her arms.

Krimsey looked back at Felice, who had stepped over the mess of wires into the cabin-like home. She hovered at his right shoulder, distancing herself from Zeph.

"She's just here to help," Krimsey said out loud, feeling uneasy and stepping over to cover Felice from Cyn's piercing gaze.

Krimsey's words did not seem to satisfy the woman because the moody presence in the room darkened. Cyn glared at Felice. "Well," she said out loud. "Don't you look just like your mother."

Cyn turned and planted herself in the chair that faced the monitor, her back to them. She began furiously tapping on a long, flat rectangle that folded out onto her lap to reveal numbered and lettered keys. Incoherent strings of white letters and numbers appeared against the black of the monitor screen in rhythm with her fingers.

"Cyn," Krimsey said, clearing his throat. "So what's the plan? My sister—Zeph said—"

"Patience, child. Don't you see I have a matter or two at hand?" Cyn hissed. "Have a seat, don't just stand there."

Stunned into silence, Krimsey clamped his mouth shut and looked at the dining area setup.

There were three chairs around the table. Krimsey pulled out the one that faced Cyn. It was positioned on the long side of the table, between the two other chairs, which were on opposite ends. Felice pulled her chair as far out as she could, creating distance. Her back bumped the tiny kitchen counter behind her. Zeph sat across from her. Both of them actively avoided eye contact by looking at Cyn's back.

Krimsey had to move a very large, dusty book onto the floor. He set it down with a soft thud.

"Not there," Cyn muttered, still working her nimble fingers and looking at the screen. "Put it on the shelf."

Behind Zeph was a stack of old books—more books than Krimsey had ever seen in his life—and somewhere buried beneath them was wooden shelving. Krimsey placed the book precariously on top of the pile, behind Zeph's head, then sat in his chair.

Krimsey's questions whirred inside him as he drank everything in. For several breaths, the only sound was the *tap tap tap* of Cyn's fingers flying over the device in her lap, the sleeping girl's whistling nose, and the absence of a low, white hum that had suddenly stopped.

"Did you check Felice, Zeph?"

"Yeah. She does not have any."

While Krimsey was biting his lip, feeling the pressure of time weigh him to his seat, Felice was slumped in her chair looking like she was trying not to nod off. She looked at the back of Cyn's head, pressing her thin lips together, then unpressing. Working them like she was chewing a word before spitting it out. "What am I supposed to not have?"

The tapping stopped. Cyn craned her body to meet Felice's eyes. "Are you fooling with me, girl?" Cyn was still enough that Krimsey noticed the soft lines of age around her eyes.

"No," Felice said softly. "I'm really not. I'm afraid I am out of the loop."

Cyn turned back around and began clacking again. "The suppressant, child. You don't have any suppressant on you. You do know what that means, right?"

Felice chewed on invisible words again, but said nothing. The expression on her face was neutral, though Krimsey could see her working at something. He wanted to ask what Cyn was talking about, himself. Krimsey tapped his finger on his chair to the passing seconds. Worried by how casually Cyn was treating precious, slipping time. Worried about his imminent transition. Worried about life and death and about his sister and fate.

"It means," Cyn said. "You don't have enough time to get to your mother for your next dose of suppressant, girly. But don't worry. We've got something for you here. No one's gonna die."

Felice's face changed, but the expression was still unfamiliar. She looked relieved. But that didn't seem right. A frown set into Krimsey's brows, the muscles in his forehead bringing them closer together. More words that made no sense. More talk of death. What was wrong with Felice? She looked tired, not sick.

"So what's your plan? Speak up," Cyn said. "If you know about the suppressant, you must have known your next dose is required in the next... what? Thirty minutes?"

"I didn't know. She told me it's just a bandaid. That's all I know."

"So you're trying to gain my trust by being truthful?"

Felice rubbed her hands together and parted her lips. She took a breath to speak, but then stopped.

More wordless tapping from Cyn. Krimsey's shoulder throbbed. "Can—" His voice cracked. From the tiredness or transition, he couldn't tell. He coughed and cleared his throat. "Can anyone tell me what's going on? You all know I'm a walking countdown, right?"

Tap tap tap tap.

"Sorry. Your friend here is dying," Cyn said, her tapping gaining velocity. "Few years back, your beloved president experimented on some of you kids to develop a gene suppressant. Start of a very slippery slope. She did it because Felice has Pneumaphage."

All the air *whooshed* out of Krimsey like he'd been punched in the gut. That's what his father had died from. And that meant... Felice was *transitus*. Felice watched this reaction in him and her lips scrunched just barely to one side, a slight twist. Krimsey blinked and the twisted look on her face was gone. Replaced by what he could only interpret as a retreating, a hunkering down somewhere cool and cold for a long summer. They watched each other for a fleeting moment.

"You're...?" He swallowed, his mouth dry.

Felice nodded slowly.

"She needs a dose of her suppressant, Krimsey. I have something here. It isn't suppressant, but it'll do the job of keeping her healthy. She'll get it so long as she behaves."

Krimsey huffed and sat back down in his chair. "Okay. But she wouldn't be here if she wasn't here to help us." That wasn't true. According to her, her mother planned for her to be here. But that didn't matter. Felice was on their side. "Can't you just trust that? Can't we just move past all this? My sister is—"

"She is currently alive. Your sister is safer at this very moment than we are right now, in this valley. Krimsey, you and Felice—" Cyn huffed. "This morning, everything was going just as I planned," she said with slow deliberation. "The only reason either of you are here is because—" she stopped tapping for a moment, held her head up at the monitor, let out a heavy sigh, then continued. "Your stunt had consequences. And my plan has had to shift."

"I'm sorry, but what plan?" Krimsey interrupted. He looked at Zeph to see how they were reacting to everything. Zeph's temples flexed, their arms crossed, but there were no emotions written on their face, or seeping out around them. He looked at the back of Cyn's head again.

"For eighteen years, the Karulis have been conducting invasive experiments on the non-viable population to reverse the *transitus* gene. And for almost as many, I have been working to put their work to a stop."

"We were working towards a cure for Pneuma—"

"You've been working towards a *reversal* of the *transitus* gene," Cyn asserted, interrupting Felice. The clacking of Cyn's fingertips suddenly felt like a very urgent, very dire act. Each key she hit amplified in Krimsey's ears. His breathing crescendoed. "Under the misguided *pretense* of curing Pneumaphage."

Felice stood abruptly, her chair scraping the floor. "That's not true."

"You know it is, Felice. Or do you…?" Cyn studied Felice's defensive expression, as if pondering her own preconceptions. "Maybe the pretense was for you. *Huh*."

Felice turned to Krimsey. Her confusion mirrored his own. "We wanted to cure Pneumaphage, Krimsey. And yes, I was a part of it. We injected kids with potentially harmful experiments. The only answer we found was that we needed to make *transitus* more human to stop the disease. No one else was even trying to cure Pneumaphage. I wanted to help. But my mother…" Krimsey could hear doubt creeping into her voice, the bewilderment of being forced to reconsider something she had always believed to be true. There was a lot of that going around lately.

"Right. *Your mother.* The one that had you take Rumi—"

"Don't say her name, please."

"Rumi Yen. You took her to her death," Cyn said, still tapping, raising her voice at the monitor, "you took her to some lab in Ross Bay and that is where she died. Is that really the best way to cure *transitus* of Pneumaphage? Reversing their genes? Killing children? What about Prae? What would happen to her if your mother got her hands around her?"

"I—" Felice began to say.

Krimsey stared silently at Felice, who cried, fighting to remain expressionless, and put her head between her knees. His lungs whistled and wheezed at her, increasing with his breath. "Is that true, Felice? Someone died?" *Elpida.* What were they doing to her right now?

Felice cried and said nothing.

"I've wanted to give you the benefit of the doubt for so long, Felice. Your mother's lies know no bounds. I've known you since you were a child, did you know that?" Cyn's voice softened. She paused her tapping, folded the device in her lap, and stood to face them. "I know you, Felice Karuli."

Felice lifted her head, spine rigid as stone. Her temples flexed. "You don't know me."

Cyn walked over and shoved a swath of wires, devices, and books into a precarious pile at the edge of the table. Then she twisted around to the shelving behind Zeph, retrieved a large stack of fibrous grey papers, and thumped it on the table in front of them all. She licked her fingertips and flipped through the stack. Faded ink covered both sides of every page. Cyn squinted at a page and lifted it to the light coming through the window.

"Felice Maybel Karuli, born July 21st, 2222. First assigned as a guide at age sixteen to Krimsey Enosh. Last guide assignment ended at age twenty-three. Official title then became Head of Medical. But you aren't *really* in Medical, now are you? No. You're not.

"You're your mother's errand girl. You do what she says and it kills you. You hate it. You hate what she makes you do. You've taken a kid in the dead of night. You've spearheaded and initiated unethical experiments on the non-viable population. And you hate yourself. Am I close?"

"Please stop." Felice was breathing hard. She closed her eyes, her lashes wet with quiet tears. "Please stop." She fell back into the chair, knocking down a wooden spoon from the counter behind her.

"Cyn, how do you know all this?" Krimsey asked.

"I've been hacking the coms and watching the HPO for almost as long as you've been alive, child. *I know everything.*"

"Cyn?" Zeph's voice dripped in concern, pointing at the blank monitor behind Cyn.

Krimsey felt a growing sensation of anxiety from Zeph and Cyn.

"Why did you stop?" Zeph asked. "You were holding off the HPO security, weren't you? Did the NWA rep find what he needed or…?"

"The HPO didn't get past my defenses. They just stopped trying to get in. Which means they found our location another way." Cyn eyed Felice.

"So, that means…?" Zeph asked.

"Lamia is on her way," Cyn said.

"What?" Felice gasped.

"Uh-uh. I don't believe your surprise for a second. I'm disappointed in you, Felice," Cyn said.

"But she wouldn't…" Krimsey halted. Felice wouldn't turn them in. Right? He scrutinized her purpled eyes. "She didn't do this."

"She played you," Zeph said with a gravelly growl.

Flickers of hot, white dots appeared in Krimsey's vision. He smelled stale wood. An intense anger rose from where Zeph sat. This was familiar. Zeph was unstable. This was exactly like the times before, when Zeph was about to attack during Survival and in the pinnacles. He clenched the sides of his chair with white knuckles.

"What do we do? What about Elpida?" He asked.

"Forget about your damn sister, what about us?" Zeph eyed Felice like a ravenous beast. "What do you have to say for yourself?"

"This is impossible," Felice said. "Are you sure she's coming here?"

"Oh, I am sure alright. We see what you are made of, Felice Karuli. True colors right on your sleeve," Cyn said.

"Krimsey." Felice looked at him. "You have to believe me. I didn't do this. I don't have a com. Your sister, we can still get her, if we work together. We still have time…"

"They call your sister Elpida 'Five' on the coms, Krimsey," Cyn said. "Felice has been injecting her with preliminary testers. Your sister became more human, and that's valuable. One step closer to the reversal of our species. Did you know that's what people did to anyone who didn't fit the status quo? Conversion therapy. Try to make them more like the brainwashed rest of society. Transitus earned our right to not be human and they're trying to erase us. They don't care about us. They don't care about Pneumaphage. Elpida could die and her death would just be considered a small price to pay. It's all right there in the papers, Krimsey." Cyn jutted her chin toward the stack on top of the table and paused. She sighed. "Felice is right about one thing, though. There is still time. Only if you work with me. Tell me. Whose side are you on? Your friend is a traitor."

The eerie silence that followed these words felt like a blanket of suffocation. Krimsey swayed in his chair with a sudden headache. He clutched his throbbing head. His entire life, he'd been played like a fool by the HPO. He had trusted the organization meant to protect him when it did the opposite. It was all a lie. On top of it all, he had put his trust in Felice. Had that been a lie, too? Had he been played again? Felice's eyes were wide, scared, unprepared. The rest of her face remained neutral. Neutral was her safe place. Neutral was familiar. She was in shock.

"Felice…" He looked from Felice, to Zeph, to Cyn. "Felice is innocent."

To his right, a flurry of movement and sound exploded.

The Plan

Before Zeph had a chance to process what was happening, their heart throttled, lighting every muscle and nerve on fire. Felice had compromised *everything*. And Krimsey was defending her! This was *her* fault. She had figured out a way to lead Lamia right to them.

Out of control, Zeph launched. Their feet slapped the hardwood floor, reverberating through their bones and energizing their legs, rocketing their body from the chair. Arms reaching, Zeph was on a collision-course dive with Felice's delicate neck. Incoherent shouts burst from their diaphragm, as if possessed. Ramming into Felice, Zeph locked fingers around her neck. The blood pumping through Felice's jugular beat like drums. The base of her skull was grimy with sweat.

Papers and cords flew from the table. Felice's spine went rigid. Zeph toppled from the table, taking Felice and her chair clattering down as well. Zeph landed on their side, gasping for breath as all the air from their lungs whooshed out. Their vision tunneled. Cyn and Krimsey disappeared from it.

Colors and sounds blurred until Zeph could not tell what was up or what was down. There was only one thing Zeph was acutely aware of: the satisfactory pulse of Felice's flesh beneath their grip.

A soft, weak hand, fist, foot—didn't matter—beat at Zeph's back with futility. Felice was weak. Her hands flapped in Zeph's face, scraping their ear.

A sharp pain shot like a knife into Zeph's belly. Stars flew in and out of the black tunnel vision. Zeph let go of Felice and heard gasps and was not sure whose they were. Rolling in the clutter strewn across the floor, they reached for Krimsey's blue foot—it escaped—then received another blow to the belly. Zeph curled up in defense.

The blows stopped. Their world was dark. Whispers from above twisted and wormed into their mind, telling them horrible things. Deeply personal, creative insults.

Worthless. Never-amount-to-anything. Only gets by on favors. Human parents. Thinks they are special. Spoiled. Only wants to be different for attention. Insecurities only their own mind had such intimate knowledge of. Zeph squeezed out hot tears.

From above, a string of words reached them, an incoherent sentence.

"Mmmf?" Zeph asked.

Cyn knelt on the floor. "Are you okay?"

A choked laugh came from somewhere else.

Distinct shapes and colors began to return. They opened their mouth. Words did not appear.

Felice crouched in the corner below the kitchen counter. She was touching her neck. It was bulging, bruised and swollen, traces of Zeph's grip left with blue-and-white fingerprints. Her eyes were red and huge and wet.

Krimsey's feet—the culprit of their agony—were nearby, and Zeph wanted to make him feel as miserable as—

Stop. Deep breaths. Cyn pressed calming, meditative thoughts toward Zeph.

Krimsey's feet shifted away, toward the open doorway. Swallowing, Zeph closed their eyes, took a breath, and began to will away their internal monster. Began to metaphorically pry its fingers from their own neck, one by one. It was somewhat comforting, though, that the monster was there at all. That at least there was someone who had Zeph's back. Even if it was imagined. Even if it was themselves. Even if the method of protection was unorthodox and scary. Zeph pushed into a sitting position on the floor. The movement aggravated the stabbing pain, like a knife buried in their belly. Glaring at Krimsey, Zeph lay back down, curling deeper into the fetal position with a groan.

"You were killing her," Krimsey said, with more than a little malice.

"Uuuh ouufff," Zeph croaked, air still settling back into their lungs. A crumb on the floor shuddered from their breath.

Krimsey's presence set their teeth on edge. He had already been getting on their nerves, with his fake niceties, his poor judgment in companions, misplaced trust, and his loud, Earthforsaken wheezes. Now, he had attacked them. This was war.

"Felice didn't do it."

With a grunt and grimace, Zeph pushed off the floor and held the edge of the table for stability. They wanted to lunge at Krimsey. They held their breath.

"Fuck you, Krimsey," Zeph spat.

"What the hell is wrong with you, Z?" he said.

"What's the matter with me—" Zeph clenched a fist on the table "—is that you are the judgiest, most pretentious, self-centered—"

"Check yourself," Cyn snapped.

"You are the most egotistical *transitus* I have ever met. You would rather die than face the fact that you are too coward to—"

"Zeph. Enough." Cyn's orders barely reached over Zeph's shouts.

"—face that Earthforsaken ocean. You are too cowardly to face that future. And you are wasting it. You are wasting yourself. You are a wasting piece of *transitus* garbage. You are throwing away your future and you are just going to die."

"You're vomiting emotion. Bring it in," Cyn said.

Zeph snapped at Cyn, shoving her reaching hand away. "I am fine. For Earth's sake, leave me alone."

"Lamia is on her way," Cyn said. This reminder glazed the room with a sobering calm. The reminder centered Zeph. There was a mission. There was a plan. They closed their eyes. They only had to work with Krimsey long enough to help finish what Cyn had started. What did Felice's betrayal mean for the plan, though? Zeph looked up at Cyn. What did it mean for Cyn?

"You two need to find a way to get over yourselves." Cyn looked right back at Zeph. Her eyes bore right through them. Like she was looking at their bones. "Not only is Lamia on her way, but Krimsey was injected almost twelve hours ago, which means he may have even less time than we actually need to pull this off."

"Injected?" Krimsey asked.

"Wing C? This morning. Your transition was *induced*. When Cyn tried to warn you, remember? Keep up," Zeph spat.

Krimsey's throat bounced down and back up and a sweaty sheen collected across his forehead. It was finally hitting him, the little invertebrate. If he had only listened to Zeph much earlier, maybe by now they would have been friends, they would have taken out Lamia, prevented her from harming anyone else, and they would have saved his sister. If he had only listened, he might even have had time to make peace with his fate. If he had only listened, he would be in the ocean. Not rattling his weak-throated voice in Zeph's ears. Not racing against time. Not about to die.

Actually, Cyn thought at Zeph. *He'd have died before getting anywhere near the ocean. He nearly died in the HPO tunnels, but Lamia was near enough, and she used her suppressant to revive him.*

Zeph looked at Cyn, forgetting to be angry at the intrusion into their thoughts. They looked at Krimsey once more, through a different light. He looked beat. His eyes were sunken. He looked half dead. *Lamia revived him?*

With the suppressant she developed at the suffering of others, yes. Saved his life, Cyn directed her thoughts at them again.

"How long do I have?" Krimsey asked.

"You might have twenty-four hours," Cyn said.

"That's what I keep hearing," Krimsey said. "But like you said, Medical was hours ago."

"You're right." Cyn looked at the ceiling and counted on her fingers. "Eleven, then. Give or take. Likely less."

A coughing whimper came from the kitchen floor. "So this has been fun and all. Does anyone else need a punching bag today? Krimsey? No? Okay." Felice's voice rasped, barely audible. Zeph looked at Felice in a new way, too. Felice had a convincing smile on but the muscles around her mouth twitched and threatened to collapse. She pushed up off the floor, wincing. "I am clearly not welcome here. I'm gonna dash before my dear mother arrives, if that's al—"

"Excuse me, you aren't *leaving*," Cyn said. She stepped in front of Felice and crossed her arms. "You're staying with me."

Felice deflated. She didn't fight back. "Thought so," she muttered.

Zeph cleared their throat. They considered what kept them here with people that they didn't like. How badly they wanted to put a stop to the HPO experiments. Everyone turned to face them.

"Cyn, why do all our paths lead to you?" Zeph asked. "Why are we all here? What is this all for? You said Lamia saved Krimsey. Why would she do that if she could just let him die? Is there another way? Can we reason with her?"

Silence followed. Cyn frowned, as if the questions hovered in the air and she was still trying to decipher them. "Lamia Karuli cannot be reasoned with."

"Why did she save him?"

"Because it served her in the moment," Cyn said. "One good deed does not undo a lifetime of terribly immoral ones."

"What makes you better?"

"What?"

Zeph pointed at Prae, who was still somehow asleep. "What makes any of us better? We kidnapped a kid. Took her from her family. Felice followed Lamia unquestioningly. Krimsey—well, I'm sure Krimsey is not a saint. And you? Cyn, you are using us. You used me and still are. We serve you in this moment. And you made a major decision about my body that I had no choice over. Why are we supposed to listen to you? Will any of this even help anyone? What if we fail?" Zeph was completely calm, now. Nearly all emotion had left them and they were determined to examine Cyn's plan with the utmost criticism. If they had to choose an emotion to describe the settling storm lining their belly, it would be pleasant, focused, amused. Zeph forgot to be disturbed by the shift in mood.

"No one said I was perfect, child. In fact, I told you the exact opposite, yet you still came. That's on you, not me." Cyn's tone was flat. "You need to find your own reasons for being here."

"I didn't say you had to be perfect. Do you even care about the lives we are messing with?" It didn't seem so, not from the way she spoke. Certainly not from the way her eyes looked like pebbles when cast in shadow. "Why are you doing this?"

"I thought you knew? Don't you see? We've been brought together to change the course of history." Cyn trembled. Either she was about to cry or flames were about to burst forth from her gaping maw. She looked at each of them, including Felice, in turn. "We are putting an end to a silent genocide. Lamia Karuli experiments on young *transitus* children in order to make them more human. But they aren't human and were never meant to be. What I did to you by making you viable, made you whole, Zeph. Do I care about the lives of the people? Absolutely I do. But it is more important to me to make them safe and whole than to worry about the small inconveniences, like being separated from parents for a few days.

"Or like you Zeph, who was at risk of being subjected to experiments if I didn't change you. You may not have been viable before, but you were still *transitus*. Not only did my solution keep you safe from being used for the HPO experiments, but it was developed without harming other people. It was a simple solution because you are not human, Zeph. We are in a war between making *transitus* disappear, and making them whole. My fight is *our* fight and it's the *honorable* one."

Cyn's speech was impassioned. She breathed heavily now. She opened her mouth as if to say more, never taking her eyes from Zeph, but she paused. She rubbed her right temple. Her eyes sparkled when they caught a glint of outside flood-lamp light. "But, dear child, I am doing this because what I really want to do is not possible."

Cyn's energy that filled the room shifted and Zeph felt it condense and land on their shoulders like snow. They sensed where this might be going, but all Zeph could think about was that a war was going on that millions of *transitus* weren't even aware of. The war on their genome. It was wrong.

"What is it you really want?" Felice asked. She leaned against the kitchen counter, her body language caved-in and unthreatening—she was someone who had given up.

Zeph cursed Felice for allowing the conversation to continue in this direction.

"I cannot go back in time." Cyn's voice cracked. She didn't look at Felice. "What I really want is to have never given you to Gina. I thought you were safer and you were, but it doesn't mean I don't regret not knowing you every second of my life. I can't get that time back, but I can make life better for you. Can you see that?"

Cyn thinks she is playing a god. "Yes. I see that." *But who am I to tell her not to? She is fucking good at it.*

Split Up

Krimsey Enosh, Tuesday, March 26, 2250, 10:07 p.m.

KRIMSEY LOOKED AT CYN. "What do we do now?"

Cyn smooshed her lower lip between her thumb and forefinger, frowning at Felice. "Same thing we were going to do, only quicker."

"What were we *going* to do? I still don't know anything over here." Krimsey flapped his arms in exasperation. The little girl in the corner was now awake, staring cross-legged with big eyes. "Let me start from the top so you can understand," Cyn overenunciated, her whole face passionately jumping into the explanation she was about to give. "And then we've really got to get moving."

Cyn paused, giving a quick side-eye to Felice.

"Originally, the plan was simple. Lamia's current desperate, downward spiral would self-sabotage." Cyn's lips pursed into an I-can't-believe-I'm-having-to-explain-myself expression.

Krimsey didn't love her condescending tone. Or her raised brows. Her intense stare.

"She's been off her game for months now. All I had to do was put enough into motion, get a very concerning message out to the NWA—concerning enough to send somebody in person—and everything would unravel." Her voice shook and grew approximately four decibels. "Taking Prae, who is one of four new arrivals Lamia still plans on taking to the lab, was part of this plan. Cause a bit of chaos. Throw Lamia off. It worked. Lamia gets exposed. The NWA swoops in."

Cyn's hands, mainly her pointer finger, joined the rant.

"Only, Lamia hasn't been exposed. She's crafty. She's smart. She's even already working on kidnapping those other three children. She's a storyteller. And when you and Felice jammed the power, it also left a gap in my defenses that I hadn't thought to close." Her voice crescendoed. Krimsey could swear that spit flew. "They were able to get into my system, like a crack they opened wider and wider and wider. Lamia used me as part of her cover-up story and it seems to be working. She has been trying to find me, expose me, and use me as a way to distract the NWA rep who arrived as a response to my message.

"What the outage also did was buy Lamia time with the rep. She's been covering up her tracks quite well with him, given the circumstances. It's like she can't be caught in a lie or something. Without proof one way or the other, the lie just fizzes. Everything she's doing to the *transitus* children on this island would have been exposed by now if not for the power outage."

Cyn was clearly riled up now.

Krimsey felt physically ill, though he knew that wasn't the guilt. It was his body changing. He imagined his lungs cocooning like a caterpillar and turning to complete goo. "I feel terrible."

"Nonsense." Cyn took another long, deep breath. "You're going to help and you're going to get your sister out of that damn lab. Lamia has the rep convinced that her death records are legitimate. We need to get her out and get her to the rep."

"How will you do that?" Felice leaned on the kitchen counter, casual, but looking like a wounded animal.

Cyn gave Felice a hard stare, inhaled through her nostrils, looked out the door to the grassy field, then returned her gaze to Krimsey as if coming back from a dream. "You and Zeph will leave. I've already shown Zeph how to get to the lab, but the transports are too risky. Zeph will need to swim to the outside of the lab and communicate door-code instructions to Elpida."

Felice laughed. Something that sounded more like a screeching or cawing bird than human.

"Swim?" Krimsey asked, looking at Felice. Felice had her lips clamped shut, her arms crossed, and a buried smile that almost looked painful.

"I'm sorry, that's just not going to work," Felice said to the floor, still hiding her smile, just loud enough to hear.

Krimsey's trust in her was diminishing. How else would Lamia have found them? Felice must have sent a signal. And now she was learning their entire plan.

Mind-speak? He projected the thought outwards, wondering why Cyn wasn't being more careful.

"The lab is an old repurposed SCUBA base," Cyn continued out loud without missing a beat. She didn't acknowledge Krimsey's request or Felice's outburst. "From before the HPO was the HPO. Zeph's going to get your sister out, Krimsey. What I need you to do is to go back to where you shut down the power. When you shut the power down, it fucked up my plan but gave me a brilliant idea. I need you to trip the coms security alarm. Everyone is trained to evacuate their homes and go Up Top when this alarm sounds. When you execute this perfectly to the timing I've mapped out, Zeph will be Up Top by the dome with Elpida. The families will be there. Lamia will be there. The rep will be there. The rep will see that Elpida is alive. Lamia will be finished."

"What about the other three kids who are in danger?"

"I don't have a handle on them because the kids don't have coms yet. Stick to the plan. I know where your sister is and that's the lab. Stick to what we know."

The plan gave him hope, but the details evaded him. Cyn and Krimsey spent the next ten minutes going over the timing, the exact instructions as to how to trip the alarms, step by step. How the aftermath would play out. He was still uneasy. Sheets and sheets of maps, codes, instructions, and data were strewn across the table.

He knew why Zeph had to be the one to communicate the door-codes to Elpida, because of Zeph's mind-speak. But he wanted to be the one to rescue his sister. He wanted to be the first friendly face she saw. And he wanted to see her one last time before he transitioned completely to a new life underwater, without her. He couldn't help but think about everything that could go wrong. For example, they had no coms. Their timing had to be perfect. So how were they going to execute perfect timing when they had no way to tell time?

"What if we're caught?" He asked. "What do we do then?"

"Then, it's over. We give up." Cyn's voice was flat.

Krimsey thought she wasn't serious. But her eyes were solemn.

"We have one chance. This is the best shot we've got," she said with a matter-of-fact shrug. "I've played out thousands of scenarios in my head and the truth is, this may not work. That's life. Is there another way? Absolutely. The world does not operate in black and white. It's black and white and all the in between."

"Chaos," Zeph said. They leaned against the door frame behind Krimsey with their arms crossed.

"Yes, well, no one can ever make guarantees," Cyn said. "But we can do our damned best."

The thought of failure raised Krimsey's temperature.

"Hey," Zeph said, poking him in the good shoulder with their elbow. "We're the heroes. Heroes win." They gave him a brief smile, then turned around and headed outside. "Come on."

Cyn nodded her head toward the doorway. "You better be on your way."

Krimsey headed outside, but as he did so, he glanced back one more time to look at Felice. Her expression was unreadable. She looked away the moment their eyes met. Krimsey swallowed, looked ahead, and saw that Zeph was already halfway to the hole in the ground at the far end of the valley. He turned and chased after them, ignoring the strong *thwaps* of reedy grass making cuts on his ankles.

When Krimsey got to the cavern, he shouted into it. "We're going to need to work together to get back to the HPO." His voice bounced back at him.

"*I* know how to get back," Zeph said.

Krimsey lowered himself down the rough rock. At the bottom of the cavern, Krimsey saw a faint highlight on Zeph's cheek. A crunchy thud echoed off the walls. Eyes looked up at him. "Come on."

Krimsey climbed down the rock, his ribcage creaking, suppressing a cough. "Are you going to tell me what your actual problem is or what? Is it because you think I'm a coward? Or is it because of our fight you say you've left in the past?" Krimsey concentrated on his footing. The rock cut into the skin on his knees and hands. He paused for a breath. He thought he was a coward, but he hoped that it was more of an internal struggle. Not one that was visible for others.

He reached the bottom. For a moment, the only sound was the thudding in his own ears. Zeph uncrossed their arms, looked away, and crawled out of the cavern. Krimsey managed to keep up and they headed down the foothills together.

The town below was dark.

"You're not a coward, Krimsey," Zeph said after a while. "If anything, you've proven to be the opposite. It's nauseating. You have no sense of self-preservation. You're risking your chance at your life in the ocean to save your sister."

"You called me self-centered and judgy," Krimsey said.

"I'm just mad, okay? Let me be mad and stop prying into my business."

Krimsey stopped prying.

Sweat trickled down his shirt as he followed Zeph through the tunnels that connected the port town to the HPO. His chest constricted. Breathing was difficult and pain spiked like needles in his lungs. Zeph stared ahead, keeping a consistent pace. Krimsey panted to keep up. Soft, echoing footsteps and labored breathing were all he had for company until Zeph abruptly stopped and turned to look at him.

"I have no one." Zeph's cheeks glistened with tears and sweat. Their eyes were puffy and actively held in a pool of tears. They were looking everywhere—the wall, the ceiling, the floor—except at him. "I am mad at you because I have no one. No one to lose. No one to save. No one who would come for me. You have everything to lose. I would give anything to have whatever it is you have that drives you."

Zeph's dark, shimmering eyes met his. They faced him, unmoving, and their bottom lip curled. The tears Zeph had been holding back spilled down their face. Krimsey held his breath, unsure of what to do.

"You don't have to do anything," Zeph said. "I just had to make sure someone knew. You are a fucking hero. Your sister is lucky to have you."

For the first time in his life, Krimsey saw it. The strength, power, and conviction that had always been inside him. "Thank you."

"Yeah." Their voice was kind and soft. Weak? Sad. Tears still flowed. "Shall we continue?"

Krimsey put a hand on Zeph's shoulder. They stiffened, but didn't push him away. He pulled them in and gave a tight hug before letting them go.

In the distance there was a metallic *bang*. Krimsey froze. Zeph stopped crying and pressed against the curved tunnel wall, motioning Krimsey to do the same.

The two of them listened. All Krimsey heard now was air. Whistling air.

"Come on. It's just the air vents." Krimsey took a step out. Zeph's arm darted out and slammed him back against the wall.

Something is wrong, they thought at him.

Krimsey waited for Zeph to explain.

Do you think we're being followed? They jabbed a finger behind them.

"No. This place is dead," he whispered.

We should split up now. Just in case.

Krimsey considered this. There was another loud crash. "Sounded like a transport car." He couldn't believe the HPO had those all this time.

Maybe they're looking for us. Listen.

Zeph tapped their head.

Go straight until you come to a fork. Stay left, go up the stairs. Continue until you see the blue lights, take the second right, then an immediate left to a dead end. There is a door at the end. It leads to more stairs. Go down the stairs and that tunnel will take you straight to the bottom of Karuli Crag. Got that?

Krimsey's head reeled.

I think so… but what if we're caught?

Don't get caught. Zeph took a tentative step, as if testing a pressure point. There was a knot in Krimsey's throat, rooted in his chest like a clump of cancer. It felt as if ten thousand kilograms of stone compressed his lungs, ribs, and spine. It was uncomfortable to swallow. He tried to press all worry from his thoughts as he split away.

But, he realized, it wasn't *his* worry. It was Zeph's. Stopping to watch Zeph leave, he tried to impart some confidence to them. He opened a tiny wall of emotion. Let out a small stream of newfound confidence. Repayment for all that they had ever instilled into him. Zeph glanced back and smiled.

The Cure

Felice Karuli, Tuesday, March 26, 2250, 10:44 p.m.

SMELLS OF MILLION-YEAR-OLD EARTH entered through the window from downdrafts in the valley outside. Prae shifted in her pile of bedding. Electronics hummed with white noise. Felice stared at Cyn from across the table; the woman's eyes had not left hers in the thirty minutes since Zeph and Krimsey had left.

The back of Felice's skull tingled; she rolled her shoulders and stretched her neck. She blinked, trying to piece together the woman in front of her.

"Why don't you leave?" she finally rasped through sore vocal cords and a burning throat.

Suddenly, Cyn stood and stepped toward the kitchen counter. She set a kettle on a little freestanding burner. "Oolong?"

"Oo-what?"

"It's tea, dear child," Cyn said.

"I've never heard of it."

"Maybe you should widen your palate."

"I have a very sophisticated palate."

"I'll make you a cup. It'll help soothe the throat."

"Thank you." Felice coughed the words into the crook of her elbow. As Cyn prepared tea on the counter, little snores came from Prae, who had dozed back to sleep. The child slept so much, Felice was beginning to suspect she might be drugged.

Cyn set a cup she'd retrieved from a cupboard onto the counter and sighed. Felice stretched her neck from side to side again, feeling hot and cold numbness spread from the base of her head down past her shoulders.

"You know this place as well as I do. Is there really anywhere for me to go?"

"What?"

"You asked me why I don't leave," Cyn said.

"Right." Felice hunched her back, then arched it, feeling the temperature of her discomfort plume and spread across her chest. "You made *this* ramshackle place. Couldn't you find another? And you could have tried to return Prae to her family. Lamia is going to take her to the lab."

Cyn turned around and gave Felice an inquiring stare. After a while, the kettle rumbled. Cyn poured the tea and plopped a cup in front of Felice and one in front of her own chair before sitting. The tea sloshed up the sides of the cup and had little bits of leaves in it still.

Felice sipped her liquid lava. The taste was soft and fruity, with a brightness that nipped the tongue. It filled her shriveled stomach but didn't help the growing discomfort.

"Have you given up?" Felice asked.

There was a twinkle in Cyn's eye. "I never give up. I'm quite looking forward to seeing your mother, actually."

"Are you? I'm not."

"I have some questions," Cyn said thoughtfully, her cup in one hand.

"Like what?"

"I guess you'd call it more of a curiosity than a question, per se. I'd like to know how she feels."

"Oh? How she feels about what?" Felice gasped when it felt like her lungs had caught fire. "Fuck. Zeph did a number on me. Damn it."

"That's not Zeph. That's the Pneumaphage. You're overdue on your suppressant."

Her insides did a belly flop, the impact rattled her chest. "Oh."

Cyn's bright eye winked at her, then her eyes moved along the wall behind her. A smile twitched into place. "She's here." Felice turned around and looked out the door.

Three figures at the end of the valley emerged from the ground like the undead and into the fluorescent circle of light. Felice looked back at Cyn and her heart skipped, seeing that the smile there had grown.

"What are you planning?"

Cyn wasn't going to tell her. But *damn*... she needed to know.

"Seriously, I'm on your side here." Felice coughed again. "What do you think is going to happen to the HPO when you take her out? What about the residents? I just want to make sure they're safe. You know..."

Felice stopped as Cyn stood and moved to the kitchen counter. One of the figures outside had a silhouette like a greyhound. Two others flanked either side of the graceful middle figure and they all made their way across the field.

"What are you doing?" Felice choked out, taking another sip of tea, hoping it would help.

"Greeting an old friend. What else?"

Cyn set down another cup of tea at the empty chair nearest the open door.

The hound-like silhouette of her mother trotted stealthily through the field and stopped at the porch awning. She barked an order to the people on either side of her, who clomped ceremoniously onto the creaking porch.

Felice shot out of her seat when she noticed what they wore. They were tall, bulky humans wearing dusty, dark green uniforms. Their exposed calf muscles and biceps bulged.

"For Earth's sake, Lamia! These are old world uniforms. Where the hell did you get these?" She eyed the guards' sides for firearms.

Her mother, outside, craned her head to see better through the open doorway as the guards barged in and seized Cyn from the kitchen. "Do those even work?" Felice croaked, spotting the guns and tasers on each hip.

One of the men grunted.

"Stop," Lamia shouted, her eyes moving to meet Felice's. There was a guard on either side of Cyn, each grasping an arm. Lamia stepped onto the porch and stepped through the doorway.

"Mother," Felice rasped.

Lamia ignored her but looked furious. Probably because Felice never sent any signal. She could tell by the twitch above her eye and by the taut skin on her face. The hot and cold sensations chased after each other from Felice's skull to her chest, as if in a race.

"Too many people in here," Lamia muttered. "You two wait outside. You stay, Felice. Sit."

"The hell is going on?" The outline of her mother's face fuzzed at the edges, then sharpened. She questioned if it had happened at all.

"When was the last time you ate? You look terrible. I *said* sit." Lamia's arm moved as if to dart to Felice's forehead, but then stopped short. Felice glanced at Cyn, whose smile twitched wider.

Lamia's booming commands aroused Prae. She wriggled and unfurled like a bleary-eyed cat amongst her cozy nest.

"I'm hungry," Prae said tearily, rubbing her eye. "Where's my mom?" Her face was wet with snot and tears.

Lamia looked down at the table. "Tea? I'm quite hungry, actually, though I wouldn't mind the tea." Lamia's voice was chipped and guarded while Prae's cries for her mom crescendoed. "What do you keep here, Cyn? Do you mind?" Cyn stood to go comfort the girl.

Lamia turned and snapped, "Let me." Still ignoring Prae, she rummaged in the tiny kitchen cupboard without any regard for leaving things in their place.

Cyn sat back down. "Are you telling her or am I?"

"About the suppressant? You're an old fool. She already knows."

Lamia scrounged in the cupboard with more urgency. She pulled open a sealed bowl, sniffed, made a satisfied sound, and turned back to the table. She placed the bowl filled with almonds in the middle of the table.

"How are you feeling, Daughter? Let me refill your tea so we can enjoy it together."

"I've been better." Felice spotted a glass-vial-sized lump in Lamia's dress pocket. Lamia plucked the tea from in front of Felice and turned to the counter, supposedly to administer suppressant to Felice.

"I wouldn't do that." Cyn's eyes were dead set on Lamia.

Lamia stopped and, instead of looking at Cyn to answer, looked at Felice. No, she didn't look. She *examined*. "Why not?"

Prae's cries were incessant. Felice pushed her chair from the table and stood. She was dizzy.

"Felice. Stop," Lamia said. "You need your suppressant."

"Yeah, well, you need to be a mother for once," Felice shouted, swaying by the table. She placed a hand on the back of her chair to steady herself.

Prae's cries hiccuped to a momentary silence. Felice walked through the mess on the floor to get to the six-year-old. Picking her up to rock her against her chest, Felice glared at Lamia.

Lamia opened her mouth, surely prepared with a snip-mouthed retort, but then Cyn pounded a fist into the table. Teacups rattled and splashed. "My only question—" Cyn's voice was like a bomb bursting. Slowly, she pulled her fist from the table—"Mrs. Karuli: *Why* on *Earth* would you keep the cure to Pneumaphage from your dying daughter?"

Felice's first thought, Prae still sniveling and wrapped against her, was that there was no cure to Pneumaphage and that there may never be a cure, should Cyn's plotting succeed. Cyn must have mixed up her words. Realization was a deep uneasiness in the pit of her belly, though, as she watched her mother's face.

Lamia's face shifted from indignant and inconvenienced to something else, heavy and burdened. Her lips shook before she spoke. "You didn't."

"Didn't what?" Felice asked, horror filling her. Her body wasn't just reacting to the lack of suppressant. Cells and systems inside her were shifting, bubbling up, and morphing.

Lamia watched Cyn, sat at the seat by the counter, folded her hands in her lap, and her face—her *face*—was unrecognizable. Whether it was the lighting, Felice's changing, blurry vision, or a true external shift in appearance, she could not see her mother in those eyes anymore. "Drink your tea, Daughter."

Felice looked at Cyn for guidance. Cyn shook her head.

"You mess with *children*, Lamia. Children." Now Cyn's gaze flicked between Felice and Lamia. Felice felt small. She hugged Prae tighter. "I've been thinking about this moment for a long time. I've watched what you've done. Tables have turned now. How does it feel to lose? Tell me, what kind of dread is it you feel in the pit of your stomach? What kind of wrenching in your heart? Or did you lose the ability to feel somewhere along the way?"

Lamia was quiet. Her lip quivered.

"Tell me, Lamia, why are you so repulsed by your own kind? Why do you want to eradicate *transitus*? Why—"

"Forgive me for believing, with every fiber of my being, that the human race is worth saving. Being *transitus* is the worst thing that has ever happened to this planet. The *transitus* genome will be just a blight on our history when I'm through with it. We deserve our humanity back. Humankind doesn't just jump ship because life is tough, or we'd have gone to Earth-forsaken Mars, you goddamn fucking cunt." Lamia stood and turned to Felice. Her eyes swam in pent-up tears. Felice had never seen her mother cry. The red-eyed tears poured harder as she examined Felice.

"Drink your damn tea," Lamia said.

Cyn blinked. "Don't."

Felice felt as if she had been injected with coals. "You gave me the same treatment as Zeph, didn't you? You made me viable."

"Suppressant will probably kill you now," Cyn said.

Felice laughed. She stared at the tea. She should have made the connection—non-viability was the inability to successfully transition. Pneumaphage was the non-viable lungs trying to become viable. So becoming more *transitus* was the cure. Cyn discovered the cure and hadn't killed anyone. "How long have you known this, Lamia?"

The edges of Felice's vision blurred. The heat in her lungs flared.

Lamia softened. Her muscles loosened. "Oh, I've always known, dear daughter. It's always been a race. Our cure or hers."

Felice turned to her mother, breathless. "But… why…?" She couldn't finish her question.

"Because then I would lose you. To the ocean. And I wouldn't want that." Lamia seemed to have already collected herself. Her focus only meant one thing—she was already plotting. "Now, will you please drink before you pass out?"

"What?" Did her mother prefer her probably dead rather than more *transitus*? Felice's last breath of fire blazed and her world tilted. She wanted to reach toward the wall behind her for support. To stop her fall. But she was too paralyzed.

Staggering, she hit the wall with her shoulder instead. Something cracked behind her and came crashing. Clutching Prae, feeling her slip, a flashback sent Felice to the night Rumi died. Back to her heart banging in her ears, looking down a black shaft, looking for Rumi. Back to the memories she did not want to relive.

A whimper echoed at her.

She blinked.

Not real.

Not real.

Except it was. It had happened. It was real. And she was opening her eyes and Prae was whimpering. Looking at her. They were on the ground. The monitor from the wall was cracked, also on the ground. Felice's chest had cushioned Prae's fall. *Thank Earth.*

The memories working their way to the surface of her mind like a rotten meal in her stomach needed to be purged. Her gaze drifted toward the table. Cyn and Lamia hadn't had time to react to the fall. Both were getting up. Felice had just enough time to form a firm—and final—opinion of each of the women.

She hated them both.

Last Wish

Artyom Simmons, 2143

Everything I knew was a lie.

I thought we couldn't have been more different. Humans and mutants.

Mutants.

The word made my skin peel as if I'd baked in the ozone for hours.

The Red Square bustled with a melting pot of them clustered at the New World Kremlin wall. Huge yellow eyes filled the chanting crowd that spilled into the streets. Dumb, sloping foreheads. Sickly shades of blue-skinned monstrosities and crops of strange red hair.

Colorfully worded signs littered my sight. Signs that said, *Human Rights are Mutant Rights!* and *STOP GOVERNING US* and *Give Us the Ocean or We'll TAKE IT.* My tenacity to get this job done was being tested because, as I shouldered through, all hell broke loose. I heard screams and dull thuds of someone being popped in the face.

Shattered glasses skittered across the brick. Spit flew into my eye. I flung out my elbows and fists. I was used to defending myself. Defending my livelihood. Defending what dignity and decency *their* kind—the *transitioned* ones—left me with after they'd desecrated all life from Ladoga Bay.

What was a fisherman without his fish?

I packed a punch, feeling the potentially fatal crunch of a nose.

A fist knocked me down. Sharp kicks to the belly and ribs sent fireworks across my vision. Chaos spread down the Square.

"Break it up! Move it!" someone bellowed. "MOVE IT."

When the torment stopped abruptly, I looked up. I blinked through blood, sweat, and blinding white spots. Code Enforcement severed the crowd in half.

Bogdan's voice cut in and out of my ear. "*Big Fish, what's your status?*" I thought I imagined it and pushed my bulky body up off the bloodied brick.

"Are you okay, sir?" a man in uniform asked me. I nodded, my heart pounding. I choked up, staining my clothes with dark red blood. "You don't look okay. Please have a seat." He took me to a raised curb.

"I'm fine," I sputtered with flecks of blood. "They just went... crazy." He checked me for signs of concussion, a clinical frown pasted to his face. I squinted at him, looking for his badge. The man caught me looking. I must have looked confused because then he said, "Just here to help."

"You a medic?" My head rolled to the side wearily.

"Street medic."

"*Shit*," I whispered just under my breath. *He's one a them.*

My eyes rolled into the back of my head and the sky went black for a moment.

A strange-looking girl surrounded by water blinked with brown-and-gold eyes behind my lids and disappeared. My heart pounded, feeling heavy.

A second later, I was staring at the street medic's eyes. They were brown, oversized, and squinting at my forehead. He daubed a stinging cut above my left brow with a cotton ball. I weakly pushed his arm away.

"Stop moving."

"You're one a *them*," I accused through gurgles of blood.

The man stopped, frowned as if *I* were in the wrong or something.

"You people ran me outta business." I hocked blood and spit dangerously close to his shoes. He made a stunted sound but then continued to tend my wounds. I looked up at him through blurry eyes.

"What are you even doing here if you don't believe in equal rights?" he asked. His hand and the disinfectant moved to a warm, trickling spot on my scalp. I sucked in breath at the sharp burn that followed. He stepped back and looked me in the eyes. I squirmed under his narrowed gaze and shifted my weight to stand.

I managed to get onto my feet.

"Where do you think you're going?" He reached for my arm.

I jerked my wrists from his, appalled. "Why are you helping me? I don' want your help. Just..." I looked him in the eye, wondering for a brief moment if he could have been human. "Keep clear of the Square," I warned him.

I slipped away, starting north through the Square. I worked my way to where the chanting mutants were the densest and slid a small object out of my pocket, tossing it close to the base of Nikolskaya Tower. Then, some sort of running occurred. Pain dulled everything. It was as if I slogged through mud.

"Big Fish! What's your status? You have ten minutes." Bogdan shouted in my ear, sounding annoyed.

My target was an inconspicuous Old World building, run-down and dirty. The building peeked around the corner from what used to be a museum. An ornate, neo-Russian building with curved nineteenth-century overhangs, spires, and red brick.

"Sorry B. I was held up. Big Fish is now on target."

"Held up? Are you at the door?"

I slipped into a narrow alleyway and came upon the side door of the building. The door had hydraulic hinge locks and was ten centimeters thick.

"Yes. Awaiting instruction."

A red smear of blood spattered my knuckles. Shaking, I wiped the fluids from my face and hands with my shirt. Bogdan guided me through the mechanics of the door. I threw all the vats of my bubbling fury into jimmying that damn door.

The door stayed shut.

Red-stained tears rushed into my palms like rivers of blood. My empty stomach lurched, like a stone had struck the pit.

"*Big Fish, get it together.*" Bogdan continued to guide me but my hands, now slick with red tears, fumbled. "*Six minutes,*" he said. It took another two minutes and a strangely calm Bogdan to get me inside. The room was dark and abandoned.

"*Four,*" Bogdan said.

I pounded down the hallway at the rear of the room. Burning pain in my ribs, stomach, shins, and forearms lit a fire in me. I traced my fingertips down the wall, counting the number of doorways they skidded over. Halting at four, I shoved the door open. Something in me cracked.

I stumbled through the doorway, grasped a small black detonator from my pocket, and raced down the dim underground tunnel.

"*Two minutes.*"

I placed the first detonator halfway down the tunnel. My surge of accomplishment was quickly stamped out by sharpness building in my stomach.

"*One minute.*"

The stone in my stomach tightened around a piercing thought. I was not getting out of the tunnels alive.

I barreled on.

It was when I placed the fourth detonator that I began to wonder why the mutant medic had been so kind to me.

I placed the fifth and last detonator.

I simultaneously wished for my pain to be gone and for—

The Test

CYN WAS STANDING STILL on the other side of the table, keeping her wide smirks in check as if she held in bursts of laughter. Despite the anger she felt toward her, Felice knew she still had to side with Cyn and do whatever it was that would best support her.

The woman was a bitch. Calling shots that weren't hers to call. Touché. Felice supposed it took someone who was ruthless, a little mentally unstable, and nearly two decades of living in a mountain alone, to checkmate an organization that was equally unfettered. At least Cyn didn't want anyone dead. Nor had she killed anyone. Which couldn't currently be said for Lamia. Felice could tell by the way her fingernails curled into her palms that Lamia was currently planning a murder.

Getting off the ground, Felice hoisted up Prae and set her on her feet. Felice swayed and her mother quickly snatched her shoulder. Felice looked at the firm, long fingers that gripped her, then followed the arm to meet her mother's face with the most neutral stare she could muster.

Her mother snatched her hand back. She looked down and straightened her dress out of habit. The way she did when she mistakenly stepped into territory that could have been deemed as motherly. Too motherly. She'd had a brief lapse earlier, but the tears were now dry. Lamia projected strength. Only strength. Control.

"I guess we won't worry about the tea, though you seem worse for wear," Lamia said.

"Okay." Felice stole a glance at Cyn, ignoring that Lamia had moments ago suggested Felice drink a tea that would have been, most likely, an action of suicide. "Now what?" Whether she liked it or not, her mother was still in control.

"You're taking this…" her mother started, flicked her grey eyes at Felice.

"How do you want me to take it? What's the plan? I know you have one." Felice needed time alone to process whatever was happening with her body. There was going to be a lot of that when this was all done.

Lamia straightened. "We go to port," she said, with her com flashing. "And rest. Where is Krimsey? And Zeph?"

"Are you worried about Krimsey and Zeph?"

"Should I be?"

"Cyn *did* send them away." Felice stole a glance at Cyn, feeling like the woman was picking her apart. Still deciding to trust her or not. Felice needed to play this just right.

"Where?" Lamia asked.

Felice shrugged. "I wasn't privy to the plan."

Felice trailed behind Lamia and watched as she clambered down into the dark hole out of the valley, one of the guards assisting her. With her dainty dress and sandals, her mother struggled, pitched a loud fit of profanities half way down, and Felice held in her laughter. Though her own clamber down wasn't the epitome of grace.

Once out of the valley, Felice caught up to her mother and the guards who had Cyn and Prae in custody. Prae cried. Cyn looked withdrawn in contemplation. Felice flexed her sore, sprained wrist. Lamia's lip curled up in a scowl. "Barbarian," she spat, lifting her dress, starting down through the foothills. "Who lives like that?"

Following the procession, Felice wanted to comment but found no words. Her thoughts had turned dark. "Will you send her to Mainland?"

"Cyn? No."

"What are you going to do with her?"

"I haven't decided yet."

"You wouldn't...?" Felice didn't really know what her mother was capable of doing anymore. She didn't want her mother suspecting she no longer trusted her. But she also wanted to be sure Cyn—and, more importantly, Prae—wouldn't be hurt. She played with this delicate ground of trust, a razor-blade edge.

"Wouldn't what, Felice?" The question was posed as a challenge. Lamia saw right through Felice's thinking. Perhaps because it was also on her mind. "I do not have plans to dispose of her, if that's what you're asking." Her laugh barked in the high wind.

Felice was quiet.

"Just how infernal a person do you think I am, Daughter?" Still, dark thoughts brooded. Lamia looked over her shoulder. Her lips curled into a dry smile. "Did you really think that? That I'd off her? She's been a thorn in my side for a long time, but I'm not going to *kill.*"

"And Prae?"

"You already know the plan for Prae."

Felice's vision streaked red. What a strange world Lamia's head must live in. To have it all so twisted. To take Prae to the lab *was* to kill. Did she really not see that?

"So if Cyn sent Krimsey and Zeph away, how do you not know where they went? You must have heard them talking."

"I didn't." She did. But there seemed to have also been an awful lot of dialogue going on without speech. Felice elaborated. "Somehow, they seemed to know things. Sharing a look felt like more than just a look. Like..." Felice hesitated, knowing that giving her mother this kernel of knowledge was risky. She avoided looking at Cyn. She had to give Lamia something. "Like they could read thoughts."

"That's nonsense."

Felice ignored her mother for the rest of the walk. If she had further questions, they'd go unanswered. She didn't care anymore. She felt sick. Her very thoughts were so disgusted with herself, with her mother, with Cyn, that they were making her physically ill. Her body was in rejection of simply existing. She should have taken the tea.

They slept in an emptied guide suite at the port town lodging. All the parents and the respective guides had been relocated by Carmak to the HPO.

It was well into the night when Felice sat up from sleep. On the edge of the bed, a vague idea touched her mind. It solidified. Dropped into her lap as a word of gratitude. *Thanks.* She knew that it came from Cyn. Though she wasn't sure how a thought in her mind could have a voice separate from her own. Just then, she knew for certain that Krimsey, Zeph, and Cyn really had been swapping thoughts. For some reason, Cyn found reason to grant Felice a space in the safety of her *transitus* mind. For some reason, it worked.

She really was *transitus.* She was changing. She wondered if this was what *transitus* emotion felt like.

Cyn was locked in a room upstairs with the guards, who were likely sleeping. Cyn's mind beckoned Felice. Felice crept up the stairs and paused at the door. Her hand hovered over the handle.

Don't speak. It was no longer the fuzzy voice from when she was downstairs. Now, it was so clear in her head, she squinted a double-take at the closed door.

"How did you—?"

What did I just say? The voice oozed ire. *Do not speak. Not out loud.*

Forsaken Earth...

The fact that *transitus* shared emotion was common knowledge. She had heard it described as a constant flow of moods in the air. She had heard that it was harder for children to control. Older *transitus*, on the other hand, easily blocked and freed their own flow of emotion.

Wishy-washy emotion, untethered and floating in the air, was one thing. Sharing thoughts, though? It was entirely unheard of. How was the woman sharing thoughts? Though she had been suspecting this incredible ability for hours now, she could hardly believe it was true. And that it was happening to her.

Unwelcome and unexpected, Cyn's mind sliced hers with an explanation through the closed door—hardly forming actual words, but Felice understood. And the explanation was shocking. Not the explanation itself, but that Cyn knew that Felice had thought a question at all. Cyn knew what she was thinking.

A numb tingle ran down her spine.

Cyn conveyed to her that this was not, in any sense, the same as *transitus* emotion. And conveyed that Cyn and her child, Zeph, possessed abilities beyond rational understanding and beyond that of a typical *transitus*.

It goes deep. As deep as thought itself. Your presence has emerged since you took the treatment I gave you in the valley. The strength of you grows as the minutes pass.

Treatment. The word felt sour. Like the foul bitterness on the back of her tongue after eating something sweet. Just another woman pulling her strings. Forcing her life into one direction after the next. She supposed that that was how Rumi must have felt. And the other non-viable *transitus* kids, if they were to discover what had been done to them. Felice looked out the foggy window at the end of the hall to calm the rising heat. Cyn could probably sense everything. She had to keep calm.

I wanted to thank you, Cyn said.

For what? Felice wondered, thinking of how Cyn, Cyn's plan, Krimsey, Zeph, and Felice were all terribly screwed.

Something resembling laughter tickled the nape of her neck.

We would be screwed, Cyn started, *if you had told your mother our plan. And you didn't. You've proved yourself.*

Proved myself. *She had been testing her. And she passed the test.* Felice took a deep breath. More strings.

I sense your frustrations and they are warranted. I'm sorry for putting this on you without consent. I'll be honest, my motives for curing you in that manner, without consent, were along the lines of a personal vendetta.

The apology was nice, and Felice could only assume it was sincere, but she was still mad. The sadistic irony of her predicament was not lost on her. She understood now, more than ever, the damage she was responsible for having inflicted upon other *transitus*.

It was a dirty move, I know, Cyn continued. *You've earned my respect, and my trust. How might I earn yours?*

There was nothing Cyn could do to earn Felice's trust. There was nothing anyone could do. Her trust in others was permanently marred. But Felice just needed to know what was next. She needed to feel less useless.

I may have a plan, Cyn's thought was pointed directly at Felice.

What's that? Felice found this mode of communication haunting. A strange, internal pressure reminding her of Lamia's big lie. Her own identity, kept from her for thirty years.

I have much faith in my child and can only hope Zeph and Krimsey will succeed. But I do have a new proposal. Something we can do to help ensure our success.

What is it? Felice asked.

Concerned Friend

Krimsey Enosh, Wednesday, March 27, 2250, 3:06 a.m.

THERE WAS AN EXTRA com in Krimsey's pocket. Before going to coms security where he would have to trip the coms alarm for Zeph and Cyn, he had returned home, hijacked his mother's com while she was asleep, and pocketed it—just in case he could find a way to hack it and use it for telling the time. Now he was down in the HPO Underground. He reached into his pocket—

There were two coms.

Who would have put an extra in his pocket? Without telling him, at that. The only people who could have done it were either people he didn't trust or people who had no reason to be sneaky.

Someone was trying to track him. He wondered if that was how Lamia found Cyn's location. He detoured down a random tunnel and tossed both coms into a dark room. Then, Krimsey returned to his route, heading carefully towards coms security.

He measured time by the changing glow coming from the blue lights lining the tunnels. Operating on the same timers as The Bowl and Gianvante Lake, at 3:30 a.m. the lights switched from a barely-visible blue to a low, dull grey.

His plan was interrupted. On his mission to trip the alarms at just the right moment, to clinch the HPO's doom, Krimsey ran into a problem.

That problem had red flaming hair.

Had a name.

Cris Langley.

Surely, Cris, who for some reason was hanging out in a dead-end hallway of the coms wing, hadn't spotted him? The moment Krimsey saw him, he knew there was trouble. Cris was a variable. A distraction. And that was the problem. What the hell was Cris doing down here, anyway?

Krimsey dashed back to the last intersecting tunnel and crouched around the corner. He held his overactive heart as still as possible. As still as a heart could get. The thing thudded so fast, he was sure it was trying to escape. It felt liquefied. Like it squeezed between rib bones.

It didn't matter, though, because he was still breathing and Krimsey knew he had to either get past Cris without being spotted—if he hadn't been already—or he had to go punch Cris in the leg and ask him, *"What the hell?"*

His brain told him to run. To carry on without delay. But his melting heart told him other things. Told him he had time to kill. And the strange, budding friendship with Cris had an allure to it. Like an Earthforsaken fish, Krimsey was drawn to the shine.

He heard a door open and close. Footsteps. He held his breath. He looked for somewhere to hide. There was a door directly across from him. He tried the knob but it was locked. There was another intersection further down this tunnelway which could conceal him as long as the footsteps weren't planning to turn this way. He could make a run for it…

The steps stopped. There was a sharp squeak—another door opening. A metallic *thwum*. The door closing. The tunnels were quiet again.

Krimsey scooched to the edge of the wall and looked around. No one was there, but that didn't mean he couldn't be caught. He had to be careful not to run into anyone working the final hours of the night shift. He put his head between his knees.

"Psst."

Krimsey poked his head around the corner again. Cris's own head peered around from the dead-end hall. Their eyes met. Cris motioned at him. He mouthed, *"Come here."*

Krimsey stood with effort, heard another noise, and retracted from view. Several seconds passed.

"*Psst.*" If Cris's calls got any louder, there would be more trouble. For a moment, Krimsey lowered the walls around his emotion and stabbed generally toward Cris with his annoyance. He snuck along the wall and shot into the hall where Cris was. Cris yanked him further into the shadows.

"What the hell are you doing here?" Cris asked.

Wondering the same exact thing, Krimsey was stunned into silence.

"After the ceremony incident, I kept hearing your name. All night, my dad was going crazy. Really on edge. Did you know everyone is looking for you?"

Krimsey blinked. "Uh." He knew that. He looked nervously back at the main hall.

"No one is going to see you," Cris said. "No one comes here. My dad works coms security. He's the only one down here."

It sounded like Cris's dad was going to be an issue.

"I followed him tonight when he left for the night shift," Cris said.

"Why?"

"He kept talking about you," Cris said, taking a small step forward.

That didn't answer the question.

Krimsey looked around. They stood in the dark corner of the hall. It looked like an unfinished tunnel that someone had just stopped building. Budget ran out. Or ran out of gas. That's what they used back then, wasn't it? His eyes landed back on Cris.

"What are you doing here?" Cris asked.

Krimsey was acutely aware of how close Cris's forearm was to his. Cris's yellow eyes, which were level to his own, made him wonder how he was only just noticing they were the same height.

"I found the ghost," Cris said.

"What?" Krimsey asked, realizing he had been staring too long at the shape of Cris's upper lip, the way it dipped a little in the middle.

"The pings on your com? I found her."

Krimsey looked out at the lit corridor again. He took half a step backward so Cris couldn't feel the bubble of heat his body generated. His mind was becoming hazy and the distance allowed him clarity. He shook his head. "Cris, what are *you* doing here? I can't be seen by coms security right now."

"Why? What's going on?"

"I just can't. I'm…" He looked back, then again to Cris for the third time.

Cris took half a step forward, closing the distance Krimsey had just created. "It has to do with your sister, right?" Cris asked.

Krimsey nodded. "She's not dead."

"I believe you." The words were like a song. Krimsey was so relieved for the friendship he had in Cris, he could have been moved to tears. Cris was an ally. Not a threat.

"Ok. Does that mean… you'll help me?" Krimsey asked. "I mean, you've already helped me. You don't owe me anything. But… I—"

"Yes."

"What?"

"I'll help. What do you need?"

Krimsey relaxed a little, but he still glanced over his shoulder to nervously check the hallway. He pressed his toes into his sandals at the same speed as his quickening heart.

Bum-bum bum-bum.

His forehead was hot.

"Are you sure? You might get into trouble." Krimsey turned back to Cris.

"Yes, I'm sure. When I kept hearing your name, I just felt like…" Cris trailed off in thought, looking away and biting his lip.

"Like you're still a *concerned friend*?" Scalp tingling.

Teeth peered from behind Cris's lips. His smile was nervous as his eyes moved across Krimsey's face. "I *am* a concerned friend… and you look like you've had a rough night."

"I have," Krimsey said, and suddenly the burden of his tired, changing body became heavy.

Bum-bum.

His chest pattered and his belly flipped. Everything felt twisted. Krimsey was staring again at Cris's lips. Why could he not stop staring at them? Cris's smile lowered to cover the slivers of perfect teeth. When Krimsey felt the heat of Cris's arm again, he realized they had gotten even closer to each other. He wanted to step back but didn't. It was like the inevitability of two magnets. Drawing closer and closer and closer.

"If we're being honest." Cris lowered his voice and shuffled very obviously toward him. Staring intently. He touched Krimsey's arm. "I didn't want that to be the last time I saw you."

What was happening to his heart? *Bum-bum.* It raced and felt weak. Whatever stirred in him, whatever was about to happen, he didn't want it to stop.

"I feel the same way." Did he really say that? And was this really happening? He wanted to tell Cris exactly how he felt—and had felt since Survival Daily. "Maybe we should…" He didn't have the words.

Cris's eyes sent everything aflutter.

Sensing his eagerness, Krimsey stepped forward to close the gap between them. He was shaking. Not externally, but everything on the inside trembled. The heat of Cris's skin brushed his arm and caught his fingers. Four of their fingers locked in a playful game. Cris smiled nervously. Tingles followed. Cris leaned his head forward, as if coming in for a kiss. Cris dipped his eyes and stared at Krimsey's lips.

"Is this alright?" Cris asked.

Heart racing, head spinning, Krimsey nodded, leaned in as well and met Cris's lips with his. Cris's lips were a warm, plush embrace. He tasted like mint and earth. Everything felt right.

What am I doing? This isn't helping my sister.

Krimsey pulled back, heart and mind jumbled. "That was—"

Cris smiled. He reached back around Krimsey's shoulder. Pulled him back in. They kissed again. His insides were hopelessly tangled. Maybe he was transitioning.

Now?

He yanked away. Doubled over, coughing into his lap. Gasping. Cris was there, touching his back, asking, "That bad, huh? Hey, are you okay?" while Krimsey coughed out half a lung. When the episode stopped, Krimsey slid heavily against the wall. Cris knelt down, but he wasn't looking at Krimsey. He looked into the other corner, just past Krimsey's shoulder. No eye contact.

Kissing was a mistake. His thoughts were fuzzy. Biting his lip, the awkward silence grew arms and legs. Did Cris realize how close Krimsey was to his death? Transition? Whatever? Krimsey didn't know what was about to happen next, but he knew that Cris was on a different sort of path. He wasn't part of Krimsey's future. Not now. Not later.

For Earth's sake, what am I doing?

He was queasy and wanted to apologize.

"It's okay," Cris said.

The knots in his belly tightened. Scrunched, then unscrunched. Krimsey hadn't checked his emotional barriers and realized they streamed forth, unfiltered. He clamped up.

"It's okay," Cris said again, in response to what was sure to have been embarrassment seeping from Krimsey's pores. "Maybe after we're both transitioned, maybe one day we'll meet again."

Krimsey brought his knees up and put his forehead against his palms. "We shouldn't have... done that." The knots threatened his stomach with upheaval.

"No." Cris looked over at him. He placed a hand on Krimsey's knee. The touch felt forced. Cris retracted. "I'm glad for it."

Krimsey's mind spun. "What time is it?"

"3:40. Tell me how I can help."

Krimsey froze. "Your com... They track those. Did you know that?"

"Of course. I'm the son of a coms security worker." He took his com out of his ear to show it to Krimsey. It was old. The plastic had gouges in it and the model was boxy, not sleek. "It's not linked to the network."

"Where is your dad?"

"He works between rooms 515 and 521."

"515. That's the room I need to get into. I need to trip an alarm. At eight a.m.."

Cris's face tensed. He said nothing.

"You'll distract him for me? Your dad."

"Of course. Will you tell me what's going on?"

Krimsey explained everything. Cris listened with patience, occasionally looking away pensively. He told him about Cyn, Zeph, the HPO, attacking Lamia, the lab, the rep, and the plan to break his sister out from it. He told him what was going to happen next. He'd trip the alarm. Everyone would evacuate. Head Up Top like obedient citizens.

That's where the HPO would fall.

Cris nodded slowly.

"You're taking this very well," Krimsey said.

"Well… there's a lot that can go wrong," he started, staring through the darkness. "I want to help you. I knew these bastards were corrupt."

"No, you didn't." Krimsey smiled. "But you're right. And I'm worried about Zeph. What if they fail? Or if I do? I just don't know what happens next."

"Well first of all, *you* won't fail. Because you have me." He smiled. "Second of all, you will have done what you can. That's all you can do."

"What would you do? If it was your sister?"

Cris contemplated his answer by staring harder through the dark. "I don't have a sister."

"What if you did?"

"I guess…" Cris looked him in the eye. "You want me to say I'd go get her. But I wouldn't. People like us… we can't just think of ourselves."

"What do you mean?"

"There's a whole society out there. Waiting to be born. Waiting for us to grow old in the ocean. Waiting to be unearthed. If I were you, I'd leave. Now."

"Oh."

"We're different."

"I know that."

Cris leaned toward Krimsey. Breath hot on his skin. A soft, firm kiss landed for the third time on his lips. One that was solid. With intention. It lingered only briefly. Then Cris pulled away.

"What was that for?"

"I want to remember the feeling."

GREY

Felice Karuli, Wednesday, March 27, 2250, 5 a.m.

WHEN FELICE RETURNED TO the guide suite from her mind-speak conversation with Cyn and quietly snapped the door closed, Lamia stirred and sat up. Despite the low light and general dishevelment, her eyes were sharp.

"Felice?" Her groggy voice croaked with a forced stiffness. "What were you doing?"

Felice distracted herself by straightening her bedsheet. Adjusting a threadbare pillow. Plucking at a thread. She climbed in. Imagining that the bed and sheets and pillows built a dam around her rising nerves. "Just getting some fresh air. I haven't been feeling well." The latter was true.

Lamia lay back down to rest.

Nostalgic as she was for the mother and HPO she once knew, what Cyn had asked of her had to happen. And she couldn't let her mother catch on. As Felice knew it, the HPO didn't work. Not for her. Certainly not for the *transitus*. Not for anyone. The community was a farce. That was clear now.

She was determined to carry out her task.

Cyn wanted Felice to make sure that the NWA rep Mr. Boyd did not leave the island. Not until he had sufficient cause to shut the HPO down. Felice was to, at all cost, make sure Mr.

Boyd witnessed Elpida Enosh reunite with her mother Up Top. Breathing. Alive. Not dead, as the falsified reports claimed.

Eight a.m. on the nose.

Easy enough.

In her darkest hours, she'd imagined NWA somehow discovering what they were doing and troops storming the place. Finding the lab. Shutting down operations. She had pictured this day—yes, *this* day—many times. The day of unraveling, unveiling, unearthing. She'd even go as far as to say she'd pictured—*fantasized*—the usurping. Usurping of her mother. Of the HPO. Of herself. Her fantasy was no longer fantasy.

Felice would have to be extremely careful in order to outmaneuver her mother. Felice had to tread lightly if today was the day Lamia was going to be undone.

While Felice had merely imagined and mused over the years, Cyn had planned. Mapped. Coded. Cyn was the mastermind. Felice and Zeph and Krimsey her willing puppets.

It was late. Or early. Depending on the perspective. Felice heard her mother's soft snores in the bed next to hers. Her own rest, as she lay down to sleep, was fleeting. Fantasy filled her head, but no dreams came.

She figured now was as good a time as any to talk to Mr. Boyd.

Before Lamia had a chance to rise from the dead of sleep, Felice readied herself. She combed her dirty hair. Scrounged a breakfast of whatever the guides had left over in the small fridge in the corner. Heaped berries, nuts, and a piece of broccoli into a bowl of powdered eggs. Breakfast in hand, she snuck out of the suite.

Two hesitant knocks on the plastic door.

"Mr. Boyd?" Felice whispered.

She knocked again.

He was lodged in the neighboring building. Probably asleep and dreaming of Mainland and well-behaved *transitus* and governing bodies that followed rules. Strict protocols.

The downstairs living space had been cleaned up by janitors. Hardly any evidence remained of the new *transitus* families. Just a forgotten hat on the hanger by the door.

Felice said the name again, knocked, waited.

She tried the knob. It wasn't locked, but she let go immediately when she heard muffled sounds from inside.

The door opened. Mr. Boyd stood in a white robe, squinting at Felice. Arms crossed over his chest. Sleep crusted his crow's-feet. His clean shave was mottled with nicks.

"Miss Karuli." His voice soured with irritation. "If you're not here to offer me coffee at this ungodly hour, then I don't—"

"Please." Felice stepped her left foot between the door and the jamb as he was closing the door and smoothly shifted her weight to the foot and slid into the room. "I need to talk to you. It's about Elpida Enosh."

What if Felice took him to where Rumi Yen was buried at Ross Bay right now? She couldn't open Elpida's locked lab dome on her own, but she could dig up the body of Rumi Yen. She could…

Careful. Felice took a deep breath. *Stick to the plan.*

Mr. Boyd uncrossed his arms and straightened his proper Mainlander robe and wrung his fingers at his side. "Spit it out, then. Your mother gave me the reports and all was satisfactory. I have a very long journey ahead of me and I don't appreciate—"

"Mr. Boyd, Elpida Enosh is—"

"It is extremely rude to interrupt."

"Oh. I'm sorry." Felice glanced at the middle of the room. Two stuffed suitcases were propped on the wall.

"Spit it out then, I'd like to get back to sleep."

"Elpida Enosh." Felice inhaled. "Her file is wrong. She is alive. And I can prove it to you. Can you meet me Up Top at eight a.m.?"

His posture deflated. "I assure you, I will not be trekking up that dreaded mountain."

"But—"

"Let this be my time to interrupt, Miss Karuli, and maybe you'll learn some manners before barging into a man's room while he's sleeping. I'm already aware of the delusions you may have in regards to what is real and what isn't. I'm aware of your condition. And I'm aware that you may *think* Enosh is alive. The situation has been explained to me *thoroughly*. The reports are quite clear."

"The situation…?"

"Indeed. Now I wish not to be the sufferer of your delirium any longer. Take care, Miss." His words were staccatoed. Felice still stood half in, half out of the swing radius of the door. He tried to close her out and the door hit her knee.

"Delirium?"

"To call the New World Alliance on baseless claims is just… such a gross misuse of power." He shook his jowls at her. "Enough of this. You clearly need rest and so do I."

"But Mr. Boyd, I didn't—this has nothing to do with me or any 'condition.'" She felt the color rise to her cheeks in a sleep-deprived, drunken sort of way. Her voice rose as high as she dare. "I'm talking about *life and death*."

"Indeed you are." Then he pushed a confused Felice out the door, which promptly slammed in her face.

She remained in a haze. Felice walked outside through thin morning mist toward the beach and found herself in the middle of what seemed to be perpetual sunrise. Antarctica tended to drink up the sun most often during the hours between night and day. The not-quite-light, not-quite-dark sky dripped in lazy, golden-red puffs. The horizon line was red and pink. The ocean beneath it had turned to blood.

Her vision shimmered and drowned in it.

The town was waking up now. People were running carts filled with recyclables over the rocky beach for loading into the ship. Shouting at each other. Felice stopped one of them, who looked startled and stared strangely at her cheeks and kept asking, "Are you ok?" Felice never answered. Instead, she asked when the ship was scheduled to leave, and the person she asked had said, "in two hours," and Felice asked, "But what time?" and, while looking for Felice's ear com and not finding one, the person said, "eight a.m."

That wouldn't do.

She'd have to delay either the ship or Mr. Boyd. Executing a plan to delay either one of them was going to be a challenge. Both presented unique concerns. Both were impossible.

Time passed. The sun stayed. That muddied red, *transitus* red, scab red, was everywhere. The whole world was dipped in it.

"What on Earth are you doing out here?" Long, unpainted fingernails curled around her shoulder, meeting the sturdiness of her clavicle and pressing against the bone. But it was the flash of movement that captured her attention. Not the sense of the touch, which had lost its intensity. Her nerves misfired. All she felt was a numb pressure. Felice looked down at her shoulder. Accompanying the long fingers were stains of color soaking on her white skin. "I've been looking everywhere for you."

Felice turned to find a caring mother's eyes that swam in crimson twilight. She wanted to see just how quickly care turned to scorn. How quickly it turned to hate. How quickly Lamia snapped *this time*. Tears spilled. The warmth of them running down her cheeks was a comfort.

"Oh dear, you're crying. Are you still feeling ill? Do you think you might be... *transitioning*? We can check your vitals as soon as we get back. I'm so sorry you're going through this..." Lamia wrapped her arms around Felice. Stroked her hair. "I'm so sorry Cyn did this to you."

A shaking anger racked Felice with sobs. She broke from her mother's embrace to face the ocean. A deep fog was rolling in. A mist of red born of the rising, bloody sun. "Am I a pawn?" Her voice was small but carried potential. "Is this a game?"

"I don't understand." Lamia's voice was flat.

"What did you tell the rep about me?" The potential in her rose.

"Oh. That was nothing. Just a bit of cleanup was all. When did you talk to the rep? Thankfully, he'll be on his way soon."

"Why did you use me like that? What did you say to him?" She didn't know why she bothered fighting. But Lamia was still her mother. Every betrayal still hurt. Every time. *Every time.*

"Of little faith..." Lamia muttered. "I have everything handled. There's nothing more for you to worry about. But if you must know, I spun two separate stories.

"I've explained to Mr. Boyd of your *condition*, all lies of course. That you experience delirium. That you think of reality as one thing when it's really another. Like Elpida Enosh being alive or dead. So I told him, that's why you called the NWA. That's why their message had come through official channels. And that's why it's unnecessary for further presence to remain."

"You... used me."

"Well I couldn't tell him that the clinically insane woman in the mountains had the ability to access our official channels, could I? Much too suspicious. I explained that Cyn's kidnapping of Prae Ogier was completely coincidental and that I had the situation under control. I took him to coms security and showed him. I told him we'd have the criminal in custody and the girl reunited with her family."

"You know…" The strength of Felice's own voice surprised her. "Had it *ever* occurred to you that I didn't want all this?" Her voice carried power. This was a new feeling. She wasn't afraid.

Lamia's eyes were the color of decay. Though they made her uncomfortable, she didn't shy from the grey gaze or fidget her feet or hyper-focus on some distracting detail. Felice didn't back down.

"My leaving for the ocean won't be the worst thing to happen to you," Felice whispered so that her mother had to strain to listen. In her mother's eyes, Felice saw only destruction. Lamia hungered for it. What would happen to Lamia once everything that mattered fell apart? Once there was nothing left to destroy? What kept her mother going, then? "My death wouldn't have even fazed you. Do you want to know the worst thing that will happen to you?"

Lamia's lips were ghost white.

"It'll be when you realize you can't live with yourself. When I'm gone, the lies that prop your perverse ways will disintegrate. You aren't doing this work for any other reason but a sick, personal crusade. You're not doing it for me. Not for Annabel. Not for the *transitus*. For *you*. There's hate in your heart. When you come face to face with that hate, that's the day. You'll see that you're just a husk."

Lamia's grey eyes avoided Felice, now. They looked toward the heavy mist and turned the color of flesh. "It's time to go."

With just four words—four mellow, measured words—Felice's backbone dissolved. The confidence held moments ago melted into her palms like wax. For a fraction of a second, her resolve shattered and she wondered if Lamia just hadn't heard her.

Her mother *had* heard her; she just didn't care. The woman had no soul. She didn't care about the pain or suffering. Felice supposed the way her mother had handled her attempts at suicide—with a pompous flick of the wrist—had been the biggest red flag of all.

"What?"

"We have to go." Lamia was steady. "Now."

"Where the hell is there to go?"

"You *know* where. To the lab. We have to—"

"Are you…?" Felice studied the stress lines and sheen on Lamia's forehead. "Are you *worried?*" Then, Felice noticed Lamia's com was blinking. Someone was pinging her. One blink. Three blinks. Five. "What's going on? Who is contacting you?"

In the flow of people trekking to and from the ship across the beach, Felice spotted Mr. Boyd with his bags coming up past Lamia's shoulder. He struggled with the luggage a good ten meters behind her.

"Was it Carmak?" Felice asked, thinking that she could throw some carefully crafted words at her mother as Mr. Boyd passed. "Are the rest of the kids taken in…?"

Mr. Boyd was five meters away, now.

"*Careful,*" Lamia hissed. "It's *fine*. Zeph just decided to interfere. And Krimsey is still loose. I had a com on him, which is how I found you all, but that's out now. He must have found it. Carmak's com just blinked out, too, but the kids are being taken in. And Zeph is in custody."

"Who is in custody, might I ask?" Mr. Boyd huffed.

Lamia's face froze. Searched the sky for some sign that she'd misheard. Then the stunned expression lit like an explosion. Lamia turned to face Mr. Boyd with a firm shoulder pat.

Felice's lip twitched and threatened to curl. This was progress.

Someone I loved

Every few minutes, Cris's dad switched security rooms, from 515 to 521 and back, and Cris and Krimsey had to pause from their idle conversation. He passed by their hiding spot in his green shirt and pants, opened a door on the other side of it, then the door clunked closed.

"What do you think he's doing that needs all the back and forth?" Krimsey asked on the fourth or fifth switch. The man was now in room 515.

Cris shrugged.

"What if he switches rooms before I can trip the alarm? What if he catches me?"

Cris's hands clasped Krimsey's. Warm. Clammy. "It's alright." Warring heartbeats knocked around the four-handed fist. "I know how to push my dad's hot spots. I'll keep you safe."

So they continued chatting. Cris's fingers left his, and ghost sensations of Cris's touch lingered. For the first time, Krimsey was excited. And hoped he didn't die. After a while, they both fell silent. Cris's dad switched rooms once more. Krimsey tilted his head against the wall and imagined what his future could be like. Before this moment, he hadn't pictured it.

He was still the same. Still terrified. Still stubborn as all forsaken Earth, holding his convictions. He had to see his little sister free. But it felt like everything had shifted. Now, the cost if he didn't make it to the water in time was clear. He saw the future Elpida had always dreamt for him.

Humans. For whatever reason, they were given countless opportunities to make amends. Fix past mistakes and heal. A million, billion opportunities. Yet they always fell short. Maybe *transitus* were born of necessity. The world was circling the drain. This was survival. Manmade or not, *transitus* were the future. The hope of the planet. This was evolution. It was terrifying. It was exciting.

"Promise me you'll get to port as soon as you can?" Cris broke their comfortable silence. "You'll ruin my fantasy if you die now."

"*Fantasy?*"

"You die now, I can't pretend I'll find you one day."

It was like he was in Krimsey's mind. "Ross Bay is quicker than port."

"Ross Bay, then," Cris said.

"Why pretend, though?" Krimsey asked. His mouth was dry, hands slick with sweat, heart beating too fast. "We could meet someplace."

"We could," Cris said. "But we won't. I'm on my own trajectory, Krimsey. But I can still fantasize. You didn't make the promise."

"I promise I will get to Ross Bay before I transition. As soon as I say goodbye to my sister."

"What if that's too late?"

"Calculated risk, then. I won't die. I promise."

Cris looked at him with a skeptical glare.

"You wouldn't understand," Krimsey said.

"Maybe I would."

"What do you mean by that?"

"I think there's a lot I'd do for someone I loved."

Krimsey was going to say something snarky, but butterflies flipped in his belly. A silly smile kept popping out of nowhere on his face.

The door down the hall clanged again. Footsteps. Krimsey's breath stopped. Cris's dad's silhouette stopped, as if pausing to listen. Half of him and the back of his feet were visible. Krimsey could be caught at any second and everything would be ruined. He had let Cris distract him from that danger. A brutal hitch caught in Krimsey's throat. Pressure in him rose.

Then the man continued. Door 521 opened and closed out of visible range.

"That was close," Cris said.

"Way too close. Is it just me or is he switching rooms more frequently now?"

"You're right."

"What time is it?"

"Way too early. It's only been half an hour. You need to do it at eight a.m., right?"

Krimsey nodded, then looked out the hall. "Maybe I should go in...."

"What? Why?"

"So I know I can do it quickly. Familiarize myself." He shouldn't have been relying on the comfort of Cris for so long. Had he wasted his time?

"I don't like that idea."

Krimsey got up anyway. Joints popped. The swelling around his heart was intense. All Krimsey could do was hope it kept beating.

Cris stood, too. He watched nervously as Krimsey clutched his chest.

"It'll go away," Krimsey said.

Cris didn't comment. "You go in. I'll stand watch. Be quick. You remember how to do it? I can explain."

"No. I can do it. Just need to see everything up close."

Krimsey pushed open door 515 into coms security and froze. He looked back. Cris nodded at him. It was Krimsey's first time looking at him fully, in the brightness of the main tunnel, since the kiss.

He really liked the way he looked. He turned away, flushing and hot.

The coms security room was dark. Dim light from the tunnel hall flooded around him. It was the same room where Felice had helped him cause the shutdown. The only thing that had changed was that now, the box Felice had destroyed was cut out from the wall. In its place, a deep hole.

The rest of the computer boxes were blinking and humming.

Tripping the alarm would be easy enough. He came up to the wall and saw the big round buttons in the middle of the machines. Exactly as Cyn had described. Toggle these controls enough and, whether an intended result or not… it turned on an evacuation alarm.

Supposedly. He must not have toggled them enough earlier when he was taking out the power.

I can do this.

He stepped out of the room and closed the door the same moment Cris's father stepped away from 521.

Not good.

The man looked up at him and frowned.

"Hi," Krimsey said.

"Hi," he said back, looking behind him, then back.

"Uh… looks good in there. I'll be on my way." Krimsey turned around in a panic. *What do I do?*

"Hey, wait."

Krimsey whirled around. "How can I help you?" *Smile.* He smiled. Bile churned at the bottom of his throat. His heart wobbled in its cage.

The man approached and squinted at him. The dark dead end hall kept Cris shrouded, but Krimsey saw his pale skin appear.

"*Get out of here,*" Cris mouthed.

"Ah, Krimsey Enosh, isn't it? I knew you'd show your face. *You're* in a lot of trouble."

Why isn't Cris helping? What am I supposed to do now? He could run. Always an option. But if he did, it would mean that he had failed. Cris could stay hidden. Wait. Sound the alarm. Krimsey liked to imagine that Cris would do that for him.

Muscles screamed at him to run. At the very least, it would cause a distraction. No one suspected Cris of anything. Why would they? He wasn't involved. And why would Cris have any reason to sound the alarm?

Krimsey tried to bolt. It was too late. The man grabbed his arm. Krimsey kicked. He was dragged down the corridor like a leashed mutt.

"Where are you taking me? My mother works in relations." It was a shallow threat. Coms security had more authority than his mother. They both knew that. Krimsey shrugged to break from his grip.

It was all over for Krimsey.

But then Cris shot out from hiding and Krimsey watched him barrel into his dad. Krimsey's arm was free.

Cris shouted, "Go!"

Cris's dad fell to the floor and shouted in surprise.

Damn, how Krimsey wanted to give Cris a huge kiss.

The next second, Krimsey ran.

DELAY

Felice Karuli, Wednesday, March 27, 2250, 6:45 a.m.

ON THE BUSY BEACH, Mr. Boyd's attention switched between Felice and Lamia, waiting for an explanation as to who was "in custody." Lamia had slipped. Lamia had so perfectly played into her hand, Felice could hardly believe Mr. Boyd's question had even happened. Her mother patted her dress and smoothed her flyaways. Composed, as usual.

But Felice saw her twitch. Her nose scrunched. A flyaway loosed, which she batted at while she zeroed her focus on the man before her and the muscle below her eye spasmed. As if her hair had caught fire.

Or as if she'd been caught with her hair on fire. And for the first time, there was nothing to douse it. Finally.

"Seeing as I was offered no assistance getting my bags back on the ship, I figured I'd get a move on… before I see Miss Prae Ogier and Miss Cyn Jones," he said with a slowness as his mind seemed to spin.

Felice could see him mentally detangling the meaning behind Lamia's stricken facial expressions. First closed off, her lips clamping shut. Then her face muscles pulling back. Her cheekbones sharpening. Her mouth narrowing. Mr. Boyd squinted, charting each detail. He was working out the meaning of Lamia's reaction.

How much did he hear? A lot, Felice hoped.

"Last night was successful, I presume, Miss Karuli?" he asked.

"Oh, yes, Cyn Jones is in custody. *Please*, Franklin, I've told you before to call me Lamia. We aren't always so formal around here."

"You may call me Mr. Boyd, Lamia."

"My apologies. Well, we were just talking about how last night could not have been any smoother. And Prae's parents are on their way here from the HPO as we speak." Her voice shook. Not perceptibly enough for him to catch it, but enough for Felice.

Her mother was in a sinking ship with a thimble as her bail.

Mr. Boyd theatrically dropped his bags on the gritty ground. Sweat collected in the folds in his face. He wiped his hands.

"Deepest apologies for the lack of service on our end. Considering your arrival was unexpected…" Lamia cast around, her fingers like a hook, landing on the shoulder of someone who appeared to be working. The worker, not surprisingly, smelled of warm sweat and trash. "Excuse me. This man is very important. NWA. See to it his bags are taken safely to the ship?"

The worker nodded and began to continue without the bags.

Lamia cleared her throat. "Now, please." She gestured at the bags in the sand. "Take them. Thank you." The burden of the heavy bags now gone, Lamia turned to Mr. Boyd. "Departure days are always a little… *rushed*. We have so much to haul off the island and so little time. And the workers are not used to any guests departing with the ship. I'm sure you understand. Well." Lamia awkwardly cleared her throat again, placed a hand on Felice, and looked around them, ready for Mr. Boyd to leave.

"Thank you," he said, not leaving. He held his hands behind his back, appearing to hold in a question.

"Something else, Mr. Boyd?" Lamia asked, holding back a grimace.

Ask the question, Felice thought. Pry. Come on and do your Earth-forsaken job.

"Apologies if I misheard, but… did you say there were *kids* being taken in?" Mr. Boyd asked.

"Oh? Well…" Lamia said.

Yes. Yes! Felice wanted to shout with glee. She nibbled the inside of her bottom lip.

"Well, yes… if you would…" She guided Mr. Boyd toward the small steps that separated the beach and town. "Let's see Prae and Cyn, yes? I'll explain along the way. Your time is precious to us."

Felice held her breath to stop her heart from hammering too loud as she followed them back into town.

"You see… another issue arose this morning," Lamia said. "Which is really what I was discussing with my daughter. I had no intention of pulling wool over your eyes, so to speak, but I hardly thought it worth mentioning."

Despite her efforts, Felice's lungs pumped two times too fast. She struggled to hear her mother over the sound of rushing blood, crashing waves, and crunching steps which all seemed to get louder and louder. Distracted, she stepped on her mother's heel and received an icy glare.

"Please. Enlighten me," Mr. Boyd said.

"Of course, Mr. Boyd. Indeed," Lamia said, hands entwined behind her back.

She was stalling. She slowed to a leisurely stroll. Mr. Boyd cleared his throat and his profile flashed to Felice as he looked at Lamia. His face was hard. Suspicious. Searching.

Lamia straightened. "Cyn Jones has an offspring, which you are aware. They were estranged. In fact, the child was unaware of Cyn's existence until the recent breaches of security. But this child has been acting out. It has come to our attention that the child helped with the kidnapping of Prae Ogier."

Mr. Boyd stopped walking. "Go on."

"Well, this morning it seems Cyn Jones's child went rogue. Kidnapped three more children. But I assure you Zeph and Cyn Jones will both be reprimanded sufficiently." Lamia spoke with renewed confidence now. Unwavering.

The man couldn't possibly believe this Earth-forsaken—

"It seems your security problem is quite a breach."

"Yes, well…"

"Larger than you've led me to believe."

Lamia sucked in a breath. "Nothing we can't nip in the bud." She laughed nervously, illustrating a snippy pair of shears with two of her fingers.

"Indeed. You seem to have it under control." He walked on down the main drag. Brisker than before.

No. The taste of metal burst in Felice's mouth. "Ow!" She had nibbled too hard. She rubbed her tongue over a raised tear in her mouth. Lamia and the rep looked back at her. "Sorry, just bit my lip. Rough terrain."

Mr. Boyd laughed. "Indeed. One would think one gets used to these things. I suppose one does not."

They passed the more rugged industrial buildings of the main path in view of the beach and turned onto a residential block.

Mr. Boyd whistled through his teeth, then stopped. "I *know* you have a handle, Mrs. Karuli. You've proven your competency again and again. And the trials and tribulations of a life… well, *here…* are not that of an easy life. But of course, you'll certainly understand that we'll be needing to delay departure. I must see these other three children safe. As for the Joneses… these are not mild offenses. I'll be needing to take them in for proper punishment."

"Take them in?"

"I know, I know. You are in your full rights to refuse me taking them to Mainland for trial and employ your own mandates but I'm sure taking them off your hands will be the best breath of fresh air you'll ever have."

"Of… course." Lamia almost stuttered.

"Between you and I," he whispered, "I am overdue for a promotion soon. Bringing in two HPO criminals to the Mainland in a sensational scandal will yield dramatic headlines for months. You wouldn't mind doing me such a kind favor, would you?"

"I'll take you to them now." Lamia smiled and looked up and to the right. "We should take the ship. They are… a bit far."

Suppressant

LAMIA DELAYED THE DEPARTING ship to take Mr. Boyd to see Zeph and the three other "missing" children. He no longer insisted on seeing Prae united with her family. All he asked for was to lay eyes on the other children and for Zeph and Cyn to be in his custody. It was both the most terrifying and the most exciting thing that had ever happened to Felice. It was also the most absurdly ignorant—how single-minded Mr. Boyd must be only to think of his upcoming promotion.

For better or for worse, Mr. Boyd was here. Felice was helpless as he flattered her mother with compliments, swooning over her rather than seeing the glaring fiasco right in front of him.

"You really turned this place around since your father," he said as Lamia prepared them all a quick bite to eat in the guide suite. Then, munching and brandishing a ruby red apple as both Karulis sipped tea, he said, "It really is a testament of your leadership that you only have two miscreants in the bunch. And the Joneses really only count as one bad one, considering their relation. You know what they say about apples and trees."

He shook his head in awe.

By the time they were ready and the ship was ready, they were standing on the beach like a dysfunctional family. Lamia and Mr.

Boyd exchanged pleasantries, laughing, while Felice pretended not to be appalled. Then there was Cyn, flanked by a guard who brought her out at Mr. Boyd's request. Cyn, now set for NWA prison, awkwardly clawed an itch under her zip-tie shackles. Despite Felice's frenzied efforts to think at the woman, Cyn didn't reach out with her mind at all.

Backlit in blue and orange, the passenger ship's launch boat ripped toward them through the pre-dawn ocean. Rocky beach sprawled before them. The plastic docking platform they walked toward broke the seamless shoreline like a comma. Today, the tide was out and the waves beyond churned. Strands of seaweed sprawled and swayed in the shallow tides.

A tan, broad man at the launch stern had one foot braced behind him and one foot propped on the stair as the launch slid carefully into place at the dock. It bumped against the rubber guard and the tan man jumped off the boat and tied up while the launch captain helped Lamia, Cyn, Cyn's guard, Felice, and Mr. Boyd onto the tiny launch in that order, seating them in a semicircle. Each of them were given flotation vests. The boat took off shortly after they donned their vests and sea spray misted their faces when they boarded the passenger ship and got underway.

They rounded the sharp, submerged spines off Kafmir point and navigated between a landmine of scattered islands.

Mr. Boyd had a lot of questions. Substantial ones. Like, "Why did the Jones kid take the children to such a remote bay?" and "How did the Jones kid manage this alone?" Questions that were magically put to rest by Lamia with a few words and two knuckle pops.

She had answered simply.

"The bay was far and shrouded. Easy to conceal people and things." Vague but also extremely true, hinting at the history of their ex-scuba-base-turned-lab and its operations. Right under his nose.

The other answer was equally as easy. "Kids love candy."

Felice couldn't believe he bought those answers.

Candy was apparently so convincing—despite candy being a rarity on the island—Mr. Boyd didn't have any follow-up questions.

In fact, he stopped asking questions entirely and simply walked up and down the rails to watch land and sea pass by like an old movie. It was infuriating. Even more infuriating was that Cyn was locked and guarded in a gutted old engineering room directly behind her, but further commentary from the woman was apparently still closed.

Outside on an upper level of the ship, Mr. Boyd wobbled by Felice a fifth time. He seemed to be enjoying himself. That, or the smile plastered across his face was a sea-sick grimace in disguise.

Felice held her tongue as he passed. She swayed as the ship lurched over a large swell. Behind her, Mr. Boyd struggled with his footing and muttered. Felice lent a hand for stability, anchoring herself to the railing, though she did enjoy the mental picture of him pitching overboard.

"Thank you." He took her hand for a second, then continued on to the front of the ship.

When the ship lurched again, Felice's white-knuckled fingers tightened around the rails. The powdered-egg-and-berry-broccoli breakfast and her later cup of tea refused to settle.

"Felice," her mother called her from the bridge. "We need to talk."

Another swell bounced. Good thing she had a stomach of steel. Thinking it made it true.

Right?

She tasted the strange breakfast combo a second time that day.

Never mind.

Fish food now.

"When you're finished," Lamia shouted. "Meet me on the lower deck." Her head disappeared from the ledge of the ship.

Downstairs, Lamia watched a pod of dolphins through a round window on the lower deck, which was half submerged. The dolphins followed the ship curiously for a few minutes. Then they veered left and disappeared into the blue.

Lamia's shoulder blades stood out like porcelain wings beneath spaghetti straps, and the bumps in her long, whip-like braid looked like individual vertebrae. Black and horrible and demon-like. Her back moved slowly, calmly, with her breath. When she turned around she looked almost serene. Pale, clouded eyes. There was no tension there.

"Thanks for joining me." Her voice was young, almost angelic. She gestured at a spot on the cold, hard metal bench beside her.

Felice sat.

"How are you feeling?"

Felice turned inward very briefly to make an assessment. How *was* she feeling? She wanted to say that she felt dead. Because it was true—and she desperately wanted a rise out of Lamia. She wanted her mother's heart on a stake. To feel what Felice felt. Numb. Hopeless. Finished.

"Fine."

Lamia touched Felice's chin. "Tell me, really." The gesture. Lamia had done it before. She usually used touch to render Felice powerless. To make her feel things. Touch was a tool. This time it was different. As if her mother were melted like a pile of butter by the warmth of her child.

It almost broke Felice. She tried to speak but her heart was in her mouth and her tongue was fat and thick. Lamia pressed Felice against her. They melded. It was both the happiest and the lowest she had ever felt. She expected her mother to say "alright" and pat her on the back and step out and leave her to the darkness. Felice was already gathering her willpower for what came next. Picturing her mother's black, braided spine leaving the room without so much as a glance back.

In her mind, she already felt the cold metal guardrail in her palms. Taking her sandals off. The desire to join the churning white froth below. Breathing in. While the ocean could still kill her.

Felice breathed. Her mother was warm. Smelled of sand and sea.

"You're not fine." Creeping back into her voice was a hard gristle that needed to be spat out.

"No."

Her mother pulled away from her. Felice stiffened. Now it was time. Time for Lamia to leave. For her to pretend her relationship with her daughter was a normal one and that Felice was, in fact, fine.

"It should kick in soon." Lamia gave a grim smile.

"What?"

"You'll be feeling better."

A rushing warmth from her armpits down to her groin exploded. Felice's eyes misted over. "What did you do?"

"Gave you something that'll help."

"Gave me *what?*"

"It was a double dose of suppressant. A cocktail of... some other things, too."

"Suppressant... you don't know what that'll do to me after... after Cyn gave me...." Raw anger, hurt, and fear were numbed by the pleasant sensation growing in her lungs. The words came out blurry and muted. Felice stood and caught herself with her back against the wall. "Is *that* why I couldn't talk to her?"

"Talk to who?"

Her vision was like a watercolor gone wrong, everything bleeding together. Even her words and thoughts bled. She didn't mean to say that about Cyn out loud. Her mouth moved.

"Why were you talking to Cyn?"

Felice didn't remember saying Cyn's name, but apparently she did. She needed to leave. To get out of the way. To rest. To die.

"I didn't consent to...."

Lamia looked startled. She moved in and out of focus.

"I thought you'd be happy. You were so stressed. Letting things slip with the rep. Saying those hateful things to me. You weren't yourself. Don't you feel better?"

"I—" Felice halted. Physically, she did feel better. Like a weight, literally, had been lifted off her chest. "No! *No.* She said it would probably kill me." She paused and pushed her cheeks around like putty to make sure they were still there. "I hate you. I hate you for this. I wish you were dead." She faltered and spoke softly because her mother was actually tearing up.

Felice touched the sparkling drop below her hollow eye to make sure it was real. She wasn't sure it was.

"I didn't want this, either," Lamia said. "You'll thank me later."

The ship was cloaked in fog when it passed between the two mountainous arms that guarded Ross Bay. At low tide, the ship would only just clear the passage without scraping the floor. It was mid-tide now and sand and rocks and weeds were just visible beneath the surface.

Felice calculated how far the fall was just to give her cloudy brain something to latch on to. Her hair ratted around her face. She tried to fix it in mild frustration. There was no point to it anymore, really.

"That's why I wear a braid," her mother commented. Lamia was damp with mist. Her tone indifferent. Comfortable. Controlled. Cool and fleeting like a bird taking off.

Felice's drug-induced delirium was almost a comfort. It hugged her in all the right places. But in the back of her mind was the reminder that kept her from fully enjoying the state of mind it put her in. She had failed. Cyn had failed. Zeph had failed. And Krimsey, too. He had probably failed. Wherever he was. Felice would leave a wreck behind her when she either died or transitioned or imploded, but fuck it.

The calming effect from the drugs intensified.

This was Lamia's wreck. Not hers. Always had been.

Besides, something was bound to rise from this. From Felice's failure. From her charred ash. Maybe Felice's departure really would crush Lamia into a million pieces and she'd blow away. *Poof.* Just a cloud of dust.

And *transitus* were fighting back, even if they didn't know it yet. At the core, their very existence was a rebellion. Each day, their numbers grew. Both above and below sea level. Her mother would have a hell of a time taking a stab at those kinds of numbers. Hundreds of thousands. If not millions.

Especially without Felice.

And Carmak? Lamia had thrown Gina Carmak's only child—adopted, but bonded by time—into the line of fire. What would Lamia do without Carmak?

Felice let her shoulders relax. This was the ultimate mess. For the first time, she was pretty calm. Somewhat at peace, ready to finally just… be. To observe. Watch how her mother worked. It wasn't often she was witness to Lamia's cleanup. Definitely not on this scale. Failure didn't bother Felice anymore.

Her serenity was cracked open like a coconut by her mother's voice.

"Get the launch ready. Quickly."

Mother

Zeph Jones, Wednesday, March 27, 2250, 8 a.m.

THE FOG ON THE beach was thick. Zeph was taken here against their will by Gina and a big man. The fog rolled in, dense, sticky, sentient, and it swirled on every inhale and exhale. Clung like sweat.

Subtle signs hinted at the presence of water. Gentle lapping. Two unseen gulls crying out in circles overhead. The splash of a fish slapping the surface. Or a bird diving for a treat. The dampness of the black sand beneath that kicked into Zeph's sandals. The salt that dried between Zeph's toes. The smell of oysters and fish and pearls.

The three kids whimpered. Zeph plopped by a tree and drew shapes in the sand.

"I can take it from here," Gina said to the man. She donned her newly acquired com, blinking.

"You sure?" He was suspicious of Zeph's quiet obedience, looking at them like they had a third eye.

"There's no reason for you to stay."

"Alright."

The man tromped back a short way into the forest that lined the beach. Zeph heard the transport door open and close. According to Cyn, the transport was like an old-world elevator. Step in. Strap in. Then *whoosh*. More versatile than any old-world contraption. Speedier, too. Efficient.

The shell of the transport was a metal room that housed it outside. It was an inconspicuous three-by-three-meter box hidden under vines and wires.

It was how Zeph was supposed to get Elpida out of the lab. That wasn't happening.

I could expose the transport and the lab... bring the people here. Let them see for themselves, Zeph thought, trying to trade in a brooding disposition for one with more optimism and hope. If half the population on the island knew of the electric-powered transport's existence, let alone the lab, there would be an outraged *transitus* mob for the HPO to contend with.

It was as impossible as the current task before them, though. As impossible as finding that lab and getting Elpida out now that they were captured.

Gina crossed the sand. Her irritating presence interrupted the impossible thought. She walked toe to heel so the grains didn't kick up and sat close by while two kids made sculptures.

"*Please.* Join me," Zeph said, body shifting toward the kids—away from the woman Zeph had once called *Mother.*

The eldest kid, hand on hip, standing, examined the beach art. Secretly keeping a side eye on Gina. The children were leery, but they *were* children and they were bored.

"Listen to me, Zeph." Gina donned a motherly voice.

It was so *her,* like a warm hug. Zeph wanted to cry.

"Lamia is coming. She's not happy. She has Cyn Jones in her custody—" at this, Zeph's finger stopped drawing in the sand, "—you've gotten yourself into trouble going after her. If you can just be quiet and good and make yourself small, I can get us out of this."

"Us?"

"What happens to you, happens to me." The words formed another tiny, warm hug around their icy heart.

Swallowing hard, they said, "What happens to me?"

"Nothing. If I can help it."

Wiping their shapeless drawing from the sand, picking black grains from their nails, Zeph wondered about Krimsey. Wondered what would happen when Krimsey set off the alarm. "What time is it?"

"It doesn't matter. Are you listening to me?"

"Where is Elpida?" Zeph met her eyes to see her reaction. Stoic.

"Give it up, Z. I'll keep you safe."

I miss her. Zeph swallowed the creeping lump in their throat.

"Oh, my love. I'm sorry you were dragged into this." Her arm reached over the expanse between them.

"Do not touch me."

"You are speaking to your mother."

"But I am not."

Voices carried on the water. Zeph's eyes dilated, part in fear, part in the simple inability to see anything other than white. Gina stood. She gave Zeph a stern stare. It said, *Don't do anything stupid.*

"What am I possibly going to do? Run?" Though the idea had crossed their mind.

Gina's face, as it blurred slightly in the mist, gave them the look. The one that said, *Don't try me. I know what you're thinking, Zeph Carmak.*

Nothing left to do but to wait.

"Carmak?" A female voice. Buttery. Presidential.

"Over here," Gina called.

From the fog, faces materialized.

That's when Zeph leapt to their feet. Gina turned back to tackle them. Zeph popped her as hard as they could in the nose and disappeared into the forest.

In The Fog

KRIMSEY CRASHED INTO THE humid heat outside of the tunnels and collapsed onto the ground. His chest heaved. His breathing filled the back of his throat with a dryness so fierce he choked on it.

It was still dark out, the promise of twilight barely perceptible. No one pursued him, but if he didn't motivate his arms and hands to push up and his legs and feet to carry him, he'd die right here. In the dirt. Surrounded by the backlit shapes of trees scraping the starless sky.

The walk to Ross Bay was supposed to be at least four hours with healthy lungs.

He lifted his head and looked down into the tunnel he had emerged from. It pushed out cool air and faded light. He blinked at the black hole opening, then pushed himself upright. He sat in an overgrown clearing. The base of the forest was gnarled. Covered in roots and brush and rock and trees and a desperate will to survive. When he stood, he realized what was missing. No waves crashed in the distance, no trickling stream, no hope to quench his cracked throat. He only heard birds and insects, pausing at his every movement.

I've failed, he thought. *However this ends, I will die here in the forest and I've failed.* He coughed. The taste of his breath was thick and metallic. Cyn said if everything didn't go just right... then it was over.

Was it over, then? *No.*

Elpida... What happens to her if she's freed but there is no alarm? They will surely recapture her. I cannot, will not abandon her. I have to find her. And protect her. Warn Z. Find a solution.

Then and only then, Body—you and I will have a talk.

Don't die. Don't die and I will give you what you need.

I will go to the ocean.

He stepped forward, feet like lead. Stepping over a root, Krimsey pushed into the thigh-high undergrowth of—well, not a path. The thing that looked closest to a path. An animal trail. And it looked like the animals had barely even touched it. Cyn had said there was a trail to the bay. What she should have said was that there was a forest, more forest, even more forest, and good luck finding water.

He brushed past a huge cobweb, its occupant somewhere out of sight. Broke a dead branch blocking his way. Waded through the greenish-dead growth. He was already out of breath. Behind him, signs of his travel—all of one meter in—was apparent. Bent twigs and stomped foliage. If Zeph had been through here, wouldn't it have looked used?

Had Zeph not made it out? Gone a different way? *Do I turn back? Find Zeph?* A rescue wasn't possible without them... was it? *Damn it.*

He had to muscle on. With or without them.

Muscle on he did. Elpida was a constant reminder. Like an old photograph he showed himself as a bribe. *Stay alive*, the reminder told his body. *Stay alive.*

He smacked his desert lips when he heard water. A river. On Cyn's map, the river had led to the bay. He wanted to leap into it and quench the fire that spread to his heart. But that memory-photograph of Elpida blinked at him, smiled. She rolled her eyes at him as if he'd done something so characteristically *him*, and he carried on. When he saw the river, he didn't even dare drink or gargle from it. He knew he'd lose control. Instinct would take over and he'd never step foot on land again.

A sodden tree lay across his path. Its rotten top rested on the other side of the river, its dead roots dangling in the brush.

Krimsey clambered over it. Wet, crumbling bits gave way beneath him. His muscles creaked and ached and he nearly licked the damp rot that stuck to his palms. He dropped to the opposite side of the heaping decay. His knees buckled under the impact, so he decided to stay there and rest, for now. Krimsey closed his eyes, just long enough to catch his breath.

His eyes opened. All Krimsey saw was white and, for a wild moment, he thought he was blind or dead. He felt intact. Blood rushed in his ears. Or was that the river? His hands reached for his face. His palms, directly in front of him, were dirty and dry. Bits of eroded wood clung in the creases.

Fog. It was just fog. Fog so thick, he couldn't see just two feet in front of him. So thick, he could almost—*almost*—breathe. The moist molecules helped dampen his throat.

He heard a noise like a tickle.

Voices.

He followed the sound. The sticks and leaves and dirt below him gave way to something soft. Sand. He heard the whisper of the ocean. For once, the beckoning was near irresistible. He persisted, though, ignoring the ocean, and crept into earshot of the voices, still shrouded in white haze.

"This is just embarrassing."

He stopped.

It was unmistakably the voice of Lamia Karuli. A voice firm, yet yielding, soft, yet sturdy, sincere, yet… *duplicitous*. It was impossible not to hear the contradictions, the rough grains of deceit.

She sounded so close, he might have bumped into her.

"Excuse me, Mr. Boyd. Sincere apologies," she said.

"You have to do what you have to do. I can learn a thing or two," a man who must have been Mr. Boyd replied. A high tenor.

"Yes… Felice, ask the launch captain to bring Cyn ashore. Tell them to hurry. And bring the guard… Wait," Lamia shouted.

"What?" Felice sounded tired and annoyed.

"Take these children to the ship while you're at it. Make them comfortable. They've been out here on their feet for so long, darling things. We'll see to it they're brought back to their families quickly."

"Why don't we just—?"

"Go on."

Krimsey? The touch of Zeph's mind was cold and reassuring. But also small. Scared. Lonely.

Z! What's going on?

Lamia continued a string of apologies to whoever "Mr. Boyd" was.

I was caught. I am in the woods now. I do not know what is going on.

Krimsey felt their sadness trickle down his spine. *Caught by your mother? Oh, Z... I'm sorry.*

We do not have time for that. You are here. That means...?

I was caught, too. He paused. *Where are you?* Krimsey heard a low, slow splashing nearby.

I am hiding. I... may have punched my mother in the face.

She deserves it.

Thanks. But they are looking for me. I think Lamia is bringing Cyn out to make me feel guilty. But, you know... I do not care enough about anyone to feel guilty. Not anymore. Except you. I failed you and Elpida...

Krimsey felt a sort of mental caressing, fingers brushing his spine, reaching in, hugging him from the inside out. He reeled back. *Privacy? For Earth's sake.*

Sorry... A pause. *Your lungs are like sand.*

I know.

So what the hell are you doing out here?

I came to help. Cyn says if we're caught, we're doomed. I don't think that way. I can't let my sister down.

She is family. I understand.

What do we do?

I am out of ideas.

Show me where you are then, he thought. It was an unfiltered thought, though, because of course they couldn't.

Well, there is fog to my left. Fog to my right. Fog to my back. And tree bark smack in front of me. Now you.

You're funny.

"Z," someone shouted. "Remember what I said, dear?"

I told you they are trying to convince me to come out. It will not work. Krimsey, we should—

"This will be much easier if you come out now."

Krimsey guessed it was Zeph's so-called mother, the betrayer, Gina.

"Took you long enough." Lamia again. "Zeph? Zeph Jones. We have your mother in custody. How painful do you want this to be? Guard."

There was a gasp. "Is that really necessary? Where on Earth did you even get one of those?" the man's voice said.

"Zeph Jones. My friend here has a gun pointed at your mother's head," Lamia said.

No. "No!" Zeph yelled.

"Come out, then," Lamia said.

Z, don't. You're my only hope for Elpida. She won't do it. Not in front of—

An explosion of gunpowder. Sand sprayed in all directions, even landing in Krimsey's hair.

"Next one will be in your mother, Zeph."

"Don't!" Krimsey rasped and stumbled toward the voices. "Don't."

Stupid. Stupid. Stupid. How is Zeph possibly going to save Ellie on their own? But what choice did he have? He was dead anyway.

Distract them, Zeph thought to him. *Keep them on the beach as long as you can. I will get her out.*

And then what?

I do not know.

The Lab

Zeph Jones, Wednesday, March 27, 2250, 8:45 a.m.

As voices shouted to their left, Zeph emerged from the forest and crept unseen through the fog to the bay. Fully clothed, leaving their sandals on the beach, they tip-toed into the water. It was eerily still; the waves rose and fell in a shallow dance from ankle to toe.

They walked waist deep, then ducked beneath the surface and kicked. Zeph skimmed the sandy bottom, searching for the underwater lab.

Nothing.

They surfaced. Wiped their face. Took several long breaths. Dipped straight back down. In less than ten seconds, they hit sand. The transport tube, which was what would get Elpida out and onto the beach, was supposed to lead directly into the lab. Maybe there would be more luck finding that than the lab itself. It covered more surface area.

Suddenly, the bottom of the bay dropped out from beneath them. The water grew cold. Patches of freezing water seeped into their bones. Zeph equalized the pressure in their ears and gazed into the blue haze.

Their extremities tingled as they descended the thermocline. A small sand shark drifted by.

Then, there it was.

A metal dome emerged from the single-color landscape. It was wedged on top of a rocky shelf. Zeph drew closer and six more domes materialized from the haze. They branched off from a rectangular middle. Chambers connected the domes to the middle section. Squat, sturdy legs anchored each compartment to the boulder substrate. From the middle structure, a long metal tube led several hundred meters toward shore before it burrowed into rock.

One of the domes, on the opposite end from the transport tube, had a single window. The metal, otherwise, was featureless. Just bolted seams.

Zeph approached each dome, feeling for the presence of Elpida Enosh. Proximity to the lab made their skin prick. On the fourth dome, Zeph peered through the single window. The room was lightly inhabited. A table in the middle. Counter space all around. A sink. And used medical supplies on the side with the sink. Tubes and boxes and jars filled with metallic tools.

No Elpida.

Breathless, lungs heaving for air, Zeph ascended to the surface.

They equalized their ears until they crackled, then they dove back.

Hello? At the fifth dome, Zeph reached out to anyone that could hear them, beginning to feel as if the place was completely abandoned. They pressed their cheek against the metal, hopeful for a reply. Any thought or emotion would do.

Nothing.

They swam to the next dome. Again, nothing, nothing, nothing. Zeph checked them all. Elpida was either not there, or the whole plan was flawed because thoughts didn't transfer through metal.

Elpida?

Nothing.

SACRIFICE

Krimsey Enosh, Wednesday, March 27, 2250, 8:46 a.m.

KRIMSEY LUNGED FORWARD IN the sand. "Don't shoot! Don't shoot." He tripped over a foot that felt like a rock and landed in the middle of everyone. Six ethereal bodies, backlit and shining at the same time, were huddled close together.

The glowing orb of sun over Krimsey's left shoulder lit everything, like being inside of a light bulb. The sun must have been covered behind clouds before, because now the fog refracted the rays in all directions. Trillions of tiny suns.

The faces seemed to be looking down at him. He imagined them blinking, stunned. He blinked back. Squinted. Cupped a hand over his brows. Some features stood out.

Blonde, straight hair. Felice.

Tight, cat-like face. Lamia.

Cyn was a dark face hidden behind curls.

The other three were unrecognizable. A short, sharp, stiff-shouldered silhouette. A thinner, womanly frame, which Krimsey almost mistook for the president. And a rigid triangle of a man, one arm held glinting metal up against Cyn's temple.

"What on Earth's name is going on here, Lamia? Who are you, boy? Are you Zeph Jones?" The short, suited man leaned down. His softly wrinkled face came into focus. He hadn't seen much of the outdoors, wherever he came from.

"Krimsey." Krimsey coughed and tasted earthy iron. He was going to stand, but it would have taken too much effort. His heart sputtered. It stopped. He thought he was dead for a moment, but then the man stood. He looked at Lamia and mouthed, "*Krimsey?*" Then he said, "As in... the brother? As in Krimsey *Enosh?*"

Then, Krimsey's heart kept beating.

"You know..." Krimsey said. Of course he knew. This must have been the man Cyn called here in the first place. The NWA rep. "Sir, if you would just listen... My sister, Elpida—"

"Your sister," he barked. "What is the meaning of—would you please put down that—that—*thing?* That gun. Put it down."

The man with the gun looked to Lamia, who made a stunted sound in reply, "I—"

Lamia was cut off by another sound. An electronic screech. Alarms. Security-breaching alarms. It grew in the distance and sounded in the ear coms of the people who stood around.

"I've had just about enough of this," Lamia cried, indignant. "Who the hell sounded the evacuation alarm?"

The alarm... The alarm!

Cris. Cris. Forsaken Earth, Cris did it. That had to have been him. It was like, somewhere, Cris was saying, "I've got you." Saying, "We'll meet again."

But what use was the alarm if Elpida wasn't Up Top? But the rep was here. The rep needed to see proof. Tangible proof that Elpida was not dead.

"Ive will handle it," Lamia said.

"I will take care of it," Felice said.

"You will not." Lamia was spiteful. "You stay."

Krimsey lowered his head to the sand. He could cry. So close. But still a failure. His face was hot. He swallowed his heart like an orange coal.

Felice split away from the group, into the fog.

"Felice," Lamia tumbled ungracefully after her daughter. They crashed into the undergrowth.

"Sir, listen," Krimsey said. "They're keeping my sister Elpida Enosh in a lab. Underwater. You have to help us."

"What do you mean in a lab? What's going on here? Miss Enosh is dead."

The man with the gun lowered his weapon with a question on his face. The thin woman—Zeph's mother?—had her face arranged into an *O*.

"She isn't dead. We were going to free her," Krimsey coughed and tripped over words to force them out. "That's what the alarm is for. We were going to show everyone what the HPO has done—has been doing to *transitus*. To get *your* attention. There's a lab. My sister is there. You have to arrest the president. You have to arrest Lamia Karuli."

Seeing the man's face working out what Krimsey said spread relief across his chest like a drug.

"Can you… show me this place?"

"I can," Cyn interjected. She lifted her wrists. They were tied together with plastic. "We have to hurry."

Then Cyn froze.

Through the brush, Lamia returned. "Apologies. Felice is taking care of it… Everything alright?"

"Mr. Enosh here says you have his sister? In a… lab? Is this true?"

Lamia looked between the man and Cyn's raised wrists. The smirk that spread across Lamia's face was sloppy as an eel. She laughed. "Oh yes." She reached across the man to the guard. Time stopped. Metal transferred fingers. The glock glistened. "It's true." And Lamia Karuli pulled the trigger. Right into the rep's chest. Krimsey's ears exploded. The man crumpled belly-first like a sack of blood and poured. The sand by Krimsey's hand soaked red.

"What the hell have you done?" Zeph's adoptive mother screamed. Pierced the fog and air. Split time.

"Carmak, go to the ship. *Now*. You and the guard both. Take the ship to port and return the children to their families."

"What have you done?" The woman didn't move. "What have you done? Forsaken Earth. What have you done?"

"I. Will. Take. Care. Of. It. Now *go*. Take Cyn with you. *Thank you*. Krimsey, you're coming with me. *UP*." She pulled him to his feet and dragged him. "I'm going to need some viable subjects to test a *new* hypothesis."

His heart took a painful leap and rattled in the cavity of his chest. Krimsey coughed up blood.

"Elpida," Krimsey screamed. The effort felt like it tore his lungs to shreds.

This was it. So this was how he died. Screaming her name. Having lost Elpida and lost the will to survive. He couldn't hold on anymore.

He screamed again; he was burning alive. His skin crawled. He was dragged over the body of the dead man. Empty eyes. Krimsey stumbled into the forest, dragged by the collar of his shirt.

The shirt slipped off. Lamia grabbed him by the skin.

I'm dying.

They went inside something metal. He was on the ground. His ears popped. Pressure expanded in his head. They were dropping, dropping, dropping.

His heart skipped. It thudded once, stopped, thudded twice, stopped again. It rattled and shook more violently than the metallic transport he was in. It came to a sudden stop and his heart forgot to pump his blood for several excruciating seconds. It was time. He knew it was time.

Then, a sound. Doors. *Whoosh.* Open.

He smelled corroding sea. His tongue tasted the blood that filled his lungs. Krimsey stumbled out of the transport. He was vaguely aware that Lamia had stopped.

Thwump... thwump-wump... wump... wumpp. His heart stopped again. Restarted and stopped.

He looked up and blinked. "Elpida?" His voice was unfamiliar.

Elpida stood half inside a small, dark chamber, hand on a door and one foot in the room he was in. Behind her, another door, closed shut. She was thin and green, her once-lush skin sallow and sick. Purple beneath her eyes as if she hadn't slept. She wore a thin sky-blue slip. Bruises were scattered across both arms.

He tried to gasp her name again, but this time it didn't come out.

Her eyes were huge, the only thing still familiar. Looking like a child caught stealing chocolate. She was frozen, watching Lamia. Frightened. She looked like death herself.

So.

He was too late. He was always too late. Elpida's knees wobbled.

Lamia turned around. Krimsey was all but choking now. He fell on his back. It was happening. The transition. It was like a living thing slithered inside him, where his lungs should have been, and sat on his heart. He couldn't breathe.

"Krimsey." Was that Elpida's voice? Sweet Ellie? Pida? She sounded surprised. Strained. Conflicted. "You found me."

Ellie, I came for you, he thought, craning his neck. Lamia shifted above him.

"Don't move," Elpida said. "I figured this place out. The tech. The doors. Your protocols."

He sensed a tensing above him. "You don't want to do that, little girl."

He wanted to tell Elpida how proud of her he was. Had she gotten out all on her own? Figured out the codes? Hacked the doors? Had she been so close to freedom? Had his efforts at rescue just sealed her doom? He blinked hard. Warm tears flooded his face. Tech… she'd have tested into that tech internship, he knew it. He was so proud. To have figured all this out in—what? Two days?

Ellie, how can I help? How do I set you free from here? She didn't hear him.

"You don't think I can do it? I'll open the door if you move." Krimsey didn't know what that meant, but Elpida was firm, despite the weak, tired fissures in her voice. He craned his neck enough to see her again, despite the pain it caused him. She quickly glanced down at him; a state of relief and gratitude crossed her face. "I love you," she whispered just to him, the words barely making a sound.

I love you, too, he thought, coughing out a garbled syllable. He focused on her face. The creature pressing against his heart moved just enough for him to take another breath. "I love you, Pida."

"I'm going to open this other door," she said to him.

"That will flood the whole damn place, you stupid girl," Lamia said somewhere up high, her voice frantic.

"This place won't hurt anyone else ever again," Elpida said with a tired smile. "This was my choice, Krim. It has been my plan since I've been here. I'm so glad I get to save you, now, too." Her eyes were red and her hand shook.

"You'll kill him if you do that. And yourself." Lamia growled.

He understood now what was happening. His vision went red, sparked black and white and red and orange like fireworks against the sky. *No,* Krimsey thought. *No, Ellie.* He didn't want her to open the door. He needed her to live.

He couldn't remember the last time his heart had beat.

"No," Elpida whispered. He heard the soft smile in her voice. "Just you." Somewhere, metal creaked. The sound of an unoiled hinge. Krimsey looked up again. She was pushing open the door behind her. She was upside down in his crackling vision, standing on his ceiling—her floor. The door flung open. There was a whooshing sound. Ten thousand tons of water came gushing up from behind Elpida.

Elpida. Framed in a silky screen of water. Framed against blue. Then she was floating. Then he was floating. And he was so irrevocably broken. So stricken with grief he didn't want to breathe. Elpida had saved them all. All along, it was her plan, her sacrifice. Her love.

Saving him.

Not the other way around.

Everything was blue.

He cried. A sob constricted his throat. He grabbed his chest and screamed.

And after he expelled all the air he had, he realized another thing. He had to take his next breath. It was the grief, not the desire to live, that made him do it. So he could continue to cry.

A rough, painful stab in his heart pumped something foreign through him.

He could breathe.

LIFE AFTER DEATH

Krimsey Enosh, Wednesday, March 27, 2250, 9:33 a.m.

DEATH WAS ALWAYS THE *beginning.*

Death always gave me a new start.

In the flash point between deaths, I could see all my lived lives. I was everyone, everywhere, all at once. Past, present, and future. I remembered that this was how it was every time, when I died. I saw all the lives—and deaths—I've ever had. At sea, on mountain tops, in the wild plains or cityscapes. Thriving. Surviving. Loving and living.

A billion, trillion times over. Captured in the pinprick of a moment.

But this time was different. This time I was learning something new. Unexpected. Because this time, my body—I, Krimsey Enosh—did not die. Yet I still saw it all flash. Diane Marion, Élodie Le Goff, Gianvante Dasulorn, Tessa Darling, Artyom Simmons, Felice Karuli, Cyn Jones, Elpida Enosh, and more....

What did it mean that my body was still alive, then?

What message was I supposed to grasp?

Maybe, in order to start something new, to shed and mourn my human experience, to evolve, to become what I am, a part of myself had to die with my sister forty meters underwater in this groaning metal prison. Maybe whatever shackled me to the constructs of humanity had to die. Maybe I had to feel that death, so I could grow. This death was not like the others. Because I was still here.

I was whole.

And new.

One day, I'd really die. Maybe then, I wouldn't see all the lives yet because they had yet to be lived. They were all in front of me. Maybe that's why I had never seen beyond human and *transitus* lives.

I had to evolve first.

Maybe.

I was still figuring it out.

I had this fleeting thought, this thought that was already fading, about death. Death and evolution and humans and *transitus* and freedom. Like I had the entire map of the universe flash in front of me for a millisecond. The Answer. Everyone and everything.

Me.

As the thought left me, feeling all my lived lives fade away, watching my sister die, my mind and body came back to the present, came back to *Krimsey Enosh*, came back to *right now*, and I began to think that maybe this was all a delirium.

What delirium?

The thought—whatever I had been thinking moments before—was gone.

And Elpida was dead. And Lamia was dead. And my life on land was dead. But I was alive. And I was not who I thought I was. I was confused. And I was grieving parts of me that were severed.

Gone. Empty. Bleeding. Dead. Death felt like an ending, but something in me, something tugged at me, telling me I was wrong. That death was something else.

At first, I only felt absence, as I swam to her. Creeping and dreadful. Crawling into me, down my throat, filling me up. The ocean pulled my breath away. Ripped it from me. Stole it. I fought. It won. It was violent. Brackish ocean filled my once-vacant lungs. Like a salty-sweet balm.

When I wrapped my arms around her and took my second breath, I felt calm. Elpida was like a fragile silk flower, suspended.

I held her hand, closed her eyes, kissed her cheek, and somehow managed to slow my sobs.

My shoulders and hands shook. My breath, sips of life now gifted from the ocean, shuddered. We had drifted to the middle of a large room and below me, I saw sand and realized I—we—were trapped.

A metal covering kept us imprisoned.

It took work to lift the thing off its hinges, but it did come loose. I braced myself and pushed the grating aside with my feet, leaving me an opening in the corner just large enough.

I took Elpida. And out of respect for the ocean and her body, I took Lamia.

I burst through the surface with the bodies but I was a stranger. The atmosphere I had grown up in rejected my lungs. It was suffocating.

Elpida's skin was cold against mine. I brought her body to shore first, put her on the beach, then Lamia.

Neither moved, but people from the beach did. People I hardly felt I knew anymore, people I hardly acknowledged. It was as if I were outside the realm of time, watching it pass. Vaguely familiar faces hurried about. Then time grew slow. Even seemed to stop.

One person watched me from the beach for a long time but I did not acknowledge them. They might have even said something to me.

Eventually, I moved because I could remember making my sister a promise. I lifted my wet, laden body from the waves. Water drained from my newly formed lungs. The pain was only bearable because I was so removed from myself that I could hardly feel. Her body against mine as I lifted her from the shore was like a soft cloud. My muscles gave out, bringing me to my knees, but I did not drop her.

I couldn't breathe. I wondered how long I could survive on land.

I had promised to take her somewhere beautiful. A hike through the flowers and grass. Through the mountains. Someone lifted Elpida from my arms and they looked at me. I did not recognize them because I chose not to. They said something, became urgent as my body convulsed.

Someone else joined in and together they shoved me back into the waves. My body gave them no resistance. I toppled backwards and breathed again.

What was I thinking?

I was alive because of her. To throw that away would be the worst, most selfish act I could do.

She wanted this for me more than anyone.

The people I now saw as Cyn, Felice, Cris, and Zeph stared at me. I stared back at them, breathing deeply each time a wave washed over me in the shallows. An unfamiliar group of kids crept up behind them to peek at me. The children seemed to be afraid. Was it my face? Had I changed in some monstrous way?

Am I even still Krimsey Enosh?

Ocean droplets fell from strands of Elpida's hair on the shore. Felice had her in her arms as they watched me, stopping to see what I would do. As if I were a creature to be regarded with caution.

I looked between the three of them. Felice's shoulders were hunched under Elpida's weight. Zeph looked, of all things, content.

Cris stepped out from behind Felice and came to me and knelt, bracing against each wave.

"Your sister..." he whispered. Cris cupped a warm hand around my cheek. I pressed into it. "I'm so sorry—" Cris broke off and turned his head to the side.

Zeph and Felice joined Cris by the water. I'd been wrong about Zeph looking content—they looked stunned, and tears were beginning to spill from their eyes. Cris and Felice, too—they were all crying, I realized—all of them.

I would have known they were all stricken had I reached out, had I felt their presence. I would have known Felice was as relieved as she was devastated by her mother's death. I would have known there was a new camaraderie between Cris and Felice. Felice must have brought him to the beach after the alarms. I would have known all this. But I was guarded. I looked at Zeph and touched their leg. They wiped their face on their shoulder.

I made Elpida a promise. Do you understand?

I pictured my sister's face. Visualized the promise I made. The hike and the mountains and the flowers. I showed Zeph.

Zeph nodded. *I do.*

I looked and nodded at each of them in turn, lingering on Cris with a small smile, then let the tide pull me out, and I wondered if I had the courage to start life after death.

Epilogue

HER MOTHER WAS DEAD.

It wasn't real until she came back to the beach to find the bodies—three horrible, grey bodies. Lamia was pulled out of the water, dead grey eyes looking at the sky. Several people from the boat came and stood around the body, just staring. At Lamia. At each other. Just blinking and staring.

Felice had nothing to wash down the bitter taste in the back of her throat. Lamia's braid had come undone. The dark mess of hair clung to her face. Felice wanted to reach out, to rearrange it as her mother had so often done to her. She would do that, but not now. For the funeral. After all had settled, she'd make her mother appear as she had always appeared before.

Now, Felice held the small body of Elpida in her arms. The fog had gone and it began to rain.

"How?" she asked. "How did this all happen?"

Does it matter? Cyn thought at her after twisting her lips to form words and failing.

"How?"

Cyn looked at her.

But she knew how. Felice had pretended not to see Elpida when she figured out the doors the first day there. Elpida—the final variable no one had thought to include. In so many ways, Elpida had reminded her of Rumi, with one major difference. Elpida had refused her role as captive. And she—amazingly, disastrously, heartbreakingly—ended the cycle.

Felice held Elpida and crammed into the transport with Cyn, Zeph, and the boy named Cris who had sounded the alarms. Zeph had barred Carmak from joining them, who still stood stricken on the beach. It was damp and stuffy and awful. Felice hugged Elpida to her chest with care. When they tumbled out, they all took a big breath of air.

Up Top, their presence and the dead girl in Felice's arms drew attention in seconds, including the devastation of the girl's mother, Sanjana. Sanjana kissed her daughter and cried, falling into place beside her. A small crowd had already gathered in the courtyard to watch the ship and people on the beach. Unable to grasp the meaning of what they saw unfold, the people of the HPO, humans and *transitus* alike, were shocked to see a dead *transitus* girl in the arms of Felice Karuli.

Felice said nothing. She didn't need to.

Felice floated through the crowd and the unfolding as if in a dream. Over the bay, the sun was set in perpetual gold-grey light just beneath a blanket of dark clouds. Rivulets of rain drained between their feet in small rivers in the black gravel. The rivers cascaded over either ledge of the mountain in mini waterfalls.

Felice, as promised and instructed by Zeph, proceeded to march down Footpath Main toward the smooth black steps that led into the mountains and valleys between the HPO and port town.

Her arms grew sore. After an hour, they burned and slipped in the rain. Felice only clutched Elpida's small body even tighter. Behind her, a curious procession had formed. Low murmurs followed Felice, who was flanked by Sanjana, Zeph, Cris, and Cyn. Hundreds, if not a thousand or more, humans and *transitus* followed them through the mountains in single file.

Golden light beneath the storm front set the wildflower valleys ablaze. Dazzling fire and rain. Port lay in the distance by the shore. Hours had passed. Felice scouted a patch of wildflowers that ran amok, several meters off the path. It was clear and open enough to fit the entire procession of people, she thought.

She stopped. They stopped, too. Watching her.

Sanjana was stoic, unable to conjure a smile or affirming expression, but she nodded, as if understanding Felice's pause. Throngs of people watched Felice as she waded into pink, violet, and yellow flowers. She walked deep into the valley, where the sun just peeked between a cleave in the mountain. She placed Elpida there, among the flowers, dropped to her knees, took a deep breath, and began to cry.

Thank Earth for Elpida Enosh.

Word of Lamia's corruption traveled quickly through the crowd. Respects were paid to Elpida. A crown of flowers had been made by two girls, which was placed gently around her head. Soon, Elpida was covered and outlined in a delicate floral design.

Scattered groups of discussion had formed across the field. Felice sat within the circle of trampled foliage that surrounded Elpida. Cyn joined her.

"There's been something on my mind." Cyn was pensive. She looked to port. Felice picked at a flower petal that was still dewy and wet.

"What?" Felice breathed, unable to remember the last time she closed her eyes.

"How did you not see it?" Cyn asked.

"See what?"

"All of it. How did you do the work and not see?"

Oh, only *that?*

"I don't know." She absentmindedly traced between her fingers. "She had this control over me. I didn't ask questions. I think it's easier to perpetuate terrible, glaring problems when you're in it than to challenge standards. Am I a terrible person?" Felice asked. "Working for her was terrifying. The way she controlled herself like she controlled her experiments. The way she controlled me. Everyone else. But even though it was all right in front of me, I never got out. I never broke the cycle. I needed help."

"Hmmm…" Cyn trailed off.

"What?"

"Nobody's perfect. What matters is that now you *can* break the cycle."

"I suppose."

They fell silent. The sun began to creep back into its place on the horizon in the sky, where night ended and day began. Together, they shared hours of silence in the valley. The people fell into a strange, contented lull.

"I think," Felice said, "it's time we rebuild." She bit her lip. There was a massive mess to clean up. So much to fix. "Do we tell the New World Alliance what happened here?"

They both looked out over the field, then looked at each other. Cyn held back a smile. So did Felice. Cyn laughed. "Hell, no."

For a sneak peek into my next book, *Transitus* easter eggs, and origin story, type in the passcode "transituseastereggs" at briaunamariah.com/transitus

You may also find the link here:

If you enjoyed this book, please consider writing a review with your honest impressions on Amazon, Goodreads, or the platform of your choosing. Your feedback is incredibly valuable for helping independent authors to reach a wider audience.

Briauna Mariah